D1198987

this book is a gift of

presented to the Library

Helen-Jean Moore Library
Point Park College

MATA HARI

Books by SAM WAAGENAAR

ASIA
COUNTRIES OF THE RED SEA
WOMEN OF ROME
WOMEN OF ISRAEL
CHILDREN OF THE WORLD
THE LITTLE FIVE
CHILDREN OF ISRAEL
MATA HARI

Mata Hari

by
SAM WAAGENAAR

APPLETON-CENTURY
New York

First U.S. edition

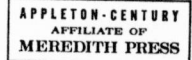

APPLETON-CENTURY
AFFILIATE OF
MEREDITH PRESS

Library of Congress Catalog Card Number: 65-21678

MANUFACTURED IN THE UNITED STATES OF AMERICA FOR MEREDITH PRESS

VAN REES PRESS • NEW YORK

Acknowledgments

Expressing thanks to people who have been helpful while doing research on a book like this is a nearly hopeless undertaking.

My involvement with Mata Hari having started over thirty years ago, a good many of those who supplied me with their intimate knowledge are no more. Foremost among these is Anna Lintjens, Mata Hari's maid and companion. Of all persons I talked to, she ranks highest on my scale of appreciation.

My old friend Leo Faust, who had met Mata Hari while being a newspaper correspondent in Paris, deserves full praise for his extraordinary memory. In the early thirties, after he had exchanged his journalistic career for the ownership and management of a renowned Dutch restaurant at 36 Rue Pigalle (where his namecard read: *"Poète et Marchand de Soupe"*), Mata Hari was frequently discussed with him over a glass of Dutch gin. And during recent years several sessions with him in Holland, plus a good number of letters received from him since, supplied more unknown details.

Mrs. Grietje MacLeod-Meijer, Mata Hari's husband's third wife, has been more than kind to me (no gin here, but much coffee and much cake), even though recounting the episodes of her life with Mata Hari's daughter at times brought back emotionally painful recollections.

Mr. Willem Dolk, of the Leeuwarden City Archives, and his predecessor Mr. Mensonides, now in The Hague, were accurate in their research and kind in giving me amply of their time. So was Mr. H. W. Keikes of the *Leeuwarder Courant,* a native Frisian whose journalistic and historical interest in Mata Hari is nearly as acute as mine. And Mrs. Ybeltje Kerkhof-Hoogslag as well as

Mrs. Buisman-Blok Wybrandt, who went to school with Mata Hari, told me about the events of those far-off days as if they had taken place yesterday.

Mlle. Lucienne Astruc, daughter of Mata Hari's lifelong impresario, supplied me with valuable letters on the artistic career of my subject. High praise is also due to Miss Ruys, chief archivist of the Dutch Foreign Ministry in The Hague, and to some of her colleagues at the Netherlands Ministry of War.

The French War Ministry, while forbiddingly uncommunicative about the secret file, has yet been helpful in trying to find information which they *were* allowed to give me. The Germans at the Foreign and War Ministries in Bonn and Koblenz, as well as some East German officials, dug deep into the meager remains of their First World War archives, most of which went up in smoke during the World War II bombardment of Potsdam.

Of those whom I interviewed back in Holland in 1932, Piet van der Hem, painter and close friend of Mata Hari, gave me some of her most valuable personal letters, simultaneously recounting much of what he knew about her. So did Dr. Roelfsema, Mr. De Balbian Verster, and the two kind Dutch ladies who are simply indicated in this book as *Mrs. K.* and *Mrs. V.* To them—in memoriam—and to the many others who are still very much alive but whom I may have forgotten to mention, my warmest thanks.

Introduction

THIS book is the first true account of Mata Hari's life. For close to fifty years the Mata Hari story has been told by authors who based their information on hearsay. Facts were not only rare, they were nonexistent. Thus rumors only were mostly used as the truth.

This book is based on fact. In doing research on Mata Hari, I have been fortunate in finding documents which for the greater part were unknown till now.

The much-discussed French secret file on Mata Hari is still secret. Only two outsiders have seen it: a French journalist who by a stroke of freakish luck was allowed to copy a large part of the file, mostly covering the pre-trial hearings only, and I. Thus, while the French government still refuses to make the file public, its information is fully included in this book.

The exact details of Mata Hari's indictment have never been known, nor the names of the members of the military jury who condemned her to death, nor the way they voted. Nor have the minutes of the proceedings of the trial itself ever been made available by the French War Department. Yet all this forbidden information is included in this book.

The part the British played in the Mata Hari story has never been told. Hitherto unpublished documents from Scotland Yard have enabled me to reconstruct this phase of Mata Hari's life in great detail.

Highly significant personal letters from Mata Hari, some dating back to the years before the First World War, and others written from her cell at Saint Lazare prison in Paris, throw a totally different light on her thoughts and state of mind. And the never before published full file of correspondence between Mata Hari and her impresario make her emerge as a woman who is totally different from the one she was supposed to be.

And then, of course, there are her private scrapbooks, which I own.

My interest in Mata Hari goes back to 1931. During that year Metro-Goldwyn-Mayer decided to produce a film starring Greta Garbo, based on Mata Hari's life and more specifically on the period of her alleged spying. As MGM's European publicity and advertising director I was very much interested, particularly since, like Mata Hari, I, too, had been born in Holland.

Mata Hari was executed by the French in 1917, after a trial that constituted the most sensational spy case of the First World War; at the time the decision was made to cast Greta Garbo in the epic about the dancer spy, only fourteen years had elapsed. I reasoned that there ought to be a good many people in the Netherlands who had known Mata Hari personally. Surely a quick trip from Paris to Holland, I thought, would deliver into my hands a lot of information that might be useful as publicity material when the film was released.

The trip was far more successful than I had anticipated, resulting in a snowballing mass of information that went far beyond my original idea. I talked to one of Mata Hari's brothers; to a doctor who had treated her in the Dutch East Indies, and to other people who had known her there; to her ex-husband's third wife; at length to lawyers, acquaintances, and people who had worked for her; to a painter and close friend who had done portraits of her; and to many others who had known her intimately—till one day someone mentioned the name of the one person who probably knew more about Mata Hari than anyone alive at that moment.

The tip took me to a hamlet in Limburg, the southernmost province of Holland. There, in a small house just outside the village, lived an old woman who had been in Mata Hari's service for years. Her name was Anna Lintjens. She had been Mata Hari's maid, companion, dresser, confidante, and general factotum.

Miss Lintjens was over seventy years old when I met her in 1932. She received me at first with misgivings, but when I explained that it was my intention to get information on Mata Hari which might illustrate that she was a real human being, although a somewhat notorious one, she became more friendly.

Miss Lintjens was only too well aware that up till then hardly anyone in the world had tried to find any justification for Mata Hari. On the contrary, nearly all writers had taken it for granted that she had been a spy in the pay of the Germans. The French, these stories pointed out, had been perfectly justified in executing her.

Was there anything she could add to the famous case, I asked Anna Lintjens, which might throw a different kind of light on the past of her former employer?

A frail and quiet little woman, Miss Lintjens had let me speak without interrupting. But once I was finished, she spoke up.

"She was never a spy," she said.

The statement, of course, did not mean much under the circumstances. Yet coming as it did from the one person who had known Mata Hari more closely and over a longer period than anyone else, the phrase seemed to crystallize the first positive declaration of Mata Hari's innocence since she herself had denied all guilt during her trial fifteen years previously.

The atmosphere in the room had lightened, and Miss Lintjens became less reticent. She had met Mata Hari in 1905, she said, and subsequently had gone to work for her.

Miss Lintjens had prepared coffee while we talked, but only after the phrase in defense of her former employer had broken the ice. She had been very ill the year before, she said, which was 1931. She had been so ill indeed that she expected to die, and had been surprised when her condition started to improve. The end of her life had been clearly in sight, and she had begun to ask herself what to do with all the letters and documents that had belonged to Mata Hari.

I felt rather tense. What *had* she done with all these personal papers which might throw a completely new light on the dancer's past? Did she still have them?

Anna shook her head. No, she said, she did not have them any more. When she had recovered from her illness, she had been afraid that the papers would fall into the wrong hands when she died. After considerable hesitation she had decided that it would be better to destroy everything. And thus one day during the preceding winter she had slowly stuffed every scrap of paper belonging to Mata Hari, every letter and every document, into the small cast-iron stove in her cottage—and had burned it all.

We looked at each other. Her face was serious, and her veined hands were folded in her lap upon the clean apron. It was as if in telling me about putting Mata Hari's papers one by one into the flames, letters from friends and lovers, seeing them disappear, that she once again saw all the years of close association that had bound her to Mata Hari.

"Have you nothing left at all?" I asked.

She looked at me intently. Then, with some difficulty, she got up from her chair and disappeared through the corridor into the room at the opposite side of the entrance hall. It took a while before she returned. She had two large books in her hands, which she carried with obvious effort.

"I have *these*," she said.

I took the books out of her hands. They were large volumes, beautifully bound in what seemed to be calf, gold-embossed. In the binding the name of the owner was gold-imprinted. Măta Hari, it said—with upturned Indian-like accents above the letter "A."

I slowly lifted the cover of the heavier of the two volumes, revealing the photograph of a beautiful woman. Anna Lintjens moved her head slightly, encouraging me to go on.

I turned several pages. More photographs. "May 1908," said one caption in French, written in a beautiful handwriting, and a little further on: "*Soirée chez moi.*"

Again I looked at Miss Lintjens. "Are these . . . ?" I asked—never finishing the phrase. She nodded, still silent, and sat down.

I waited for her to speak, for it was clear to me that it had not only cost her physical effort to bring these books out, but considerable mental effort as well. If she had burned all other documents belonging to Mata Hari, then why not these, which from all indications contained as much information as the destroyed papers?

"They were hers," she said after a short pause, "I just could not burn them. She pasted every bit of paper that was written about her in there: letters, newspaper clippings, every photograph that was ever taken of her, telegrams, notes—*everything*—all annotated in her own handwriting. She always kept them with her."

"On all her trips?"

"Even when she went to Berlin in 1914," said Miss Lintjens. "She was supposed to start dancing at the Metropole Theater, but then the war broke out." A pause. "I had no idea where she was, till I heard that she had arrived in Amsterdam."

Somehow I felt lost for words. These were Mata Hari's private scrapbooks, kept alive as if by miracle in a small cottage in a hidden Dutch village.

"What are you going to do with them?" I asked.

"I don't know," said Anna Lintjens, "I really don't know. Ever since I burned those other papers I have been wondering what to do about these. It is her life that is in these books, the years she really cared about—that is why I could not destroy them. And now I don't know. I don't want them to fall into the wrong hands when I die, and ever since I was so sick last year, I know it will inevitably happen some time. I am seventy-one years old, so who knows how long I still have to live?"

There was nothing I could say—nothing I could suggest, or dared suggest. So we talked some more, till I felt it was time to leave. I could not impose any longer on this woman, who during one afternoon had opened up a great part of her life to me— perhaps the most important part.

We sat silently, Miss Lintjens looking out of the window. She then turned back to me.

"Take them," she said. "I somehow feel I can trust you. If *you* do not take them, there is nothing for me to do but to destroy these too."

The offer was startling.

"I believe what you told me," continued Miss Lintjens. "I know these books will be safe. Promise me one thing only. Promise me that you will not let go of them while I am still alive."

I promised and we shook hands. I walked to the door in the fading light of the Limburg evening. Turning around once more, I found Anna Lintjens still sitting in her chair, only a few steps away, hands folded, alone. I was taking along the last tangible objects that had tied her to Mata Hari. For a few years she would still have her memories. Then, with herself, these too would disappear—and all that would be left of Mata Hari in the world would be these books.

That evening, in my hotel room in Amsterdam, I went through the two volumes. They were complete scrapbooks, crammed with papers that dealt with the artist's career, the dancer's lifetime. There were letters and cards from persons whose names were known throughout Europe. Letters from Jules Massenet, the French composer, and a note from Giacomo Puccini. Drawings and telegrams dating back to 1905, from shortly before she danced at the Guimet Museum in Paris, which had been the real beginning of her fame—and the last item a photograph taken in The Hague in 1915, when she appeared for the last time professionally on the stage.

The books remained with me. The war years they spent in a safe at the Bank of America in Hollywood, while I was overseas. But meantime the world had begun to think of Mata Hari as she had been personified by Greta Garbo, a glamorous dancer who was shot by the French in Vincennes.

In the late fifties I started to read more about Mata Hari, first haphazardly, then with ever increasing interest. Every article and every book I found added to the confusion, till I finally felt that, with the wealth of information I already had in my possession, a thorough research job was indicated to bring Mata Hari's life into focus—cut clear from myth and fantasy.

I spent six months on constant investigation, mostly in Holland and France, but also in Germany and England. I sent hundreds of letters to governmental and city archives, steamship companies, hotels, banks, Scotland Yard, firms, to ministries in nine countries, and to scores of individuals in Dutch and French towns and villages. The more I went on, the more I became convinced that the Mata Hari story had never been completely and truthfully told.

This book is the result of patient labor, of refusing to take anything for granted and of a constant endeavor to go to the original sources of Mata Hari's story. It is the first true account of her life. Being completely documented, including the information from the secret Paris file at the War Ministry, much of it contradicts the so-called facts which have previously been published.

MATA HARI

Chapter 1

THERE were two periods in Mata Hari's life that made her famous—one of dancing, the other one of alleged spying, the two of them compressed within a time span of twelve years and seven months. When news of her success as a dancer reached her estranged husband's ears, his comment was brief: "She's got flat feet and can't dance." And years later, when at the age of thirty-eight she appeared on the stage of his home town and he was asked whether he was going to the theater, his reaction was as blunt and to the point: "I've seen her from every possible angle, and I don't need another look." After her death in front of the firing squad it was again he who had the last word: "Whatever she's done in life, she did not deserve *that*."

It is questionable whether Mata Hari's dancing alone would have been sufficient to make her name a household word in the English language, and it is undoubtedly only the combination of dancing and spying that made "She's a real Mata Hari" a commonly used phrase.

Yet when Mata Hari was born in the city of Leeuwarden in Holland's northern province of Friesland, not one among the 27,000-plus inhabitants would have bet on her career as a celebrity. The date of the birth was August 7, 1876. The future Mata Hari started life as a Dutch girl named Margaretha Geertruida, daughter of Adam Zelle and his wife Antje van der Meulen.

Mata Hari's past remained a mystery for many years, both during her lifetime and afterwards. The place of her birth, the identity of her parents and the events that brought her fame on the Paris stage had as many versions as there were writers to put them on paper. It was said that she was the daughter of a Javanese prince; that she was born in the (then) Dutch East Indies as the child of a Dutch officer and a native woman. Mata Hari herself did not mind adding places and names. Her facility for improvisation was as astounding as it was endless. Talking to newspapermen she displayed a sixth sense for a good story; not only did she constantly embellish her historical past, but she never denied inventions of even more startling details. As such her life became a continuously varied and brilliant mixture of fact and fiction—mostly the latter.

The fantasies of her imagination, which—while she was alive—added mystery and glamor to her reputation, gave even more spice to authors who wrote about her after her execution. The literature about Mata Hari grew as the years went by. Most of these writers gave free rein to their imagination, as well as to their liberty to adopt as fact the stories of others, who had already put on paper what they thought had been Mata Hari's private life and her activities as a spy.

One of the first fables about the later Mata Hari was started by Margaretha herself, and it clearly shows how apt she was in mixing fantasy and reality even when very young. Her mother, Margaretha one day declared, was a baroness. We owe the story to Mrs. Ybeltje Kerkhof-Hoogslag, who was a pupil at the same grammar school in Leeuwarden. At the time of the story Margaretha lived in the university city of Leiden, attending a training school for kindergarten teachers, and the news about the suddenly created baroness was sent back home by another girl from Leeuwarden, a Leiden classmate of Margaretha's.

If her mother was a baroness, her father, Adam Zelle, obviously had to be a baron. Which he was indeed—but only in the imagination of the good-natured people of Leeuwarden, who jokingly referred to him as "the Baron" on account of his rather peculiar ideas and the way he tried to climb the social ladder.

As the daughter of a baron, Margaretha had to be born in a castle. This too was easily supplied, when she was already known and famous as Mata Hari. Her aristocratic cradle stood in Caminghastate, she said, an old Frisian estate belonging to her illustrious forebears. Reality was a bit different. Caminghastate still exists. It is a lovely building in the center of Leeuwarden called the Amelands Home, which for a great many years belonged to the Camingha family. Mata Hari's cradle stood in another home on the same street and from her bedroom she could look across at the old building. But the baronial past, the house, the title, the cradle, it all fitted neatly into Mata Hari's—and Margaretha's—fertile imagination.

Yet Margaretha's father was a well-to-do man. Born in 1840, he had spent all his life in Leeuwarden. Living on the Kelders, one of the main streets in town, he owned a hat store where the occasionally sober window displays were a subject of discussion among the citizens; imitating the chic shops of Amsterdam, Papa Zelle had only a few specimens of his wares showing, yet always including a silk hat, a bowler and a kepi—all three signs of the times.

Business was flourishing, and having successfully speculated in oil shares, Father Zelle on January 1, 1883, when Margaretha was six years old, moved into a newly bought house at 28 Groote Kerkstraat, an old patrician home which even today is looked upon as one of the best buildings in the town.

The new home required more servants, and another maid was added to the growing household, in which Margaretha's younger twin brothers Ari Anne and Cornelis Coenraad were now just over a year old. There was also a third brother, Johannes Henderikus.

But even long before this, Adam Zelle was a man to be reckoned with in Leeuwarden. If he was a social climber, an early status seeker, he was a tall and good-looking social climber, and his company was tolerated by the more aristocratic circles of his home town.

Adam Zelle's day of glory came in the year of his marriage, in 1873, when King William III paid a state visit to Leeuwarden. The city fathers had decided to form a horse guard of honor, and the well-to-do burghers, all belonging to the town's elite, asked Adam Zelle to join them in this endeavor. Adam was only too pleased. He was so pleased indeed that he asked a local painter,

A. Martin, to do a portrait of him in his full glory of standard-bearer—black beard, top hat, cutaway, white breeches and horse. The painting today is owned by the Frisian Museum, a present from Adam Zelle himself.

A Dutch journalist, Alexander Cohen, who was born in Leeuwarden and who lived to be close to a hundred, remembered Adam Zelle well. "I have never seen him without his top hat," he wrote several years ago, "leaning against the doorpost of his shop, his hands everlastingly in the armholes of his flowered waistcoat."

But Adam Zelle could afford to look down upon his fellow citizens from the doorway of his hatshop. In 1877, a year after Margaretha was born, he earned 3500 guilders (comparable to approximately 25,000 dollars today) and there were few citizens in Leeuwarden at that time who could claim a higher income.

The fact that her father was well off may have been one of the reasons why Mata Hari was not able to live without luxury later on. Adam spoiled his four children, and specially Margaretha—the only girl. While she was still very young, Papa Zelle gave her an exquisite four-seater carriage, drawn by two beautifully horned goats. The gift was Margaretha's pride and joy. Although she was only six at the time, she was enabled to be admired, which was already important to her.

The goat carriage created a sensation. Not even the children of the richest people in town had a toy like this! Mrs. Buisman-Blok Wybrandt, now well over eighty and a former classmate of Margaretha, whom I saw in Leeuwarden in 1963, vividly remembers the carriage and called it "an *amazing* bit of foolhardiness, which put Margaretha absolutely in a class by herself." It was an impression Papa Zelle had undoubtedly hoped for.

Mrs. Kerkhof-Hoogslag, Margaretha's other contemporary, told me how keenly that carriage was remembered. A few years ago, she said, she met a former classmate of hers, and simply in order to recall their schooldays of more than seventy years before to her friend, Mrs. Kerkhof said: "You remember, that was the school Margaretha Zelle went to." The other woman's reaction, jumping back two-thirds of a century, was immediate and sharp: "Yes," she said, "she had a carriage drawn by goats." It was the one clear memory of that school—Margaretha Zelle and her *bokkenwagen*.

Leeuwarden, which even today is a placid community where on Fridays traffic in the center of the town is diligently re-routed, when farmers from all over Friesland bring their prize-crowned cattle to the city's market, was during the latter part of the last century a small provincial town, where people on the whole had small provincial ideas. They all lived—or were supposed to live— within their means and according to their social standing, and Mr. Zelle's horseback riding, his baronial airs, and the quite excellent education he gave his children were all factors that irked the Leeuwarden citizens to a certain extent.

Margaretha was a good-looking child, and Adam Zelle's financial standing allowed him to send her to Miss Buys' school on the Hofplein opposite the city hall, where she joined the daughters of the socially established citizens. The only foreign language taught by Miss Buys was French, the fashionable language of the time. Later on Margaretha continued her studies at the high school for girls on the Groote Houtstraat, where English and German were also part of the curriculum.

Miss Buys, according to H. W. Keikes, today an editor of the city's daily newspaper the *Leeuwarder Courant,* was quite a remarkable person, much loved by her pupils. A rather tiny unmarried woman with a slight limp, she insisted on good manners, an erect walk, and ladylike behavior. She also taught her girls to write properly: Mata Hari's excellent handwriting was due to the years she spent in grammar school—most of the other pupils' penmanship shows the same strong characteristics, the typical product of Miss Buys' teaching.

Writing poetry and having albums filled with poems by friends was one of the sentimental games young girls indulged in during those years. When I visited Mrs. Kerkhof-Hoogslag, she pulled out her own grammar-school poetry book and showed me—and

subsequently made me a present of—the poem Margaretha Zelle
had written in there on February 16, 1889, when she was twelve
years old. It is dedicated to "Dear Ybeltje," and reads in free
translation:

> If your eyes in reader's quest,
> Seeking joy among these pages
> Upon this sheet have come to rest,
> Remember that the writer's best
> Wishes are yours throughout the ages.

And, this being a poem, she signed it with her full name: "In
memory of Margaretha."

"She preferred to be called that," Mrs. Kerkhof-Hoogslag told
me, "because she considered it dignified. We, on the other hand,
always called girls whose name was Margaretha by the usual
diminutive, which was 'Greet.' So we compromised: Margaretha
signed all her letters and poems with her full name, and we settled on calling her M'greet" (pronounced "M'great").

Mrs. Kerkhof-Hoogslag had made a poetic effort of her own
as well, dedicated to M'greet—and after all these years she was
still able to quote the opening lines to me:

> "Amidst a thousand dandelions,
> One shining orchid stands."

She had always had "a silent admiration for M'greet," she confessed, and remembers her as "a slender girl with black hair and
cheeky eyes."

"She knew that she was different from all the other children,
and many of us could not stand that and were jealous," Mrs.
Kerkhof-Hoogslag told me. "She had a good voice and dared to
wear extraordinary clothes—and we didn't. It obviously created
jealousies, but I always defended her and explained that she
didn't do it to outshine us, but simply because that was the way
she was. It was in her nature to shine. The others sometimes saw
her behavior as impudence—I saw it as something very special."

When Mata Hari many years later became the toast of the Paris salons, no one was probably less surprised than she herself, because she automatically continued to do what she had always done: to be different. Margaretha Zelle, even during those schooldays in Leeuwarden, loved the dramatic. To amaze her friends, to find herself the focal point of their admiration, or bewilderment, to be considered extravagant, strange, to be discussed, to shine, to be special—it was all part and parcel of her nature.

She was the only girl in town, as Ybeltje had mentioned, who came to school in what were then considered daringly flamboyant clothes. One summer she wore a yellow-and-red-striped dress, another time she came to school in red velvet, whirling and turning in front of her classmates, who were greatly impressed. But as Mrs. Kerkhof-Hoogslag explained to me: "A girl simply didn't *wear* such a dress to school." Yet the impression she made on her girl friends must have been a strong one indeed, to be remembered so vividly after more than seventy years.

Her sense of the dramatic was once again made acutely clear a few years later, when Margaretha's mother died in 1891, her daughter being fifteen. In the afternoon of the day of the funeral piano music was heard coming from their apartment on the Willemskade F30. A few days later Ybeltje Hoogslag met M'greet in town, and inquired rather hesitantly after the source of the music.

"*I* was playing," said M'greet dramatically, "it was the *pain* I felt"—and the word *pain*, Ybeltje told me, was heavily underscored in the gravely and slowly spoken sentence. Was it sadness expressed in music? Real pain? Or could it simply have been M'greet's excessive and overdeveloped sense of the dramatic which prompted her to give this answer?

After Mr. Zelle had been prospering for a good number of years, his financial circumstances suddenly took a turn for the worse, and in 1889 he went bankrupt. This unfortunate incident was the beginning of the dispersal of the Zelle family. Having nothing more to do in Leeuwarden, Adam Zelle left the city of his birth and on July 15, 1889, moved to The Hague. His wife and the children, including M'greet, went to live in the modest upstairs apartment on the Willemskade.

Adam Zelle was no more fortunate in The Hague than he had been in Leeuwarden, and on May 31, 1890, he rejoined his family. But things were no longer what they used to be, and the relationship with his wife—as well as with M'greet—worsened to such an extent that on September 4, 1890, a legal separation was pronounced between Adam and Antje Zelle. She died nine months later, on May 10, 1891—and the breakup of the Zelle family was completed.

Margaretha's legacy from her mother was her poetry album, in which Mrs. Zelle had copied poems mostly religious in character, which she liked—plus one poem about love. M'greet kept it till she became Mata Hari, and then left it with her husband.

Before his wife's death, in March 1891, Adam Zelle had left Leeuwarden for the second time. He moved to Amsterdam. Margaretha stayed on in Leeuwarden till November of the same year. On the twelfth of that month her twin brothers too moved to Amsterdam, and M'greet went to live with her godfather, Mr. Visser, in Sneek, a small town not too far from Leeuwarden. A few weeks later her third brother, Johannes Henderikus, moved to Franeker, where his mother's family lived.

In Sneek Mr. Visser had to decide what to do with his ward, who by now was fifteen years old, and who had to start thinking about her future and the making of a living. It was decided to send her to Leiden to be trained as a kindergarten teacher at the only school of its kind then in existence in Holland.

"The choice," Mrs. Ybeltje Kerkhof-Hoogslag told me, "could not have been worse, for she was definitely not fit for such a career." Ybeltje and her friends in Leeuwarden decided "that it was nothing for her. Such a job was good for a 'motherly' girl, and M'greet was a *personality*."

At Leiden Mr. Wybrandus Haanstra, the headmaster of the

school, fell in love with her. What might have happened if he had *not* fallen in love, no one can tell. But it is fairly sure that in that case there would never have been a Mata Hari, and Margaretha Geertruida Zelle might have finished her life as a kindergarten teacher somewhere along a quiet Dutch canal.

Chapter 2

To bring the Leiden episode to a speedy end, Margaretha was sent to live with another uncle of hers, Mr. Taconis, in The Hague. She was by now seventeen, and—like every girl of that age—romantic.

The Hague was then, towards the turn of the century, a town where many officers from the Colonial Army in the Dutch East Indies used to spend their leave. Also, The Hague is close to the Netherlands' most famous beach resort at Scheveningen, where there were plenty of opportunities to meet young men, especially in uniform. Margaretha consequenlty enjoyed her stay in The Hague to the fullest, falling for the first time in love with "The Uniform," a love which—as she was to claim so strongly in self-defense many years later at her trial—was never to leave her.

Again nothing might have happened if a certain officer of the Colonial Army had not returned to Holland on August 14, 1894, to spend two years' sick leave at home. His name was Rudolph MacLeod, often officially written as Macleod, and sometimes Mac-Leod. He was about five feet ten, sturdily built, rather round-faced, wore a long sweeping moustache and ditto saber, and was nearly completely bald, the hair having disappeared during his more than sixteen years of uninterrupted colonial service.

MacLeod was of old Scottish descent, one of his forefathers having arrived in Holland early in the eighteenth century. A later

forebear, returning to England during Napoleon's occupation of
Holland, had come back to the Netherlands for good when the
French Emperor disappeared from the European scene. He had
been, as were nearly all of his Dutch descendants, a soldier.

Rudolph MacLeod's uncle had been a general and adjutant to
King William III, and, although old, this uncle was still alive
when his nephew returned from the Indies. The general's son—
Rudolph's cousin—was a Dutch vice admiral, whose photograph
makes him resemble another member of the MacLeod family,
also a vice admiral, but this one a Scotsman: Angus MacLeod,
c.v.o.

Rudolph's father had been John van Brienen MacLeod, a retired Dutch captain of infantry, and his mother was Diana Louise
Baroness Sweerts de Landas—aristocratic, but poor. Rudolph Mac-
Leod, having been born on March 1, 1856, was on his return
to Holland thirty-eight years old.

His military career had been an excellent one. Following in his
father's footsteps, he enlisted in the army at the age of only
sixteen. Four years later he was a sergeant and, finally, having
come up through the ranks, he was promoted to second lieutenant
in 1877, to leave soon afterwards, aged twenty-one, for the Dutch
East Indies.

The idea of going to the colonies scandalized aristocratic
members of the family on his mother's side. They had no love
for the army, and indeed the prospect of serving in the colonies around the eighteen-eighties was not an undertaking many
Dutchmen looked forward to with pleasure. The common soldiers, all volunteers, who left for the Indies as "colonials," were
often the riffraff of Holland, or poor boys who did it to make a
living as mercenaries, plus the sons of well-to-do families who
had gone wrong. Consequently, when young Rudolph MacLeod
came to say good-by to his mother's sisters, they were shocked
and suggested pulling strings to get him out of what they considered his predicament. Young Rudolph soon put them straight
as to his own feelings: his was a soldier's family; he had now

earned his second lieutenant's grade the hard way, and his future lay, obviously, in the colonies. And to the colonies he went.

Dealing with the mixed characters who made up the colonial army, the officers themselves had to be tough, or they would not last. Thus Rudolph MacLeod, from the age of twenty-one on, and for nearly seventeen years without interruption, had to deal with tough specimens of the human race, and the experience hardened him, as might be expected. His language became the soldier's language, and as his third wife—with whom I had talked for many hours back in 1932, and again several times in 1963— described him to me, he was "an outspoken, hard-bitten, tough but thoroughly straightforward soldier, with a heart of gold."

His third wife, of course, had not yet known him when he met Margaretha Zelle on his return from seventeen years of colonial duty on Java, Sumatra, Borneo, and elsewhere. His service included many years of hard fighting in what was known in Holland as the "Atjeh war," the terrible struggle in the extreme northern part of Sumatra, in which he participated for a total of ten years in the eighties and nineties. Rudolph, till the end of his life, proudly carried both the Officers Cross and the Atjeh Expeditionary Cross. He never received the Colonial Army's highest award, the much-coveted Military Williams Order, which, he said, "they had finagled not to give him."

In May 1890 he was given two years' home leave, but at his own request the order was canceled two months later. But by 1894 Rudolph MacLeod's return to Holland had become imperative, his health having been seriously undermined by those seventeen years of uninterrupted service. He had moreover suffered for years from diabetes, and his physical condition now became even worse with the aggravation of lingering rheumatism of the joints. His condition was so serious that on leaving the Indies on June 27, 1894, he had to be carried aboard the S.S. *Prinses Marie* on a stretcher.

While he was recuperating in Amsterdam, riots broke out on the East Indies Island of Lombok, just east of Bali. The news which reached Holland about the fighting was vague and for the greater part government controlled. The Dutch press was anxious for more direct information, and one journalist, J. T. Z. De Balbian Verster, writing during the first half of 1895 for the Amsterdam *News of the Day*, had left instructions with his editorial office to get him the names of all officers returning from the colonies who for some reason or other would contact the paper. As De Balbian Verster rightly thought, they would be an excellent source of uncensored news. Rudolph MacLeod having been one of these officers, the two men met and became rather close friends.

One day, over a quiet cup of coffee in Amsterdam's Café Americain, De Balbian Verster noticed that his friend was not his usual self. His friends jokingly tried to analyze the situation and decided that MacLeod was lonely. What he needed, they figured, was feminine company, and he should get married. Indeed for an officer nearing the age of forty and returning to the tropics, a wife was not a superfluous commodity.

Officers and civilians going to the Dutch East Indies on their first trip usually went unmarried. All of them were young, often just out of school or university. These civilians, on their return home at the end of their first four or six years' contractual colonial period, would feverishly look for a wife, their salaries by then usually having reached a level which could afford such a luxury. By the time the prospective bride was found, the husband-to-be often would have to return to the Indies. The marriage would then take place by proxy ("with the glove," as the Dutch called it), the groom waiting impatiently under the tropical sun, and his wife still home under the gray Dutch skies.

For officers in the colonial army the situation was more difficult and financially far more precarious. If they married back in Holland without the permission of their superior officer, their paycheck would not be increased to that of a married man, and even when after a good number of years their family would include several children, they would still be known officially in the service as "bachelor," and would have to make both ends meet on their meager bachelor army officer's salary. The charming face met in Holland would often become a financial burden back in the Indies.

After MacLeod's sad interlude in the Amsterdam coffeehouse, De Balbian Verster, entirely on his own initiative, put an advertisement in his newspaper: "Officer on home leave from Dutch East Indies would like to meet girl of pleasant character—object matrimony." The advertisement had been put in as a joke, and according to most accounts MacLeod, as soon as he heard about it, instructed De Balbian Verster to return all letters unopened. MacLeod's third wife, on the other hand, told me that he did open them. A great many letters were from girls who offered handsome dowries, including one from a minister's daughter. "He could have married money," she said, "but instead he picked the wrong one." De Balbian Verster's joke would have far-reaching consequences.

About two weeks after the advertisement appeared, two more letters arrived. De Balbian Verster happened to be out of town, and the newspaper's office forwarded the letters directly to MacLeod. One of them came from Margaretha Geertruida Zelle, all by herself in The Hague, schoolbenches far behind her, with nothing much to do and with time to read the classified ads during that cold month of March 1895.

MacLeod was intrigued. M'greet by now was a strikingly good-looking girl, who had been intelligent enough to enclose a photograph. MacLeod kept his discovery secret for a while. De Balbian Verster did not hear about it till Rudolph told him that as a belated result of one of the letters received, he had started corresponding with its sender, "who seemed to be quite a girl." The quote is De Balbian Verster's, whom I saw in 1932.

Rudolph did not get in touch with De Balbian Verster just to give him this news. He also wanted help, or at least advice. His correspondence with the charming young lady had reached the point where a meeting seemed indicated. Living in Amsterdam, and Margaretha in The Hague, MacLeod wanted to know where they could meet.

De Balbian Verster suggested the Amsterdam Rijksmuseum as a convenient place. At that moment, however, MacLeod suffered a recurrence of his rheumatism, and the rendezvous was canceled. From his sickbed Rudolph—or John, as he was called by all his friends and relatives—continued to correspond with his as yet unknown girl friend.

The day MacLeod and Margaretha did meet was a decisive and fateful one for both of them. Instead of looking at paintings in the museum, they looked at each other, and they liked what they saw. MacLeod was, especially in uniform, a handsome man, and Margaretha—who had disliked being called M'greet, but whom John from here on never called anything but plain "Griet" (pronounced "Greet")—was a charming young woman, gay, dark-eyed and black-haired, looking several years older than her age. Love or physical attraction, or both, was the immediate result and six days after their first meeting, on March 30, 1895, they were engaged.

For the first few months Griet stayed on in The Hague at her uncle's home, making frequent trips to see her fiancé in Amsterdam. During this period John had another attack of rheumatism, making several appointments with Griet impossible. The attack was so serious that he was unable to write to her personally, and he asked his sister with whom he was living to do so for him. Griet, in The Hague, answered in loving letters, clearly written by an enamored eighteen-year-old girl.

"My dearest *Johnie*," she wrote one Wednesday evening of that year 1895, "Oh, darling, I feel such pity for you, and I am so terribly sorry that our plan once again has gone wrong. All accidents happen at once, don't they? Well, John, don't feel too bad about it, *tootie*. When I come to see you on Sunday I hope the pain will be gone.

"Did you suffer much, and couldn't you write me yourself? I

guess not, could you?—for otherwise you would have done so. Do you think you'll be able to walk again on Sunday? I do hope so, darling, but do not try to overdo it. Yes, it made me feel very sad at first, but I considered it from the gay and sensible point of view, for if I just sit here and feel dismal, that won't help you a bit, will it?

"Louise wrote me: 'I hope for both of you that in a few weeks at the city hall everything will be floating in sunshine.' Well, I hope so, too, and you, John? What do you think? You'd better be brave and gay, for that brings the best results. Your little wife always does that, and if I had not, my gaiety would have worn off a long time ago. Do you expect me Sunday?

"When you are able to, will you write me and let me know how you are feeling? Just give me a wonderful kiss, and just imagine that I am with you, that's what I do too.

"Well, *Johnie,* adieu with a delicious kiss from your so very loving wife—Greta." *

Not much time was lost between their engagement and marriage. On July 11, 1895, three and a half months after they had first met, Margaretha Geertruida Zelle became Mrs. MacLeod. Her husband was thirty-nine years old, Margaretha not yet nineteen. It was a simple civil ceremony at the Amsterdam city hall with only a few friends present, as well as a last-minute-introduced Papa Zelle. Two fellow officers acted as witnesses for MacLeod, while De Balbian Verster and the publisher H. J. W. Becht were Margaretha's witnesses.

But all had not been smooth during the days preceding the wedding. There had been a close inspection of the bride, an attempt to stop the proceedings, and especially one surprise meeting which had seriously threatened to cancel, or at least to postpone, the so happily planned occasion.

In the first place no one in John's strictly military family could get married without the official sanction of his uncle, the retired old general. Although himself by now a veteran of many years'

* Another Dutch diminutive of Margaretha.

service in the army, John had to follow family tradition and dutifully took his young future bride to see the doyen of the Dutch clan of the MacLeods, hoping that she would pass inspection.   ·

Uncle Norman silently looked at the new family recruit. He mumbled a few words and for a moment the situation was tense. But at closer inspection the old soldier could only agree with his nephew's choice. "Young but good-looking," he said repeatedly, "damn' good-looking." Griet had made the grade, and the first obstacle to their marriage had been passed successfully.

Though the possible opposition within the MacLeod family had thus been averted, there were still members of the Zelle group who as yet had not been brought into the picture, and John had a surprise waiting for him.

Griet told him one day that she had a father, and according to the third Mrs. MacLeod, he had answered that this "happened in the best of families." Dramatically Griet had said: "But he is *alive!*"

The estranged father Zelle had been kept a secret, and Griet had told her fiancé that she was an orphan. But now, the wedding day constantly approaching, Griet needed her father—or at least his consent. Being under age, she could not marry without it, unless she could bring a death certificate along. As it happened, Papa Zelle, still very much alive, was living with his second wife in one of the poorer sections of Amsterdam, at 148 on the Lange Leidschedwarsstraat.

John did not look forward to a meeting with his suddenly emerged future father-in-law. He was an officer, of excellent family. Mr. Zelle was a bankrupt traveling salesman, living in a decrepit neighborhood. John was marrying the daughter, not the whole family, and his interest in Griet's relatives was fairly well nil.

But John was in love, and was contemplating his marriage with appropriate joy. As a man of thirty-nine who had spent all of his adult life in the tropics, the women he had known had mostly

sions such as "your loving little wife," as used in Margaretha's quoted letter, would point to the same conclusion. According to Heymans the eighteen-year-old Griet wrote her thirty-nine-year-old beloved: "You ask me whether I would like to do silly things? Rather ten times than once! Just do whatever you want, for in a few weeks I'll be your wife anyhow. Isn't it wonderful that we both have the same fiery temperament?" And again: "Don't be afraid that I am unwell. It happened exactly on time, and that was a few days ago, so tomorrow you can ask me anything you want."

If MacLeod, as Heymans claims, really gave him these letters freely, then one might well wonder about the delicacy of a man of over seventy who hands a total stranger such letters from his fiancée, written thirty years previously. The only generous deduction is that John MacLeod having, as his third wife told me, "got fed up with Heymans' insistent questioning," handed him the letters without remembering their contents, and unfortunately without checking them first.

As matters stood, Margaretha had made overtures to her father in order to find out on what terms he would consent to her marriage. Papa Zelle's first demand had been a visit from the betrothed couple; he had, after all, the right to meet his future son-in-law.

The visit to his humble dwelling turned out to be a day of victory for the fifty-five-year-old father. He had insisted they come and see him in a large carriage instead of in a simple one-horse cab, and the presence of carriage and horses in the narrow street created a sensation. But Adam Zelle did give his fatherly benediction, and was promptly asked to come to the city hall the next day, where his presence was necessary from a legal point of view.

On the morning of the wedding John's sister Frida, who was known in the family as "*Tante* (Aunt) Lavies," the colloquial Dutch pronunciation of her name Louise, made a last-minute

been natives. His beautiful young wife would cut an impressi
and striking figure at the garrison clubhouses in the Indies, ai
the twenty years' difference in age was, for the moment at leas
of no concern whatever.

John's decision to marry Griet had not been prompted by hei
pregnancy, as various authors have written. According to Dutch
writer Charles S. Heymans,* Mata Hari's son Norman had been
born on January 30, 1896, barely six months after the wedding.
One writer after another (Baumgarthen, Newman) took up this
theme. As Newman put it, their marriage "was not based on
sacred, but on profane love—she was already pregnant on her
wedding day." †

For several years I myself accepted Mr. Heymans' bland as-
sertion, till I received a copy of the child's birth certificate from
the Vital Statistics Bureau of the city of Amsterdam, which gave
the year of his birth as 1897 instead of 1896. Surprised, I asked
Amsterdam to please verify the dates. The reply came back
within a week: "The birthdate of Norman John, son of Rudolph
MacLeod and his wife Margaretha Zelle is: January thirtieth
eighteen hundred and ninety-seven (1897)."

I triple-checked with the archivist of The Hague, who previously had been head of the city archives of Leeuwarden, Margaretha's birthplace. Mr. Mensonides, who consulted the records
of the Netherlands' Central Bureau of Genealogy, also found that
the year of Norman's birth was inscribed as 1897.

"It is thus without doubt," wrote Mr. Mensonides, "that the
long-lived tale about Margaretha Zelle having been pregnant well
before her marriage must be relegated to the land of fairy tales
as one more of the many fables that have been spun around her."

Still, as can be easily deducted from John and Griet's correspondence, their relationship had been an intimate one. Expres-

---

* *La Vraie Mata Hari*, original edition in French by Editions Prométhée,
Paris, 1930.
† Bernard Newman, *Inquest on Mata Hari*, published by Robert Hale
Ltd., London, 1956.

effort to keep her brother from making a fatal mistake. "Johnny," she said in the words related to me by Grietje Meijer-MacLeod, "Johnny—don't do it."

But Johnny did, and left his sister's apartment in the company of his radiant-looking bride to go and pronounce solemn vows. The ceremony at the city hall was a quiet affair, but afterwards it grew into a boisterous demonstration—all of Papa Zelle's neighbors thronged the pavement along the canal, wildly cheering the newlyweds, who quickly proceeded to their favorite Café Americain for a wedding lunch. The bride's father did not attend. Evil tongues claim that John had given instructions to the driver of his father-in-law's carriage to take him to another part of town.

For their honeymoon the young couple went to Wiesbaden, a favorite spa then as well as now, and a city that would crop up later again and again in Mata Hari's imaginary tales about how and where she had spent her youth. But Wiesbaden also gave John an inkling of what might be in store for him in having married a very young and very pretty girl. The town was full of arrogant young officers, who did not refrain from making overt advances to and loud remarks about the appealing-looking Dutch girl. John very soon had enough and stepped up to what he considered nothing but young whippersnappers. "Gentlemen," he said, "that lady is my wife"—and off he walked, arm in arm with his Griet.

On their return to Holland John made his first matrimonial mistake: he accepted his sister's hospitality and went to live with his wife at 79 Leidschekade, practically around the corner from the Café Americain. Tante Lavies had been married to *Notaire* Wolsink of the small town of Loppersum, but by now was a widow. She and her brother had grown apart through the years, yet remained devoted to each other. And from the beginning no love was lost between her and Margaretha.

It was, of course, cheaper to live with relatives than for the young MacLeods to take an apartment of their own. But the strained relationship between the two women, as well as Mac-

Leod's further extension of his home leave, soon afterwards made them decide to move.

The decision to stay with Tante Lavies had been greatly influenced by John's financial circumstances which were rather precarious at the time. Pay in the Dutch Colonial Army, even for officers, was meager, and John's salary was far from sufficient to sustain the mode of life he was leading in Holland. And Margaretha's courtship, followed by the expenses of the wedding and honeymoon in Wiesbaden, had drained his ready cash even more. The situation was not a desperate one, but these fluctuating financial difficulties were not a good omen for a happy life in the Dutch East Indies, and they played their part in the unfortunate marital developments that took place later on.

Margaretha's greatest moment during the married months she spent in Holland was a reception at the Royal Palace given by Queen Regent Emma, mother of Queen Wilhelmina. The young bride wore her long yellow wedding gown for the occasion, and with her good looks, dark complexion and black hair, she was to her husband's great pride to some extent the belle of the ball.

To a few close friends of the MacLeods the first cracks in the marital bliss appeared very soon after the wedding. Mrs. V., the wife of a doctor, had met John after his return from the Indies in 1894, when he brought her greetings from her son, also stationed in the East. Mrs. V. found him rather rude, and later, when she met Margaretha shortly after her engagement, she wondered whether the planned union would work out.

Margaretha had made the impression on Mrs. V. of "being a young woman with the best intentions, who suffered greatly from her husband's rude manners and neglect, which was already in evidence during the first weeks after her return from their honeymoon."

These first impressions of Mrs. V. seem to have been correct. John MacLeod, who mellowed so thoroughly in later years during his marriage to Grietje Meijer, in the late nineties still lived the life of the rough colonial officer. His first marriage did not change his manners overnight, nor did it limit the attraction he felt for other women. De Balbian Verster confirmed these stories to me.

Only a few weeks after the wedding John asked De Balbian Verster whether he would mind keeping his wife company that evening. He had a date with two girls, he said, and expected to be home rather late. De Balbian Verster directed his steps towards the MacLeod home and found Griet playing the piano. Late that evening John returned home, was his charming old self, and apologized for having stayed out that late—"he had been detained."

In March and again in September 1896 John's home leave was extended, each time for a period of six months. Firstly this was for reasons of health, but also because by now his wife was really pregnant. On January 30, 1897 Margaretha's son was born. He received the name of Norman John, after his paternal grandfather John van Brienen MacLeod, and his great-uncle Norman, the retired general.

A few months later, on May 1, the MacLeods left for the Dutch East Indies on the S.S. *Prinses Amalia*. The departure found Margaretha in a buoyant mood, for this trip was an adventure. She was on her way to a new country, was going to meet new people, and there was the lure of the tropics to be looked forward to. She was twenty years old, and her husband by now was forty-one—a tremendous difference in age for a couple going to a part of the world where white women were scarce, and where beautiful white women were absolutely at a premium.

For a short while the MacLeods lived in Ambarawa, a village south of Semarang in the center of Java. Then John was transferred to Toempoeng, near Malang, on the eastern side of the large island. The transfer was a great improvement, because Malang was a city with many Europeans and, what was more important, the pleasures that appeal to Europeans.

The MacLeods lived in Toempoeng for one year, during which period, on May 2, 1898, a second child was born, a girl, who was named Jeanne Louise after Tante Lavies. The MacLeods immediately started to refer to her as "Non" (and Non she remained till the day she died), an often used abbreviation of the Malay word *nonah*, which simply means young girl.*

It was, however, not a happy time. The matrimonial trouble, which had started so early in Holland, took on a far more serious aspect under the blazing tropical sun. Griet therefore was quite relieved when her husband on December 21, 1898, received his orders for transfer to the city of Medan on Sumatra's east coast, opposite Malaya on the Strait of Malacca. The separation—for MacLeod was to leave fairly immediately and his family was to follow shortly afterwards—would give her a breathing spell from squabbles and unpleasant situations.

MacLeod, with his usual brusqueness, made a simple arrangement for his wife's and children's stay in Toempoeng during his absence. One morning he rode up to the house of the government comptroller, Mr. van Rheede, and, never dismounting (I was told the story by Mrs. van Rheede), explained to him about his imminent departure, which was already known in the small Dutch settlement.

"My wife and children are coming to stay with you in a few hours, till I get them over to Medan. You don't mind, do you?"

Hospitality was openhanded in the Dutch East Indies, and transfers being a common occurrence in the Colonial Army, such hospitality was frequently requested and granted. Consequently Mr. van Rheede "didn't mind," and later that day Griet and her two chlidren moved into the friendly home. One additional reason for Margaretha's staying on in Toempoeng was the fact that the disposal of their furniture had to be supervised. Since the government did not pay for the moving of the household goods, they had to be sold at auction, which was cheaper for the owner than to pay for the shipment over long distances out of his own pocket. MacLeod, who went through an infinite series of transfers

* Th. Baumgarthen, in his book *Mata Hari,* calls her Louise Giovanna and speaks about Rudolph as Renato, obviously copied from an Italian writer.

during the years he was in the Indies, was constantly plagued by the financial burden the multiple auctions put on him.

After Margaretha and her children had been installed at the van Rheedes' for a while, there was—according to Mrs. van Rheede—no more news from John MacLeod, nor did any funds arrive for the trip from Java to Sumatra. The situation, as Mrs. van Rheede told me, "was becoming quite embarrassing." Mrs. van Rheede was partly wrong, as I found out later. While it was true that John MacLeod did not send any money for a while, he did write to his wife. In fact, he was a most prolific letter writer, who made handwritten copies of every letter he sent out, no matter its length.

On March 28, John wrote one of his many letters to Griet, giving her detailed information on the city of Medan and on the events that took place in the community. With his flair for journalistic description which he used so eloquently in the writing for various newspapers that later on supplemented his meager income, he ran off pages on end to give his wife an impression of the city she was to come to.

"It is strange to see this city with its many multiple-storeyed homes and its excellent roads: electric lights, beautiful *tokos* (shops) that outshine those in Batavia, wonderful horses and carriages. They have had to kill 739 dogs during two days on account of rabies, but Blackie (their own dog) is inside the house and feels fine; and now, dear Griet, adieu!, and be sure to give my regards to the van Rheedes—your husband, John."

A month later, when letters from Margaretha's side had been lacking, John tried to explain to his wife some of the intricacies of correspondence between the many islands of the archipelago, which spreads out over thousands of miles. "You mention that 'after having written me two letters, you are waiting for my answer from Medan.' Come now, Griet, I bet that by now you are laughing about your stupidity. 'To wait for an answer from Medan'—but Griet, that takes about sixteen days, and you mean to say that you intended not to write during all this time? That is really typical of you!"

Since Margaretha was staying with the van Rheedes (where she was dressed, like many Dutch women in the Indies at that time, in native *sarong* and *kabaja*, skirt and blouse), the hostess had an excellent opportunity to get better acquainted with her. The later Mata Hari proved to be a charming and intelligent person. "She may have been a bit frivolous," said Mrs. van Rheede, "but that was nothing extraordinary in such a young woman."

Money was one of John's constant preoccupations during all these years, and the thoughts about financial trouble hardly ever left him. He mentioned it to his wife in that same letter of April 24, 1899, in which he chided her about her lack of correspondence: "The thing that makes me so often inwardly complain is the fact that we absolutely never have any financial luck, and what a great many rotten things we have been obliged to do on account of all that lack of money."

John MacLeod in this letter then jumped to another subject of preoccupation, caused by something his wife had mentioned. "Who is that naval lieutenant you write about, who photographed the children and how did he happen to be in Toempoeng? You never explain things of that sort, Griet, and you can perfectly well understand that when I read this, I start thinking: 'Well now, who is that again, and how did he get to Toempoeng?' It's funny—you suddenly jump from Jan Pik's sailor suit and Fluit's affectionate nature ('Jan Pik' and 'Fluit' were his nicknames for his two children) to that lieutenant and then I do not hear a word about him any more! . . . And so Pik is very much in love with his little sister? That perpetual urge for kissing he certainly has from you!"

He then touched upon a subject which had been the cause of much friction between him and his wife: "Yes, Griet, just try to understand that when I rave and swear, this is caused principally because I am afraid for the children, for do not forget that our characters differ tremendously."

It is clear from John's wondering about the lieutenant that he had been both jealous and suspicious of his wife for a long time. It was a jealousy and suspicion that had been feeding one another, not altogether unusual in a marriage where the husband was old enough to be his wife's father. Perhaps there was some reason for John's jealousy, because through the years Margaretha grew constantly more attractive. On the weekly Saturday night visit to the local club—then about the only form of entertainment in the Indies—Margaretha was always surrounded by a score of young bachelor officers and planters, who paid a great deal of attention to the attractive Mrs. MacLeod. And even married men, often joined in matrimony in those hasty proxy weddings between East and West, were not averse to flirting with the good-looking Margaretha.

John finally had made the necessary financial arrangements for his wife's and children's trip to Medan, and on May 14 he wrote her the last admonishments for the voyage, and told her about what to expect on arrival.

"I am glad to have received your letter of 25 April this morning, with your description of the children's illness. There is a lot of work waiting for you here, Griet, for these houses are dangerous to live in if one is not constantly clean. If one is not continuously busy with sweeping, moving of flowerpots and tarring of the premises, all kinds of vermin crawl around. Thus last night I saw a scorpion the size of which I had never before seen in my life. Although the bite of such a beast is not immediately fatal, it does cause a high fever and for small children it is very dangerous. Therefore you'll have to inspect the rooms every day *yourself*, clean the children's beds and move the flowerpots. I am glad to note from your letter that you are perfectly aware of your heavy responsibility with the children and that you take care of them with devotion."

In Medan, MacLeod was promoted to garrison commander and as such held an important post in the Dutch community, where at times, as Chief Netherlands Military Officer, he had to

be host at official receptions. Griet, of course, loved these func-
tions, at which she could glitter as the wife of the army commander. According to the third Mrs. MacLeod, John often ran
into difficulties on these occasions. MacLeod had ordered clothes
for Griet all the way from Amsterdam. Margaretha felt like a
queen, said the third Mrs. MacLeod, and acted like one. When
older officers' wives came to pay their respect, Griet refused to
leave her husband's side to meet them halfway. She was of the
opinion that as the wife of the garrison's commander it was the
visitor's duty to come to *her*—and age played no part in this.
Petty jealousies being what they are, especially in small tropical
garrisons, Griet's behavior created both immediate difficulties and
a latent unpleasant situation for the Major.

However, the matrimonial situation of the MacLeods in Medan
was bad enough without such incidents. Then, quite suddenly, a
tragic event brought husband and wife closer together again, at
least temporarily. On June 27, 1899, their two-and-a-half-year-old
son Norman died. Both he and his little sister had been poisoned,
and only Non could be saved through the desperate efforts of
the local Dutch doctor.

Two stories circulated in Medan as the reason for the poison-
ing, one recounting the beating MacLeod had given a native soldier who was in love with the children's nurse, and who in turn
had poisoned the children to take revenge. The other version
had a more intimate connection with the married life of the
MacLeods, but was probably less true; it was rumored that John
had made successful advances to the nurse, whose native lover
had then poisoned the children.

Whatever the cause of the tragedy, for a while it seemed as if
the death of the boy might result in a happier marriage. The
improvement, however, did not last long. MacLeod had dearly
loved his son and his death was a tremendous shock to him. But
soon his quick-tempered character got the better of him again.
He reproached his wife for their son's death and their relations
became more strained than ever. At this very moment MacLeod

was transferred back to Java, another move which he blamed on his superior officer General Biesz, whose antipathy towards him he believed had been the cause of his not being promoted to lieutenant colonel.

This time the MacLeods moved to the village of Banjoe Biroe, and once there, a legal separation seemed to be the only solution. But as long as they were in the tropics, such a solution presented certain difficulties, of which the financial ones were not the least important. Moreover, towards the middle of March 1900, Griet had an attack of typhoid fever. While she was away to recuperate, John wrote a forty-eight-page letter to his cousin in The Hague, all copied by hand. Dealing with the political and military situation in the Indies as well as with John's own manifold troubles, he also dedicated many pages to his wife and only remaining child.

"Two and a half months ago Griet got an attack of typhoid fever and her condition got constantly worse," he wrote on May 31. "All the care for the little girl fell on me, and the whole situation was one of endless misery. Ten days ago Griet was finally able to travel and she is now on the coffee plantation Kroewoek near Ulingie to regain her health. You can understand that her illness was an expensive business when I tell you that we needed five bottles of milk a day at 30 cents each ... and now again that trip to Ulingie. I have kept the little girl here. She is a lovely child, but she reminds me constantly of my lost darling.

"My dear cousin, the loss of that wonderful little boy has cracked something inside of me which will always remain there. The boy loved military music, especially the Monte Carlo march, and every time they play that here I get a pain in my eyes and chest."

Banjoe Biroe was not a tropical paradise, and the situation in the *kampongs* (native villages) surrounding the nearby Willem I military establishment, where a good many Dutch enlisted men cohabited with their Javanese wives or mistresses, did not create a healthy atmosphere. John gave an excellent description of the

situation to his cousin: "One has nothing to look at but the mountains, and at night it is incredibly quiet, with only here and
there a badly functioning lantern spreading an uncertain twilight
at the crossroads. Someone who would have the pen to describe
the situations in the nearby kampongs would give a picture of a
'bête humaine' that is totally different from the one Zola has
given us. Tonight we have another invasion of butterflies, plus
flying ants and termites, and millions of little insects that drive
one crazy."

It was not a pretty picture, and not an atmosphere that would
induce a feeling of happiness in a young wife. According to John,
one of his lieutenants "had become an old man in two years time
on account of the deathly monotony of life around here," and
"without an almanac one would not know what day or date it is."
He then finished his diatribe in commenting that "Sundays here
are absolutely miserable and people who have a suicidal tend-
ency could easily put it into practice on a day like that."

No wonder that John MacLeod himself felt rather fed up with
army life, and that he too was thinking of Holland, as he had
already mentioned to Griet a year and a half previously from
Medan, before his wife had joined him there: "I would like to go
back home and am yearning for that moment. I would prefer
anything to this life here, now that I cannot be promoted to
lieutenant colonel anyhow."

On October 2, 1900, a major since 1897 and only forty-four
years old, John decided to resign from the army, the long and
hard tropical years having taken their toll. He had been a soldier
for twenty-eight years, which entitled him to his full pension of
2800 guilders. The unhappy couple went to live at Sindanglaja, a
small village between Buitenzorg (nowadays called Bogor) and
Bandung. The mountain climate here was healthy, and life was
fairly cheap—certainly a lot cheaper than in Holland, which was
the main reason why John stayed on in the tropics. But neither
climate nor her husband's retirement by now could deter Margaretha from talking about going back to Amsterdam. In fact, the

retirement was an inducement. The situation—from her point of view—was far from a stimulating one. She was still in her early twenties, was living in a small village in the Indies with hardly enough money to get by, and with a much older husband whom she did not like.

To all those who knew the MacLeods during this period it was clearly apparent that their relationship had become intolerable. There was hardly a day without trouble. Tempers flared, and voices were raised in bitter arguments.

Dr. Roelfsema, who from March 1900 till June 1902 was medical officer for that part of the Preanger Province in which the MacLeods lived, had a decided opinion about the responsibilities in the nearly continuous disputes between the MacLeods.

"Neither for the one, nor for the other did I have any specific feeling of friendship, nor enmity," said Dr. Roelfsema. And he went on to say that "during the year and a half I used to know the MacLeod family, the conduct of Mrs. MacLeod, notwithstanding the many rude insults she had to endure in public from her husband, was perfectly correct.

"I have often wondered whether Margaretha Zelle might not have grown into a good wife and mother if her husband had been a more equable and sensible man. Her marriage to the uneven tempered and excitable MacLeod was doomed to failure."

Dr. Roelfsema made this statement in a letter to the editor of one of Holland's principal newspapers (the Amsterdam *Algemeen Handelsblad*), shortly after publication of Heymans' book on Mata Hari, which put all the blame for the trouble on *her*, whitewashing the husband. A few days later he received a letter from Mrs. V. in The Hague, the same one who had first met John on his return from the Indies in 1895.

"My mother and I had the same impression you had," wrote Mrs. V., "and we felt deeply for the nineteen-year-old girl. And when later on everything finished so tragically, we too said to each other: 'Who knows what a good wife and mother she might have become if she had married someone else.'"

John MacLeod, looking at it from *his* side, years later came to a similar conclusion. Many a time he said to his third wife: "What a pity I didn't know you sooner, it would have saved me a lot of misery." But by then he had been back in Holland for nearly twenty years, and perhaps the more temperate Dutch climate had changed his outlook on life.

When I talked to Dr. Roelfsema in 1932, he elaborated on some of the painful scenes he had witnessed in the MacLeod home in Sindanglaja. At one time, he recalled, Griet started to talk about Europe, about Paris. The conversation became general and Mac-Leod grew noticeably nervous. Finally, unable to contain himself any longer, he yelled at his wife: "What the hell! If you want that much to go to Paris, why don't you just go and leave me alone!"

Paris indeed must have been quite a bit on Margaretha's mind. Years later, by then a famous woman and being interviewed in Vienna, she was asked why she had gone to Paris—why not somewhere else.

Mata Hari innocently raised her eyebrows. "I don't know," she said, "I thought that all women who ran away from their husbands went to Paris."

At another time, said Dr. Roelfsema, during a party at the home of a mutual friend, Margaretha was dancing while her husband was talking on the sidelines. Passing close by with her dancing partner, Griet said: "Hello, darling." The answer was short. "You can go to hell, bitch," said John.

Neither John nor Griet by now were particularly bashful in enumerating each other's finer qualities. John accused his wife of badly neglecting their daughter and, writing to his sister in Amsterdam—as quoted by Heymans—described his wife as "a stinking wretch," a "beast" who had "the totally depraved nature of a scoundrel." He had only one wish left: "If I could only get rid of that bloodsucker," and added, "I sometimes chuckle all over when I think that someone else might marry her, only to find out that he sold himself down the river as I did."

Griet, writing to her father, accused her husband of maltreating her, and used such words as "stingy," "adultery," "brute," "cruelty"—summing it all up in one big scene in which she claimed John threatened her with a gun.

Obviously, even MacLeod understood that under the circumstances they could not continue to spend their lives in the colonies, and finally, in March 1902, he gave in to his wife's request to return to Holland, making the trip back by naval transport. John now by force of necessity wanted to economize, and once again moved in with his sister, Tante Lavies. But as before, the two women did not get along, and the MacLeods took an apartment of their own at 188 van Breestraat in Amsterdam, quite a pleasant part of town.

The marriage now collapsed completely, and the long-contemplated separation seemed the only solution. It was, to some extent, precipitated by MacLeod himself, who felt that his wife's presence was more than he could bear.

Coming home one afternoon, Margaretha found the apartment empty; John had left for a friend's house at Velp near Arnhem, taking four-and-a-half-year-old Non with him. Margaretha lost no time. She too went to Arnhem, staying with one of John's cousins. Then, on August 27, 1902, she asked for a legal separation. It was granted three days later by the Amsterdam tribunal, entirely in her favor; Margaretha was to keep their daughter, and MacLeod was to pay her 100 guilders a month alimony. When the first payment was due on September 10, he claimed to have no money—and never paid his wife anything, then or later.

After the separation had been granted, and after John had put the usual advertisement in the newspapers requesting all and sundry "not to supply any goods to my estranged wife, Margaretha MacLeod-Zelle"—a short reconciliation took place, during which John wrote his wife several tender letters. There followed intermittently a few happy moments, and towards the end of 1902 Margaretha and her husband were seen ice-skating at the Amsterdam "IJsclub," an open-air skating rink that was located behind the Rijksmuseum, where they had met in 1895. According to one eyewitness, Non—"an adorable little girl"—was with them. The same eyewitness, who had skated a few rounds with John MacLeod, judged him "an old gentleman," and described Margaretha, "who was dressed in a dark green suit," and who, like most Frisians, "skated wonderfully," as "an absolute beauty."

The reconciliation, of course, did not last long. Margaretha was young and thoroughly theatrical, John, middle-aged and thoroughly distrustful. And both were disgusted with each other.

Margaretha, for a while, stayed on in Amsterdam—then went back to her uncle Taconis in The Hague. But in Holland she faced a difficult future. She had never done any work, and getting a sensible job was hard. Moreover she had no money. Her daughter Non had gone back to her husband for a while, and MacLeod, unloving husband but loving father, never again gave her up. To Margaretha it was a fairly convenient solution—it facilitated her freedom and lessened her financial trouble.

Neither in Amsterdam nor in The Hague did she find work—and Paris was still strongly on her mind. With the exception of her short trip to Wiesbaden, and the long one aboard a Dutch ship to and from the East, she had never been really abroad. On her way to the Indies she had made the usual short stops at Tangiers, Genoa, and Port Said. But her fellow travelers had been Dutchmen. She had never *lived* in a foreign country, with the exception of those years in the Dutch East Indies, and even there she had been surrounded by her countrymen only. The thought therefore was an obvious one. Why not Paris?

With Margaretha leaving for the Ville Lumière, fable and fantasy later on took hold of a good many writers. H. R. Berndorff, who wrote about Mata Hari in *Le Grandi Spie* ("Great Spies")*—had her retire for hours to temples in the Indies before her arrival in Paris, where "she lives outside reality." Then on her return to Holland, according to Berndorff, "she went back to live with her parents, selling hats and keeping the house clean."

A Dutch folk singer, Koos Speenhoff, as famous for his songs

* Italian edition by Mondadori, original German title *Spionage*.

as for his tall stories, has an even better tale, which he gleefully described in a book of his.* According to him, Margaretha arrived at his house in Rotterdam in the middle of the night. Shedding her coat, she told him she would like to dance with his company, and proceeded to give him an Eve-like demonstration, Speenhoff accompanying her on his guitar, with his mistress sleepily looking on from the sidelines, in bed. The following Sunday Mata Hari danced for the first time with his company, Speenhoff claims. "There was champagne, flowers—and a gentleman," wrote the Dutch bard, "and a few months later she danced in Paris."

Chapter 3

MARGARETHA's first trip to Paris was not only a great disillusion, but ended in utter disaster. She arrived in France without a penny in her pocket, and in order to make a living decided to pose as a model. But there was neither fun, nor any future in this, and hardly any money. Paris did not seem the solution after all, and Margaretha MacLeod went reluctantly back to her own country.

For one week she stayed with one of her husband's uncles in Nijmegen. John, hearing about it, intervened—and the uncle asked her to leave. Having no friends to turn to, no money to live on, and no financial support from her husband, she started to think once again about Paris.

Frisians are known as the most stubborn of Dutchmen, and Margaretha was no exception. Having been defeated in Paris once, she was determined to try again. And without any doubt her second trip brought her more luck than the first.

* Dutch title: *Daar komen de schutters.*

This time Margaretha arrived in Paris in 1904. She had, as she told a newspaperman the next year, "half a franc in her pocket and went straight to the Grand Hotel."

But what to do? Confiding in another journalist, she told him that "there was no one to help her." Should she try modeling again? The painters' studios had proved to be a failure. Night clubs, the Folies-Bergère, where good-looking women were always welcome? She would have to dance, she thought, and she had never done any professional dancing in her life. Yet to dancing she turned, thanks to the suggestion of M. Molier, the owner of a famous riding school in the Rue Benouville in Paris, himself a renowned horseman. Margaretha, who had learned to ride in the Indies, had found a first engagement with M. Molier, who was of the opinion that with a body like hers she might have even more success in dancing than with horses.

But dance how? Besides the waltzes and quadrilles she had known in the clubs in the Indies, and the dancing lessons she had as a young girl in faraway Leeuwarden, Margaretha had no experience. Many years later in The Hague, during the First World War, she once remarked to a friend of hers, Dutch painter Piet van der Hem, who told me the story, "I never could dance well. People came to see me because I was the first who dared to show myself naked to the public."

Margaretha, however, knew by now only too well that she was beautiful, or at least most attractive. She knew from experience that men liked her, and she knew how to be charming. Many women artists have started with less. Also, she spoke a fairly decent Malay, and had seen some native dances in Java and Sumatra. But that was all. The stories, as told by herself and repeated by others, as to her initiation in sacred dances in the Buddhist temples of the Far East, are utter nonsense. But being a clever nobody, she played for high stakes—and won.

Of course, the later Mata Hari could not have arrived in Paris at a better moment to startle the pleasure-seeking high society with her dance innovations. The year 1905 was the bubbling heyday of *la belle époque*, during which Paris yearned for excesses, lived a life of gaiety and charm, the men complimenting their own closely corseted wives while courting those of others, and where the joy of being both alive and rich often seemed to be the one and only reason to flit from dinner to supper and from one conveniently located bedroom to the next. Margaretha took to this life like a budding flower to sunshine; she developed, opened up, and blossomed forth.

Margaretha made her debut as an oriental dancer at the salon of Mme. Kiréevsky, a singer who was active in Paris society in the organizing of benefit performances. Her success was instantaneous, and as early as February 4, 1905, the English weekly *The King* published an enthusiastic article about her. The writer explained that he "had heard vague rumours about a woman from the Far East, who had come to Europe laden with perfume and jewels, to introduce some of the richness of the Oriental colour and life into the satiated society of European cities." According to these same rumors, there were supposed to be scenes of "veils encircling and discarded," and he felt "there was just a suggestion of naughtiness" about the attempt to have a display like this in a private drawing room.

After several more performances at other private Parisian homes, Margaretha danced in the beginning of February at the forty-fifth celebration of the *Diner de Faveur*, where her name for the first time was given as Lady MacLeod. Mata Hari was not born yet, but already the *Courrier Français* was of the opinion that "this unknown dancer who comes from far-off countries is a strange person when not moving, and an even stranger one when she does."

At Mme. Kiréevsky's recital one of the guests took a very special interest in Margaretha. M. Guimet was an industrialist who had turned to collecting on a grand scale. To house his private collection he had the Museum of Oriental Art built on the Place d'Iéna, and he was considered an expert on all things eastern. But was he? One thing is certain—both he and his director, M. de

Milloué, were utterly captivated by our Dutch dancer. M. Guimet immediately conceived the idea of treating his friends to a special demonstration of her truly oriental art. Once again a chance meeting became a point of decision in Margaretha's life.

But could M. Guimet present an oriental dancer under the name of Margaretha Geertruida Zelle, which even pronounced *à la française* would sound dubious, or as Lady MacLeod? No one would have believed in the authenticity of his effort. A new name had to be invented, and after a soul-searching conference between the two, Margaretha Zelle stepped into the background and Mata Hari emerged.

All reports state that the name was the idea of M. Guimet. It seems from my own research that it was a long cherished invention of Margaretha herself. According to rumors, I had been told, there once had been a letter in circulation in Leeuwarden, sent by M'greet herself from Java, in which she chimerically claimed to have become a dancer with the name of Mata Hari. The rumor was confirmed when I visited Mrs. Ybeltje Kerkhof-Hoogslag in Holland. As she remembers it, she was walking in Leeuwarden some time before 1898 (because that was the year she herself left the city), when a friend told her to have just received a letter from M'greet "who says she has changed her name to Mata Hari." Ybeltje, the constant defender of M'greet, was obviously interested and started to read the letter on the spot. The two girls were quickly surrounded by other school friends, all of them hilariously impressed with this new twist in M'greet's life, which they found perfectly in line with her own sense of fantasy, as well as with the lofty ideas of her father, "the Baron." They unanimously agreed that "it was just like M'greet—another one of her crazy inventions."

Yet Mata Hari seemed a strange name for a dancer from India, whence, according to M. Guimet, she hailed. Of course, the owner-director of the Museum of Oriental Art was far from being the great expert people thought he was. He had made a trip to Japan, and brought back the first and very much acclaimed woodcuts; he had been in Egypt and various middle eastern countries, and had succeeded in assembling an imposing collection. But his fundamental knowledge of eastern languages was slight. If not, he would have known that the name Mata Hari was not Hindu but Malay. But no one in Paris knew any better, or cared. India, the Dutch East Indies—it was all the same, it was all somewhere way out east. Mata Hari herself was unconcerned. For all she cared they could make her Indian, Siamese, Chinese, or Laotian—as long as it was oriental. Mata Hari sounded mysterious, and that, under the circumstances, was what counted. Only she knew that *Mata* means eye, *Hari* means day—and that in the simple Malay language *Mata Hari* is the very prosaic way of talking about the eye of the day: the sun.

The name stuck, and the evening of March 13, 1905, became the definite turning point in Margaretha's life. Before coming to Paris, she had been on the stage only once. Back in Malang on Java, in a show put on at the local *Societeit* or Club House, she had played the role of the queen in a musical adaptation of *The Crusaders*. Even at that time "it would have been difficult for the public not to be charmed by this elegant amateur" was the opinion of the local correspondent of the *Weekly for the Indies*. But back in 1899 the success of the performance had been short-lived. Now, in Paris, the unknown girl from Leeuwarden metamorphosed herself permanently into a dancer from the East, and overnight she became the sensation about whom all Paris raved. The good-looking young woman from Holland had succeeded where her baronially inclined father had failed; she found herself the center of a new world—a world that adored, admired, envied, and finally killed her.

M. Guimet had done well by his new artist. The museum's rotunda on the second floor, which housed the library, had been transformed into an Indian temple. Its eight columns were garlanded with flowers, stretching upward towards the round balcony on the floor above, from where, at the top of each column, statues of barebreasted women were to contemplate Mata Hari's

nakedness in Galatean envy. The light of candles deepened the
atmosphere of mystery, while one of M. Guimet's most prized
eleventh-century bronze statues, a three-foot-high, four-armed
Siva Nataraja from southern India, surrounded by a circle of
flames and crushing a dwarf with one of its bronze feet, emerged
floodlit from the background. The very carefully selected small
group of guests (the library had a diameter of only twenty-five
to thirty feet) would be able to have a good look at the eastern
dancer. In the meantime an off-scene orchestra played music "inspired by Hindu and Javanese melodies."

Mata Hari, the new bayadere, was dressed in what could pass
for an authentic oriental costume, selected by M. Guimet from
his rich collection. Surrounded by four black-togaed girls, she
wore a white cotton brassiere covered with Indian-type jewel-
studded breastplates. Bracelets of similar design were worn on
wrists and upper arms, while her head supported an Indian dia-
dem that curled up backwards above her black hair, knotted à
l'espagnole. Jeweled bands were clasped around her waist, holding up a sarong which from the hollow of her back descended
around her hips towards a point on her belly about halfway down
below the navel. The rest was bare. It was a startling costume,
and M. Guimet's aristocratic guests, grouping the cream of Paris
femininity in all its dazzling bejeweled charm, grace, and seduc-
tivity, and including among its men the Japanese and German
ambassadors, were duly impressed with what they saw.

The newspaper critics outdid themselves in finding words of
praise. They glorified the "oriental woman." They praised her
knowledge of sacred dances and her perfection in performing
them. Paris was soon at her feet, put flowers at her stage door,
jewels into her hands, and Mata Hari readily clasped the city,
including some of its men, to her bosom.

At the beginning of her lucrative career, Mata Hari, while
being flattered by what happened to her, must also have been
staggered by her cunning, which enabled her to conquer Paris
with imitation oriental dances.

All the letters, all the words of praise that were pouring from the pens of the overwhelmed critics, and all the photographs that were taken of her, were carefully pasted into her scrapbooks, which as such constitute a unique documentation of her career as an artist. They contain the already mentioned letters and calling cards from Massenet and Puccini. There are photos of her at the races, letters of admiration from the most famous people among Paris society. And with all this came money and luxury in abundance, for there was never a lack of admirers, of whom a good many became her lovers.

The fascination she exercised over the public is perhaps best expressed in a poem which was sent to her by one of her multiple worshipers:

To Siva

When before your altar she has thrown off her veils,
And inclined in front of you her svelte and nude body,
Siva, dear God, do you feel burning in your marrow
The all-powerful Desire evoked by her beauty?
Do you rush to press your mouth against her flowering lips,
Do you take her voluptuous body, to press it against yours
So as to wallow in love?

Here lies the secret of Mata Hari's earlier successes—the public, under the guise of art, was erotically fascinated. It was a daring exploit and therefore no wonder that she was invited over and over again. Another important factor was, of course, Mata Hari's perfect knowledge of how to behave in highly civilized company. She was not the simple vaudeville dancer to be left alone after the performance. With her clothes on she could easily, and with charming grace, mix with her hosts and their guests.

The first newspaper clipping Mata Hari pasted in her books after her public debut was a page from *La Vie Parisienne*, which mentions her as "Lady MacLeod, that is to say Mata Hari, the Indian dancer, voluptuous and tragic, who dances naked in the latest salons. She wears the costume of the bayadere, as much simplified as possible, and, towards the end, she simplifies it even a little more."

But *how* did she dance? *La Presse* of March 18, 1905, tells us quite in detail. She danced "with veils, bejeweled brassieres, and that is about all." The tall Mrs. MacLeod, the paper wrote, wore the dress of the bayadere with incomparable grace. "From Java," the paper continued, "on the burning soil of which island she grew up, she brings an unbelievable suppleness and a magic charm, while she owes her powerful torso to her native Holland.

"No one before her has dared to remain like this with trembling ecstasy and without any veils in front of the god—and with what beautiful gestures, both daring and chaste! She is indeed Absaras, sister of the Nymphs, the Naiads and the Walkyrie, created by Sundra for the perdition of men and sages.

"Mata Hari does not only act with her feet, her arms, eyes, mouth and crimson fingernails. Mata Hari, unhampered by any clothes, plays with her whole body. And then, when the gods remain unmoved by the offer of her beauty and youth, she offers them her love, her chastity—and one by one her veils, symbols of feminine honor, fall at the feet of the god. But Siva wants even more. Devidasha gets closer to him—one more veil, a mere nothing—and erect in her proud and victorious nudity, she offers the god the passion which burns in her."

And, writes the paper, "sitting around her, the Nautsches excited her further in uttering terrible 'stâ-stâ-stâ' sounds—and finally the priestess, gasping for breath, sinks down at the feet of the god—where her dancing girls cover her with a golden sheet. Then Mata Hari, without any feeling of shame got up gracefully, pulled the holy veil around her, and, kindly thanking both Siva and the Parisians, walked off amidst thunderous bravos!

"Afterwards Mata Hari, now dressed in an elegant evening gown joined the public and, playing with a Javanese *wajong* puppet which she held in her hands, told us gaily the story of the prehistoric drama of Adjurnah."

Maybe Mata Hari did mention the story as being prehistoric, or maybe the innocent writer thought it would make his article more interesting. As it happens, the story of Adjurnah is far from prehistoric but deals with one of the characters in a several-centuries-old Javanese folk tale from the Hindu religion. It is still a very popular story today, often told at night in the Indonesian villages, and illustrated by the shadowy characters of the *wajong* puppets, projected from behind on a white screen. It was undoubtedly from these *wajong* plays, enjoyed by Indonesians and Westerners alike, that Mata Hari had got her "prehistoric" information.

An English correspondent in Paris, Frances Keyzer, gave the following account of what her admiring eyes had seen:

"The door opened. A dark figure glided in, her arms folded upon her breast beneath a mass of flowers. For a few seconds she stood motionless, her eyes fixed upon the statue of Siva at the end of the room. Her olive skin blended with the curious jewels in their dead gold setting. A casque of worked gold upon her dark hair, she was enshrouded in various veils of delicate hues, symbolizing chastity, beauty, youth, love, voluptuousness and passion."

Having been enchanted by her dance of the veils, the writer continued: "The next dance was equally impressive. She stands before us as a graceful young girl, a *slendang*—the veil worn by Javanese maidens—around her waist. In her hand she held a passion flower, and she danced to it with all the gladness of her sunny nature. But the flower was enchanted, and under its charm she loses command of herself and slowly unwinds the *slendang*. As the veil drops to the ground, consciousness returns. She is ashamed and covers her face with her hands.

"Nothing inanimate will render the emotion conveyed by the performer, nor the colour and harmony of the Eastern figure. It was a tropical plant in all its freshness, transplanted to a Northern soil. The Parisians who witnessed the performance were struck with the unconscious art of the dancer, and with the intelligence and refinement she displayed."

That much for a phlegmatic English correspondent living in the Paris of 1905, who apparently was not only fascinated by Mata Hari's dancing, but also by her "dark figure" and "dark hair." Where, one might ask, did this daughter of the province of Friesland, where most people are blond, get her dark complexion?

According to one Frisian expert it might have come from her mother's branch of the van der Meulen family, who were descended from the Woudkers, a tribe that once lived in the forests of Friesland, and who all had dark complexions. She certainly did not have it from her father's family, since the earliest Zelle, Herman Otto, a weaver from the city of Rheda in the German province of Westphalia, had arrived in Leeuwarden around 1770, where, on March 25, 1780, he was accepted as a *burgher*.

Mata Hari could be most thankful to her Woudkers ancestors for that dark complexion, for as a blond dancer from the East she would hardly have found acclaim among the Parisians.

Few modern artists can look back on a debut that was applauded so warmly. The Parisians accepted Mata Hari because she brought them something excitingly new—and perhaps because she so demurely covered her face after dropping that *slendang*. They continued to call her Lady MacLeod, and Mata Hari was clever enough not to say that she had no right to a title.

After her second evening of dancing at the Guimet Museum, on March 14, *Le Matin,* the influential Paris morning paper, wrote that on the previous night "the mysterious and sacred India, the India of the Brahmans and the bayaderes has been revealed to us by Madame MacLeod, an oriental dancer." The paper continued to say that Mata Hari "evoked admirably the ceremonies dear to Vishnu, to Indra and to Siva, while dancing the 'Poem of the Princess and the Magic Flower,' a 'War Dance of Subramaya' and 'that magnificent Invocation of Siva,' which travelers returned from the Indies have described so often."

Another Paris theater critic, Edouard Lepage, gives us some more details about the sensational appearance at the museum. "Suddenly Mata Hari appears," he writes, "the 'Eye of the Day,' the Glorious Sun, the sacred Bayadere whom only the priests and the gods can claim to have seen in the nude. She is tall and slim and supple like the unrolled serpent which is hypnotized by the snake charmer's flute. Her flexible body at times becomes one with the undulating flames, to stiffen suddenly in the middle of her contortions, like the flaming blade of a kris.

"Then, with a brutal gesture, Mata Hari rips off her jewels, tears her veils. She throws away the ornaments that cover her breasts. And, naked, her body seems to lengthen way up into the shadows! Her outstretched arms lift her unto the very tip of her toes; she staggers, beats the empty air with her shattered arms, whips the imperturbable night with her long heavy hair . . . and falls to the ground."

The clawing in the nude in midair must have been an eyebrow-raising demonstration, but it certainly seemed to excite the artistic—if not the sensual—appetite of the Parisians. What could have been more extravagant than a woman from the Orient, supposedly married to a Scottish nobleman, who dared to show herself in public in a far-advanced state of undress that was pronounced "art"?

The *Gaulois*, another newspaper, wrote on March 17, 1905, that seeing her "so feline, extremely feminine, majestically tragic, the thousand curves and movements of her body trembling in a thousand rhythms, one finds oneself far from the conventional *entrechats* of our classic dancers."

Mata Hari danced, continued this enthusiastic writer, "like David before the Holy of Holies, like Salammbô before Tanit, like Salome before Herod!" He waxes even more lyrical when leaving the museum this slightly foggy March evening after the show.

Lost in thought while crossing the Place d'Iéna, he poetically mixes literature and ancient Egypt, and quotes:

"Among all the pageant with its legendary pomp
I did not look once upon the proud Pharaoh,
But admired instead the amber bodies of the Bayaderes."

The following evening, March 15, Mata Hari continued her conquest of French society during a concert, again organized by Madame Kiréevsky, for the benefit of the Russian Ambulances. It was during the middle of the Russo-Japanese war, and the Russians had just suffered a catastrophic defeat at Mukden. A good many members of the Parisian nobility, including princes, counts, dukes, and duchesses, both French and Russian, were seen among the audience.

During that year 1905 Mata Hari danced in all about thirty times at the most exclusive salons of Paris, plus six times at the Trocadero Theater, where arrangements had been made to represent her in a setting that approximated as closely as possible the atmosphere of the Guimet Museum. She danced three times at the home of Baron Henri de Rothschild, at the home of Cécile Sorel, celebrated actress of the Comédie Française, at the Grand Cercle, where she shared the program with the famous soprano Lina Cavalieri, the Cercle Royal, and elsewhere—always among oriental carpets, palm trees, flowers, and incense burners.

Cécile Sorel, who later married the Comte de Ségur, was as enchanted with Mata Hari as any of them. Among her guests was M. Gaston Menier, the French chocolate king, and after the performance of May 14, Cécile Sorel sent a letter to Mata Hari, which she dutifully pasted in her scrapbook:

Mademoiselle,

Your beautiful dances have enchanted my guests, and M. Menier would love to see them once more at his own home on Friday. Are you free? You will dance amidst an atmosphere worthy of your great art, a large enclosed veranda filled with the rarest plants and flowers. Write directly to him, or if you prefer, to me. I am, with my most artistic greetings,

C. Sorel.

Mata Hari was free, and danced that following Friday, the nineteenth, at the Meniers'. Her host was not only enthused by her performance, but even turned out to be as good in the taking of candid photographs as in the making of chocolate. Several of the tiny photographs, showing Mata Hari quite in the nude, were interspersed among the lines of a letter he sent her a few days later:

Chère Madame,

I have not forgotten my promise to send you the photograph of the *serre* where you have danced so deliciously the other night. I am expecting the print any moment—and it will remind you of one of your evenings of dancing. But for my guests and myself it will be the souvenir of an ideal artistic event in which you represented the true antique beauty—and the small photographs which I have pasted on this letter describe better than words the impression which your beautiful appearance, like an oriental dream, has left among us. I, for my part, am happy to have contributed the setting of lights and art objects, which—I am told— harmonized so deservedly with the lines of your beautiful body.

There is only one note of discord in the general acclaim. When she danced at the home of Emma Calvé, the French soprano who at New York's Metropolitan Opera House was famous for her Carmen, the *Echo de Paris* mentions that her dances "are not of a moving or impressive interest or perfection." Just the same the newspaper acknowledges that it is pure art, for "Mata Hari dances in the nude, but do not believe that her dancing is indecent or that the sight of the beautiful Indian woman might provoke inappropriate thoughts—even though she danced naked from head to foot, with big eyes, and with a smiling mouth that is set into her face like a cut in the flesh of a ripe apple."

Some people in Paris were shocked that a "lady" would show herself in the nude to more than one person at a time. While for her performance at the home of the Comtesse de Loysnes she had put on a *soupçon* of clothes (dancing before a group of venerable members of the French Academy, which made the *Journal Amusant* remark that she danced "naked as a speech by an académicien"), she had danced without anything on at the Cercle Artistique et Littéraire. Since the public was composed of nothing but artists, she danced "naked as Hassan in the Thousand and One Nights, naked as Eve before she committed the first sin, with no other fig leaf but an illusive bit of jewelery."

The same nudity was displayed at Emma Calvé's where Mata Hari was accompanied on the violin by Georges Enesco, the already famous composer of the two *Romanian Rhapsodies,* and later on teacher of Yehudi Menuhin.

Colette, the French novelist, was among the spectators that evening. In an article in the Paris *Figaro* in December 1923 she described her impressions: "I have seen her dance at Emma Calvé's. She did not actually dance, but with graceful movements shed her clothes. She arrived fairly naked at her recitals, danced 'vaguely' with downcast eyes, and would disappear enveloped in her veils." And, wrote Colette as an added note of interest about a performance she saw elsewhere, "in another dance she sat on a white horse."

This strange performance took place on May 5, 1905, at the house of Miss Natalie Clifford Barney, an American expatriate author known as "The Amazon of Letters." Miss Barney lived in Neuilly, from where later on she moved to a house in the Rue Jacob in Paris. Here her salon was frequented by such literary figures as Gertrude Stein, Ezra Pound, Colette, André Gide and

Rilke, and visiting American authors could meet some of the most illustrious French poets of the day.

In the spring of 1965 the now eighty-eight-year-old and still extraordinarily bright Miss Barney told me that after Mata Hari's soiree at Emma Calvé's she had invited her to dance in the garden of her home in Neuilly. It was here that Mata Hari made her entrance "sitting on a white horse," and Miss Barney, an enthusiastic horsewoman herself, "had lent her one of her own turquoise-studded bridles for the occasion."

"The thing that struck me most when she made her entrance," said Miss Barney, "was the fact that, contrary to what I had expected, Mata Hari's skin was not dark, but quite purple." Natalie Barney explained that "it was an extremely cold spring day, and the fairly nude Mata Hari, greatly exposed on her white horse, had turned numb with the cold."

Mata Hari's second performance at Natalie Barney's took place indoors, thus eliminating the capricious twists of the Parisian climate. This time she had agreed to appear entirely in the nude (with the exception of her inseparable brassiere), but on the strict condition "that only women be present." Miss Barney had invited a dozen of her friends to this intimate display of pseudo-Javanese girations. Included in the group was Dorothy Rockhill, an American who quite recently had been married to a young British violinist, Arthur Larkin. Distressed that her newly acquired husband would miss Mata Hari's exhibition of nudity, Miss Rockhill refused to accept Natalie Barney's invitation if the violinist were not included in the party. To solve the delicate problem, it was decided to dress the Englishman in women's clothes. But Mata Hari, who probably knew more about the male body than any of the other women present, spotted the manly spectator immediately, lunged at him with the outstretched spear that was more or less the only added appurtenance of her war dance, and, frightening the poor man nearly to death, shrieked: "There is an intruder in the house!"

At ten o'clock in the evening of April 1, 1905, Mata Hari danced at the Salle Mors in the Rue des Maronniers in Passy, "with 326 people present," as she did not fail to record in her scrapbook. According to the *Revue Musical*, the evening, which had been organized by the Society of Amateur Photographers, had various other attractions on the program. Before "Lady MacLeod Mata Hari" showed herself in dances which made the magazine comment that "these Indian gods have undoubtedly strange ideas and some very peculiar customs," the audience could enjoy "cinematographic projections by M. Gaumont," who from this rather humble beginning branched out to become the czar of the French motion-picture industry.

Paris not only accepted Mata Hari, marveled about her and admired her, but now that she was an established artist and the novelty of her nude dancing had been described in all details, new fields of feature-article writing about her had to be explored. Parisians started to compare their daring artist with predecessors in the field of the dance. First and foremost to mind came Isadora Duncan, who had arrived in France from the United States in 1899, to display flowing Greek robes in dance movements that were accompanied by classical music. Isadora Duncan, whose private life was about as erratic as Mata Hari's, then left Paris for the applause of Berlin, where she established a school of dancing in 1904. But in the controversy about the two dancers in the Paris newspapers Mata Hari came out as the winner. "Miss Duncan is Vestal," was the opinion of Frances Keyzer, "Lady MacLeod is Venus."

La Vie Parisienne, the undress-loving humorous Paris weekly, was more elaborate on the subject. "Miss Duncan reincarnated Greece," wrote the magazine. "On music of Beethoven, Schumann, Gluck, and Mozart she restored the pagan dance movements. All Paris salons wanted to have Miss Duncan. Then, like everything on earth, she disappeared. She, her mother and her long-haired brother who accompanied her on the violin, went to conquer Berlin.

"This season we have Mata Hari. She is Indian, with an English

Portrait of Margaretha as a young girl.

Painting of Mata Hari's father, Adam Zelle, as a standard-bearer of the Leeuwarden Horse Guard of Honor, for the visit of King William III.

Left: Poem written by Margaretha on February 16, 1889, in the poetry book of her girl friend, Ybeltje. She was then twelve years old. *Right:* Birth certificate, reading: "On the 7th of August 1876, was born in Leeuwarden, Margaretha Geertruida, daughter of Adam Zelle and his wife Antje van der Meulen."

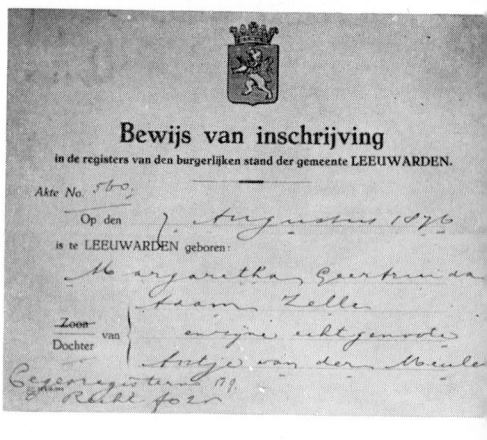

Margaretha (sitting, first from left) and her husband (standing, second from left) aboard the S.S. *Prinses Amalia*, leaving for the Indies on May 1, 1897.

Left: John MacLeod with his and Mata Hari's daughter, Non. *Right:* Margaretha and her husband on the eve of their departure for the Dutch East Indies.

Paris, February 1905.

Left: Mata Hari at the Guimet Museum, March 13, 1905. *Right:* In Paris, 1905.

Mata Hari dancing at the home of M. Menier, the chocolate king.

Mata Hari dancing in Paris, 1905.

Mata Hari in Paris, 1905.

"The dance is a poem, of which each movement is a word"; from Mata Hari's scrapbook.

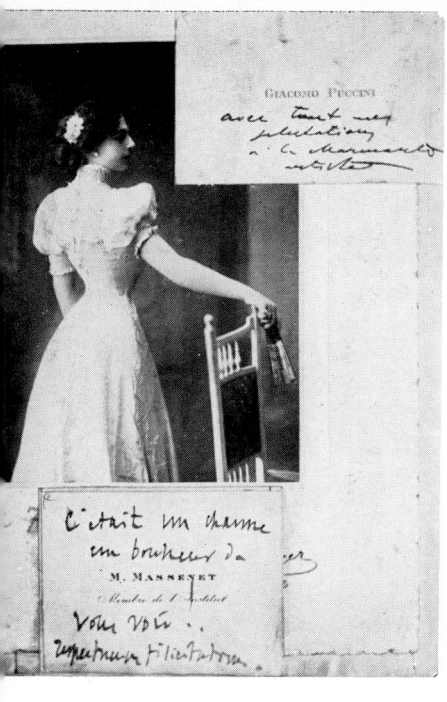

Left: Page from Mata Hari's scrapbook, with cards sent to her by Massenet and Puccini. Puccini wrote, "With all my compliments to the charming artist"; and Massenet, "It was charming and it made me very happy to see you." *Right:* In Vienna, December 1906–January 1907.

In Paris, 1908.

At the Longchamps racetrack for the *Grand Prix d'Automne* on October 4, 1908.

Mata Hari riding in the Bois de Boulogne on Cacatöes, one of her favorite horses, May 3, 1912.

The Château de la Dorée at Esvres-sur-Indre, where Mata Hari lived in 1910–1911.

In the garden of her home in Neuilly-sur-Seine, 1911.

Above left: Mata Hari's portrait by Paris artist Paul Frantz-Namur, 1909. *Above right:* At La Scala during the season 1911–1912; from her scrapbook. *Below:* Page from the Italian weekly *Illustrazione Italiana* on the occasion of the opening of La Scala. Mata Hari indicated herself in pencil, as well as conductor Tullio Serafin.

Above: Mata Hari with her orchestra under the direction of Inayat Khan in the garden of her home at Neuilly-sur-Seine, October 9, 1912. *Below left:* At La Scala in Milan, January 1912. *Below right:* In Habanera costume, Paris, 1913.

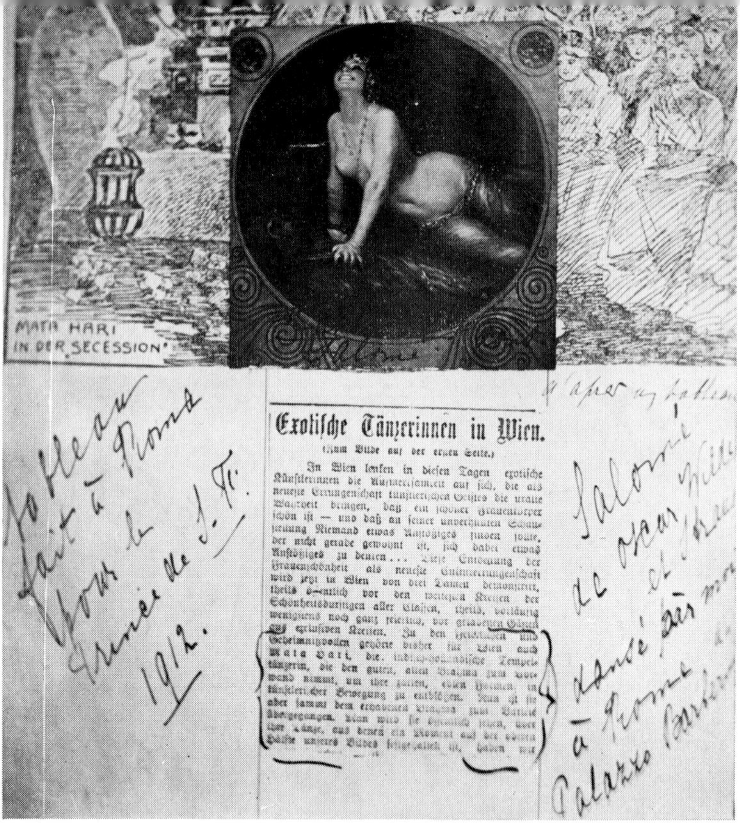

Above: From her scrapbook: Mata Hari as Salome, with review of her Vienna performance. *Right:* Mata Hari on the cover of *Nouvelle Mode* magazine, December 21, 1913.

TWO CHARMING POSES IN THE DANCE

Above: A page from *Vogue* magazine of September 24, 1913, showing Mata Hari in four poses in her dance at Neuilly. Photographs were taken in 1912. *Left:* Advertisement for Mata Hari's appearance at Palermo, Italy, September 1913.

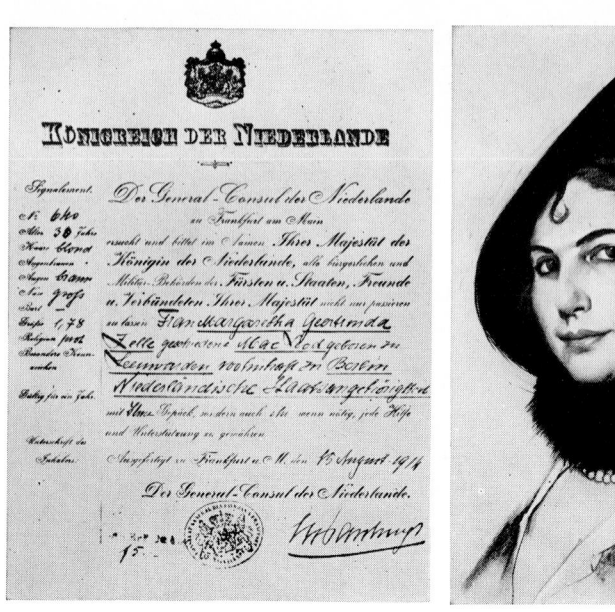

Above left: The "passport" Mata Hari received from the Netherlands consul in Frankfurt am Main on August 15, 1914. *Above right:* Painting of Mata Hari by Dutch artist Piet van der Hem, The Hague, 1915. *Below left:* Dramatic entry in the scrapbook, August 1914: "War— left Berlin—theater closed."

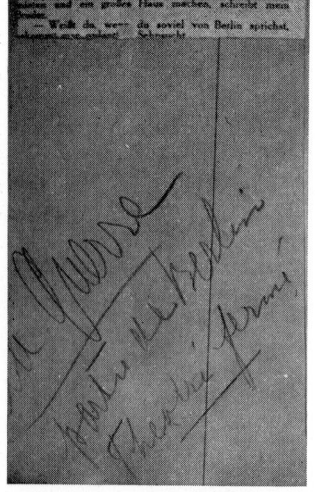

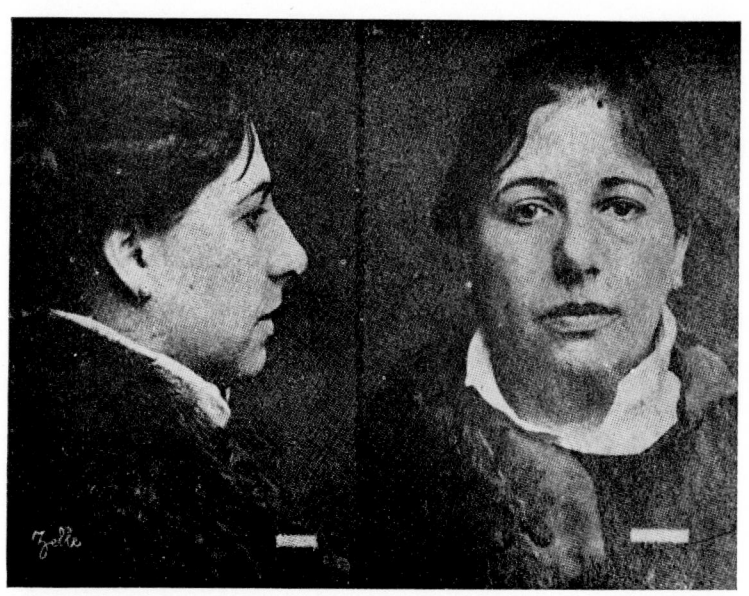

Prison photograph of Mata Hari on the eve of her execution.

Mata Hari's execution on October 15, 1917, at Vincennes.

Last photograph of Mata Hari in her scrapbook:
Holland, March 13, 1915.

mother and a Dutch father, all of which is a little complicated. Yet she is Indian. Miss Duncan apparently danced with only her feet and her arms showing, while Mata Hari is entirely naked, with only some jewels and a piece of cloth around her hips and legs. She is charming—a rather big mouth, and a pair of breasts which make many a spectator, too heavily provided for comfort, sigh with envy."

Mata Hari's breasts have been highly scrutinized by a good many people, and have come up for a great deal of comment. According to most witnesses they were never shown in public. When Edouard Lepage wrote that during her debut at the Guimet Museum "she throws away the ornaments that cover her breasts," he added that she was "naked." Yet no report indicates that she touched the cotton brassiere which she wore under her breast-plates. It seems indeed that Mata Hari was rather self-conscious about her breasts.

Gomez Carrillo relates in his book how John MacLeod, in a fit of jealousy, bit off one of his wife's breast nipples, which then induced her to hide them so carefully from the public eye.* Not so, said her prison doctor Leon Bizard in 1925 in his own book *Souvenirs d'un Médecin.* "The truth was much more simple: Mata Hari had small breasts with highly discolored overdeveloped nipples, and she was not interested at all to show them."

Yet still another eyewitness story contradicts both these versions. In 1964 one of Mata Hari's rare surviving lovers confided his knowledge in these words: "Those people know nothing about Mata Hari's breasts. I agree that they were small, but they were very delightfully shaped. In fact, I would call them quality-breasts."

* E. Gomez Carrillo, *Le Mystère de la Vie et de la Mort de Mata Hari.* French translation published by Eugène Fasquelle, Paris, 1925.

Chapter 4

MATA HARI had learned to understand the value of publicity by now and took good care never to tell the same story twice. She easily elaborated on the subjects of her art and past, interchanging the two with flowing ease, fictionalizing facts, and succeeding magnificently in getting everybody thoroughly mixed up.

Dancing at the Trocadero Theater in a benefit performance for *Les Yeux du Soldat,* she was interviewed by Paul Hervier, for whom she spun a lovely yarn: "I was born in the Indies and lived there till I was twelve years old. My childhood memories are very clear. I remember the slightest events of my first years amidst that civilization that is so different from yours. At the age of twelve I went to Wiesbaden. I got married. With my husband, a Dutch officer, I returned to my native country. I have become a woman, and my eyes enjoy once again the sights of my youth."

She had not explained her art yet, but did not lose much time in doing so.

"Shall I tell you how I see my art? It is really very simple, the most natural in the world, for nature itself is simple, and only man complicates it. One does not need things that have been complicated to the point of being ridiculous; the sacred Brahman dances are symbols, and all the gestures must correspond to thoughts. The dance is a poem, and every gesture is one of its words."

The last phrase must have greatly appealed to Mata Hari, whether originally hers or quoted from someone else, for many pages further in her scrapbook she repeated it in large letters under one of her own photographs.

Getting ahead in the world, she could no longer be married to a simple major, and consequently she promoted her husband to full colonel, the rank he had coveted for so long. For, talking to a writer for the British *Gentlewoman,* who published his impressions on March 25, 1905—calling his charming artist constantly Mata Kari instead of Mata Hari—she explained how she had arrived from Java only one month previously (instead of three years, in March 1902), where "she was born of European parents and married Sir MacLeod, a Scotchman, a colonel in the Dutch Colonial Army."

While the French and British press thus praised Mata Hari outrageously, ably assisted by the Paris edition of the *New York Herald,* which, on May 11 of that year wrote, in French, that "it is impossible to make the mysteries of the Indian religions come to life in a more chaste manner," it is obvious that Dutch correspondents in the French capital were cocking an ear when they heard about that famous countrywoman of theirs.

Holland, at that time, was still a rather chaste country. At Amsterdam's beautiful Zandvoort beach female water enthusiasts were most decorously taken into the sea inside a horse-drawn dressing room on wheels, and sunbathing was strictly separated according to the sexes. Therefore the rumor that a Dutch woman had the temerity to show herself undressed to the naked eye was news indeed.

The *News of the Day* was the first paper to draw the attention of its readers to their famous compatriot—or was she?—who was having such a success among the French. Quoting from one of the French newspapers, the correspondent finished his article by asking the question: "Who can Mata Hari be?"

The answer did not take long in forthcoming—and added more fiction to the ever deepening mystery about Mata Hari's past. The day after the article was published, a letter to the editor gave the quick answer, received, wrote the newspaper, "from a friendly source":

"Mata Hari's real name is Mrs. MacLeod. She was born on Java and married an English officer. Being a passionate lover of the dance, she studied its movements with never ending patience.

Through cunning behavior, which, had it been detected might have cost her her life, she managed to be admitted to the secret temples of India, where far beyond the reach of profane eyes the bayaderes, nautches and vadashis dance before the altar of Vishnu. Her sense of postures and poses was so amazingly innate, that even the fanatical priests who guard the golden altar regarded her as a holy dancer."

It could hardly have been more beautifully masterminded by Mata Hari herself, and if she had not been in Paris and the newspaper published in Amsterdam, one might have wondered whether her own embellishing initiative were not behind this delightful bit of fantasy.

It would have been normal if only French newspapermen, whose knowledge of the East was rather embryonic, were taken in by such nonsense. Mata Hari's own countrymen should have been fully able to differentiate between truth and fiction. Nothing of the sort.

A second Dutch correspondent approached Mata Hari, and what he wrote in one of Holland's most serious newspapers, the *Nieuwe Rotterdamsche Courant* of May 31, 1905, is more than mythical:

"Mata Hari! Strange well-modulated name, which suddenly resounded through Paris, through the smart and political Paris—a name that floats on the lips of the common man like something secret, unbelievable, far out of reach.

"Priestess, dancer, lady? People ask—and guess. It is said that four ministers of state invited her to supper and that in the intimacy of their dining room she regaled them with her art."

The writer then went on to say that he had visited the mysterious woman in the pension where she lived near the Champs Élysées, in a room that is overflowing with flowers, "flowers everywhere, a forest of flowers in large costly bouquets."

Then he meets the person he has come for, "a tall and slender chic young woman, beautiful, with dark complexion, gay, dressed in a smart suit, straw hat with dark-red flowers, who smiles, talks, who moves gracefully and with ease through the room—Mata Hari!

"Yes, she says, she is Dutch, she is Mrs. MacLeod." And yet at the same time she is oriental, "because she was born in the Indies; she also knows the Ganges, Benares, she has Hindu blood in her veins. She acts as if all this means nothing to her, as if all this knowledge about the customs and art of these mysterious countries is perfectly commonplace."

Just the same the author does have his little doubt, but then reflects that M. Guimet after all was not born yesterday. He asks her whether it is true that she assisted Guimet in the preparation of his lecture which preceded her dancing at the museum. Mata Hari "finally has to confess," he says. "Yes, she studied orientalism, lived with it, thought in it and dreamt about it; she knows the music of these countries, indicates variations for the harp that accompanies her dances, and she even composes."

He wants to know how she arrived so suddenly in Paris, and how she was able to become a success so quickly.

She answers that she arrived only half a year ago from Holland, and "it is quite a story, oh, not a very pleasant one!"

Mata Hari tells him about her troubles, which he records dutifully: "She did some modeling for a while, and rode horses in a circus. But she felt she could do better, that the glow and the arts of those holy countries were deep within her.

"Suddenly she is no longer the plain young woman, suddenly she becomes a strange, energetic, proud human being—proud indeed, too proud to accept defeat, too proud to be ugly, or small or helpless, too proud to be without talent. She laughs about herself and talks about a thousand things, about all the people she has met so suddenly in the very center of that high society, among the fabulously glittering crowd that constitutes Parisian life."

At that moment there is a prosaic interruption, and the interviewer is called back from his short dreamy sojourn among the temple dancers and high society by the ringing of a bell. Even priestesses must eat, and this high priestess has not yet reached the dining room of her own villa—she is still living in the simple boardinghouse off the Champs Élysées, where all the guests eat together around the table d'hôte. The Dutchman has a few last questions—about plans, about the theater.

"Plans? Oh, she has so many of them! She wants to get an apartment of her own, with her own furniture, she wants to get away from the uninteresting atmosphere of the boardinghouse. And she wants to work—work and study.

"The theater? She does not know yet—and with a mocking gesture she pushes aside the letters and proposals from impresarios, long lists of figures that protrude from among heaps of books on the table."

There is another and more persistent interruption; the maid puts her head around the door—dinner is really ready.

"Mata Hari tries to put all serious and important things into the background; suddenly she is gay again, lighthearted, joking. She shakes my hand—strongly, proud and very friendly—and the visitor walks slowly back into town, lost in thoughts. But the image of this young woman remains with him, sharply outlined— this young woman for whom Paris as yet has not been able to find any name but: Lady Mata Hari."

Reading these articles in the Dutch press, both John and Father Zelle must have had some strange thoughts. The little girl who had driven around Leeuwarden in her goat carriage now a famous dancer; the young woman who had answered an advertisement in a newspaper now living in Paris, the city she had talked about so frequently, and a success; it was all a far cry from Frisian fields and Javanese hills. Something which neither father nor husband ever had seen or suspected had been hidden in that head of their daughter and wife.

Now Mata Hari's fame started to be noticed elsewhere. To the army of foreign correspondents in Paris, always eager to find a story with a light romantic touch that might interest the readers back home, the arrival of the mysterious Hindu dancer was a good story indeed.

The correspondent of the *Indépendance Belge* went all the way back to the sixteenth-century Ecumenical Council of Trent to find a festival which was "half profane, half religious," and which thus could be compared to Mata Hari's pseudo-religious dancing. He reminded his readers that close to four centuries previously Cardinal Pallavicini, who was the historian of the Council, had mixed religion and pleasure. He had invited "all the women of Trent and surrounding countryside to a great ball, where they danced with cardinals, prelates and doctors of philosophy." At the same time a colleague of this Belgian writer confessed that "he and the spectators had felt an emotion which defies analysis and which leaves one with the impression of a dream."

It was an Italian correspondent (for *La Patria*) who had to come up with yet another comparison with religion, although in this instance he preferred Brahma to the Church of Rome. "Mata Hari combines the theological science of a Brahman with her charm as a dancer." And he was immediately seconded by a writer who found that "no one before her has been able to give such a complete impression of sacred art."

A Romanian correspondent in Paris was far more romantically inclined. Mixing the sounds of the Orient with the gypsy music of his own country and—as any Romanian—always apt to rave about a beautiful woman, he found in Mata Hari "a strange philosophy in the subtlety of her body, in her pyrrhic rhythm, in her indolent and voluptuous movements, in the tragic menace of her eyes and arms, in the slow prayer of her amorous gestures, in her imaginary caresses, her provocative retreating, her perverse abandon, her innocent triumph over both instinct and sensuality.

"It was like an evocation," the Romanian continued, "and it seemed as if the walls of the museum would come crashing down, as if outside were no longer the Avenue d'Iéna but a far-away and moving horizon, the eternal forest trembling under the fiery kisses of eternal summer, the sculptured and pyramidal pagoda at the end of a large avenue bordered with flowering rose bushes, and, amidst the haze of perfumed incense, this beautiful woman, so eloquent in her studied silence and in her shrieking pantomime, symbolized innocent nature with all its seductions, all its weaknesses and all its joys!"

Even for a romantic writer from Bucharest this was quite an exhaustively enthusiastic performance. He was, however, not as lucky as his colleague who wrote for the *Journal* of St. Petersburg, because unlike him he had not met the mystical woman personally. The Russian writer, on the contrary, "had the chance to speak to this young Hindu," and Mata Hari showed herself from her most imaginative side.

The correspondent asked her what she thought of European society in general and of Parisian society in particular. Her impressions, he wrote, "were not flattering," and he then went on to quote the always-out-for-a-new-angle Mata Hari.

"Having remained for so long close to nature, which is simultaneously innocent and simple, she looks upon our worldly behavior as if it took place on a stage where everything is false and on the surface only. Women wearing make-up and false hair, compliments that are nothing but lies, all this inspires in her an amazement that borders on hilarity. She is astonished that our women do not have the customs of her country, where women may have to suffer inferior treatment like being whipped, but where at the same time they are superior on account of a far more stimulating and higher education which leaves nothing indifferent to them—because they can sew, make their own clothes, are good cooks, can shoot straight, can ride horseback and are capable of doing logarithms and talk philosophy."

There was, indeed, never an end to Mata Hari's imagination; the bigger the lie, the more the interviewers were impressed. To Paul-Louis Garnier, who wrote for the *Courrier de la Plata* in Buenos Aires, she confided details of her initiation into the temple dances: "In Batavia I often came in contact with rich princes who would invite us, my husband and myself, into their homes.

These men, who are very religious, have famous dancers whom they hardly show to anyone. They know the most secret Brahman dances, which are executed around the altar, and I have been able to study with them for a long time."

What must have gone on in Mata Hari's mind when telling these amazing stories one can only imagine. She had never been in India, had never been whipped—unless the stories she told about her husband were true—and had never been initiated in temple dances nor in higher mathematics. Yet she distributed these tales with the ease and self-assurance of the accomplished storyteller from the East.

Her success was such that an Englishman living at the Moscow Gates in St. Petersburg postponed his return to Russia for several days, simply to see Mata Hari dance. His name was Harold Hartley, and his letter, written in Paris at the Hotel Meurice, and preserved by Mata Hari, reads as follows:

"A great—but diffident—admirer of you who, in order to look at you, has stayed five days longer in Paris than he intended, ventures with great deference to ask you to accept on his departure the accompanying flowers as a sign of his admiration."

During all that year of 1905 there was only one man in Paris who actually doubted about Mata Hari and about her art. François de Nion, who wrote for both the influential Buenos Aires daily *La Prensa* and for the *Diario* in Cadiz, talked to someone who had been living in the Indies for years, "a true Orientalist" as he qualified him.

This man explained that dancing girls in the Orient, instead of showing themselves in the nude, are always dressed in white and that their chastity is proverbial in the lands of the Brahmans.

It set M. de Nion thinking, and he wondered whether Paris was the victim of an impostor. "Are we still living in the times of Louis XVI," he asked, "who arranged a majestic and enthusiastic reception for a foreign ambassador who turned out to be none but a Marseilles shopkeeper?"

While M. de Nion was still wondering, Mata Hari took meas-

ures that might at least supply part of the answer, for now the
scene changes. Although disdainful about theatrical engagements
when talking to her journalist countryman from Rotterdam, Mata
Hari soon afterwards changed her mind. She was after bigger
things. Following in her father's footsteps, she needed a wider
range of appreciation, and a meeting with an elder gentleman
gave her a start in that direction. The gentleman was a civil
lawyer, *Maître* Clunet, who from this point on would play a part
in Mata Hari's life that would only end at her death.

Mata Hari explained her aspirations to Maître Clunet, who sent
her with a warm word of recommendation to a friend of his,
Gabriel Astruc, one of the best known impresarios in Paris. Astruc,
who a few years later was instrumental in bringing Diaghilev's
Russian Ballets and Chaliapin to France, and who in his memoirs
described Clunet as Mata Hari's "true and trusty friend," immediately set to work, and remained her manager and agent till the
end. Quickly weakening in front of the figures Astruc had thrust
at her, she accepted an engagement at the Olympia Theater on
the Boulevard des Capucines. She was going to embrace the
Greater Public. Paul Ruez, director of the theater, made sure to
present his star attraction amidst a number of the very best international variety acts, among whom was Fred Karno, one of the
foremost mimes of his time, under whose guidance Charlie Chaplin five years later was to make his debut in *A Night in an English
Music Hall.* On the program were furthermore Arabian dancers,
a juggler, "Leo and his Infernal Violin," and some acrobatic acts,
plus the by then more and more popular "cinematographic projections." Mata Hari received the enormous salary of ten thousand
francs for her performance.

The result was stupefying. Had the press been lyrical when she
danced at private homes and clubs, Mata Hari's appearance in
Le Rêve ("The Dream") by Messrs. Ryan and Howden, with
music by George W. Bing, was a sensation. Parisians, who had
been made curious by the stories in their newspapers, now were
able to see the oriental wonder for themselves.

On August 18, 1905, Mata Hari made her first appearance at the Olympia during an *avant première.* On the twentieth the first performance for the public took place. The result justified Monsieur Ruez' financial investment to the fullest. It was a complete triumph.

La Presse, already greatly enthusiastic before, now wrote on the twenty-first that "one would need special words, new words, to explain the tender and charming art of Mata Hari! Maybe one could simply say that this woman is *rhythm,* thus to indicate, as closely as possible, the poetry which emanates from this magnificently supple and beautiful body."

Other newspapers followed suit. Jacques Vanzay, in the *République Française,* mentioned that "she is a real artist." And *Le Journal,* one of the most influential morning papers, wrote that "Mata Hari personifies all the poetry of India, its mysticism, its voluptuousness, its languor, its hypnotizing charm. To see Mata Hari in a rhythm and with attitudes that are poems of wild voluptuous grace is an unforgettable spectacle, a really paradise-like dream."

Le Figaro had similar comment, but put it in a more practical form. "If India possesses such unexpected treasures," wrote its art critic, "then all Frenchmen will emigrate to the shores of the Ganges. Mata Hari is a prodigal success."

While the performances were continuing amidst such intriguing applause, it became clear why Mata Hari had accepted to appear in a music hall. In the first place the Olympia was the best theater Paris had to offer, having been entirely renovated by M. Ruez when he took over the management from the Isola Brothers. But secondly, and it had surely been the deciding argument, money beckoned and could be used to advantage.

Being a true daughter of her luxury-loving father, Mata Hari, in her first flush of success, had spent far more money than she had made during these first six months of her Parisian acclaim. Now that she was receiving a large and steady salary, a Paris

jeweler caught up with her and had her paycheck attached for
unpaid bills totaling twelve thousand gold francs.

When the case came to court, Mata Hari suddenly remembered
her husband, all alone in Holland with her little daughter. The
agreement with the jeweler was made, she told the judge, "without the consent of my husband, a Dutch officer."

The judge satisfied both parties: Mata Hari was allowed to
keep her jewelry, and the salesman was told that he would receive two thousand francs a month from his client's salary.

And again it was a compatriot of Mata Hari who wondered
whether she had chosen the right career. This Paris correspondent for the *Nieuwe Courant* paid her a visit towards the end of
September, when she was still dancing at the Olympia. Mata Hari
had made good her promise to leave the simple pension, and had
rented an unfurnished apartment in the same neighborhood, at
3 Rue de Balzac.

The apartment, according to the correspondent, was on the
mezzanine floor, with a large sitting room and a piano with lots
of music. Talking in both Dutch and French, "which Mrs. Mac-
Leod speaks very purely," Mata Hari explained that "she had
dancing in her blood."

The correspondent was impressed but wondered what Mata
Hari would have done if, without a penny to her name on her
arrival in Paris, she had not succeeded. The answer was charac-
teristically Mata-Harian: "I had a gun ready and my decision was
taken." To which she added that she had a character which was
always apt "to follow a sudden impulse."

She had several offers from abroad, said Mata Hari, including
London and St. Petersburg, and she was preparing three new
Brahman dances. She differed from other artists, she said, in that
she was one with her public, on the same social level. She not
only *danced* in the best Paris salons, but was received there as an
equal, and she herself at times entertained her hosts.

The correspondent, by now even more thoroughly impressed
by the studiously religious character of Mata Hari, was curious to

know whether she did not look forward to an ideal that went way beyond dancing in public. He must have thought of meditative retirement in a Buddhist monastery—India, Tibet, or somewhere in that area.

Mata Hari fully agreed. She did have such an ideal. But it turned out to be different from what the serious correspondent had expected. Mata Hari confessed that she might say good-by to her dancing career soon, because better prospects had appeared in her future. She had been asked in marriage by Count T——y, a Russian officer attached to Grand Duke Michael.

"À *la bonne heure*," said the laconic Dutchman to himself on leaving, "a Dutch Salome has not been born yet."

In the meantime, what had happened to John? He had gone on living in Holland, and now wanted to get a divorce from his estranged wife. But for this he needed her consent, and for the time being Mata Hari had not the slightest inclination to give in— the marriage proposal from the Russian count apparently having fallen through. Yet without the wife's agreement, a Dutch court of law would not give its approval to a divorce.

At last John decided to send his lawyer, Mr. Heijmans, to Paris, to try and convince Mata Hari. John wanted to get married again, not only for his own good—he was now fifty years old—but also to have a second mother for his daughter Non. While MacLeod may have had his faults as a husband, especially during the earlier years of his first marriage, his behavior as a father had always been excellent.

The lawyer had a conference with Mata Hari and enjoyed his stay in the French capital to the fullest. He came to see her nearly every day, talking about a thousand and one subjects. And Mata Hari, still feeling very Dutch, liked his company. But every time the divorce was brought into the conversation, she would say that she just *loved* to talk Dutch again, and Mr. Heijmans should not spoil that pleasant experience by reminding her of such unpleasant a matter as a divorce.

The lawyer, convinced that he would never get any results

from conversation only and perfectly well understanding that he had not come to Paris at his client's expense just to have a good time, finally pulled an ace out of his briefcase in the form of a nude photograph of Mata Hari. The picture, he explained, had been sent to her husband by a friend who had obtained it in Paris.

Mata Hari was astonished and angry. The photograph, she said, had been taken privately for a friend of hers, and was not to be put on sale. This, said Mr. Heijmans, might well be the case, but a stern judge in Holland might be of the opinion that an honorable woman and mother "should not have herself photographed in the nude for a friend." Mata Hari, knowing only too well what a Dutch judge might think, understood that she had little choice. She did not want to be mixed up in a scandal, especially on account of her daughter, and finally accepted a divorce. It was granted in Amsterdam on April 26, 1906.

John MacLeod's next matrimonial venture did not bring him much more luck than his first. On November 22, 1907, he married Elisabeth Martina Christina van der Mast, who was twenty-eight years his junior, from which marriage he had one daughter, Norma.

MacLeod, who eked out his meager military pension with the writing of courtroom reports for the Arnhem daily newspaper, had sent Mata Hari's daughter Non to live with another family. On weekends she used to come home to have her meals with her father and his second wife. The latter was hardly a loving stepmother, and the results were not long in coming. MacLeod and Elisabeth separated in 1912, and a divorce was finally pronounced in 1917.

Chapter 5

AFTER the success at the Olympia Theater, Gabriel Astruc continued actively to promote his client's career, and in January 1906—four months before her divorce—Mata Hari left for a two weeks engagement in Spain, her first appearance abroad. Dancing at the Central Kursaal in Madrid, the press found her dances "discreetly voluptuous." But they regretted that Mata Hari danced in tights, "although of minimum proportions." Just the same she was "sensationally" applauded.

She had not left for Madrid without the necessary introductions. Maître Clunet had given her a letter to a friend of his in the Spanish capital, who was none but the French ambassador, Jules Cambon—again a person who would play an important part in Mata Hari's life for the next twelve years.

While in Madrid, a surprise letter from Astruc brought her probably one of the first great artistic shocks of her life. Till now she had only appeared in oriental dances of her own invention, even after she had moved from the intimacy of the Paris salons' small audiences to the larger setting of the concert hall. Now Gabriel Astruc informed her that he had signed a contract with his friend Raoul Gunsbourg, director of the Opera in Monte Carlo, to have Mata Hari appear there in the ballet of Massenet's *Le Roi de Lahore*. Mata Hari answered Astruc's letter immediately, and asked him please to send her the score of the opera.

M. Gunsbourg, who had been born in Romania as the son of a rabbi, had come to Monte Carlo via the theaters of Moscow and St. Petersburg, to reign as the uncontested czar of Monte Carlo's theatrical life for fifty-nine years, till 1951.

Staging *Le Roi de Lahore* under the active sponsorship of Prince Albert I of Monaco, the season promised to be an outstanding one, as the Monte Carlo Opera was at the time—next to the Opera in Paris—the foremost lyric theater in France, with many first performances to its credit. Chaliapin was to sing in Monte Carlo that season, but as yet it was not sure whether the great Russian basso would appear. In June 1905 the sailors of the cruiser *Potemkin* had revolted in Odessa, and in the great Russian October upheaval that followed—as Mata Hari neatly informs us in her scrapbooks—Chaliapin "had been wounded on the barricades of the Tverskaya in Moscow, and had promptly been carried off to jail by the Czar's police."

The performance of *Le Roi de Lahore* on February 17, 1906, with composer Massenet present in the Prince of Monaco's box, was a huge success. Mata Hari, "whose presence in Monte Carlo," according to one newspaper, "was causing considerable comment," danced in the ballet of the opera's third act in the company of the famous Mademoiselle Zambelli. The role of Sita was sung by none other than Geraldine Farrar, one of the most glorious voices that had ever come out of the United States.

Thus Mata Hari had gone one step higher. She had arrived at the serious theater. Dancing in the nude belonged to the past— for the moment at least. This time she was not acclaimed because she lost her veil and covered her face—in an early version of what nowadays might well be called an artistic striptease act—but because she could dance. Really dance, and not just move and pose.

While the press, calling her "a seductive star," said that she had brought to the ballet "the troubling charm of her strange dances," they also reported her as making a happy off-stage appearance at the Nice Carnival, dressed as Venus.

Her friendship with famous personalities continued. Puccini, who was present in Monte Carlo, sent her flowers with a card on which he transmitted his greetings to the *"charmante artiste,"* and Massenet himself was entirely won over by her. "I was charmed and happy to see you dance—my respectful congratulations," wrote the sixty-four-year-old composer of *Le Roi de Lahore,* who already had such operas as *Manon, Thaïs,* and *Werther* to his credit.

Mata Hari's friendship with Massenet grew through the years, as is shown by a letter from the composer in which he says he is "very proud of your proposal and so unhappy to be for several months already in the middle of feverish work." (Mata Hari had probably asked him to compose a special ballet for her, an endeavor she pursued for a great many years.) Still later, when she was living in Berlin, Massenet sent her an exuberant note just before returning from the German capital to Paris. It is one of the most impressive messages in Mata Hari's scrapbooks. In fact it was not pasted *in* the books, but was one of the very few documents Anna Lintjens had handed me separately in 1932. Perhaps Mata Hari had thought the note of too intimate a nature to be joined to newspaper write-ups and other letters. Indeed the content of Massenet's letter is strikingly revealing as to his feelings for Mata Hari. Although he was known as a very warm and rather overwhelmingly friendly person, causing one of his close male friends in the music world to say, "Every time he embraced me, I felt I had to go and wash my face," his note to Mata Hari was written in such an expansive mood that it must have been the result of more than just a friendly feeling. Writing with the impetuousness of a young lover, the French composer had the following message delivered by hand: "How happy I have been to see you again! Mata, Mata—I am leaving for Paris within a few minutes! Thank you, thank you—and my fervent admiration."

Written in 1906 on blue notepaper with perforated gummed edges as was then in use, the letter was addressed to "Madame Mata Hari—Berlin." There is no mention in the literature about Massenet of any voyage to the German capital. In his own book *Mes Souvenirs*, which was published during the year of his death in 1912, he recalls the only known trip he ever made to Germany, the one to Bayreuth. But the composer's interest in the weaker sex was well known, and Mata Hari might have attracted him enough to make a quick trip up north.

In Berlin, Mata Hari had become the mistress of Herr Kiepert, a rich landowner whose estate was just outside the city. A lieutenant in the Second Company of the Eleventh Westphalian Hussars Regiment who was married to a Hungarian beauty, he had installed Mata Hari in an apartment at number 39 in the Nachodstrasse, within walking distance of the Kurfürstendamm, main artery of (what is now) West Berlin. With Lieutenant Kiepert she attended the Imperial Army Maneuvers at Jauer-Streigau in Silesia from September 9 to 12, 1906, an event that was seriously considered as a link in her presumed espionage career when she was on trial in Paris eleven years later.

On August 29, 1906, Mata Hari wrote a letter from Berlin to Gabriel Astruc in Paris, informing him about an offer she had received from London to appear in a pantomime, "which pleases me enormously." But she would much prefer to do it in Monte Carlo, "where I have had such a great success." And referring in the same letter to Massenet's visit, she told Astruc that the composer had "given her an introduction for the opera in Vienna."

She did not dance at the Opera in that city, but to Vienna she did go, where—towards the end of 1906—she started her conquest of the Austro-Hungarian Empire. Her arrival was nearly immediately the cause of a "tricot" war. For her first appearance at the Secession Art Hall she danced in the nude, after which she wore tights for her appearance at the Apollo Theater. This induced the press to publish a long series of polemical articles on the merits and demerits of dancing in close-fitting tights, in the seminude, and with nothing on at all. There was, indeed, plenty of exposed and unexposed flesh available in Vienna to keep the opposing factions feuding.

Mata Hari was staying at the Hotel Bristol. At the Hotel National was the American dancer Maud Allan, and none but Isadora Duncan stayed halfway in between. Maud Allan was dressed on-stage in "nothing but gold." Still another dancer had appeared on the Vienna stage dressed in a mere handkerchief, "which she held in her hand." Even the lighthearted Viennese were slightly taken aback, and once Mata Hari appeared, the "war of tights" was waging on all newspaper fronts.

But Mata Hari won. Although some dowagers were of the opinion that "things were going a bit too far," it took only a very few appearances and everybody found things highly satisfactory.

Late in December Mata Hari was eagerly awaited at the Vienna Christmas Bazaar, where she was to sell autographed photographs. Young Vienna had breathlessly hoped she would come in Javanese costume, in tights perhaps, or—who knows—attired in a fluttering handkerchief only. To some extent they were disappointed, for Mata Hari came as everyone else—fully dressed. Just the same she delighted the audience with her "slender shapely appearance," and once they got over their initial disappointment, they found that "she looked as adorable with her clothes on, as off."

Entering the German-language area professionally, Mata Hari felt that a few new angles had to be added to her already highly varied autobiography. "My parents were Dutch," she explained, "but my grandmother was the daughter of a Javanese Prince, and as such I have real Indian blood in my veins." Mata Hari's grandmother had never had as much as even one single glimpse of the Indies, but was born, as were all her relatives, in the stolid province of Friesland.

The interviewer of the Vienna *Fremdenblatt* gave an excellent description of the dancer as she appeared to him at the Hotel Bristol.

"Slender and tall," she seemed to him, "with the flexible grace of a wild animal, and with blue-black hair," which surrounded "the small face that makes a strange foreign impression. Forehead and nose are of classical shape—as if copied from antiquity. Black long lashes throw a shadow on her eyes, and the eyebrows are so finely and so gracefully bent that it seems as if they were drawn by an artist."

She first spoke to him in French and then continued in "enchanting English-German," while she invented another portion of her life story. Now her father did not sell hats in Leeuwarden, but was a Dutch officer. According to this new version she was born in Java, spent two years at a girls' school in Wiesbaden (her honeymoon serving at last *some* purpose), and married an officer when she was sixteen years old. In 1904—two years after she and her husband had already returned to Holland—she "still lives in Deli on Sumatra." The elimination of those two years of trial and error in Europe occasioned a quicker transfer from the temples of India to Western civilization, a time-dissolve which Mata Hari must have felt made her appearance on the European stage more interesting.

The next day she talked to another newspaperman in Vienna. Now her husband suddenly became a descendant "from an old Dutch family, which was naturalized in the Indies"—although how a Dutchman could become naturalized in Holland's own colonies must have been a mystery even to Mata Hari.

Her charm captivated this writer as all others. He found her "a striking beauty with the tender lovely face of a young girl." She made him think of Baudelaire's poems, "Bizarre goddess, dark as the night," and "Even when she walks, she seems to dance."

Then, to get things *really* mixed up, she contradicted the stories published in the Paris newspapers, which proclaimed her to be a former Indian priestess and the widow of a colonel. "And my husband is still living in Malang," she added.

There were more interviews before she showed herself on the stage to the eagerly waiting Viennese, for by now Mata Hari fully understood that publicity was an important part of her career. To the correspondent of the *Deutsches Volksblatt* she talked in "quite fluent excellent German," and while the words flowed from her mouth, he had time to qualify her lips as being "like a blooming rose."

"In my dancing one forgets the woman in me," she explained, "so that when I offer everything and finally myself to the god—which is symbolized by the slow loosening of my loincloth, the last piece of clothing I have on"—Mata Hari had indeed become a master in the art of dropping interesting items about her act—

"and stand there, albeit for only half a second entirely naked, I have never yet evoked any feeling but the interest in the mood that is expressed by my dancing." The demure Mata Hari must have had a naïve idea about her Viennese public, or more likely, was out to give them a little foretaste of what they might expect.

We are now in the year 1906, a fairly long period removed from the First World War. It is therefore interesting to note what Mata Hari told her interviewer in Vienna when the latter asked her whether she was going to dance in Berlin. It may well be that her lover, Kiepert, did not want her to appear in public in the city which he shared with his mistress and his wife. Or perhaps Mata Hari did not like the Germans particularly at that moment, although several years later she changed her mind—at least artistically.

"Berlin?" answered Mata Hari, "I wouldn't dance in Berlin for *any* amount of money!"

She then finally made her appearance—the one in the nude— at the Secession Hall, for which invitations had been sent out to come and see "Mata Hari, Lady Mac-Leod." The public was highly select, including the Austrian Minister of the Interior, Count Julius Andrassy, and the Countess, as is indicated by a visiting card which Mata Hari carefully preserved in her scrapbooks. The card was sent to her by La Princesse Léopold de Croÿ, née Comtesse de Sternberg, who, writing in English, asked her: "Dear Lady MacLeod—If it is not indiscreet, I should be so thankful if you would be so kind as to send two more cards for Saturday to Countess Andrassy, Wallnerstrasse No. 6."

From the following day, December 15, 1906, till January 16, 1907, she entertained the Viennese at the Apollo Theater. Perhaps to put the public in the proper religious mood, the conductor of the orchestra had the wild idea of playing Martin Luther's "A Mighty Fortress Is Our God" as the musical introduction to Mata Hari's dancing!

The opinion of the critics was divided, and there were indeed some very critical words from the newspaper *Die Zeit* (which did not deter Mata Hari from putting them in her scrapbooks), in which the writer wondered whether "these dances, in their oriental calm, are real—whether they even have anything Indian at all."

But even if they had not, there was yet much to admire, for "this body, which is formed like a work of art, and which moves with gestures that are full of caressing charm and yet priestlike, is highly provocative." And, having a second thought about seeing a naked woman on the stage, the paper added: "Whether it is provocative in the artistic sense only is a matter of taste."

Had anything gone wrong, or were the Viennese expecting more and longer nudity? Mata Hari apparently did not care too much, for next to write-ups that were only slightly unfavorable, she did not hesitate to paste entirely negative opinions in her books, like the one from the *Wiener Deutsches Tageblatt*, which was short and far from sweet: "I would have to lie if I were to say that the performance is more than that of an amateur."

Of course it might well be that the gentleman who wrote these lines had never seen any dances from the East, be they Indian, Javanese, or from Bali. Mata Hari most likely based her movements on what she had seen in central Java, where the dances of Jogjakarta are fairly stylized and slow, with positions held for a considerable length of time, contrary to the dances of Bali, which are all movement—and which island Margaretha Zelle MacLeod had never visited.

The *Arbeiter Zeitung* and the *Deutsche Zeitung* were in the same corner of the critical field—both negative. While the former paper was of the opinion that "the new art of the dance, which Mata Hari for the moment more feels than expresses, is still waiting for its great exponent," the latter wrote "if she had not had the advantage of 'nude publicity,' she would not have been a success."

Negative or positive, Mata Hari was not dismayed, and indeed there was not much reason to be, seeing how the crowds came to deposit their money at the box office of the Apollo Theater.

"Isadora Duncan is dead!" proclaimed the *Neues Wiener Journal,* "long live Mata Hari!"

"The public is a bit amazed," wrote another journalist, "they had expected something different." But the public was soon satisfied. In a second dance Mata Hari dropped her veil. In the third one she unwrapped all seven, and "aristocratic women with endless forebears as well as the chosen representatives of the fine arts brought the exotic artist a thunderous ovation."

Happy Mata Hari. She had won over the Austrians like the French and the Spaniards. Had there been some unfavorable criticism, it was easily forgotten before the supreme applause of the rest of Vienna. And if her popularity can be measured by the contents of the feature articles written about her, then she had definitely made a hit in the Austrian capital. The *Deutsche Volksblatt* dedicated the following highly amusing poetical folderol to her:

> ... and there, in front of this holy spot,
> Where gods surrounded another god,
> Sat the audience, which would not falter
> When seeing a woman swoon at the altar.
> The ritual, a slow-motion safari,
> Would be danced by half-Indian Mata Hari,
> Who soon arrived, her veils a-flowing,
> While Indian music started echoing,
> Played on a snake-charming violino,
> And a melody-stomping pianino.
> It was, since Duncan, our first chance,
> To see such an amazing dance,
> For while Mata Hari showed legs galore,
> And even a little-little more,
> It did our eyes a lot of good
> To watch her daintily stepping foot
> And lovely head, which was set upon
> An enticing body, with so little on.

And Mata Hari, dressed as before,
First lost one veil, then lost one more,
Till finally, with little to hide,
She was ready to be Siva's bride.
At which point, like a girl of tender age,
She quickly stood up—and disappeared backstage.
Each person now was a Mata Hari fan,
But then appeared a fully dressed man,
Who said: "We're turning off the light,
Mata Hari will show no more tonight."

The success of Adam Zelle's daughter, which had first hit the Dutch press from Paris, now was confirmed from Vienna. Papa Zelle started thinking. He had never liked Rudolph MacLeod, had always enjoyed high living, and now found himself, through no fault or merit of his own, the father of a famous woman, a "lady," an internationally known and acclaimed dancer. His job as a traveling salesman was not a lucrative one, and he was living with rather limited means at the Da Costakade 65 in Amsterdam. Might it not be possible to make some money out of this windfall? Would a book help? It was at least worth trying.

During the second half of 1906, shortly after Mata Hari's divorce, Adam Zelle took some notes, letters, and papers to an Amsterdam publisher, and asked him to arrange the material into a biography of his daughter. The subject looked interesting, but when the publisher went to see John MacLeod to get some of the facts straight, the latter contradicted the quite fantastic tale presented by his ex-father-in-law. Mr. Zelle, however, was not dismayed, and soon found another publisher. The result was an amazing concoction of 266 pages, published in December 1906. Its lengthy title was *The Life of Mata Hari—the Biography of My Daughter and My Grievances Against Her Former Husband.* Its contents nowadays would constitute a nice case for libel.

It is quite evident from the book that Mata Hari had not learned her love of fantastic invention from a stranger. In Father Zelle's biography Mata Hari became related to dukes, kings, and many simpler noblemen. In a foreword Adam Zelle decided to have Mata Hari travel even farther afield than France, Spain, and Austria. He claimed that the first half of the book was written entirely by his daughter, "who had sent it to him from the United States of America." As always, the Zelle fantasy knew no boundaries.

Soon the facts as supplied by Mr. Zelle were contradicted by another Dutchman, Mr. G. H. Priem (a lawyer), who took the side of Rudolph MacLeod in the marital conflict. His ideas were represented in a short treatise as "The Naked Truth About Mata Hari."

Finally appearing in print, Adam Zelle took advantage of the occasion to air some of his long-slumbering dreams about his aristocratic extraction, delving into those dukes and kings—in which, of course, there was not a word of truth.

The name Zelle is well known in Friesland, and according to one of Adam Zelle's uncles some ancestor of his might have been living in the vicinity of a Celle castle or "Celle burgh" near Hanover in Germany, which later on developed into the city of Celle, still there today. But to deduct from this that the Zelle family had been the uncontested masters of Celle is as far fetched as to claim that Jack London's ancestors once owned the capital of Great Britain. And as to the kings and dukes, they all existed in Papa Zelle's vivid imagination only.

The writings of Adam Zelle and Mr. Priem, plus yet a third pamphlet written by someone else, very quickly lost the public's interest. The only financial benefit from the controversy was reaped by a Dutch cigarette manufacturer who saw his chance to cash in on the Mata Hari fame. He put a "Mata Hari" cigarette on the market, advertising it widely in the Dutch press. Mata Hari herself was clearly interested in this proof of her being a celebrity, and, as usual, pasted one of the advertisements carefully in her scrapbook. It offers "the newest Indian cigarette, which will be satisfying to the most refined taste, made from the best Sumatra and choice Turkish tobacco." The "Mata Hari" came in a Russian model exclusively, then considered to be very refined, was available in both yellow and white, and the price of one hundred "Mata Haris" was one guilder and twenty-five cents.

Chapter 6

THE curtain on her last performance in Vienna having been rung down in the middle of January 1907, Mata Hari spent the next two and a half months traveling, most likely in the company of Herr Kiepert. Passing through Paris, she went quickly on to Marseilles, where she embarked on the North German Lloyd steamer *Schleswig*, which together with the *Hohenzollern* for two years previously had provided a new luxury service to Alexandria. It was a cold and miserable Wednesday with a slight rain falling when the ship left the new Marseilles Harbor at three in the afternoon on its five-day trip to Egypt. Two competing Italian fanfare orchestras played the "Marseillaise" and "Santa Lucia" simultaneously on the windblown quay of the port.

By the end of March Mata Hari was back in Rome, from where on the thirtieth she sent a long letter to Gabriel Astruc in Paris. Informing him that she had made "a long voyage to Egypt as far as Assuan," she wrote that she had hoped "to find classical dances, but unfortunately everything that is lovely has disappeared and the dances that are left are insignificant and not graceful."

Then she came to the point. She had heard that Astruc would put on the first Paris performance of *Salome* by Richard Strauss at the Châtelet Theater on May 10, and she would like nothing better but to dance in that opera. "The music by Strauss is powerful and I would love to create and interpret the meaning of the dance, which usually is the weak point of an opera. A badly executed dance," she informed Astruc, "cuts all effect."

Writing her letter from the old Hotel Bristol on the Piazza Barberini (now the Bernini-Bristol), Mata Hari told Astruc that she would be back at her apartment at 39 Nachodstrasse in Berlin "within a few days," and would he please let her know his decision. At the same time she sent her impresario a letter which she asked him to forward to Richard Strauss. Astruc, who probably had his own ideas on how to produce *Salome,* apparently judged it unnecessary to send the letter on to the composer of the opera, for a good many years later I found it still in his own file in Paris. In the letter Mata Hari had asked Richard Strauss please to see her on her return to Berlin. "I would like to create 'The Dance,' and above all I would like to dance it in Paris, where I am well known, and only I will be able to interpret the real thoughts of Salome." To entice Richard Strauss still further, she informed him that "in Monte Carlo I interpreted the 'Air Hindou' by Massenet, who can tell you more about me." Although Mata Hari's German by now must have been excellent, the letter to Richard Strauss was written in French.

The idea of being able to dance *Salome* became an obsession with Mata Hari, and during the next few years she would repeat her request to Astruc time and again, but while she did interpret Salome's "real thoughts" later on, it was never under Gabriel Astruc's sponsorship.

It was not till the end of that year 1907 that Mata Hari finally returned for good to Paris, after having broken with Kiepert. She was now living at the expensive Hotel Meurice, as indicated in an interview in the *New York Herald's* Paris edition of December 23. She explained that she had been away "on two years of travel for pleasure," although her absence in reality lasted less than one year. During this time, she said, "she visited Egypt and India on a hunting trip," thus grandly extending her trip across the Indian Ocean to the country of which she claimed to interpret the dance, but which she actually never visited. She was now ready with three new dances, of which she considered "The Legend of the Rose" the best, and she expected to renew her dancing activities on February 1, 1908, at the Salle Fémina on the Champs Élysées.

A preview of this new dance was given at the New Year's party of Arlette Dorgère, who was playing *L'Ingénu Libertin* at the Théâtre des Bouffes Parisiens. Shortly afterwards she displayed her graces at a benefit performance organized by Leon Bailby—later on owner of the morning paper *Le Jour,* and the driving power behind the fabulous yearly *Bal des Petits Lits Blancs* at the Paris Opera—which gala took place at the Trocadero Theater.

Mata Hari was in good company at the Trocadero. Among her colleagues were Sacha Guitry, Cécile Sorel, and Mary Garden, the Scottish singer who in 1900 had made a sensational Paris debut in Charpentier's opera *Louise.*

Yet the return to Paris had brought Mata Hari a disillusion. While she was abroad, she had been imitated back in the French capital. There were numberless naked dancers to be seen at theaters and cabarets, because a good many women had suddenly discovered that a well-shaped body could find easy admirers if shown in comparative undress.

The situation posed a serious problem for Mata Hari. Should she go on dancing as before, dropping her veils? By now her body had become highly attractive in and out of bedrooms, resulting in ermine capes, though probably not (as a German writer later claimed) in the use of the Château d'Etiolles, which apparently once belonged to Madame de Pompadour, and which was to have been a farewell present from Herr Kiepert. (The French government's Bureau for Historic Monuments informed me that there is no château at Etiolles any longer. It had been destroyed during the French Revolution, and the only landmark of interest during Mata Hari's time in or around the village was a church.)

Mata Hari was now over thirty and began to wonder whether her body still had the same appeal on the stage. She was seriously considering throwing her past totally overboard, and dancing in a dress with a long train.

In fact, Mata Hari was fairly bitter about being imitated in music halls all over Paris. At a benefit performance for the Old Actors' Home on September 20, 1908, at the village of Pont-aux-Dames, organized by Benoît Constant Coquelin (the actor famous for his interpretation of Cyrano de Bergerac, and who later played with Sarah Bernhardt in *L'Aiglon*), she gave vent to her indignation in a little speech, which was remarkable enough to be reprinted in *The Era*, a British publication:

"Two and a half years ago I made my first appearance at a private performance at the Musée Guimet. Ever since that memorable date ladies styling themselves "Eastern Dancers" have sprung out of the ground and honour me with their imitations. I would feel highly flattered with this mark of attention, if these ladies' performances were accurate from a scientific and aesthetic point of view. But they are not."

And then Mata Hari's wondrous imagination opens up again. "Born in Java," she continued, "in the midst of a marvellous tropical vegetation, I have been taught from my earliest childhood the deepest meaning of these dances, which constitute a cult, a religion. Only those born and bred there become impregnated with their religious significance, and can impart to them the solemn note to which they lay claim. I have travelled all over the East, but can honestly say that nowhere have I seen women dance while holding a snake or some other object. This I first saw when I came to Europe, and it struck me with dumb amazement. The Eastern dances such as I have witnessed and learned in my native Java are inspired by the flowers, from which they take their poetry [which was, of course, good publicity for her dance 'The Legend of the Rose']. Last year in the interior of Russia I came upon a lady—also a pseudo-Eastern dancer—who modestly styled herself an oriental pearl, and I could not help remarking to her that if there are real pearls, there are also imitation ones."

The speech is the only indication that Mata Hari had possibly made a trip to Russia between the time she returned from Egypt and her reappearance nearly eight months later in Paris. But she had also claimed to have been to Egypt *and India*. In Mata Hari's own mind fact and fantasy were so inextricably mixed that in the end nobody knew what was true and what was not, and consequently the cocktail of her life became more and more a composite of truths, half-truths, and pure imagination.

Thus it is not at all amazing to find still another story from the same period in her scrapbooks, which leads off in yet another direction. While she reaffirmed to be born in Java—Leeuwarden by now seems to be entirely forgotten—she added that she had "been sent to Holland at the age of twelve, accompanied by an officer and an old Indian woman. By this time (her) parents were dead." After she had married at the age of sixteen, she returned with her officer-husband to Atjeh on Sumatra, where she spent the time "horseback riding, gun in hand, and risking her life."

What a wonderful story one writer received from Mata Hari when she explained to him why she danced only intermittently. One wonders whether she was thinking of her lost son when she talked to Edouard Beaudu of the magazine *Fantasio*—or whether the name of the magazine was an inducement to let her own fantasy range even more freely than usual.

"Out there," wrote Beaudu, "on that island where battles were raging, a drama, a violent drama spread its darkness amidst the gay clarity of this ardent life. She returned to Europe, very sad, very somber, and, distressed in body and soul, she found consolation in the dance, which is the hallucination of the body. She danced much and often, subject to her melancholy moods. That is the reason why this artist only dances when it pleases her, when her nerves are perhaps exasperated—when she suffers too much."

Mata Hari was a well-kept woman by now, with large amounts of money at her disposal. On October 4, 1908, she appeared at the Grand Prix d'Automne at Longchamps in a magnificent velvet dress with large muff, the delight of Parisians and photographers. Shortly afterwards she was seen, again at Longchamps, "in a sensational clinging robe of antique blue chiffon-velvet trimmed with chinchilla."

Gabriel Astruc was not kept too busy to find her lucrative engagements during these years, for Mata Hari did not have to dance for money any longer. Thus she appeared at one benefit after another: the Gala des Pupilles, a performance at the home of M. and Mme. Guimet in honor of Baron Kurino, the Japanese ambassador; in August she danced for the local poor of Houlgate in Normandy; and some time towards the end of the year she claimed to have made a second, but this time totally imaginary, trip to Egypt. At least that is what the press wrote—as an untruth —shortly before she appeared at the Théâtre Fémina on February 6, 1909, participating in a benefit performance for the Clémentine Hospital in Sofia. There was Bulgarian music on the program, Bulgarian dancing, Bulgarian students in Bulgarian costume, a Bulgarian rhapsody, even cinematographic views of Bulgaria, and then there was a dance entitled "The Orchid" by the famous dancer Mata Hari, in whose veins ran amalgamated Dutch-Javanese-Maduran-Balinese-Indian blood, none of which was very Bulgarian.

Through all this, Mata Hari had become an established "Star of the Dance," taking her place (according to a page from the art revue *Musica,* carefully pasted into her books) among such famous names as Cléo de Mérode (Belgium's King Leopold II's "official" mistress), Isadora Duncan, Loie Fuller, Lola Montez (the Irish-born dancer who became both the mistress and down-fall of King Ludwig I of Bavaria), and La Belle Otero. She had added another dance to her repertoire, the "Ketjoeboeng." This, according to the *Daily Mail,* is a flower "that blossoms and dies in a night," and which in Mata Hari's interpretation became "a beautiful illusion."

What did Mata Hari do during the rest of 1909? Nothing much apparently, except—the only thing that her scrapbooks reveal—posing for a painting by Paul Frantz-Namur. She had probably tired of all the benefit performances, the flowers that blossomed and faded, and the long every-night dinners. She was waiting for bigger things, and a change.

The change came in 1910, when the stage called her once again to Monte Carlo. M. Antoine, director of the Paris Odeon Theater, had prepared a play by a French-Algerian writer, Chekri-Ganem. Called *Antar*, and its action taking place "in Arabia," the third act featured a ballet danced by a single person: Cleopatra. What, Monsieur Antoine must have thought, could fit Mata Hari better?

The premiere took place on January 7, and, helped by the music of Rimsky-Korsakov, it was—as usual—a success. Mata Hari's "Dance du Feu" prompted the Paris *Matin* to write that she "gave a beautiful performance that was successively smiling, mystical, and impressive."

Coming on top of an article in the Paris *Comoedia* which praised her as "the uncontested Queen of the dances of yore" on account of her appearance at a New Year's Eve benefit at the Apollo Theater in Paris, there seemed to be no one left to doubt the dancer's ability.

Yet there was alway M. Antoine himself. Having brought Mata Hari to Monte Carlo in January, he was now going to stage *Antar* at his own theater in Paris, the Odeon. Once rehearsals had started, M. Antoine claimed that Mata Hari was difficult; she was often late and her "proud character" had made life impossible for the director of the play. M. Antoine sent Mata Hari packing, and the latter promptly sued for breach of contract, asking payment of three thousand francs salary, and five thousand francs damages.

It took the court nearly two years to finish the case—in favor of Mata Hari. M. Antoine, charging that Mata Hari was obstreperous, had made the mistake to say that she had not been a success in Monte Carlo. Mata Hari's lawyer, Jules Jung, was quick to show press clippings from the scrapbooks, hailing his client's success on the Riviera, and at two hundred gold francs a night for fifteen performances, Mata Hari received her money.

On December 23, 1911, M. Jung sent her a telegram to the Grand Hotel in Milan (telegram dutifully in books) notifying her of the successful outcome of the trial.

M. Antoine was a bad loser. Nearly eight years later, and two years after Mata Hari had been executed, the Netherlands Legation in Paris received a letter from lawyer André Regnier, written on August 14, 1919. Acting on behalf of M. Antoine, he asked information on possible property left by Mata Hari. She had, after all, been found guilty of spying and had been executed as a result of this verdict. According to M. Antoine's reasoning it was therefore quite obvious that a woman who had been found guilty of such acts had been equally capable of fooling the judge who had put M. Antoine in the wrong. And maybe, if any funds were left, M. Antoine could convince the Paris tribunal to refund him his three thousand francs. . . .

Yet not everything was won. Notwithstanding Mata Hari's eloquence, the requested five thousand francs damages remained in M. Antoine's pocket.

"*Monsieur le juge,*" her lawyer had said in court, "my client is born in Borneo, in those mysterious Dutch East Indies." And while Maître Weyl here and there put in a word to the contrary in defense of M. Antoine, Mata Hari explained the reasons why she felt entitled to get those five thousand francs:

"M. Antoine wanted not only the presence of a dancer of name, but he also wanted to give his public an original Hindu dance, of which the secret has been handed down through the ages without ever having been put on paper. As such I possess a real secret, and this knowledge of the ancient Hindu dances constitutes for me a precious property."

She complained furthermore that M. Antoine had tried "to arrange her dances despotically" and that he had had the audacity to ask her to rehearse in front of another dancer, Mme. Mariquita, who could thus study the details of her art.

The judge was not impressed, perhaps—as one newspaper put

it—"because he may have been of the opinion that a dancer who was used to dancing in the nude, could not, without difficulty, hide any secrets!"

Chapter 7

WE now come to an amazing period in the life of Margaretha Geertruida Zelle Mata Hari Lady MacLeod, the famous Indian Hindu dancer. Mata Hari suddenly disappears. There is a total void as to her whereabouts, which apparently escaped the many writers who have tried to bring light into the darkness of her past. For over a year there is utter silence. Had Mata Hari gone abroad? Was she ill? Where was she?

Bernard Newman, in his *Inquest on Mata Hari*, made unwittingly one of the most serious mistakes of his mystery and travel-writing career. In his last paragraph he discusses an interview which took place in 1933 between the French journalist Paul Allard and Captain Bouchardon, the *rapporteur militaire* of the trial in 1917. In his closing line Mr. Newman writes:

"Finally, in a case which teems with fantastic as well as unanswered queries, *here is surely the most fantastic statement of all.** When Allard was interviewing Bouchardon, the latter turned an awkward question by suggesting that the dead Mata Hari was not the Dutch Margaretha Geertruida MacLeod, née Zelle, but a Frenchwoman named Mme. Rousseau from Buzançais (Indre)!"

Undoubtedly Allard shrugged off the statement by Bouchardon, just as Newman did. Yet Mata Hari did spend most of those many "lost" months of 1910 and 1911 as Mme. Rousseau, the nonofficial one. The real Mme. Rousseau had married M. Rousseau on October 14, 1903, and Mata Hari was the man's mistress.

* Italics mine.

The Rousseaux did hail from Buzançais in the Indre department of France. Old Madame Rousseau, the nearly mother-in-law of Mata Hari, still lived there in 1910 and 1911, sixty-five years old.

For years I had been intrigued by a page of photographs in Mata Hari's scrapbooks which she described as belonging to *"Mon Château de la Dorée."* And Anna Lintjens, when she trusted me with the books back in Holland, had given me a picture postcard of this very same château.

In 1962, when I started to look seriously into Mata Hari's papers, I wrote a letter to the mayor of the village of Esvres, in the *Indre et Loire* department, asking whether the château still existed, and whether he could inform me who had been the owner around 1911. The mayor, M. Germain, answered me immediately. "From 1910 till 1914," he wrote, "the owner of the château was *Madame Mata-Hary."* And, he added, the château existed *toujours.*

Driving from Rome to Paris late in 1962, I decided to stop off in Esvres, south of Tours, in the heart of the château country. The château existed indeed, a lovely eighteenth-century building, situated at the end of a majestic tree-bordered lane which is nearly a third of a mile long.

M. Germain, the mayor, turned out to be a pleasant farmer who had not known Mata Hari personally, but who had heard various tales about her. And, as it turned out, he had made a mistake as far as ownership of the château was concerned, as well as to the years Mata Hari had spent in Esvres. She had *not* been the owner, and had been living in Esvres from about the middle of 1910 till almost the end of 1911—not 1914.

We talked for a while in the simple living room of his farm, and I wondered whether there was anyone left who might have known Mata Hari. The mayor's wife mentioned a woman in the village. *"Eh, oui,"* said the mayor, "true enough; Pauline worked for Mata Hari in the château."

That evening and the next morning I had long talks with

Pauline Bessy, who was now the widow Piedbout, but who had only been twenty-two years old when she was Mata Hari's maid and as yet unmarried.

Pauline had served Mata Hari's meals, had brought her breakfast, polished the silver, made the morning coffee. She had been engaged by Mata Hari around the month of June 1910, and had remained till her final departure towards the end of the following year, when Mata Hari told her: "I'll be back in two weeks." But she never came back, and even though Mata Hari had asked her to come and work in Paris, Pauline had preferred to stay in Esvres—and by 1962 she had *still* not been to Paris.

Although the photographs I had seen of Mata Hari always showed her as a beautiful woman, there have been several reports to the contrary. Again it is Newman who makes the most definite statement. "Mata Hari was not beautiful," he says, "her photographs are misleading." I asked Pauline for her opinion. After all she had seen her for many months every single day, with and without make-up. Her statement was as definitely positive as several of the others had been negative: *"C'était une belle femme, vous savez!"* ("She was a beautiful woman.")

The Château de la Dorée had been owned by the Comtesse de la Taille-Trétinville. In 1910 she had rented it to a certain Rousseau, a banker in Paris (he was actually a *coulissier*, a stockbroker), and shortly afterwards Monsieur Rousseau had brought Madame Rousseau down. Only it turned out that Madame Rousseau was really the famous dancer Mata Hari, while the official Madame Rousseau went on living in Paris.

Rousseau had met Mata Hari at a soiree where his son, who was a musician, had played. The love affair must have been one of the great passions of Mata Hari's life, for how else can it be explained that after having been feted for so many years in various European capitals, she had suddenly decided to bury herself in the French provinces? Surely, the surroundings of the château were pleasant enough. Mata Hari daily went riding "on one of the four magnificent horses she had in the stable," Pauline Bessy told me, adding that this stable was "red-velveted—*un vrai bijou.*"

But besides this daily exercise there was little to do. The weekdays Mata Hari spent entirely alone, except for the presence of Anna Lintjens, who had followed her to Esvres. The love affair with M. Rousseau, who was three years older than his mistress, was only kept going over the weekends. On Friday evening the banker used to arrive by train from Paris at the Tours station, and would take a taxi from there to Esvres. Early on Monday morning the château's coachman would bring him back to Tours, and Mata Hari would spend the next five long days waiting for him to return, mostly riding in the surrounding countryside on the one horse she preferred: Radjah.

Mata Hari's skill as a horsewoman had been denied by various writers, but had already been proved by her engagement at the Cirque Molier. At Esvres one day, she gave another example of her excellent riding qualities. A sixteen-year-old boy, relative of the owner of the château, brought a letter for Mata Hari down from Paris and arrived from Tours on horseback, a journey of which he was very proud. He mentioned his exploit to Mata Hari, who suddenly jumped into the horse's saddle, rode up and down the outer staircase of the château, and, handing the reins back to the astonished boy, said: "When you can do *that* you can say you know how to ride."

Pauline, discussing the liaison between Mata Hari and Rousseau, said that "they seemed to get along beautifully. There never was any quarrel, and they used to go riding together a lot." And, unasked, she offered some more information: "They had separate bedrooms, but surely managed to see each other."

Mata Hari's bedroom was large, said Pauline, about sixteen by twenty feet, "with a mauve-canopied bed on a raised platform in the center. You had to walk up a few steps to get into it."

Mata Hari, accustomed to luxury, stayed in her large bedroom in a château that had neither bathroom, nor running water, nor electricity—and not even gas. M. Rousseau must have had a great hold on his mistress, about whom his mother was fully informed, as was—as I found out later—his wife. The old Mme. Rousseau, living in Buzançais, one day paid a visit to her son's mistress, trying to convince her to give up her lover.

According to Pauline, "she did not have a chance. The moment she saw Mata Hari she began to feel very friendly towards her, and remained with us for six months off and on. When she left, Mata Hari stayed on—she was *Madame*."

Rousseau, when renting the château, had actually said that Mata Hari was his wife, as explained in a letter to the owner from her son, in which he gave her references about Rousseau, whom he had seen in Paris, and whom he described as "honest and serious, with good silent partners." Director general of his private bank since 1908, and having put up 125,000 francs of his own money as part of the operating capital, Rousseau had declared that "he had married for the second time a certain Madame van Zellen, the widow of an Englishman, Lord MacDonald (I believe), a former governor general of the Indies."

Mata Hari was *très gentille*, said Pauline, adding that "she was very good to us"—Pauline, the cook, the gardener, the coachman, and groom. And, of course, to Anna Lintjens, whom everybody at the château knew as "Anna." But while getting along excellently with these servants, it had been different with those Mata Hari had found on arrival, one of whom, a certain Delacôte, wrote to the owner of the château on July 31, 1910: "We are very glad to leave the employ of M. Rousseau and his mistress, and we are not the only ones, for the situation at La Dorée at this moment is deplorable."

Guy d'Aulby, now living in New York but at that time a fifteen-year-old boy whose father, known professionally as Edward Maryon, was to compose a ballet for Mata Hari, spent one month of his summer vacation with her at Esvres at her request, undoubtedly to diminish her loneliness. One may assume that M. Rousseau did not allow his mistress more mature companions.

The loneliness of Mata Hari at Esvres must have been hard to endure, and possibly only her love for Rousseau made it bearable. Not even Anna shared her meals. Mata Hari had lost the old Dutch habit of having a solid breakfast, and instead started the day on coffee only. For some strange reason she was strictly economy-minded about this morning coffee, which none of the staff was supposed to have before she had her own, between nine and ten in the morning.

"I made coffee just the same," said Pauline, "and used to yell out at everybody: *'Le jus est prêt!'*—I am sure she heard me, but she never said a word." It was the only revolt that took place at the château during those many months Mata Hari lived at Esvres.

I asked whether she ever mentioned her daughter.

"Once," said Pauline. "She had bought a gold watch and told Anna to mail it to Holland, but her husband sent it back."

"And M. Rousseau?"

"He died during the war of '14."

Trying to find out more about banker Rousseau, this last bit of information led me off on a wrong track. At the Bourse in Paris, a few days after my talk with Pauline, I noticed the commemorative marble slabs that carry the names of all bankers and exchange agents who had died during the First World War. I glanced down the names till I got to the R: *"Rousseau—Auguste,"* it said, *"mort pour la Patrie."*

Only six months later, after endless correspondence with mayors in a good many French towns and villages, did I discover that Mata Hari's lover's first name had not been Auguste but Xavier, and that he had not died during the First World War, but quietly in his own bed in 1946. Having been born in Buzançais as Felix, he had always been known as Xavier, and had done business under the name of Xavier Rousseau & Cie at 41 Rue Vivienne. Later, in 1963, his wife confirmed his relationship with Mata Hari to me. "He was a skirt-chaser," she said, "and very good-looking. He and Mata Hari finally had a quarrel, and when at long last he came back to me, he was totally ruined." He then became a salesman for Heidsieck champagne, and when he died, his wife said bitterly, "he did not leave me a penny."

Still, this was Mata Hari's grand period. Returning occasionally from Esvres to Paris in 1911, her photographs, taken at all principal race courses, were invariably printed in the newspapers and magazines. In August 1911, taking the cure at Vittel, she was present at the Concours Hippique. Six years later this same city would be named frequently when Mata Hari for the third and last time in her life appeared in a Paris courtroom—this time for espionage.

She had now moved to an unpretentious but extremely charming house just outside Paris proper, situated at 11 Rue Windsor in the suburb of Neuilly-sur-Seine. Installed by Xavier Rousseau, he was never able to pay for the furniture for, as his wife told me, *she* finally received a summons to pay up—and never did either.

The house was not destroyed to make room for a modern dwelling, as has been claimed, but exists today as it was originally constructed around 1860. Built in Normandy style, the plaster walls crisscrossed with wooden beams, its gate with double doors gives entry into a small courtyard. The ground floor has two fairly large rooms, of which one has an open fireplace, and both look out on the garden. This same garden can be seen from various bedrooms on the first floor, where, until a few years ago, the present occupant enjoyed his morning ablutions "in Mata Hari's bathtub." And, a strange coincidence, the name of the present owner is the Count de *Mata*rel.

The quite large garden was, when Mata Hari occupied the house, approximately sixty by one hundred feet, and not being surrounded by other homes, it was large enough for Mata Hari to entertain her guests with her dances—in the nude if need be.

Now that she had every luxury in the world, Mata Hari's thoughts went back once again to her daughter in Holland. The gold watch had been returned—but why not try something better? Non was thirteen years old, and the estranged mother had seen her only once since she was a baby. Shortly after her early triumphs in Paris, Mata Hari had paid a short visit to Holland, where she had made an appointment with John to meet Non at a strange meeting place—the Arnhem railway station. Mata Hari was accompanied by a liveried servant; her husband came in old clothes. The interview was short. Mata Hari asked the little girl, who had no idea who the chic-looking woman was, whether she would like to come with her. "If Daddy allows me to," well-brought-up Non had answered. Daddy did not, and that had settled the issue for the time being.

But now Mata Hari's ex-husband lived separated from his second wife, and Norma, the daughter from this unhappy union, had remained with the mother. Why then could not Mata Hari's own daughter come and live with *her* mother in Paris?

Being a woman whose impulses were always followed by drastic action, Mata Hari sent Anna to Holland, instructing her not to care about money, but to return with Non. It was a fair attempt to kidnap her daughter from right under the father's nose.

John MacLeod lived in Velp, a small town near Arnhem, not far from the German border. Miss Lintjens was supposed to take Non by car to Antwerp, to continue from there by train to Paris and Neuilly.

Anna, by then in her early fifties, told me that she did not cherish the mission, and that she was at a loss as to how to go about it. It was the first kidnap-attempt in her somewhat haphazardly regulated middle-aged life, and the first fifty years had passed without a policeman being involved in her affairs.

On her arrival in Velp Miss Lintjens took up her watch in the neighborhood of Non's school, having posted someone else close to the school's exit. This person was to inform her when Non would be approaching, and point her out. What she was to do next was not very clear in the Lintjens mind, but at least it was a start. As Mata Hari's emissary she had bought some candy to keep the girl interested—if not in coming along, then at least to keep her talking.

Luck was not with her. Her informant came back from the school building to say that Major MacLeod himself had come to fetch his daughter. As the Dutch saying goes: Holland—or rather Anna—was in trouble.

She probably made the worst move she ever could have made: she went up to MacLeod and explained that "a lady" had given her a present for his daughter. MacLeod was immediately suspicious and answered gruffly, in his best commanding officer's voice, that "if presents are to be given, I am the one to give them." With that he stalked off, Non's hand solidly in his, leaving Anna standing with a red face and a mind that was racing one hundred miles an hour. She could find only one solution in this most uncomfortable predicament: get out of Velp, and get out fast. She did—and took the first train back to Paris.

Chapter 8

Now came the moment which must have flattered Mata Hari more than anything in her career. Gabriel Astruc arranged for her to appear at La Scala in Milan, and at the same time did his best to try and get her to dance with *Les Ballets Russes*, which, appearing for the first time in Monte Carlo, had been brought to France through the combined efforts of Astruc and Raoul Gunsbourg. Leon Bakst, the painter and stage designer who was the decorative power of the dance group and the intimate collaborator of Serge de Diaghilev, apparently had offered to create some of Mata Hari's costumes for her Milan appearance. But through Rousseau's financial debacle her ready cash had suddenly dwindled, and from her house in Neuilly Mata Hari wrote to Astruc declining the offer: "We do not need Bakst." At the same time her publicity sense prompted her to inform her impresario that even before leaving for Milan she would have some photographs made as Venus, the part she would dance at La Scala, which Astruc would then be able "to send to newspapers abroad." Having a contract for the greatest opera house in the world, Mata Hari already had her eye on similar performances elsewhere.

Artistically she felt she had reached the top. If Monte Carlo had been a golden contract, the Milan invitation put the jeweled seal on it. She had indeed "arrived." In 1905 she had started dancing as a rank amateur, without any training. For close to seven and a half years her fame had spread from the private salons of Paris and through the music hall, now to find its apotheosis in Milan. She had finally and indisputably been accepted as a dancer, not because she produced a ripple of eroticism in her audience, but because she could dance—as a professional.

During that season of 1911–1912 Mata Hari danced in two ballets at La Scala, where, as she was to inform Astruc, she met Preobrajenska, one of the most famous ballerinas of her time, "who gave me some precious advice." At the season's opening performance she mimed her by now well-known fantasy of "The Princess and the Magic Flower" in the fifth act of *Armida,* an opera Gluck had composed in 1777. *Bacchus and Gambrinus,* a ballet with music by Marenco, showed her on January 4, 1912, as Venus. Mata Hari was highly pleased with her appearance, as well she might have been, and some of the loveliest pictures in her scrapbooks date from this period. Annotating these photographs, she looked at herself as from a distance, and wrote in the third person: *Mata Hari comme Venus à la Scala de Milan.*

While this was her second trip to Italy, it was the first time that she had come to perform, and it is obvious that a new chapter had to be added to her biography: she now came from an old soldier's family; her grandmother was the daughter of the Regent of the island of Madura in the Dutch East Indies, who married an officer. Her mother too married an officer, and so did she herself —the latter item being the only bit of truth in the whole story. Being born on Java, she informed the Milan press, she became an orphan at the age of twelve, after which her family decided to give her an international education, which led her to spend alternately a year each in England, Germany, and France.

In an interview with the *Corriere della Sera*, Italy's foremost daily, she managed to live up at least to her "one year in France." For, says the writer, she speaks "a harmonious and perfect French." And, this interview taking place in midwinter immediately after her arrival in Milan, the gentleman can assure his readers that her "Venus" will be all they may expect. "One sees immediately," the journalist writes, "that notwithstanding Mata Hari is enveloped in a fur coat and hat, the part of Venus will fit her magnificently."

Being an Indian dancer, the interviewer then wonders about the color of her skin. "Is she not yellow?" he asks somewhat incredulously, and immediately proceeds to give the answer himself. "Not in the least," he says, "because she is really descended from Europeans."

Mata Hari then distributes some philosophic thought: "There is an Indian proverb," she confides to her interviewer, "which says: 'When a dance is well performed, it extinguishes in those who watch it exactly *those* desires which they would like to be stimulated.'"

The Italian to whom she told this bit of wisdom commented to his readers: "In India, perhaps."

The opening performance at La Scala was conducted by Tullio Serafin who, even then, at the age of thirty-three, was already famous, and who in 1963, at the age of eighty-four, was still one of Italy's foremost opera conductors. He remembered Mata Hari well. She was *"una creatura adorabile,"* he told me, "very cultured, and with an innate artistic disposition, who gave the impression of being a simple member of the aristocracy." She was moreover "a serious artist," said the Maestro, who then, trying to find one single expression to describe her, called her *"una personalità."*

The Milan newspapers, taken quite by surprise, did not know

what to make of Mata Hari's performance, which was so different from the ballets they were accustomed to. The *Corriere della Sera* thought her dancing somewhat slow, yet appreciated these "plastic movements." But it also called her a "choreographic artist, a mimic wit with inventive intelligence and with quite an exclusive strength of expression." The *Lombardia* of January 5, 1912, judged these same slow movements "executed in perfect harmony, worthy of our admiration."

Mata Hari was quick to inform Gabriel Astruc of her success. "All newspapers are unanimous in saying that I am an ideal Venus," she wrote him. Judging from what the newspapers *did* write, her statement seemed to contain a bit of exaggeration, but exaggerating was one of Mata Hari's weak, or perhaps strong points. She then proceeded to tell Astruc how she had danced, and what impression this had made on the Milanesi and the ballet master at La Scala. "I play Venus with my own hair, therefore dark. They were astonished, but I answered that Venus is an abstract personality who is the hyperbole of beauty, and that she can be brown, red-haired or blond, and they said I was right."

The *Uomo di Pietra*, a rather humorous weekly in Milan, took a different view of the matter and thought that "inasmuch as so many mimes are dancers, La Scala judged it opportune to import a dancer who could also mime." At the same time it suspected the management of La Scale of the sinister plan of fattening up Mata Hari, so they could produce an opera in which she could perform the *danse du ventre*.

Mata Hari perhaps missed her chance in Milan, for had she mentioned her yearning to dance *Salome* to the director of La Scala, he might have taken her up on it. Yet she was now more convinced than ever that she could do better yet, and the idea of having a ballet specially composed for her, based on one of her own Indian tales, did not leave her. Having first tempted Massenet, she now tried Umberto Giordano, composer of *Andrea Chenier* and a good many other works. But Giordano too was busy. He promised, however—as she wrote to Astruc—to give her an introduction for Saint-Saëns.

Gabriel Astruc had not been sitting still. Having succeeded in getting his artist accepted at La Scala, the situation had to be further exploited. The conversations about joining the Diaghilev Ballet Group, which had started before she left for Italy, had been continuing. Mata Hari now found the preliminaries well enough advanced to work out the details of a contract, which from Milan she sent to her manager in Paris. She already had signed her own copy before forwarding, and all Gabriel Astruc had to do was to get Diaghilev to add his signature.

Astruc had also been contacting Berlin impresarios, and he wrote Mata Hari to bring her up to date on how things were proceeding. But she, being only too well acquainted with the situation in Berlin, was skeptical. "As far as Berlin is concerned," she wrote in answering Astruc's letter, "I am perfectly willing to perform one of my classical dances there, but do not believe that I can have the stage arrangements of plants and moonlight that is indispensable to my dancing."

For the moment therefore Mata Hari did not return to Berlin. Instead she made a quick trip to Rome, where she finally danced her *Salome* and, although in private, with considerable success.

The performance took place at the home of Prince di San Faustino. The Prince lived in the magnificent Palazzo Barberini on the Via delle Quattro Fontane, nowadays a museum. Thus, contrary to the Dutch newspaperman's expectations in Paris in 1905, who had written "À *la bonne heure,* a Dutch Salome has not been born yet," Mata Hari succeeded even here. It was not, of course, what she had hoped for. There was no huge stage and no thousands of spectators to applaud her interpretation of "the meaning of this dance," as she had written to Gabriel Astruc five years previously. But her demonstration was indeed accompanied by Strauss's "powerful music," and was based, as the opera itself, on Oscar Wilde's play—which, after Wilde had originally written it in French, had promptly been banned by British censors, for which reason Sarah Bernhardt had played its world premiere in Paris.

Mata Hari took advantage of her performing *Salome* in a private home to dance it with as little on as possible, and the Prince di San Faustino was so taken by her that he had her preserved for posterity in a painting, made while she was in Rome. As shown in color in her scrapbooks, it displays the Dutch Salome seductively exposing herself in a half-leaning pose, a transparent veil hardly obscuring anything from the waist down, with lots of breast and *ventre* in a most revealing close-up.

With Rousseau gone out of her life, Mata Hari, on her return to Paris, found herself rather short of funds, and on February 8, 1912, she turned for help to Gabriel Astruc. Writing from her home in Neuilly, this letter is the most revealing document about Mata Hari's sudden financial crisis, and, as always, she was not interested in small amounts of money, but wanted a big lump sum for which she offered her house as collateral.

"I wonder whether you know anyone," she wrote to Astruc, "who would be interested in the protection of artists, like a capitalist who would like to make an investment? I find myself in rather difficult circumstances and need immediately about thirty thousand francs to pull me out of this unpleasant situation, and to give me the tranquillity of mind which is so necessary to my art. It would really be a pity to cut such a future short. As a guarantee for this loan I offer everything I have in my home, including horses and carriages."

She continued to say that all money would be paid back within two or three years, out of the fees which Astruc would be able to get her. And to make sure that Astruc himself would not be the victim of such action, the contract would specify that the agent's commission would first be deducted from all amounts refunded.

There is no indication that Gabriel Astruc was able to find a Maecenas to shower his financial gifts on Mata Hari, although outwardly everything during that year 1912 pointed to an ample supply of funds on her part. The stables of her villa in Neuilly-sur-Seine housed the thoroughbreds which she had brought along from the Château de la Dorée, and which she had offered as a guarantee to whoever would come forward with those thirty thousand francs. She went riding in the nearby Bois de Boulogne, dressed immaculately, as might be expected from a European who descended from the Regent of Madura.

Riding sidesaddle in habits that alternated between dark and pure white, her thick hair covered with either a *chapeau melon* or top hat, she cut a beautiful figure on the lanes of the Bois, where—according to one magazine—"those who see her pass by daily on one of her magnificent horses, and who are impressed by the grace, nobleness and beauty of this aristocratic *cavalière,* would certainly not imagine that this admirable amazon is none but Mata Hari, the holy dancer!"

The preliminary talks with Diaghilev had now reached the point where it was deemed necessary for Mata Hari to make a trip down to Monte Carlo. There, in March, she met not only Diaghilev himself, but also Fokine and Nijinsky. But things were not going well, and one can only wonder at Mata Hari's innocence in believing that Diaghilev would sign a contract with her, sight unseen. While her dancing or miming was greatly attractive within the framework of operas and ballets that fitted her special gifts, the Russian Ballet had different requirements, with the exception perhaps for such works as *Scheherazade* and *Cleopatra.* Consequently Diaghilev first wanted to judge her dancing, and this was something Mata Hari had never before come up against. She was the accomplished artist, so why should she have to show what she was capable of? Mata Hari aired her bewilderment and disappointment in a letter to Gabriel Astruc, explaining that Diaghilev wanted her to work first, and only then would he perhaps sign a contract—a procedure which she considered equal to Diaghilev's having asked her to "come down to Monte Carlo for nothing."

Mata Hari wrote her letter after the Russian maestro had

broken an appointment with her, sending her a note at the hotel instead, in which he said that he had been rehearsing late "and was sorry not to have been able to work on the dance of the Goddess."

Then Bakst got into the picture again, and in a strange way indeed. The part of the goddess apparently required Mata Hari to be seen in the nude or at least in the seminude, and Bakst perhaps wanted to see what kind of body he was going to dress—or undress. For on April 2, Mata Hari, keeping Gabriel Astruc closely informed, wrote him: "I undressed *completely* before Bakst in my room, which is sufficient. And I find it unnecessary to start all over again on the stage of Beausoleil, where all stagehands can freely pass by."

Having her nudity inspected by Bakst was as close to dancing with *Les Ballets Russes* as Mata Hari ever came, and it was a disappointed goddess who returned to Paris. The prospect of dancing with the most sensational ballet group then performing in western Europe had made Mata Hari voluble as usual, and having spread the stories of her coming debut with the Russians far and wide, she was now reaping the unpleasant aftereffects of her premature statements. Writing to Astruc on April 30, she said, "I must tell you that the story of the Ballet Russe has put me in a most awkward position, because I talked too much about it."

Yet life had to go on, and Mata Hari took up where she left off before her trip down south. At Easter she was seen at the Auteuil races at the occasion of the running of the Grand Prix du Président de la République, and in May she put a photograph of herself on horseback in her books, which she marked, "On Cacatöes, 3 May, 1912, morning in the Bois de Boulogne." Cacatöes ("Son of Upas," she carefully mentioned under another photograph) and the lovely Radjah were still her favorite horses. In June she added one more photograph, again riding in the Bois, and shortly afterwards she made an appearance at the Grand Steeple Chase at the Auteuil racetrack.

All this display of luxury and financial abundance was, however, purely for show. Like her father, who only stopped playing the grand seigneur when he was completely bankrupt, she continued to look at the world with a smiling face and to act with the bravado of the great artist. Yet all the time she was needling Astruc and expected him to get more work, now that the Ballet Russe contract had come to naught. Vienna attracted her, but if this did not succeed either, she was perfectly willing to go elsewhere, as she wrote her impresario on May 16: "Will you please try London and the United States if Vienna does not succeed? But that would amaze me, for it is there that I have been acclaimed the most."

But since Gabriel Astruc was busy with a great many other projects and could not devote all his time to just one artist, Mata Hari got annoyed and finally wrote him that every time she came to see him he got up from his chair as if to show (that, at least, was her interpretation) that it was time for her to leave. Things got so bad that, on June 21, she asked Astruc to cancel the contract signed so many years before, when he became her manager.

Gabriel Astruc considered that he had probably gone a bit too far, and the ruffled feathers were soon smoothed down again, although without resulting in many contracts.

The performance at La Scala still haunted Mata Hari. If Vienna had not succeeded, if the Ballet had fallen through and nothing had come of London and the United States, then what about Berlin? Not just any theater in the German capital, but the Berlin Opera, of course!

In 1917 the French Military Court insisted that Mata Hari had powerful friends in Berlin all the way back to 1906. Yet by 1912 she had lost all her contacts with Germans to such an extent that she addressed herself to an old French friend in Berlin in an effort to get a contract at the Opera: Mata Hari wrote to Jules Cambon, by now French Ambassador at the court of Kaiser Wilhelm II.

It was six years since the two had met in Madrid in 1906, and the French envoy obviously did not want to commit himself on paper. His answer to Mata Hari, written from Berlin on July 26, 1912, on embassy stationery, was therefore couched in prudent phraseology.

"I remember meeting you in Madrid," wrote Jules Martin Cambon, "where you came to see me with a letter of introduction from Maître Clunet. You now would like to dance at the Berlin Opera. The Opera is the Court Theater and is governed entirely by His Majesty's Household." The moment is bad, Cambon reminds his friend, for in midsummer the imperial family is out of town. But if she insists, he writes, he will speak to the superintendent of the Opera and see what he can do.

Not wanting to leave a stone unturned, Mata Hari forwarded Cambon's letter to Gabriel Astruc, asking him to "please write to His Excellency von Hülsen [Count George von Hülsen was the superintendent of the Prussian Court Theater] in Berlin and mention Cambon's letter. I would like to change my place of residence and do hope I shall succeed."

She continued to entertain royally at her home in Neuilly, for nothing came of her efforts to get an engagement in Berlin. On October 9, she gave a lavish garden party for a small group of friends, where she enchanted them with a delightful rendering of her "Magic Flower Dance." Wearing her hair in three long plaits—"the famous coiffure of the most beautiful women of southern India, the Dravidians"—and, as she herself wrote—"accompanied by my orchestra under the direction of Inayat Khan," * a dozen

---

* Inayat Khan's association with Mata Hari is quite extraordinary, inasmuch as his own daughter, Noor Inayat Khan, became a British agent during the Second World War. An officer in the WAAF (Women's Auxiliary Air Force), she later on worked as a secret radio operator in France, and in 1944 was shot by the Germans at the Dachau concentration camp. More remarkable yet, a close friend of Noor, British author (and Noor's biographer) Jean Overton Fuller, after seeing a photograph of Mata Hari dancing with Inayat Khan's orchestra, declared that she and Noor looked so much alike that they might be mistaken for one another.

photographs in her books show her as a charming person, gracefully pirouetting amidst two long white tulle veils, attached to the very center of her famous—but now oh, so slightly bulging —*ventre*. The evening was such a success that even a year later, in September 1913, the London *Tatler* devoted two pages of photographs to it, headlining the article "Lady MacLeod dances in the light of the moon to her friends." And in order to give its readers an idea of what the dances really were like, the captions under the photographs read "such stuff as dreams are made of," and ". . . a gossamer, a breath."

In December—the fourteenth, to be exact—the Université des Annales in Paris had asked Paul Olivier, music critic of the newspaper *Le Matin,* to address its members on the subject of Japanese, Indian, and Javanese temple festivals. Mata Hari seemed the most appropriate artist to underline his words in movement, and both she and her orchestra, directed by Inayat Khan, who was billed as Music Master of the Maharajah of Hyderabad, participated in the proceedings. Mata Hari not only danced her interpretation of the "Princess and the Magic Flower"—by now an old standby in her program—but also a new dance, which she called "Chundra," to be danced by moonlight.

During his lecture, Paul Olivier told his audience that Mata Hari was not the first bayadere (from the Portuguese word *bailadeira:* dancer) to come to Paris. In 1768 the beautiful Babaiourn had preceded her. Babaiourn became both friend and confidante of Marie Antoinette, he said, and could have married any of the nobles of Paris—which probably would have brought her life to an untimely end under the guillotine. Instead, she changed one veil for another, and became a Carmelite nun.

Introducing Mata Hari, who most likely was not inspired by the nun story, Olivier said he was sure that all those present were fully aware of the noble birth of the lady they were soon to admire, and that her name was only a pseudonym. Born along the shores of the Ganges, he went on, she now divided her time between her tropical fatherland and her small villa in Neuilly where she isolated herself in pure Brahman fashion among her animals and flowers.

Better than anyone, the lecturer explained the story of the Magic Flower, which he called one of the most popular and poetic of India: "A young priestess walks in her garden, which is full of flowers. 'I am walking in the garden of life,' she sings. Suddenly she notices a beautiful flower, representing Love. Should she pick the flower? The movements of the veil in her hands explain the struggle of her emotions. Finally her hesitation comes to an end. The princess picks the flower . . . and drops her veils."

The evening was marked by an amusing incident. Mme. Brisson, *directrice* of the Université des Annales, realized only at the last moment that the dropping of the veils might show a bit too much body, which in turn might shock some of the more reserved *mères de famille* present. Mata Hari was already waiting backstage. Inayat Khan had started the introductory music. Rummaging frantically through the dressing rooms, Mme. Brisson reached Mata Hari just in time with the only bit of appropriate clothing she could lay her hands on—a long piece of red flannel, which was hurriedly applied diaperwise to where diapers usually go. The flannel, it was said, had belonged to Mme. Brisson's father, Francisque Sarcey, eminent art and theater critic of *Le Temps*. By then quietly reposing in paradise, Sarcey must have looked down benevolently on the application of his tummy-warming flannel—for while on earth, it was said, he had always been averse to the display of too much feminine charm in public.

Paul Olivier, who had to leave immediately after the lecture, next day sent Mata Hari a superlative letter, in which he assured her that she had been "the unforgettably radiant and living centerpiece of this all too short festival, a festival of exquisite and unique art, which to all of us, and in particular to your lecturer, will remain a scintillating souvenir."

Signing off, the last phrase of his letter is a masterpiece of French *politesse*. "I put at your feet, dear Madame," wrote Olivier, "my most fervent and grateful homage, and beg of you to consider me sufficiently worthy to accept the certitude of my profound and absolute devotion."

Chapter 9

LESS than a week after the performance at the Université des Annales Mata Hari felt the necessity of more dancing—at whatever price. On February 20 she sent off another letter to her manager, expressing the hope that she would be able to dance at many private parties. Astruc apparently had told her that it was impossible to obtain the very high salary she had been accustomed to, for she mentioned in her letter that she "leaves the question of money entirely to [him]. If you feel that one thousand francs is too much, ask for six hundred."

Not succeeding in contracting the many evening performances Mata Hari had hoped for, Gabriel Astruc found her work in a field she had not tried yet: musical comedy. The Théâtre de la Renaissance had started an extremely successful run of *Le Minaret* by Jacques Richepin, in which the later famous French film actor Harry Baur played the part of Mustapha. For the fiftieth performance Mme. Cora Laparcérie, producer of the play, wanted to treat her public to something special, and thanks to Astruc she engaged Mata Hari to brighten the Nuptial Festival in the third act.

The applause was great on account of her "irresistible grace, beauty, and harmonious gestures." This applause also prompted Leo Maretis, art critic for the daily *L'Événement*, to send her a more than enthusiastic note: "Brava, bravissima, amiga! Your dance is an admirable vision of art!"

The success was such that Mme Laparcérie * decided to keep Mata Hari in the show for a full month, from April 18 to May 18, 1913.

In June of the same year Mata Hari declared that she was tired of appearing in public. During a conversation with Eugène d'Aubigny of the *Moniteur Théâtral,* which took place in her dressing room at the Comédie des Champs Élysées (Gabriel Astruc was director of the Théâtre des Champs Élysées, while Leon Poirier, later a famous motion picture director, ran the Comédie in the same building), she explained that the only reason which had made her decide to appear that day at a lecture delivered by Hughes le Roux was that she did not want to disappoint the speaker.

"People here do not understand," she said. "The public sees only the gestures, but does not understand the meaning. To execute our dances, one needs our education which was shaped through three thousand years. Our dances require moonlight and palm trees—they are lost on the stage."

She then let her fantasy run rampant and distributed some delightful information on the sexual habits and desires of her adopted countrymen under the palm trees. "In our country too we have dancing girls who serve the pleasures of men. But the real dancing girls, the sacred ones, are respected and never touched. If a Hindu feels any sensual emotion when contemplating a dancing girl, he reserves it for the woman who is accompanying him."

Monsieur d'Aubigny, being sure that there were no moonlight and palm trees on the stage of the Comédie des Champs Élysées, wondered after this conversation whether it would really be worth his while to stay for the performance, but finally his curiosity overcame him. He was not disappointed. He saw the same

---

* On December 3, 1921, *La Danseuse Rouge,* a play by Charles-Henri Hirsch, opened at the same Théâtre de la Renaissance. Based on his own book *La Chèvre aux Pieds d'Or,* published in 1920, the play was a highly sympathetic story of a spy, unmistakably modeled after Mata Hari, although carrying another name. The title role of "The Red Dancer" was played by Cora Laparcérie.

Magic Flower, which Mata Hari had explained to him as being "one of the dances the Spaniards saw when they first arrived in the Indies." His mind, "perfectly charmed," followed "the development of the symbolic and ideal poem," which was danced by Mata Hari "with expressive gestures."

Now there was a most sudden change of scenery. Her decision not to dance in public any longer was suddenly and fairly dramatically thrown overboard, for whom do we find at the new revue at the Folies-Bergère on June 28 "for the summer season"? Mata Hari, of course.

The show was called "La Revue en Chemise," but Mata Hari's own chemise was well extended this time. Gone were the dances of the East. Forgotten were the temples of India and Java. Mata Hari switched to Spain, and the opening-night public—very chic, with the Brazilian Ambassador leading an audience that included princes, counts, and the foremost actors, actresses, and intelligentsia of Paris—saw her in a Habanera, danced against a backdrop copied from a painting by Goya. But the movements remained slow, still reminding her admirers of the temple dances. Her body was tightly enclosed in a corset, and a wide Spanish skirt hid her legs, but luckily, wrote one critic, "her arms, supple as lianas, have been preserved for us, as well as her face with the large eyes, and the fine feline lips." Again the public of a sold-out house liked what it saw, and Mata Hari had to give an encore.

"It is Art," wrote the press, "Art beautiful and pure; Art with a capital A, and this one scene, this magnificent 'living painting by Goya' is all by itself worth going to the Folies-Bergère for." From the Indies to Spain was apparently only one step, and Mata Hari could do no wrong.

The next step Mata Hari took was, however, more startling. For two weeks, finishing September 15, she performed at the Trianon Palace in Palermo, Sicily. Situated at the extreme south of Italy and Europe, Mata Hari found herself both in geographical location and in artistic environment at the opposite end of La Scala in Milan, for the Trianon was a "Café-Chantant-Cinema," the kind of theater that had become more and more popular. Mata Hari appeared twice daily, heading a program of ten numbers, which in addition to the ever-present "cinematographic projections" also included a trained dog act.

Why had she gone to a far-off Italian provincial town? Most likely for two reasons: she was really short of money, and probably some wealthy friend of hers was behind it, and had made the arrangement via Astruc's office.

Palermo, before the First World War, was a city where the social life was governed by the wife of Signor Florio, a rich shipowner and one of the wealthiest men in Italy. His wife, born Princess Lanza di Trabia, of an old and aristocratic Sicilian family, was very beautiful, and some of the cream of international society used to flock to the Sicilian city to be present at the parties for which the Florios were famous. Her husband, Ignacio Florio, was, as it happened, also owner of the Trianon—and whatever Mata Hari's duties may have been, she performed them to everyone's satisfaction.

Her obligations under the Sicilian sun fulfilled, Mata Hari returned to Paris. She started to prepare three Javanese dances, which she expected to bring before the public in January or February 1914 at the Galliera Museum.

Vogue, the fashion magazine, interviewed her and headlined its article "Concerning Lady MacLeod, the Mata Hari, who brought the sacred dances to the Uninitiated West."

Her childhood at the home of her grandfather, the Regent of the island of Madura, was once again featured by the innocent writer. Through his influence, wrote *Vogue*, "entrance to the most sacred temples was made possible, and the secret rites were thus observed. Like a child of the people she passed from one temple to another, until the different gods and their wondrous fêtes were as familiar to her as to a native. Little by little, never thinking of a future career but merely from the love of beauty and the appeal made to an artistic nature, she schooled herself in their ways, and gained an understanding of the hidden meaning and the deep-seated influence of the Buddhist religions."

She then "married Lord MacLeod when barely seventeen, and left her native land to go with him to Scotland." But things, as indeed they did, went wrong with her marriage—only it did not happen in Scotland—"and when it became necessary for her to support herself, her unconscious training stood her in good stead."

Mata Hari told about her imagined experiences in Spain, where "she was regarded as a goddess." It made an excellent story in the style of Sir Walter Raleigh, for "when she appeared in the streets, every man with the instinct of a cavalier laid down his coat for her to walk upon. 'And thus,' said Mata Hari, 'while I was in Madrid, my feet were never on the ground.'"

Yet that is where they were, and that ground, in the early days of 1914, was getting dangerously hot. Mata Hari finally made her move and shifted from the one center of the coming conflict to the other—from Paris to Berlin, where we find her towards the end of February.

She had new plans and wanted to stage an Egyptian ballet. Not knowing how to go about it, she wrote a letter to her original sponsor, M. Guimet in Paris, who answered on March 9.

"*Chère Madame*," wrote the by now seventy-four-year-old director of the museum under whose guardianship Mata Hari had made her official debut nine years previously. "To stage an Egyptian ballet is an excellent idea, on condition that it is really Egyptian. If you were in Paris, you would find at the museum all the information you want. You are in Berlin. Kindly see Professor Erman at the Museum of Egyptology."

Mata Hari was serious about the project, immediately looked up the Professor's address, and added it to Émile Guimet's letter in a penciled footnote, then left the letter in her scrapbooks: "*Geh. Regierungsrath Prof. Erman, Peter Lennestrasse 72, Dahlem.*"

It is unknown whether Mata Hari ever saw the director of the Berlin museum, but it is sure that she never performed the Egyptian ballet, nor another ballet for which she herself wrote the script, as nearly always, and which she called *Chimère ou Vision Profane*. It was to portray the anxiety of a young Hindu priest who is haunted by the vision of a woman. World events interfered—world events that were to bring another sudden change into Mata Hari's life, the last and most tragic one.

But in that spring of 1914 life still seemed good, at least on the surface. Mata Hari was finally going to dance in the German capital, where, as she said so many years previously, she would not dance for any money in the world. She had moreover met her old friend Kiepert again, with whose money she was supposed to have bought, but never did buy, the Château d'Etiolles.

According to the Berlin papers, the two were seen "talking very animatedly and confidentially in a booth in one of the most fashionable restaurants in town." The writer wondered whether Mata Hari had lost "her several hundred thousand which she had once received from Mr. K. as a farewell present, or whether it was love that brought her back to him."

The identity of the friend, who was indicated by the Berlin newspaperman simply as "Mr. K.," set several writers guessing. Some thought that he might have been the Kronprinz, who lived at the Caecilienhof in Potsdam, and of whom it was said that he had been her lover, a story that has no truth whatever.

On May 23, 1914, Mata Hari signed a contract with Director Schulz for her engagement at the Metropole Theater on the Behrenstrasse, to start on September 1. Mata Hari mentioned this fact immediately in her scrapbooks, writing it down, as always, in French: *Metropole Théâtre, Berlin, Allemagne, Direction Schulz*. The play she would appear in was *Der Millionendieb*.

Mata Hari lived at the Cumberland Hotel, and her Berlin publicity campaign was already starting. One of the magazines gave an amusing, and as usual entirely mixed-up version of her past:

"Is Mata Hari already in Berlin?"

"Sure—seems to be a remarkable woman—she is the new dancer at the Metropole."

"What is her real name?"

"Lady MacLeod. Her husband is a descendant of an old Scottish clan."

"Still married?"

"Not a chance. There seems to have been some wild story in Java. Nobody knows what really happened. It is only known for sure that her husband shot a friend of hers, and that they were subsequently divorced."

"Shot him in a duel?"

"No, not in a duel. Killed him in cold blood right in front of her. She herself was shot in the shoulder, it seems. But it hasn't done her any harm. She can still dance."

She could. But she would never dance in Berlin. Four weeks before her engagement at the Metropole was to start, war broke out.

Chapter 10

In describing Mata Hari's life at the start of the First World War, a good many writers threw themselves with enthusiasm into the realms of fantasy. Nothing could stop them. Many authors, faced by the problem of not knowing, simply invented. Others, less inventive—copied. As such a whole series of Tales of Mata Hari came into being, hardly any of them authentic.

It was of course far easier to write about things that were not true than about those that were. In the first place nobody could criticize, because nobody knew. And in the second place there was little to tell, because little was known.

Major Thomas Coulson, OBE, whose book *Mata Hari—Courtesan and Spy* served as a sort of bible to many other writers, portentously theorizes that she "inherited her amber-tinted body not from her Hindu parents, but from Jewish progenitors." He must have obtained his bizarre information from French Major Émile Massard's book *Les Espionnes à Paris*, in which the idea was put forward that she was "of Jewish origin, converted to Protestantism." Major Coulson then claimed that Mata Hari's mother, the always Protestant Antje van der Meulen, sent her daughter "to a Catholic convent," where she "remained until she had reached the age of eighteen."

On the artistic side Major Coulson describes how "her prosperous and highly respected burgher father (who by then was bankrupt) put up the funds for her first trip to Paris," and how she later danced in London, where her performance was "a reflection of her Paris success." Unfortunately for Major Coulson there is not a word of truth in this; Mata Hari was only once in her life in London—in jail. And she never set foot on a London stage, nor did she ever dance anywhere else in Britain.

Major Coulson then goes on to set the tone for his book: "Scarcely any capital of Europe escaped her poisonous presence. Like her favourite reptile, the serpent, the slime of her writhing body coiled from one city to another, leaving its track of debauchery and treacherous betrayal."

Could it be that such inventions were only distributed during the first ten or twenty years after Mata Hari's death, before the Second World War? Certainly not. As late as 1959 a woman writing under the pen name of Monique St. Servan, in a book published by Gallimard in Paris (*Mata Hari—Espionne et Danseuse*), tells us how "Margarethe spent her holidays with her Aunt Astrid, her mother's sister, at the Castle of Camingha-State near Arnhem." There, writes Mlle. St. Servan, "she waits for her parents, Anton Zelle, a rich fur merchant from Leeuwarden, and her mother, the very beautiful and very rich Gertrud, daughter of Baron and Baroness Winjebergen." Since the story takes place in Holland, Monique St. Servan brings in the delicate Dutch touch: the Zelles live "on Tulipstreet, looking out on a canal," and after the engagement to MacLeod, the latter "every night plays cards with his father-in-law in Leeuwarden."

As if all this were not enough, the young couple then leave for the Dutch East Indies on the good ship S.S. *Gravenhage* ("official" name for The Hague, but unfortunately wrong ship)— and the ship sails from "Het ei." For those French readers who are not familiar with Dutch, the writer gives the translation: "*Het ei*" means "*l'œuf*" (the egg). She had, as the Dutch saying goes, heard the ringing of the bell, but did not know where the church was located. Amsterdam's harbor is indeed called the "Y," pronounced "Eye," exactly like the Dutch pronunciation for "ei"— egg. Only "Y" has nothing whatever to do with "ei."

Having discovered the real name of Mlle. St. Servan, I wrote her and asked for information on some of her more amazing details in the book. Her answer was amusingly illuminating, and shows how Mata Hari history—and other history unfortunately— sometimes is made: "I wrote the Mata Hari book in a completely fictional vein, needing money right then to finance much time-consuming studies . . . and I enjoyed accumulating the most bizarre details, which I suspected of being totally untrue."

Among all Mata-Harian inventions the most absurd one is due to the spy specialist-author, Kurt Singer. In his book *Spies Who Changed History* he has Mata Hari's daughter grow up in Batavia (now Djakarta) on Java. He tells us that her name is no longer Non, but that this unblemished child of the tropics is now called Banda.

On a November day in 1917, says Singer, poor Banda, in the last letter received from her mother, is delicately informed that she is now an orphan. Banda, "having no tears in her eyes . . . left the house and went to church." Which, inasmuch as Singer gives the full text of the letter, should not surprise anyone.

Banda then develops into a Japanese spy before, and an Indonesian patriot during the Second World War, and is finally shot by Chinese communists in Korea. "The time," writes Singer, "was 5:45 A.M., the same hour her mother, Mata Hari, had been executed." As it happens, even the time was wrong.

And then, of course, there is Peter Brandes. While doing

research on my own book, I read the Dutch translation of Heymans' *La Vraie Mata Hari*, having been acquainted with the French original for years. In preparing a pocketbook edition, Mr. Nijpels, the Dutch publisher, had added many footnotes on subjects that had come to light since 1929, when Heymans finished his work. All through these notes the "expert" opinion on Mata Hari by one Peter Brandes cropped up, quoted from a series of articles published in a German magazine in 1951. To my surprise Mr. Brandes described himself as the man who, working for Metro Goldwyn Mayer around 1932, had been sent to Europe to find material for the Garbo film, at which time he had stumbled on Mata Hari's scrapbooks. It set me thinking.

Then the solution dawned on me. In 1950 I had put a number of true facts about Mata Hari at the disposal of an old friend of mine, Curt Riess, to be used for a German magazine. I had then left on a six months' trip to Africa, and the articles were published while I was abroad. Curt Riess, writing under the pseudonym of Peter Brandes, suddenly had to extend the series to nine articles and, having run out of material, had consulted other books on Mata Hari, mostly full of fiction.

Mr. Nijpels in Holland, as happened so often in the literature about Mata Hari, had then made his public acquainted with the "expert" opinion of the fictional Peter Brandes, and his readers were thus presented with "true facts," based on material that was slightly true, partly invented, and mostly fiction. Mata Hari herself could not have done any better.

But back in the summer of 1914 these developments were still to come, and Mata Hari, finding herself in Berlin, for once in her life was not very sure of how things would turn out. The war, or at least the immediate effects of war, had taken her by surprise, and the German march into Belgium found our dancer totally unprepared.

The most dramatic entry in Mata Hari's scrapbooks took place on this day. During all the foregoing years she had steadfastly written her notes and remarks in ink in that strong and very positive handwriting of hers, learned at the school of Miss Buys. Now she must suddenly have grabbed a pencil, and in an obviously highly nervous state of mind she wrote, right next to a newspaper clipping that informs us that "Fräulein Mata Hari, the first character dancer of La Scala in Milano, has been engaged from September 1st by the Metropole Theater": *"War—left Berlin —theater closed."*

Most investigators of the Mata Hari story have declared that she was already in the service of the Germans when war broke out—and, in fact, had been working for them for quite a while by then. According to my own information she was definitely not.

On the day war was declared, Mata Hari was reported to have had lunch in Berlin with Traugott von Jagow, who since 1909 had been Chief of Police of the German capital. Von Jagow was an intelligent person, and a man of quick decisions and words. One of his favorite expressions was: "Streets are for traffic. Others keep off."

By 1914 von Jagow was forty-nine years old, and had been active as a civil servant since 1895. He had held responsible positions before he became Chief of Police of Berlin. At her trial in 1917 the court considered Mata Hari's lunch with the German a serious factor in her alleged position as a spy.

The Mata Hari–Jagow angle has been exploited by nearly every author who has dealt with the spy's story, and the only thing that was not mentioned about that lunch was the menu, it seems. Bernard Newman, who constantly declares "this is legend" and "this is the Naked Truth," says about the incident: "It is true that she lunched with Herr von Jagow, the Berlin Chief of Police." And later on he adds, "She admitted this."

Unfortunately for expert Newman and the others, Mata Hari never did anything of the kind. She did admit that she had eaten a meal in Berlin, but never said it was lunch, because it was dinner. And she admitted that she shared this meal with someone in the Police Force, but never mentioned him as the Chief of Police. And she never even mentioned von Jagow, for the very simple reason that the man *was not von Jagow*. The police officer's name was *Griebel,* and he was not the *Chief* of Police, but *"un chef de police."*

The whole mix-up about von Jagow, which by now has persisted for nearly fifty years, was probably started by someone who had heard a *"chef de police"* mentioned. (In France the Chief of Police is called the *"préfet de police."*) He had then looked up who had been Chief of Police in Berlin in 1914, and very rightly had come up with von Jagow—who was the wrong man.

Mata Hari called the spy-angle of her meal with the police officer wholly ridiculous. She had known Griebel, she said, as she had known scores of other men with whom she had had lunch, dinner, and sometimes breakfast. Most writers state that Mata Hari had met the "chief" of police when he came to check the decency of her costumes. It was a typical fabrication, since she was not to start dancing till one month later, and by the time the meal took place (as Mata Hari said herself) she had known Griebel, who was one of her lovers, for quite a while.

This is what Mata Hari declared about that dinner during the first interrogation by Captain Bouchardon after her arrest in Paris:

"Towards the end of July 1914 I was dining one evening in a private restaurant room with one of my lovers, the *chef* of police Griebel, when we heard the noise of a disturbance. Griebel, who had not been informed about the meeting, took me along to the place where it was held. An enormous crowd was staging a totally mad demonstration in front of the Emperor's palace, yelling *'Deutschland über Alles.'"*

(The office of the Chief of Police in Berlin wrote me in June 1963 that "the personnel data of former police officers had for the greater part been destroyed during the last war, and in what is left, there is no mention of Herr Griebel." He was not the Chief of Police, the post held by von Jagow, but probably a section chief.)

But whatever Griebel's position, if he really had anything to do with espionage, he would certainly not have taken the risk of showing off in public with one of his own—or one of his country's —spies, after first having taken the trouble of dining with her in a private room of a restaurant.

Increasing the Mata Hari confusion by one more degree, author Kurt Singer, who already had changed Non MacLeod into the famous Indonesian spy, Banda, looked on the wrong page of his encyclopedia when he came to look up von Jagow—not knowing, of course, that he was dealing with a totally wrong man. He made him Germany's Foreign Minister, whose name was also von Jagow. Only his first name was Gottlieb, while the Chief of Police was called Traugott.

Mata Hari, perhaps as an aftermath of this Berlin adventure, seems to have remembered the Germans with not too loving thoughts. People who knew her in Holland during the following year and a half told me that whenever the subject of the Germans was brought up, she used to say: *"Ah, ces sales boches!"*

But what did really happen during those first days of war in Berlin and on those that followed? Mata Hari wanted to get out of war-delirious Berlin, and back to Paris. She left Berlin with all her baggage on August 6, for Switzerland, not knowing that in the meantime new border regulations had been put into effect by the Swiss. As she was to explain during the pretrial hearings in Paris later on, her baggage—sent as freight—went across the border, but she herself was refused entry into the country, not having any valid papers. And on the evening of the seventh Mata Hari found herself back in Berlin—without her clothes.

(According to the Swiss Federal Police, a law on border control—including stamping of identification papers—was only passed in Berne on November 21, 1917, but from the moment war was declared, official identification papers were needed to enter the country.)

By now Mata Hari was quite desperate. Mr. K., a Dutchman who was on business in Berlin and whose departure had been delayed by the outbreak of war, met her in the lobby of his hotel.

I have the story from K.'s wife, a charming gray-haired woman whom I met later in Amsterdam.

Mata Hari, in a highly agitated frame of mind, was nervously pacing up and down the lobby of the hotel. Mr. K. noticed her because she was exotic-looking, and very beautiful. Asking whether he could be of any assistance, she explained that she was a Dutch dancer, and since it was known that she had been living in France for years, she was afraid of being followed by the German police, who might suspect her of being unfriendly towards their country. She then told Mr. K. about the loss of her suitcases and clothes. And as if this were not enough, she said her manager had skipped with her money, and a fashion house had disappeared with her valuable furs. As it was, she had no more to wear than what she had on her back.

Could it be that Griebel, who otherwise could easily have protected her, had been told to be careful about the long-time Paris resident? Whatever the reason, Mata Hari had her fill of Berlin and the Germans, and now wanted to go to Holland—but did not even have the money for the train fare!

Mr. K., who had explained that he too was Dutch, said that he would be pleased to help her and that he would leave a ticket for that night's train at the desk of the hotel. Later that day he had second thoughts about this plan, judging it unwise to travel in the company of a woman who might indeed be suspected by the German authorities and be arrested during the journey or at the moment of boarding the train. Also, he felt that his wife might not approve of his traveling with such a good-looking woman. All things considered, he left Mata Hari's ticket with a note at the hotel, and took off for Holland on an earlier train.

Mata Hari said later in Paris, during her interrogations, that she had stayed on in Berlin till August 17. As happened on several occasions during the hearings, she got her dates wrong. She must have left Berlin on the fourteenth, because on the following day she happened to be in Frankfurt am Main, requesting a travel document from the Dutch consulate in that city.

Passports as we know them today were not yet universally used, but Mata Hari needed an official paper that would facilitate her getting across the border. The document, which was dated August 15, consisted of one sheet only. It is clearly indicated as a means of identification, and does not carry any photograph. This requirement only came later. On the printed form, on which only name and other details had to be filled in, the "Consul General of the Netherlands in Frankfurt am Main requests all friendly governments, in the name of Her Majesty the Queen, not only to let pass—with *her* baggage—*Mrs. Margaretha Geertruida Zelle, divorced wife of MacLeod, born in Leeuwarden and living in Berlin,* but also, if necessary, to render *her* all assistance" —signed H. H. F. van Panhuys. The word *her* of "with *her* baggage" (like all other words in italics) was filled in by hand. It was the one part of the request Mata Hari had absolutely no use for—she had no more baggage.

The travel document, valid for one year (the 640th delivered by the consulate), mentions two curious details. One has to do with Mata Hari's age. It was originally written down as thirty-eight, which was true. Having been born on August 7, 1876, she had attained her thirty-eighth birthday just one week before she went to the consulate. Then the eight was changed into a zero, which must have been more pleasing to her.

Giving her religion as Protestant, and indicating that she was five feet eleven inches tall, with big nose and brown eyes, the physical description on the document tells us that her eyebrows and hair were blond. In fact, Mata Hari was blond (again) in Paris in 1916, one report indicated. She did not intend it as a disguise, for she kept the name Mata Hari, and remained Margaretha Geertruida Zelle. Perhaps it was simply that peroxide— and a few gray hairs—had come her way. Yet one of her later pseudo-biographers immediately came to another conclusion. She had, after all, been born in Friesland, and in Friesland, the author must have thought, all girls are blond. The false conclusion sounded logical: not from brown to blond (it was really very black—"blue-black," as one of her Leeuwarden school friends had described it), but from blond to brown.

Chapter 11

ARMED with her identification paper Mata Hari soon afterwards arrived in Amsterdam and immediately went to see Mr. and Mrs. K. at their apartment. Adam Zelle had died in 1910, and Mata Hari had not kept up any contact or even correspondence with her brothers. She knew no one in town, was without funds, and was glad to spend many an evening at the K.'s residence. Mrs. K. had the impression that she was very unhappy and very lonely. The world had indeed crashed around Mata Hari. Paris was, for the moment at least, out of reach, the men with money whom she had known were far away, and there was no immediate theatrical engagement to look forward to.

When Mrs. K. got to know Mata Hari better, she asked her why she had not tried to seduce her husband that day in Berlin. Mata Hari's answer was delightfully direct and instructive: "Because I had only one chemise left, as everything else had been taken away from me—and really, I didn't feel clean enough . . ."

She had moved into the Victoria Hotel in Amsterdam, although her financial circumstances were worse than they had ever been. As always, however, a man came to the rescue. The story again comes from Mrs. K. Walking in town one day, Mata Hari noticed that she was being followed, or at least she thought so. She entered a church to find out, and coming back into the street, the man was still there. He came up to her and started talking in French. Could he help her? Mata Hari had not needed help so much in a long time, and caught on to the situation immediately. If she answered in Dutch, the spell would be broken. So she answered in French, and said she was a Russian visiting the strange city, which once before, many years ago, had been visited by her Czar, Peter the Great. Ah, yes, said the gallant Dutchman, who turned out to be a banker named van der Schalk—*all* Dutchmen knew about Peter the Great. He had come to Holland just before 1700 to learn shipbuilding. Mata Hari nodded. He had lived in Zaandam, a short distance from the Dutch capital, and the little house was still standing, known to all Dutchmen as the Czar Peter House. Mata Hari nodded again. Would she like to visit Zaandam? He would love to take her there and show her a few things. Some other time, suggested Mata Hari.

And so it went for several weeks, till one day a friend of Mr. van der Schalk met him in the company of his paramour, and enlightened him on her nationality. The shock was too great. To a Dutchman, a liaison with a Russian woman was an adventure; with a countrywoman of his, all glamour was lost. He was, however, said Mrs. K., a gentleman after all, and paid all of Mata Hari's hotel and other bills. For a while at least, she was back on her feet.

Living once again in the same country as her daughter, Mata Hari suddenly got an attack of motherly love. It was eight years since she had been divorced, and just about as many since she had seen Non for some minutes only at the Arnhem railway station.

Non, by now sixteen years old, had been told fairly little about her mother, and whatever she had heard was not very good. It is therefore difficult to explain why her father, while Non was still a child, had kept a daily reminder of her mother around the house. After the Mata Hari cigarettes, a Dutch biscuit manufacturer had put biscuits on the market, packed in a luxury container that showed photographs of Mata Hari on all sides. Non, after she had graduated from teachers' college in The Hague, spent a first year as a schoolteacher in Velp. Living at the time with her father in nearby De Steeg, she had to go to school by streetcar, and took her luncheon sandwiches along in her mother's biscuit tin. Non's stepmother, Grietje MacLeod, still has the tin at home.

Mata Hari asked a friend for advice. What would be the best

way to see her daughter? The friend suggested she write a letter to her ex-husband. Any contact with him being anathema to her, she wrote the letter directly to her daughter, explaining that she supposed Non had heard all kinds of rumors about her mother, but that by now she was old enough to hear *her* side of the story.

As could be expected, Non turned the letter over to her father, who sent it on to his lawyer, that same Heijmans who had visited Mata Hari in Paris at the time of her divorce. MacLeod added a postscript: "What a stinker!"

John MacLeod answered the letter for his daughter, saying that if Griet wanted to see her, she might take the trouble of writing directly to him, the father. She did so, in French. Written from the Victoria Hotel in Amsterdam on September 18, 1914, the letter is both tragic and pathetic. It reads:

> My dear friend,
>> Because you ask me to, I beg you personally to be good enough to let me see my daughter. I have become too much of a Parisienne to lack any tact, in whichever way or subject. Tell me what I should do, and I thank you beforehand for according me what I want so much.
>
> Very truly yours,
>> Marguerite.

Adding a postscript, she wrote: "In answering me, please use the name Mata Hari."

In his answer John expressed surprise in discovering that she had forgotten her native Dutch, though he had noticed from other letters—the one to Non—that she was still perfectly familiar with it. He did agree to a meeting, he said, which he thought could take place without any feeling of hatred, since he felt that the old bitterness had died out in the meantime. In his opinion the projected meeting should not take place in The Hague or Amsterdam, and he proposed Rotterdam instead.

As the third Mrs. MacLeod told me, John believed that Mata Hari's only reason for seeing Non was that she had heard her daughter was good-looking—long-legged, same dark color of skin as her mother, and with Mata Hari's black hair. Also he felt that she wanted to show off with her in Amsterdam or The Hague, where she was known. No one, on the contrary, would know her in Rotterdam.

Mata Hari in some subsequent correspondence suggested taking care of Non's education at a later date—perhaps she could take the girl to Switzerland for a while. Again MacLeod disagreed: if Mata Hari wanted to spend money, he said, it would be better to put an amount of five thousand guilders on deposit in a bank, so Non would be able to take singing and piano lessons—luxuries which he, on his slight government pension supplemented by his journalist's pay, could ill afford. He was urged on in this endeavor by a friend at the city hall in Arnhem, who told him that "there was money." But MacLeod had lost all confidence in that direction, and said: "I know all there is to know about the Zelle fortunes."

Thus went the argument for a while. When John finally informed his ex-wife that, not yet having received his monthly check from the government, he could not pay for the trip to Rotterdam, Mata Hari gave up. She never saw her daughter again.

Though John MacLeod did not mind his daughter's carrying her mother's pictures to school every day, he was reluctant to talk about her. Non, while still attending teachers' college in The Hague, was once asked by a friend what she thought of her mother. "I can't talk about my mother the way I'd like to," she said. "I have heard so many rumors about her life in Paris, but every time I ask my father about what happened, he gets terribly vague."

Yet she was intrigued by her mother's presence in The Hague, to which Mata Hari had moved in 1915. According to Grietje MacLeod-Meijer, Non used to write letters home with statements like: "I passed the house yesterday—there were no men around, but lovely curtains in front of the windows." Yet there were apparently no efforts on her side to get in touch with her mother, nor did Mata Hari—who obviously knew that her daughter went to school in The Hague—make any move of her own.

Back in Holland during those autumn days of 1914, it was difficult for Mata Hari to get readjusted to life among her countrymen. The country she came back to was quite different from the one she had left ten years previously. Although neutral, the declaration of war had thrown Holland into near panic. The Germans had wanted to march through the narrow strip of Dutch Limburg which hangs like an appendix into Belgium. The Dutch government had refused and had been able to enforce its refusal. Bypassing Holland, the Germans marched just the same, and immediately the Belgian refugees started to stream across the Dutch border into Holland, where they were hospitably received in tens of thousands.

British soldiers were interned in Holland. German soldiers were interned in Holland. Refugee camps sprang up like early crocuses. Schools were closed, to the delight of their pupils, and with straw blowing around in the wind, the hurriedly mobilized Dutch soldiers slept where children were supposed to learn the peaceful principles of life, the boys and girls instead admiring the field kitchens in front of their school buildings.

All of Holland had gone on a buying spree when war was declared; war bulletins and maps appeared overnight in every cigar store, of which Holland has many, and the Dutch Minister Postuma soon launched his austerity program, which made all of Holland sing wryly: "And Thursday we eat porridge, Friday porridge, Saturday porridge, and Sunday we again eat porridge, and Postuma, oh! how I loathe you!"

It was an atmosphere which, even without its war affiliations, was difficult for Mata Hari to accept. She had become very French during those years of absence. Her early life in Holland had known only two phases—the first one as a young girl, and the later one as an unhappily married woman. Except for business purposes, she continued to write in French, even to close Dutch friends.

Dancing being her profession, she approached theatrical producers and signed a contract with Mr. Roosen, a Dutchman who was director of The French Opera, a company which, with a mixed roster of Dutch and French singers, was highly popular in Holland. Roosen engaged her to dance in a ballet at the "Koninklijke Schouwburg"—The Royal Theater—in The Hague on Monday, December 14, and Mata Hari was quick to frenchify the name of the theater in her scrapbooks to "Théâtre Royal Français."

The Dutch were curious, especially those Dutchmen who had spent a large part of their life in the colonies, and who had now retired to The Hague. They came to the theater in droves, making it—according to the newspapers—"the most packed house we have had this season." The ballet Mata Hari danced, and which followed a performance of Donizetti's *Lucie de Lammermoor*, was "a living painting" based on Lancret's work "La Camargo," the original of which was then in the collection of Kaiser Wilhelm, and is nowadays part of the Mellon Collection in Washington, D.C. The ballet itself was called *Les Folies Françaises*, with music by François Couperin.

Mata Hari danced and mimed a series of eight "moods," among which were her favorite virginity, ardor, chastity, and fidelity. It sounded peculiarly like the dance of the seven veils which she had done at the beginning of her career, but without dropping them this time. She wore a yellowish period costume for the appearance in The Hague, embellished with white and dark-red veils, "which fluttered transparently around her."

The Hague newspapers found her dancing "an idyllic pastoral flirtation," and although Mata Hari "tripped while on stage, which made the audience hold its breath for a long moment," the Amsterdam *Telegraaf* assured its readers that the performance "was a caress to our eyes and showed a lot of good taste."

A few days later, on December 18, a repeat performance of the ballet took place at the municipal theater in Arnhem, this time following *Le Barbier de Séville*. John MacLeod, living in what was practically a suburb of Arnhem, and who, as he had said, "had seen her previously from every possible angle," did not attend. Yet his ex-wife's presence as a famous dancer in the community where he lived must have been a strange sensation for him.

Mata Hari pasted a print of Lancret's painting—which local set designer Manceau had used for the model of his backdrop—in her books, and wrote about herself: *"Ballet des Folies Françaises, dansé par Mata Hari, Théatre Royal Français."*

It was the next to last entry in her scrapbooks. On the last page she pasted the cover of a Dutch magazine which had splashed her photograph in front of its readers. It showed Mata Hari as a mature and beautiful woman with long earrings and a string of pearls. She wore an elegant wide-brimmed hat and a white, low-cut dress. The date of the magazine was March 13, 1915. Mata Hari must have looked at it for a long time before she picked up her pen to write across the photograph: "13 March, 1905–13 March, 1915." It was ten years to the day since she had made her debut at the Guimet Museum in Paris.

But back in December 1914, on the Wednesday following the Monday evening performance at The Hague, Mata Hari, in a letter to painter and close friend Piet van der Hem—born, as she was, in Leeuwarden—showed a keen sense of both business and humor.

"Dear Piet," she wrote in French, "I am sorry you were not there. I had a lot of success and a great many flowers. People begin to understand that it is more refined than Max Linder at the cinema.* All seats were sold. Roosen was happy, the cashier as well, so it could not have been any better."

---

* Max Linder, a French film comedian, was in those early days of the cinema as popular on European screens as Charlie Chaplin.

By September 1914 Mata Hari, shortly before having reestab-
lished contact with an accidental Dutch lover of hers, had decided to go and live in The Hague, and had rented a small house
at 16 Nieuwe Uitleg, along a quiet canal. But a lot of work had
to be done inside the building before she would be able to move
in. While waiting, she left Amsterdam in the beginning of 1915
and took rooms at the Hotel Paulez. (The hotel was bombed
during the Second World War, and since 1959 the new Breuer-
designed American Embassy stands on its site.)

The house on the Nieuwe Uitleg was quite old, and the work
of redecorating, installing a bathroom, and setting up the furniture took much longer than Mata Hari had expected. The job
might have been speeded up if she had been able to pay cash.
But her funds were extremely limited during all this time. She
had discovered that there was no future for her dancing in Holland. The "French Opera" changed its program daily, and moreover it had few opportunities to offer ballet.

Yet the army of writers who took such pains to fill books about
Mata Hari claim that she was a spy by now—a highly paid spy!
Reality proves that the situation was quite different. Mata Hari
was terribly short of money during those first eight months in
The Hague. The contractor, a Mr. Soet, who was also to take care
of the furniture, stalled constantly, not being sure whether he
would ever be paid.

In September of the previous year, Mata Hari had made a
verbal agreement with him by which he promised to finish the
job, and she would be allowed to pay him the full amount of
his bill over a period of two years, starting from the moment she
would move into the house. Not only that, but she was so unsure
of her future finances that she made it a condition to be allowed
to pay whatever amount she would have available at any given
moment—and even those pay dates were left entirely to her own
choosing. Now the contractor asked Mata Hari to sign a statement in which she had to confirm that she owed him money. But
even before he had this paper in his possession, he tried to get

the promise of countersignatures from some of her friends, which would have enabled him to use it as a promissory note at a bank —cashing it immediately against real money.

Mata Hari was furious when she heard about it and on August 8, 1915, wrote an eight-page letter—in Dutch this time—to her lawyer, another Mr. Hijmans, who had his offices only a few doors away on the same Nieuwe Uitleg.

"Dear Mr. Hijmans," she started her letter, written on stationery of the Hotel Paulez,

I am enclosing a bill from the carpenter, intended for Mr. Soet, but sent to me. I am sorry these people come bothering me with it at the Hotel Paulez. After all, I do not know them. I do hope this matter will be cleared up soon. If Mr. Soet does not want to keep his word, I would rather he took everything he brought into the house out again. His extra cost is perhaps 400 guilders, but mine is 4000. I have the receipts from the Hotel Victoria and Hotel Paulez to show him. Such people are dangerous and I did not come here to have law suits and all kinds of trouble. He trusted me when he started, and now, a year later, he should not try and get my signature as a guarantee. He has tried to get a loan on this paper even before he had it in his hands, and none of my friends want their names used for such purpose. Now, of course, no one will sign, because they have been warned.

Mr. Soet does not have to worry. His honest and approved bill will be paid if he keeps his word—paid within two years from the day I move into the house, and when he has delivered all he still has to deliver.

I must be free to pay the amounts I have at my disposal, whether large or small. It was on *these conditions* that I accepted his proposal in Amsterdam, in the presence of Mrs. K., and he had better keep his word, or he can remove everything, but—I reserve the right to sue for damages,

and! for his insulting me in Wurfbain's office,
and for the dirty work with the bill
and for the long sojourn in hotels.

Since yesterday I have gas—and Vanburgh has installed
the bathtub. The gas company has fixed the meter—but I
shall only move in when I know where I stand with Soet.
Please do point out to him how unfair it is to do business
this way.
                                        Sincerely yours,
                                        Mata Hari.

Mr. E. Hijmans must have been able to help, for three days
later, on August 11, 1915, Mata Hari was registered as a resident
of The Hague at the Vital Statistics Office, where her registration
has not been removed to this day. Once again, she had a home of
her own.[*] Just the same, her precarious financial situation did
not improve immediately, for as late as October 8 of the same
year—nearly two months after she had moved out of the Hotel
Paulez—she wrote a letter to the hotel's director, informing him
that she would "pass by one of these days, probably next week"
in order to settle her accounts. In a previous letter, of September
28, she already had complained about the many visits to her new
home by the hotel's bookkeeper, assuring the director that he
could have "full confidence" in her. Now, in October, she added:
"You know yourself that money matters are difficult for all of us,
but you can rest assured that everything will be settled." (Mata
Hari never owned any of the houses she lived in, notwithstanding the claims put forward to the contrary. As was the case with
the house in The Hague, her home in Neuilly-sur-Seine had been
rented from its owner, M. Maget, while the Château de la Dorée
was shared with M. Rousseau, who had rented it—in his own
name—from the Comtesse de la Taille-Trétinville.)

The difference of opinion between Mata Hari and the contractor had come to a climax during the three days that passed

---

[*] From 1923 till 1938 the occupant of the house at 16 Nieuwe Uitleg was
Dutch actress Fie Carelsen, who on the occasion of her Silver Jubilee in 1932
starred in a Dutch play called—*Mata Hari.*

between the writing of the letter and the taking possession of the house. It was an incident that showed only too clearly how true Mata Hari's claim had been when, years before, she had told a Dutch correspondent in Paris that she was a woman who frequently "would follow a sudden impulse." Anna Lintjens, who by now had rejoined Mata Hari in The Hague, told me the story in 1932.

Having a final look around the house, Mata Hari's attention had been directed towards the bed. It was not, she told Mr. Soet, the kind of bed she was accustomed to. The contractor had his own opinion about the bed, which he declared to be of excellent quality, filled with the best horsehair he had been able to lay his hands on in Holland. Mata Hari said it was not so. The argument grew hotter, and when Mr. Soet stuck to his statement, Mata Hari flew into a rage, rushed to the kitchen, came back with a huge knife, ripped open the mattress in one big slash, and, holding a bunch of horsehair under the nose of the astonished contractor, said: "So *that's* what you call good quality?"

Anna Lintjens' son, with whom I had an interesting conversation in 1963 when he was seventy-seven years old, told me of another episode of temper on Mata Hari's part, the story also coming from his mother, and having likewise taken place during that period. According to this tale, the contractor's men had just carried a wardrobe to the top of the stairs, when Mata Hari asked him to move it through a door into a certain room.

Mr. Soet took a good look at the door opening, and said: "It won't go, Madame." Mata Hari said it would, and once again the contractor stuck to his guns. After the conversation had continued along these lines, another explosion of temper took place inside Mata Hari, and with a big push she threw the wardrobe down the stairs. Then, turning to the flabbergasted contractor, she said: "It won't go? It *went!*"

There was, for a while, a strange gap during the months that followed. In all writings on Mata Hari dates are constantly mixed, and events that took place in one year are transposed to another. It was well known that she made one trip to France from Holland during the war, the one which ended in her arrest. However, she had been in France before—towards the end of 1915, in December. How she went and when precisely she left The Hague on this second trip (which actually was the first) remained a mystery for a long time. Even Mata Hari herself was confused when this trip to France was discussed during the hearings with Captain Bouchardon. She mentioned that she had returned in May 1915, and had stayed for three months, having made the trip via England and from there across the Channel to Dieppe. (She obviously could not go via Belgium, which since August 1914 had been occupied by the Germans.) She was totally mistaken, and only much later she discussed it as having taken place in December 1915, which was the right month. From the time Mata Hari left Paris for Berlin in the spring of 1914 till that trip in December 1915, she had never set foot in France.

But whatever the date of that first wartime trip to Paris, it was without any importance to the French. The judgment as pronounced on July 26, 1917, simply mentions that she had been there in December. The first question which the members of the War Tribunal had to answer *yes* or *no* was: whether Mata Hari "was guilty, in December 1915, of entering the entrenched camp of Paris." And the answer was *yes*.

One writer only, Dr. Leon Bizard, who during Mata Hari's stay in prison in 1917 was in medical charge of that institution, mentions the 1915 Paris period in his book *Souvenirs d'un Médecin*. (Dr. Bizard also writes that he had met Mata Hari before the war in a Paris house of prostitution, without indicating whether she was there as part of the establishment or as a visitor. The story seems unlikely, Mata Hari having been far from destitute at that time, although always in need of money—and if she did any "receiving," she certainly received at home.)

On her arrival in the French capital in 1915, Dr. Bizard informs us, the police had a card on file which wrongly said that she was born in Belgium, and that she had to be watched. The police followed instructions, but—always according to Dr. Bizard —discovered nothing suspicious. "She did a lot of shopping and bought a lot of shoes," * writes the doctor, "and after a while the police stopped following her."

It may well be that Dr. Bizard's statement is correct. But how very casually statements—totally imagined ones—by other writers, also dealing with this same year 1915, have been accepted as equally correct and as such have started a flood of false rumors is born out by an episode that was originally mentioned in a newspaper. It was quoted by Gomez Carrillo, picked up by Alfred Morain in French in *The Underworld of Paris*, to be translated into English by Richard Wilmer Rowan in 1938 in *The Story of the Secret Service*. It then cropped up in Edmond Locard's *Mata Hari* in 1954, after which it was fully, sensationally, and wrongly followed up by Kurt Singer, the creator of Banda, who mentioned it in capital letters in one of his stories, to underscore its importance heavily.

In July 1915 Mata Hari was still trying to get her house in The Hague furnished. Yet at the same time she was supposed to be in Naples. For in July of that year the Italian Intelligence Service, according to these various writers, sent the following secret message to Paris: "While examining the passenger list of a Japanese vessel in Naples, we have recognized the name of a theatrical celebrity from Marseilles, named Mata Hari—the famous Hindu dancer, who purports to reveal secret Hindu dances that demand nudity. [All this, of course, in a secret-service message.] She

---

* Mata Hari used to have her shoes made at a shop called Smart, owned by a French art student, Lucien Grandgérard, who styled himself years later as the *bottier attitré* of Mata Hari, something like *"Shoemaker to the Queen."* Monsieur Grandgérard, in 1965 a somewhat older but active portrait painter, still has a visiting card from Mata Hari's lover Xavier Rousseau, which indicates the latter's reverence for his mistress' fake title as well as Mata Hari's constant reluctance to pay her debts on time. On his card Monsieur Rousseau informed the shoemaker that he "would talk to Lady MacLeod about her bills."

has, it seems, renounced her claim to Indian birth and become a Berliner. She speaks German with a slight oriental accent."

I asked the War Ministry in Rome whether they would be kind enough to go through their files and find the telegram. Notwithstanding all efforts, as Colonel Broggi, chief of the Ministry's Historical Division informed me, they could not locate the mysterious telegram. And for good reason, as I soon afterwards discovered, for the story is a total invention.

René Puaux, correspondent of the Paris newspaper *Le Temps*, traveling to Egypt early in 1907—coming from Marseilles—on the S.S. *Schleswig*, had reported Mata Hari's presence aboard the ship in Naples. His article was published in the supplement of *Le Temps* on March 21, 1907, in just about the same words as quoted above.

Then the mystery writers got hold of it, for good measure added the Italian Intelligence Service, made the nationality of the ship Japanese instead of German, and moreover made two slight changes in the text: one in the year it happened, and another one due to probably insufficient knowledge of French. The year 1907 became 1915, and what had been mentioned in the original French article as *"elle parle l'allemand avec un accent aussi peu oriental que possible"* ("she speaks German with an accent as un-oriental as possible") became simply, "she speaks German with a slight oriental accent." From there on the story was established, and Mata Hari for nearly forever after was sighted aboard a Japanese ship in Naples in 1915, provided with that German-oriental accent.

To improve even on this story, another Mata Hari writer, Mrs. Lael Tucker Wertenbaker, in a novel published in the United States early in 1964, *The Eye of the Lion*, transferred this Naples episode to Mata Hari's trial in Paris. Elsewhere, Mrs. Wertenbaker borrowed Kurt Singer's equally imaginary tale about Mata Hari's nonexisting daughter Banda.

But while not in Naples in July, Mata Hari did turn up in Paris in December. The trip was a quick one, for she was back in Holland in the beginning of the following year. As Mata Hari herself declared later: "I returned to Paris to recover my personal effects and household goods which I had left in storage with the firm of Maple at 29 Rue de la Jonquière. I went back to Holland via Spain with my ten packing cases, the British frontier at the time being closed on account of troop movements." Later on she indicated that most of her belongings which she had left in storage after having closed her house in Neuilly-sur-Seine consisted of table silver and linens.

Although Mata Hari's only idea when she left for Paris was the collecting of these household goods which she needed for the new home in The Hague, traveling back and forth across war-shattered Europe in her nonchalant way as if no world conflict existed, she was quick to discover a chance of possibly staying on and appearing once more on the Parisian stage. She heard that Diaghilev was still in France, and thought there might be a chance now, where there had not been any three years previously, although experience should have told her that the Russian Ballet and her own oriental dancing were worlds apart.

Staying at the Grand Hotel and writing on that establishment's stationery, Mata Hari on December 24, 1915, sent off a letter to her old friend, mentor and impresario Gabriel Astruc. She thought she had something new to offer, perhaps the "living painting" she had done in Holland, and was careful to point out that she really did not mean to make a comeback on account of the money, for she was a well-kept woman in Holland. She, moreover, rather childishly, asked Gabriel Astruc to inform Diaghilev that he would not have to worry—he could *use* someone like Mata Hari.

"I am in Paris for a short while only," she wrote, "and shall be returning to Holland within a few days. I see that Diaghilev is still around. Inasmuch as I have some new and rather strange dances, could not you get me a contract with him?"

"As you know, I create all these dances myself. It is not for the money, for I am well kept back in Holland by one of the aides-de-camp of the Queen, but I would like to do it as a matter of interest, and for the prestige. He [Diaghilev] will not regret it, for I believe that I can bring him something new."

Asking Astruc to answer her at the Grand Hotel, she mentioned that he would have to write her under the name of MacLeod-Zelle because she was traveling incognito on account of her official name being mentioned in her passport.

Of course, nothing came of the Diaghilev plan, and via Spain and Portugal Mata Hari returned to her well-to-do lover in The Hague. He was the aforementioned occasional friend, she was to disclose during the Paris hearings, a most distinguished member of the Dutch aristocracy, Baron Edouard Willem van der Capellen. Born in 1863, he was seven years younger than John MacLeod, which made him fifty-two when he met Mata Hari for the second time. Again it was the uniform that made him attractive—as well as his money—for Baron van der Capellen during those years of the First World War was a full colonel in the Dutch cavalry, a branch of the service he had been attached to ever since he had entered the Royal Military Academy in 1879.

Commander of the Corps of Hussars since May 1914, Baron Edouard, who finished his military career in 1923 with the rank of major general, often came to the house of his mistress on the Nieuwe Uitleg. Anna Lintjens' son, himself a soldier stationed in The Hague in 1916, remembers him well—and also remembers Mata Hari as "having blonde hair, although not light blonde." According to Mr. Lintjens, Mata Hari had only one continual complaint for the Baron: there were not enough theaters in Holland.

But Holland was getting on Mata Hari's nerves. She disliked its quiet, since notwithstanding the war nothing much happened in the small town atmosphere of The Hague. She needed the excitement of the big city and longed for Paris and for a certain Marquis de Beaufort whom she had met at the Grand Hotel in December 1915, and whose memory was still very much on her mind, as hers was on his.

She requested a new passport from the Dutch government, which she received on May 15, 1916. It is still in the French secret file of the Ministry of War, where I saw it. Again only one sheet of white stationery, it now has a photograph attached—the same photograph, but smaller in size, as the last one Mata Hari put in her scrapbook: large hat with white feathers, earrings and pearls.

Chapter 12

MATA HARI had no trouble getting an entrance visa for France from the French Consul in Holland, but there were difficulties with the British. She wanted an English visa for a possible stopover in Great Britain, and the consul in Rotterdam refused to give it to her.

She could not understand the gentleman's attitude and, even before getting her passport on May 15, she went to the Foreign Office in The Hague to ask for assistance. It was promptly given, and on April 27, 1916, a telegram was sent to the Netherlands Legation in London, signed by Dutch Foreign Minister *Jonkheer* Loudon. His signature did not mean that he personally intervened for Mata Hari. It was the standard signature on all Foreign Office telegrams, which carried either Loudon's name, or the name of Mr. Hannema, the Secretary General.

Addressed to *Jonkheer* De Marees van Swinderen, Chief of the Dutch Legation in London, the telegram said: "Well-known Dutch artist Mata Hari, Netherland subject whose real name is MacLeod Zelle wants to go for personal reasons to Paris where she has lived before the war. British consul Rotterdam declines put visa to passport though French consul has done so. Please beg British government to give orders consul Rotterdam that visa may be granted. Wire." The Dutch Foreign Office's number on the telegram was 74.

Although it arrived in London the following day, the twenty-eighth, the person who handled it did not go to the Home Office —according to a handwritten note "H.O." on the original tele-gram—till six days later, on May 3. It took the British twenty-four hours to give the answer, and it is the first indication of trouble for Mata Hari—though she did not know it. The Dutch government officials, on the other hand, who did know the contents of the answer, must have raised their eyebrows.

The British, as the Legation in London wired back to The Hague on that May 4, at six in the evening, refused the visa. "Authorities have reasons why admission of lady mentioned your 74 in England is undesirable," said the message.

The British answer marks a most important point in everything that happened from here on, and has been totally overlooked— being totally unknown—by all those who have written about Mata Hari. It means that the British suspected Mata Hari long before the French. It is true that Captain Ladoux, head of the French *Deuxième Bureau,* the Intelligence Service, did mention later on that his colleagues in London had sent him reports "for over a year," but that is all. The British had no specific information whatever, or they would have informed Captain Ladoux. But as late as August 1916 Ladoux knew nothing incriminating about Mata Hari, as he himself stated afterwards. There was suspicion on both sides of the Channel—and the suspicion had started in London.

In June 1963, after some correspondence with Scotland Yard and the British Foreign Office, I paid both these offices a visit. There was total ignorance about any British implication in the Mata Hari case, and this ignorance extended to the Home Office.

At Scotland Yard it was explained to me that while they han-dled British Intelligence during the First World War, this work was later on taken over by a newly created separate office. And if any papers dealing with Mata Hari had ever been in their files, these files were now elsewhere. Documents from the British Ministries would be made available to the Public Records Office "after fifty years," I was informed, "but certain documents which deal with the security of the state or which otherwise might be deemed to be unpublishable, might be withheld for far longer periods." And it was thought that if the British were involved in the Mata Hari affair, such information might indeed be considered as unpublishable. But as far as they themselves believed, said the gentlemen at Scotland Yard (later on seconded by a spokesman at the Foreign Office), the British really had had nothing to do with the Mata Hari case.

I then showed the persons I was talking to photostat copies of some letters written on official Scotland Yard stationery. The letters, as was only too clear from their contents, dealt most categorically with Mata Hari. The gentlemen at Scotland Yard were surprised at seeing these documents, but insisted that nothing about them was known at their headquarters. A similar statement was made at the Foreign Office.

British suspicion of Mata Hari was most likely based on reports from their agents in Holland, who had informed their superiors in London about a visit she had received in The Hague on her return from her first wartime trip to France. The visit, which Mata Hari would mention at the pre-trial hearings in Paris more than a year later, was from one of the German consuls in Amsterdam. Nothing about what was discussed at that meeting was known to British Intelligence, and in fact there was nothing that could prohibit a Dutch national in neutral Holland from talking to a German subject. But the meeting apparently raised definite suspicion in the British mind, and from then on London considered Mata Hari suspect.

The visa refusal remained unknown to Mata Hari, or at least the reason *why* it was refused, because the Foreign Office in The Hague did not disclose the contents of the wire received from London. She was therefore undismayed and went to France just the same. How? Again there was a question mark for a long time. The Dutch steamship *Zeelandia* was mentioned by Mata Hari herself in an interview with Captain Ladoux that took place in Paris in August 1916, but it was not officially confirmed till I read Mata Hari's own testimony in the French secret file.

According to information received from the Amsterdam head office of the Royal Dutch Lloyd, the *Zeelandia* left Holland on May 24, 1916, which consequently must be the date Mata Hari started on her fateful voyage. It checks entirely with the various date stamps in her new passport, which, as we have seen, was issued in The Hague on May 15, 1916. The simple document has only half a dozen stamps indicating her appearance at some consulate, border crossings, and a visa for Spain. The first date among these proves her presence in Madrid on June 12, 1916, nearly three weeks after the *Zeelandia* left the harbor of Amsterdam. There is no stamp for the entry into Spain at Vigo; the time had not yet come when at every border a uniformed gentleman affixed his rubber stamp to one's passport.

On June 14, according to another stamp, Mata Hari left Madrid for Paris, where her passport was marked on the sixteenth—but not until after an adventure at Hendaye, on the French side of the border, where she was stopped.

The Intelligence Service in Paris, prompted as we have seen by the British, tried to keep an eye on their suspect, and had given orders not to let her back into the country. Why? asked the indignant Mata Hari. The Frenchman at the border answered that he did not know, and advised her to go and ask for help from the Dutch consul in San Sebastian. Mata Hari was furious. According to her own statement she wrote a letter to her old and intimate friend M. Jules Cambon, ex-Governor General of Algeria, ex-French ambassador in Washington, ex-French ambassador in Madrid, ex-French ambassador (till the war broke out in 1914) in Berlin, brother of the then French ambassador to London, and at that time secretary-general of the French Foreign Office. In the letter she aired her indignation at being barred at the border of France, and would M. Cambon please arrange to let her in?

Had she been a spy, her being prohibited from entering France should have set her thinking. Not so Mata Hari. The fact that she had frequented Germany before the war never struck her as anything that might be suspicious to the French. This was her private affair, perhaps an incongruous thought in wartime, but Mata Hari was a citizen of a neutral country, and after all, that was just the way she was. Her capricious behavior should have been a warning to the head of any espionage service—French as well as German—not to consider her for a spy-job. She had glamour, yes—she had the knowledge of languages and she knew a great many people in high places on both sides of the Rhine. But she lacked the elementary basic intelligence.

An old friend of mine, Leo Faust, who was a Dutch newspaper correspondent in Paris from 1912 on and all through the war, had met Mata Hari on several occasions and is in total agreement—as he wrote and told me in 1959 and afterwards. He clearly remembers a meeting late in 1915 at Pré Catelan, a restaurant in the Bois de Boulogne which was used as a Dutch Red Cross hospital ("it was winter," he recalls, "but no snow and not very cold"), and both he and his wife saw her for the last time in a box at the Folies-Bergère "only a few days before she was arrested in 1917. She was in the company of a Polish officer in dress uniform."

"Through the years the conviction has grown in me that she was not a spy," was Leo Faust's opinion. "She did not need to be and could make a fairly large amount of money in other ways. Moreover she was far too stupid to be considered as 'adequate' by anyone who might have thought of employing her as a spy. On the contrary, such a person would have considered it a danger to himself to trust her with any secret."

Back in Hendaye, when Mata Hari returned to the control post, the man she had met there had either been relieved, or he had forgotten all about his instructions. She had no more trouble, did not have to send the letter to Jules Cambon, and continued by train to Paris with a clear conscience.

By now Mata Hari had become uncompromisingly promiscuous, but in a ladylike sort of way. Some of the men she was genuinely fond of, others kept her in money. In Holland there was still Baron van der Capellen, but he was far away. From his bank account in The Hague, however, he continued to send her funds. In France, in the meantime, she had met a Russian officer, Vadime de Massloff, whom she believed she really loved. But he was not in Paris, so she consoled herself fleetingly with the company of a man she had known before the war, Jean Hallaure, who was now, as most of his countrymen, in uniform—the uniform which, since she was a young girl, had always held such fascination for Griet Zelle. The fascination had not worn off.

Vadime de Massloff (whose name is given by various writers as Marrow, Marlow, Marzow) was a captain in the first Russian Special Imperial Regiment. Mata Hari liked him, indeed claimed to have been more in love with him than with any man in her life. When six months later she was arrested in Paris, several photographs of Vadime as well as his visiting card (Mata Hari was inordinately fond of keeping visiting cards as souvenirs) were found in her room. One of the photographs, included in the unpublished secret file, has the following inscription on the back: "Vittel, 1916—In memory of some of the most beautiful days of my life, spent with my Vadime whom I love above everything." The picture had never been sent. Did Mata Hari keep it, waiting for an opportunity to hand it herself to Vadime, or was it purely for personal reference and intended to be stuck at some later date in that part of the second volume of her scrapbooks which is still blank? No one will ever know. But Mata Hari in any case had taken care to bring the photograph up to date: according to all reports Vadime wore an eye patch, and with ink this eye patch had been carefully drawn over the left eye on the photograph.

Towards the middle of August Mata Hari started to formulate plans to go to Vittel, a trip which attracted her for two reasons: her health, and the possibility of spending some time with de Massloff. She knew the place well. She had been at this spa at the foot of the Vosges Mountains before, drinking its water which is said to be good for arthritis and other such maladies, but which most French prefer for the sake of their liver. During her sojourn at Vittel in August 1911 she had been photographed in a lovely long lace dress, holding a parasol, gloves of elbow length, and wearing a huge hat with sweeping ostrich feathers.

Mata Hari, exploiting men for her own benefit whenever it suited her, decided to get help from one lover to get to the next, which would thus take care of her heart and her liver at the same time. Jean Hallaure, her temporary friend in Paris, was a lieutenant in the cavalry who had been wounded at Guise early in the war, which left him with a slight limp and kept him from further active duty. A close friend of his, *Capitaine de Vaisseau* Léon Corblet, who notwithstanding his naval rank was an Intelligence trouble-shooter for the French army, had found a place for Hallaure at the Ministry of War's Intelligence Office, which was then just being started. According to Monsieur Corblet, Jean Hallaure, the very tall and good-looking son of a prominent *notaire* in Le Havre, had never done a day's work in his life before entering the army. Twenty-five years old in 1914, after the war Hallaure married an American girl in New York, and then returned to France to spend the rest of his days in the village of Ste. Marine en Finistère in Brittany, where he died a few years ago.

Hallaure explained to her that Vittel was situated in the Zone of the Armies, for which a special permit was needed. He advised her to see a friend of his at the Military Office for Foreigners on the Boulevard Saint Germain. Perhaps it was Hallaure's design, or maybe Mata Hari's mistake, but she opened the wrong door and found herself in the wrong office—that of Captain Ladoux, Chief of the French Intelligence Service. A career officer, he had been named for his post by General Joffre, supreme commander of the French Forces. But Captain Ladoux had needed some help to get his appointment, and the help had come from Jean Hallaure, who, being lower in rank, thus became not only his superior's secretary, but his left and right hand as well.

Ladoux himself tells about the interview in his books *Mes Souvenirs* and *Les Chasseurs d'Espions*. The conversation was pleasant, and Ladoux informed Mata Hari that he knew about her friendship with Hallaure. When he told her that Hallaure was severely wounded, that he was a *grand blessé*, Mata Hari smiled. She was perfectly familiar with his wounds.

From here the conversation got on more dangerous terrain. Ladoux said that he also knew about Vadime de Massloff (whom Ladoux, mystified as most, indicates in his writings as Marow, Malsoff, and Malzov) and for the first time Mata Hari was surprised and remarked: "So you have gone through my papers?" This was followed, according to Ladoux's version, by his telling Mata Hari flatly that he did not believe the British claim that she was a spy, and he agreed to arrange for her permit to go to Vittel.

But now Captain Ladoux changed his tune and his conversation. He wondered what Mata Hari's feelings were about France, and inquired whether she would be willing to help the country which she claimed to love so much. Mata Hari was fairly noncommittal, but when Ladoux asked how much she would request for her eventual services, she told him that he would get her answer if she decided to accept. With which remark the conversation ended for the day.

Mata Hari's next move only confirms Leo Faust's impression that "she was too stupid to be a spy." Having returned to Ladoux two days later and been given her permit for Vittel, she went to see an old friend of hers. He was Henri de Marguerie, who from 1901 to 1904 had been attached to the French embassy in The Hague, when Margaretha had started off to seek her fortune in Paris. De Marguerie was now an accomplished diplomat with an important post at the French Foreign Office. And Mata Hari, instead of keeping the fact that she had been asked to spy for France a deep dark secret, went to de Marguerie to ask for advice.

Mata Hari herself supplied Henri de Marguerie's reaction to her startling revelation, which should have been kept hidden in the most secure section of her conscience. "Monsieur de Marguerie," she told her interrogator in February 1917, "said that it was very dangerous to accept missions of the nature that had been offered to me. But he added that, judging as a Frenchman, if anyone would be able to render services to his country, it was I."

Setting off on her cure, Mata Hari had a charming time in Vittel, where she saw a lot of her beloved Vadime—as was dutifully reported by Ladoux's counterintelligence agents. While the cure which she had indicated to Ladoux and Lieutenant Hallaure was indeed the main purpose of her trip, she could hardly have told either man that at the same time she hoped to see her lover Vadime de Massloff.

(Bernard Newman writes that Mata Hari stayed in Vittel for two months, whereas in reality she only remained two weeks. He then states in italics, *"And Captain Marov was not there."* Captain *Marov* probably was not, but Captain *de Massloff* surely was.)

In the back of his mind Ladoux may have been wondering whether Mata Hari, if she *was* a German spy, would be trying to get information on the French airport then under construction at Contrexéville, only a stone's throw from Vittel. This airport, due to Mata Hari's stay in the neighborhood, has come in for lots of comment, and its importance—as exemplified in the old Garbo–Mata Hari film—had been highly exaggerated. Neither airplanes nor airports during the First World War were anything like those in the Second World War. There were no runways, but only grass or mud. The planes were constructed of wire and canvas. They were excellent for reconnaissance, but long-range sorties were unknown. Bombing was inaccurate and most of their battles were fought in the air, especially after the invention which made it possible to synchronize the machine-gun bursts with the movements of the propeller. But the pilots were dashing young men in uniform, superbly attractive to Mata Hari.

However, notwithstanding all efforts by Captain Ladoux's men, they were unable—according to Ladoux's own assertions—to find even the slightest indication that Mata Hari did anything suspect during the few weeks she stayed at Vittel, neither there, nor in Contrexéville. Her conduct was exemplary, her mail—

which was uninterruptedly checked—was void of secret ink or other incriminating detail, and on her return to Paris, where she had rented an unfurnished apartment on the Avenue Henri Martin, Captain Ladoux knew just about as much as before—which was nil, except for his suspicion.

Ladoux's watch of Mata Hari had started, as we have seen, in 1915—at the request of Scotland Yard, and the file presented at the trial contains copies of the daily reports supplied by Ladoux's agents. There is nothing suspicious in these reports as far as Mata Hari is concerned: she went shopping, had tea, saw friends, at one time visited a fortune-teller—but as is the case with Ladoux's own memory and conclusions, the reports frequently throw a strong suspicion on the men who wrote them.

They claim, for instance, that when Mata Hari was in Paris in December 1915, she had made arrangements to leave on two successive days and both times she had canceled her departure. According to Ladoux's agents, the ships she was to have taken were then torpedoed and sunk, and after her arrest Mata Hari was severely taken to task for having caused these sinkings. She was most emphatic not only in denying having known anything about the ships, but—as we shall see—everything points to the agents' claims being totally fabricated.

"I do not recall having postponed my departure from Paris in January 1916," Mata Hari declared at the hearings, "or having changed that departure after my baggage was brought down. I had my passport visaed in Paris on January 4, and I crossed the border at Hendaye on the eleventh. It may be that after I had received the visa I was obliged to leave a few days later than I had intended to, because Mme. Breton was late in delivering my dresses. I do not know whether the ship that left Vigo before mine was torpedoed. I am not afraid of such possible accidents. I never even think about them."

Alain Presles and François Brigneau, who in March 1962 wrote a series of four articles on Mata Hari in the French weekly *Le Nouveau Candide,* also mention these reports: "Both times the ships of which the date of departure coincided with her own canceled departure from the hotel, were torpedoed and sunk."

Studying the Mata Hari file, the members of the jury who in 1917 condemned her to death must have been greatly impressed by the reports from Ladoux's Intelligence Service. But as can easily be seen, they are without foundation and only spread suspicion where none was indicated. For it is evident that the agents' references to the coincidence of canceled departure and torpedoing were pure fiction.

Mata Hari was living at the Grand Hotel in Paris. Due to the war, there were no passenger ships of neutral nations leaving from the French Channel ports. Thus on leaving the hotel, Mata Hari could not take a train which a few hours later would deposit her at either Le Havre or Cherbourg or even Bordeaux, from where the boat would then leave for Holland. To take the boat, Mata Hari had to go by train from Paris to Madrid, a journey of a minimum of twenty-six hours, and then take another train from there to Vigo or Lisbon, again a full night's trip. Thus the very minimum of forty-eight hours would be needed to reach the harbor of embarkation, which time would even be greatly increased if she stopped off in Madrid.

There is still another argument proving the fictional connection between the departure from Paris and the sinkings: Mata Hari would travel on a Dutch ship, belonging to a neutral nation, and there were no daily departures, because these ships came all the way from Latin America. A great many Dutch ships *were* sunk by the Germans. But it can hardly be expected that Mata Hari, having her luggage brought down in the hotel, would make a quick phone call to some secret agent in Paris, who would then advise her: "Don't take that ship—we are going to sink it!"

It is strange that Captain Ladoux did not discover the discrepancies in his agents' reports. It is even stranger that his own intelligence was entirely mixed up, for at times facts stated by him, as well as the conclusions he draws from them, are either totally untrue or at least highly doubtful. In *Mes Souvenirs* he writes that "since January 1915 she attracted the attention of my services through her numerous trips outside France." Yet in January 1915 Mata Hari was not in France, had not been there since early 1914, and would not be back on French soil till December of 1915! In January 1915 Mata Hari was still in Holland.

Chapter 13

ON her return from Vittel, Mata Hari's meeting with Captain Ladoux started off quite pleasantly again, and at times the conversation took on a nearly bantering aspect. Mata Hari told him that she had been followed on her way to his office, and the Chief of Intelligence confessed that this was the way his organization worked. His spy-suspect felt that the man who had trailed her must be tired, and suggested he be allowed to go to the nearest café and get a drink. Ladoux agreed entirely, which must have been a great consolation to the weary agent.

Then the conversation once again became more serious, and Mata Hari informed Ladoux that she was perfectly willing to help France—on condition that she be paid adequately. When she mentioned the price of her cooperation, a million francs, Ladoux was fairly surprised. But Mata Hari, never timid when it came to money, explained that she needed that much in order to be able to marry Vadime de Massloff, whose family fortunes and relations would only accept her if she could show sufficient capital. Ladoux was not immediately agreeable to the idea, but Mata Hari told him that her services would be worth it—she knew, after all, a great many people—Wurfbain, for instance.

The name must have popped into Mata Hari's fertile mind from somewhere way back, waiting for a convenient moment to be made use of. Wurfbain was the man at whose offices she had been insulted by the contractor in The Hague, as she had explained in her letter to Hijmans, her lawyer. He now lived in Brussels, said Mata Hari, and could be of great help to her. (The Brussels Chamber of Commerce informed me that they could not verify Wurfbain's business address in 1917, all archives having been destroyed during the great fire of the Palace of Justice in 1944.) Mata Hari's unbridled fantasy brought ideas into her head at exactly the moment when they might seem like the truth and making as always immediate use of them, she little realized that some day she would weave her web into such a complicated pattern that she was going to be caught right in the middle of it.

Ladoux, however, found Brussels an excellent idea, and already Mata Hari must have had visions of the Dutch coast and her house in The Hague—and perhaps even of some quiet moments after the hectic months she had behind her. According to the French's own version, Ladoux told her to get her passport for her trip to Holland via Spain.

Mata Hari also used the word passport frequently during the pre-trial hearings, but it is obvious that both of them meant *visas*. Not being a diplomat she did not have to go to the Foreign Office for a passport, but she did need a permit to cross the border in the form of a visa. Mata Hari had her own passport, the one that had been delivered to her in The Hague. To provide her with a French passport was not necessary, and it was moreover never delivered, for—proved by the stamps on her Dutch passport —she used this when she left the country.

There is great confusion as to what happened next. The plan which had developed in Ladoux's mind to catch his victim has several versions: Ladoux's own, Major Massard's as explained in his book *Les Espionnes à Paris*, a third one about a rendezvous in The Hague (again Ladoux's), and a fourth involving a British agent. The French knew nothing whatever about this British agent, and the first time he was mentioned it was purely casually by Mata Hari herself, certainly not suspecting that the French afterwards would use her own testimony to condemn her to death.

The British agent was a Belgian citizen by the name of Allard. When interrogated later on, Mata Hari was to tell Captain Bouchardon that she had met him and his wife aboard the Dutch ship *Hollandia* on her way back from France to Holland in November 1916. The captain of the ship had mentioned that Allard was a British agent, while his wife was working for the Germans, and on arrival back in Spain, Mata Hari had told this story in Vigo to the Dutch consul's secretary, who happened to be a Frenchman. That was all Mata Hari knew about the British agent, and she was not *asked* about him, but *told* the French. Yet Allard was incorporated in the trial, where the jury had to answer *yes* or *no* on whether Mata Hari "had divulged the name of an agent in the service of England."

The version most writers were attracted to was Massard's, the one involving six spies who were supposed to work in Belgium, and to whom Mata Hari—on Ladoux's instructions—was to deliver certain messages. Five of them were double agents, spying for both France and Germany, and therefore known to the enemy. The sixth was spying for France only, and is said to have been shot several weeks later by the Germans. This made Mata Hari suspect of having delivered all six names to the German Intelligence Service, who then picked out and shot the one man whose name they were not familiar with. Nowhere, however, neither in Massard's nor in Ladoux's books—the most accurate ones—is this executed agent mentioned as working for Britain, and the much publicized case of the Belgian spies was never even mentioned at the trial.

The rendezvous in The Hague was Captain Ladoux's own invention, all of which make the events of the weeks following Mata Hari's departure from Paris seem even more complicated, fabricated, and suspicious.

Major Coulson put his foot even deeper in it. He makes Mata Hari responsible for the battles both at Chemin des Dames and Artois, which he says took place "shortly after she left Vittel." Since she had been in Vittel in September 1916, it seems hardly possible that Mata Hari had anything to do with the German capture of Chemin des Dames in 1914, with the French forces' finally dislodging them from there in October 1917, or with the Germans' unsuccessful counterattack in the spring of 1918. As to Artois, the battles raged there in May and June 1915—more than a year before Mata Hari ever got to Vittel.

Then the Major gets even farther afield trying to prove how guilty Mata Hari really was. Before she took off for Spain he has her go to the Netherlands Legation in Paris, where she handed in a letter with the request to have it forwarded to her daughter in Holland.

According to Major Coulson, the man she talked to was a French agent, who opened the letter, and after deciphering it he discovered that it contained "information of primary importance on the matter of espionage arrangements by which the French were trying to repair the huge damage caused by the formidable coup delivered by their enemies." Obviously there never was such a letter, nor did any such information ever exist, except in Major Coulson's mind.

One of the other rumored accusations frequently made against Mata Hari is her informing the French about the German refueling base for submarines at Mehidiya in Morocco, locally known as Mehdya. Situated about six miles north of Kénitra (formerly called Port-Lyautey), it is problematical whether the Germans would have chosen the site for their secret base. But the French, upon hearing that Mata Hari had been able to give them the information, concluded that this proved that she was a German spy "because such information could only have been obtained from the Germans." The deduction was about the easiest any counterintelligence agent could make—*all* such information had to come from the Germans, and it was exactly to obtain it that the French *Deuxième Bureau* used spies, both French and foreign.

Bernard Newman, in his book *Inquest,* misses the point about the Moroccan submarines about as much as any of his colleagues. He argues whether the Germans would have used Mehidiya, and because it sounds illogical, he—as most other writers—dismisses the whole incident. But the point is not whether the Germans did or did not use Mehidiya, or even whether they used any place in Morocco as a base. The point is whether Mata Hari informed the French about it. And that she did indeed! She did it as a spy *for the French,* and part of the information, no matter whether it was true or not, was obtained by her *at the request of the French,* even though the Frenchman involved in the episode, in a dubious statement made during the pre-trial hearings, declared to the contrary. The gentleman was Colonel Denvignes, chief of the French Intelligence Services in Madrid. Yet when Mata Hari repeated her information on the German submarines to Captain Ladoux himself in Paris, the latter was so surprised about the news that he said: *"Les bras m'en tombent,"* meaning: "I can't believe it—I'm stupefied!" Captain Ladoux never denied Mata Hari's statement in court, all other opinions to the contrary.

Having accepted Captain Ladoux's proposal to return to Holland and spy for France, Mata Hari asked him, according to Ladoux's own confirmation in *Mes Souvenirs,* whether she was allowed to inform the Netherlands Legation in Paris of her imminent return home. Ladoux had no objections, but drew a curious conclusion from her request, in line with other hasty and illogical conclusions he had come to before, and still would come to later.

Ladoux writes that he "was now convinced" of her being a spy, although one wonders why. Did the fact that Mata Hari wanted to inform the Legation of her own country about her return to Holland prove that she was a spy? For some mysterious reason Captain Ladoux thought so. It would seem that to the Chief of the French Intelligence Service *any* move by Mata Hari proved that she was a German spy.

Without having received her million from Ladoux, in fact without having received anything, Mata Hari finally left Paris for Madrid and Vigo, where she was to board the Dutch steamship

Hollandia, on which Captain Ladoux had told her he would have a cabin reserved. The date was not, as has been variously reported, early or late in October. She crossed the French-Spanish border on November 6, 1916, as is clearly indicated by the fourth of the six stamps on her Hague-issued Dutch passport in the Paris file.

Captain Ladoux now was hot on her trail. Mata Hari was to take the 8:13 train from Madrid to Vigo, and came into the lobby of the hotel at 7:05. One of the two secret agents who had followed her from Irun on the Spanish side of the border apparently was not as clever as he thought he was, for Mata Hari walked right up to him and said that she had immediately recognized him in Irun. She would stay another day in Madrid, she told him, and asked not to be followed that afternoon because she "was supposed to meet a countryman of hers between 2 and 4." The agent, a discreet gentleman after all, promised to leave her alone —but sent his colleague instead. According to this man, as retold by Captain Ladoux, she took a horse-drawn carriage, while the agent (only thirty-six years old but disguised as a man of sixty) followed her on a bicycle. He reported that she went to the Café Palmario and made two phone calls, which he traced as having gone to the German Bank in Madrid and the German consul in Vigo.

Considering the easy conclusions Ladoux's agents had come to when describing the sinkings of the two ships Mata Hari was supposed to have sailed on, one wonders how much credence should be given to the report of the telephone calls—even though they do not prove anything immediately incriminating. One wonders even more when discovering how seriously Captain Ladoux contradicted himself later on.

(The Spanish National Telephone Company informed me that all telephone books of the then existing companies have been destroyed, but that no one at the head office remembers any café by the name of Palmario. The same negative information was received from the daily newspaper ABC of Madrid, where none of the elder journalists remember the café, even though newspapermen in the Spanish capital spend a great part of their lives in the coffeehouses of the city.)

In his book *Chasseurs d'Espions* Captain Ladoux accurately says that Mata Hari took the SS *Hollandia*. Yet in *Mes Souvenirs*, where he relates the same story, he tells it totally differently. Now he explains how Mata Hari was *supposed* to have taken the *Hollandia*, but was requested by the British to take an English ship. Ladoux is quite angry at the British, and explains why: "Captain Paul, chief of our Intelligence Service at Hendaye ... informed the British Admiralty of his suspicions, but the latter, once the dancer had gone aboard the Dutch transport at Vigo which was to bring her to Rotterdam, transferred her without consulting us to the British ship *Marvellous*. And," adds the mixed-up Captain Ladoux, "she afterwards continued from Liverpool to Holland." As we shall see, Mata Hari never went aboard the *Marvellous*, never saw Holland again, and only went to Liverpool to return to Spain—for now follows one of the strangest episodes in the life of the ex-dancer.

Bypassing the various versions of all the imagined stories, we find that even in the official reports there is nothing but contradiction, both on the part of the French *and the British*. If one can believe the reports from Scotland Yard—and there is no reason *not* to believe them—then either the French and the British between them concocted a trap for Mata Hari, or the British Secret Service was muddle-brained at the time, or both.

Chapter 14

EVEN if the British fleet had not been the master of all the oceans in 1916, it certainly was the uncontested master of the Channel. As such, a great many neutral ships were constantly directed to British ports for purposes of cargo and passenger investigation. This fate befell the *Hollandia,* on which Mata Hari was hoping to reach Holland—and perhaps even was planning to continue from there to Brussels to do the job she had promised Ladoux to accomplish. Nothing extraordinary happened till the ship was berthed at Falmouth, in Cornwall.

Now it should be kept in mind that the British had been suspicious of Mata Hari well before the French, that they had refused her a visa in April 1916, and that in fact the French had only started to shadow her after they received a message from their colleagues across the Channel. Consequently the Secret Service officers who climbed aboard the *Hollandia* at Falmouth must have had a list of suspects in their pockets including the name of Mata Hari. Perhaps even one of their own agents had already informed them from Vigo that she was aboard. Ladoux, apparently, had not told them.

Yet not one of the British Intelligence agents recognized Mata Hari. They read the name Margaretha Geertruida MacLeod-Zelle on her passport, but this did not mean a thing to them, they claim—although it might conceivably be imagined that they knew this to be Mata Hari's real name. But, even stranger, they accused Mata Hari of being Clara Benedix, a German spy-suspect whom the British very much wanted to get their hands on, and who came from Hamburg.

Mata Hari, as can be imagined, was amazed to the point of being frantic. Matters got worse when, after a thorough search, Scotland Yard officer G. Grant put her officially under arrest. The British Intelligence agents took her off the ship and started her on the long journey to London, a trip that even today takes six and a half hours by fastest train. And they took her straight to Scotland Yard and put her in jail, on the morning of November 13.

As it turned out, Mata Hari had every reason to be frantic in Falmouth, for from here on the British involvement in the Mata Hari case became a tragedy of errors.

When, in June 1963, I first contacted Scotland Yard, I was told that Officer Grant had died a few years previously. A resurrection apparently followed, for in December 1964 I found out that Mr. Grant on the contrary was still very much alive, an extremely spry gentleman of seventy-eight whose full name was George Reid Grant. When I finally met him and he started to talk, the British Mata Hari episode became far clearer.

Officer Grant had only rejoined Scotland Yard in 1915, having been in the British army in France since the outbreak of war. Both he and his wife, Janet, were then sent to Falmouth, she as a special agent for the interrogating and searching of suspected female passengers aboard neutral ships which put in at that British port.

George Reid Grant admitted that he had known Mata Hari. He had met her a first time when she returned with her packing cases from France early in January 1916, and their second short meeting took place aboard the SS *Zeelandia* on its outward-bound voyage in May 1916. On both occasions the Dutch ships had put in at Falmouth. Officer Grant had been introduced to Mata Hari, whom he qualified during our conversation as "one of the most charming specimens of female humanity I had ever set eyes on," with what he called "a commanding carriage."

George Grant had no inkling of any suspicious activities on the part of Mata Hari. But shortly after the *Zeelandia* had left the port of Falmouth towards the end of May 1916, sailing for Spain, "a message came down from Scotland Yard in London," said Grant, "instructing me to detain a certain woman if she ever happened to pass through Falmouth, and to bring her to headquarters for interrogation." To make recognition easier, headquarters had attached a photograph to the message. The name of the woman to be detained was Clara Benedix.

When examining the photograph, George and Janet Grant immediately recognized Mata Hari—or at least they thought so. The likeness was remarkable, Mr. Grant told me, "especially in the Spanish-oriental costume the photographed woman was wearing." Officer Grant put the photograph aside for future reference, and started to be on the lookout.

Late one evening during the second week of November 1916, the *Hollandia* arrived at Falmouth, on its way from South America —via Vigo—to Amsterdam. As usual at these late hours, Officer Grant made a cursory inspection, discovering to his surprise that the woman to be arrested, Clara Benedix, was aboard. To Mr. Grant there seemed no possibility of a mistake. The woman he had been introduced to so many months previously might indeed be Mrs. Margaretha MacLeod, born Zelle, and she might be Mata Hari, but according to the likeness on the photograph she was also Clara Benedix, which name was probably an alias, maybe only *one* of Mata Hari's assumed names.

Early the next morning George Reid Grant and his wife went back aboard the *Hollandia,* and while Mrs. Grant "stripped Mata Hari and searched her thoroughly," George Grant inspected Mata Hari's—or Clara Benedix'—cabin with the assistance of the ship's carpenter, who unscrewed the wooden wall panels, looking for hidden documents. The search brought no results. In fact, said Officer Grant, "we found absolutely nothing incriminating in her baggage."

Then George Grant, with a certain Mr. Adams, son of the pre-war director of the Mission to Seamen in Rotterdam, acting as interpreter, interrogated his suspect. Mata Hari protested vigorously, showed her passport in the name of Margaretha Zelle-MacLeod, and tried in every way to prove that she was not Clara Benedix.

The protests were of no use, and George Grant told her that she "was going to be taken to Scotland Yard to investigate her movements." At which announcement Mata Hari, according to Grant's story as related in 1964, "got into one hell of a state."

The ship's captain protested as well, and—as was both his right and his duty in the case of the arrest of a neutral passenger aboard his ship—he informed Officer Grant that he would bring the matter to the attention of the Netherlands authorities. To which he added: "You are making a terrific mistake this time; this woman is the most popular passenger aboard."

Yet nothing could make Mr. Grant change his mind: Clara

Benedix had to be brought to London. So by ten o'clock that morning, escorted by Mr. and Mrs. Grant, Mata Hari and all her baggage were taken off the ship, and spent the rest of the day at the Grants' lodgings in Falmouth, waiting for the evening train to London.

"How can you do this to me?" Mata Hari asked several times, "what do you want from me?" Next to taking her to London, the Grants actually did not *know* what they wanted from Mata Hari. After all, as George Grant told me, they were only doing their duty. Mata Hari wept a few times during the afternoon, "drank an awful lot of coffee, and refused all food."

That evening the three of them, Janet Grant acting as official chaperone, boarded the train for London. During the night Mata Hari took off her skirt to cover a light that bothered her in the compartment, and in the morning, after the women had first gone to a hotel to freshen up, Officer George Reid Grant took his "detained" person to Scotland Yard, where he turned her over to Chief Inspector Edward Parker.

In the meantime prisoner and captors had grown rather fond of each other. On leaving, Mata Hari gave Janet Grant several photographs of herself, and a small glass toy dog which Janet later left to her husband, and which Officer Grant still had in 1964. Mata Hari also gave them her name card, which read "*Vrouwe* Margaretha Zelle-MacLeod." *Vrouwe,* in Dutch, is an aristocratic title similar to "Lady." Above the name on the card which gave the Nieuwe Uitleg in The Hague as her address, a small crown had been printed. Even in 1916 Mata Hari had not yet forgotten her father, the "Baron."

The Grants, by now having accomplished their mission in the detention of Clara Benedix, returned to Falmouth with serene minds. Meanwhile Mata Hari remained at Scotland Yard a case of mistaken identity that eleven months later would end in her death.

Sir Basil Thomson was at that time Assistant Commissioner of Police and head of its Special Branch, better known as Scotland

Yard. Educated at Eton and New College, Oxford, Sir Basil had been a top-ranking civil servant for a good many years, including a period during which he was Prime Minister of the Fiji Islands. He became a barrister in 1896, till 1913 had been governor of several large British prisons, and finished this part of his career as Secretary to the Prison Council. Born in 1861, he was fifty-five years old when Mata Hari arrived at Scotland Yard, and, in view of his education and past, he must have been an intelligent person, with a keen sense of organization. Yet on November 16, he signed two contradictory letters, both addressed to the Netherlands Minister in London. The first letter was dictated by a person whose initials were E.R., while the initials on the other letter were K. P. But both letters were signed by Sir Basil.

Either the agents who had taken Mata Hari off the ship or those who first questioned her on her arrival in London were not good at languages, or they were just not very clever—a serious thing to suspect a Scotland Yard agent of. Because in letter number one Margaretha Zelle MacLeod is said to be the bearer of a *French* passport issued in *The Hague,* while only in the second letter did they discover that Madame Zelle MacLeod's passport was really Dutch. Her name is spelled differently in the two letters: the first time it is MacLeod, then it becomes McLeod, the way Mata Hari used it in her signature.

Meantime the Dutch authorities in the British capital as yet knew nothing of the case. Mata Hari of course could not understand why the British told her that she was not the person she was, and asked to be allowed to write to the Dutch Legation, for which Scotland Yard obligingly supplied pen and paper. But although she wrote her letter immediately on November 13, the day of her arrival in London, Sir Basil Thomson did not communicate it to the Netherlands Legation till the afternoon of the sixteenth.

Nowhere in his writings—books and magazine articles—does Sir Basil mention the mix-up of the Clara Benedix incident. He only relates that he had no real proof against Mata Hari and that he advised her to go back to Spain, instead of continuing to Holland. Reality was different. Once they had discovered that she was not Clara Benedix after all, there remained "a grave suspicion of un-neutral acts" against her.

In the morning of November 16, 1916, Sir Basil Thomson sent his first letter to the Netherlands Minister in London, who received it that same day. It was marked *confidential*, and my photostat copy gives the following text:

Sir—

I have the honour to inform you that a woman carrying a French passport bearing the name of Margaretha Zelle MacLeod, No. 2603 issued at The Hague on the 12th of May 1916, has been detained here on suspicion that she is a German agent of German nationality named Clara Benedix of Hamburg. She denies her identity with this woman, and steps are now being taken to establish it. The passport bears signs of having been tampered with. She has applied to be allowed to write to your Excellency, and materials for the letter have been furnished to her.

I am, Sir, Your obedient Servant—B. H. Thomson.

Scotland Yard sent their second letter—again signed by Sir Basil —in the afternoon of that same November 16, and it reached its addressee the following morning. There is no further mention of Clara Benedix, but now there is suddenly the suspicion of "un-neutral acts." And while the first letter kept silent on where she came from, only mentioning that she had been "detained," full information on the ship is now included. Also included is finally the letter which Mata Hari had written three days previously. Having informed the Netherlands minister that very morning of the sixteenth that "materials for the letter have been furnished her," it is strange that it was only sent after having been lying around for seventy-two hours.

Again the letter was marked *confidential,* reading:

Your Excellency—

We have the honour to inform you that a lady bearing a Dutch passport, named Madame Zelle McLeod, has been removed from the Dutch ship *Hollandia* on her arrival at Falmouth, there being grave suspicion of un-neutral acts against her. She has asked me to forward to you the enclosed letter.

Inquiries are being made as quickly as possible by cable, and she will not be detained longer than necessary. If, however, she proves to be a person suspected of un-neutral acts, it may be necessary to take further action against her.

Now, according to this second letter, the writer (Mr. K. P.), had apparently not been informed about the story of Clara Benedix, because he states that she was *removed from the Hollandia as Madame Zelle McLeod,* the reason being the "suspicion of unneutral acts." Either it had taken Scotland Yard three days to come to the conclusion that Margaretha MacLeod-Zelle was indeed herself and not the German woman from Hamburg (after which they decided to forward the three-day-old-letter to the Netherlands Legation), or they knew from the beginning who she was, and the Clara Benedix story was a hoax.

The text of Mata Hari's letter—and the fact that she spells her name both Mac-Leod and McLeod in the same letter—speaks only too clearly of the state of mind she was in. Dated in large letters "November 13, 1916," she wrote in Dutch—in that bold handwriting of hers:

Excellency,

May I beg Your Excellency politely and urgently to do everything possible to help me.

A terrible accident has happened to me. I am the divorced

Mrs. Mac-Leod, born Zelle. I am traveling from Spain to Holland with <u>my, my very own</u> passport.

The English Police claim that it is false, and that I am not Mrs. Zelle.

I am at my wits' end; am imprisoned here since this morning at Scotland-Yard and I pray you, come and help me.

I live in The Hague at 16 Nieuwe Uitleg, and am well known there as well as in Paris, where I have lived for years.

I am all alone here and I swear that <u>everything is absolutely</u> in order.

It is a misunderstanding, but I pray you, help me.

Sincerely
M G Zelle McLeod.*

Again one wonders why Sir Basil Thomson, signing this second letter, had not given orders to change its contents, inasmuch as it really was—but failed to mention so—a follow-up to the one sent earlier that morning, contradicting it in one way, and elsewhere duplicating its information. Writing to the London representative of a foreign nation—especially on such an important subject as spying by one of its nationals—it may be assumed that Sir Basil did not scrawl his signature without reading the letter first.

In the meantime he had talked to his subject, and once he had come to the conclusion that she was really the person her passport indicated her to be, he wanted to know what she was doing on that ship, and why she was going to Holland. Mata Hari, in her usual way, first seesawed from one explanation to another, till finally, feeling herself pushed into a corner, she must have thought that the best answer was the truth—Great Britain, after all, being an ally of France.

---

* The underlining in the letter is Mata Hari's own.

Thus she blurted out that she was on a mission to Holland for the French. Basil Thomson was rather surprised at this, and advised her on his own account—he wrote—to give up what she was doing and to return to Spain. The idea, of course, was not his. As he had already informed the Dutch Legation—and as Captain Ladoux later confirmed in his own book—he had "made inquiries by cable," and had contacted his French colleague.

Sir Basil's discovery that his counterpart across the Channel had engaged a woman as a spy whom he had been warned about by Sir Basil himself, must have fairly astonished him. And when Captain Ladoux found out that Sir Basil knew, he must have felt rather silly. His pique was such that his grudge against Mata Hari most certainly started from that day. And once he felt that he had made a fool of himself in the eyes of Sir Basil Thomson, his bearing down on Mata Hari could not show any letup. Captain Ladoux, from here on, was set on taking revenge—and his revenge would be terrible.

Thus the Captain, answering Sir Basil's inquiry, and in a complete reversal of all he had personally planned before, suddenly pretended that the whole case was a mystery to him—that he did not remember anything about the mission to Holland which he himself had suggested. DO NOT UNDERSTAND, he cabled London, and added, SEND MATA HARI BACK TO SPAIN.

Here, starting with Gomez Carrillo and Heymans, and as usual copied by others, the case of the double agents in Belgium is brought up once more as the real reason behind Ladoux's tactics. According to them, the sixth agent, the one working for France, or Britain exclusively, was shot "two weeks after Mata Hari left Spain."

If for a moment we accept the thesis that Mata Hari divulged the names of these agents to the Germans, then Heymans' and his fellow writers' theory is still wrong. The proof lies in the already mentioned seventh question put to the jury at the trial: "Was Mata Hari guilty of having divulged the name of an agent in the service of England *during the month of December* 1916?" If therefore any agent in Belgium *was* shot in November, then Mata Hari had nothing to do with it, and Captain Ladoux had no valid argument when he cabled Sir Basil requesting him to send Mata Hari back to Spain.

Another confusing factor in this amazingly strange episode is the total silence of the Netherlands Legation. One of its nationals having been arrested by Scotland Yard on suspicion of espionage and having requested assistance from the Legation, it seems a fair surmise that a report should have been sent to the Foreign Office in The Hague—the more so, since their own London file on Margaretha Geertruida MacLeod Zelle already contained a copy of their wire to Holland, informing them about the British refusal to grant her a visa in April. Yet there is no such report. There is no possibility of the report having been mislaid, since all documents in the London file are numbered in perfect sequence.

It was not till several weeks later, probably after arrival of the *Hollandia* in the Netherlands, that someone brought Mata Hari's arrest to the attention of the Dutch Foreign Office. Most likely the *Hollandia's* captain by now had made his report to the Netherlands authorities, for it is not till November 25—twelve days after the arrest—that the Ministry of Foreign Affairs sent a telegram to its representative in London, *inquiring* about Mata Hari. Again there is no lapse in the correspondence; it was the first message they sent on the subject of their compatriot since they had received the visa-refusing cable from England, which had carried the London Legation number of 62.

Again addressed to "DeMarees Van Swinderen, Netherland Minister, London," the message said, "Your sixty-two. Mata Hari traveling from Spain to Holland on board Dutch steamer *Holland(ia)* taken from board by British authorities Falmouth please investigate and wire—London two hundred eighteen." The Hague, as the telegram clearly indicates, thought it was telling London something new.

This time the Dutch Legation acted with more speed. The telegram had been received on the morning of the twenty-sixth, and at one o'clock that same day it was answered. Mata Hari had been arrested, said the cable, "suspected having committed un-neutral acts," but she was "released however after few days" and was "now staying Savoy Hotel." After which the Legation added that Mata Hari "returns to Spain."

Full details on the strange proceedings were then sent to The Hague by diplomatic bag a few days later. On December 1 the minister himself sent a report, which follows in full:

"Further to my cable of November 26, I have the honor to inform you as follows about the dancer Matahari.

"After I had been informed by the Assistant Commissioner of Police, in a letter which was sent by messenger, that a Mrs. McLeod-Zelle had been arrested in Falmouth on suspicion of having committed un-neutral acts, and having received at nearly the same time a letter from the arrested person herself requesting my intervention, my findings on the following day led to the knowledge that this Dutch national originally had been arrested because her passport was considered to be false, and that her real nationality was German, being a certain Clara Benedix from Hamburg.

"These suspicions soon proved to be without foundation, but an official communication which in the meantime was received from Paris caused reason to believe that Mrs. McLeod neverthe-less occupied herself with activities which were undesirable to the police. She was liberated from prison but remained under police surveillance. During the interrogations she was submitted to, she explained that in Paris she had been assigned the task by the Allies of transmitting certain information to Holland. The police distrusted these communications and were confirmed in this opinion by further information which in the meantime had been received from Paris, which made it clear that the indicated mission had not originated on the Allied side, but on the enemy's.

"Following this, a new interview with the suspect took place, which resulted in her voluntary agreement to return to Spain.

"I do not know whether Mrs. MacLeod might have preferred to

continue on her trip to Holland; after the first and only afore-mentioned communication she has refrained from any further contact with the Legation, and from a private letter which I *most confidentially* was given to read, I understand that she wants to avoid everything which might spread the knowledge of this 'adventure' (I quote) any further."

Thus this letter shows that not one, but several cables had been exchanged between London and Paris. And Captain Ladoux, as he wrote in his books and as he declared during the pre-trial hearings later on, had not simply informed Scotland Yard that he "did not understand," but he had clearly and irrevocably committed himself: Mata Hari from now on was a German spy. He moreover most conveniently forgot to inform Sir Basil Thomson that Mata Hari had told him the truth, that she had indeed been charged by Ladoux with a secret mission—as he himself confirmed later. Captain Ladoux told the British that Mata Hari made the trip by order of the Germans. It was a deliberate lie and falsification with only one idea in mind, and with only one purpose—to trap her.

Contrary to fact, Major Coulson invented the story that the British Secret Service allowed her to continue to Holland, where she went to the tobacco store of a certain Max Neuder, known to the German agents as a "letter box." Her visit, says Coulson "was promptly reported to headquarters in London and Paris, confirming the existing suspicion against her." Then, to get her back to France—for after all, not even Major Coulson could change history to the extent of having her arrested in *Amsterdam*—he writes that the German authorities in Holland "wanted their powerful spy back in Paris, where she had to make the fullest use of her wiles in obtaining information on the production of tanks as weapons of war."

Mata Hari, in the meantime, prepared to make good her promise to Sir Basil Thomson, and applied at the Spanish consulate in London for permission to go back to Madrid. It was granted her on November 29, as indicated by yet another stamp on her one-sheet Dutch passport: "Good for Spain."

The return trip did not take long. On arrival in the Spanish capital Mata Hari reported to her own country's representatives, and had what turned out to be the last official stamp printed in her passport: "Madrid, December 11, 1916—seen at Dutch consulate."

Mata Hari's arrest by the British was followed by the imprisonment of a countryman and close friend of hers early in 1917. Dr. Bierens de Haan was director of the Dutch Red Cross hospital at Pré Catalan in Paris, where Leo Faust had met Mata Hari during the winter of 1916. According to another Dutch Red Cross doctor whom I happen to know well, Dr. A. van Tienhoven, Mata Hari a few times entertained the patients entrusted to the care of Dr. Bierens de Haan.

When the latter went back to Holland via England in 1917, a photograph of himself and Mata Hari, taken at the hospital, was found in his baggage. This made him highly suspicious to Scotland Yard, who detained him for more than six weeks. At the end of it he was luckier than Mata Hari—he was allowed to continue on his trip to Holland.

Chapter 15

CAPTAIN LADOUX, whose statements in his own books, as we have seen, must often be taken with a grain of salt, informs us that Mata Hari "stayed on in Spain for two months for sentimental reasons." Again he was wrong—it was only three weeks, from the second week of December till the very beginning of January.

In the meantime the Captain, now working at a feverish pitch to take full advantage of the web which he had so successfully spun between Paris and London, had given instructions to the powerful Eiffel Tower radio station to intercept all messages which a secret German transmitter near Madrid communicated directly to Berlin. (It seems strange that Captain Ladoux only thought of this now. Being familiar with the existence of a German station, one would imagine that the French were constantly engaged with such interception, having deciphered the German code some time previously.) The results, according to Captain Ladoux, were not long in coming. Two telegrams, one a question, the other one the answer, were caught by the Eiffel Tower, and they were the trumps in Ladoux's further game.

The Germans, Ladoux writes, sent the following text to Berlin: AGENT H-21 ARRIVED MADRID HAS BEEN ENGAGED BY FRENCH BUT WAS RETURNED TO SPAIN BY BRITISH AND NOW ASKS FOR MONEY AND INSTRUCTIONS.

The answer from Germany came forty-eight hours later. It was a very clear message: TELL HER TO GO BACK TO FRANCE AND CONTINUE HER MISSION. SHE WILL RECEIVE CHECK 5000 FRANCS FROM KRAMER ON COMPTOIR D'ESCOMPTE—which was, and is, a bank in Paris.

The Paris file on the trial gives some additional text that was contained in these telegrams, all dealing with the spy whom the Germans—according to the French—indicated as being known to them as H-21. This spy, the telegram said, belonged to the Cologne Center of Espionage, and had been sent to France for the first time in March—when Mata Hari was still back in Holland. H-21 had taken the *Hollandia* from Spain to England with a mission for the French, had been returned by the British, and was now waiting for instructions. But that was not all. The telegram added considerably more particulars about H-21's discoveries. He (there is a constant interchange in the variously quoted texts between "he" and "she") had told the German chief of espionage in the Spanish capital some colorful international political gossip, such as the preparation of an Allied general offensive which would take place in the spring of 1917.

Other information concerned King Constantine of Greece. He was a troublesome character, married to Kaiser Wilhelm's sister, and extremely pro-German. His brother, Prince George, lived in Paris and was the husband of Princess Marie Bonaparte. According to the telegram, spy H-21 had reported to her superior in Madrid that the princess had been talking to Aristide Briand— the French Prime Minister—about substituting Prince George for King Constantine on the throne of Greece by war's end.

There seem to be as many loopholes in these telegrams as there are facts, at least if we follow Captain Ladoux's version, which certifies that Mata Hari was a spy. One might expect that von Kalle, the Chief of the German Intelligence in Madrid, who by then had been in the service for nineteen years, including periods of work on the General Staff in Berlin and Strasbourg, was a competent officer. Yet several items in his telegrams—even in cipher—were totally unnecessary, and made them read much more like dime-novel messages than like the cryptic coded telegrams they were supposed to be.

Nearly all the information was written so as to make sure that whoever would read the text would come to the conclusion that only one person was being discussed: Mata Hari. Only she at that moment had gone to England (or Holland) with a mission for the French. Only she was stopped by the British and had been returned to Spain.

And, if Mata Hari were indeed a German spy and in possession of valuable data, why would the efficient officer in Madrid have waited a month before transmitting his information to Germany? It could only mean that he did not receive it till then. By then Mata Hari would have been of little use, because any other spy would have wanted these facts to get into German hands as quickly as possible, and would consequently have disposed of them immediately on arrival in Madrid, on the way out to Vigo. It would have been totally illogical to hold on to this information for another month, till the arrival in Holland.

Then the Chief of Intelligence in Madrid found it necessary to inform Berlin that H-21 belonged to the espionage center in Cologne. Why? The German Intelligence Service, with its mania for efficiency and detail, must have had a filing system in its Berlin Central Office indicating details on all of their spies, and the code number H-21 in itself would have been sufficient. All that was missing in the telegram was the full name of the spy and her place and date of birth.

And where would Mata Hari have found the gossip about Princess Marie Bonaparte and Briand? On the *Hollandia,* or at Scotland Yard or the Savoy Hotel? Because if she were a spy and had actually picked up this bit of news about making Prince George a king, then she must have heard it in Paris *before* she left France on her unfinished trip to Holland, and again she would have disposed of it immediately upon her arrival in Madrid. (King Constantine was indeed deposed in 1917, but his son Alexander followed him on the throne, instead of Prince George.)

Yet the French themselves claim that the royal news was mentioned in the telegram of December 14 only—a month later. It was the one time the French were right. Mata Hari had never spoken to the German Chief of Intelligence before her return from England, because she did not know him.

The same mystery prevails on the subject of the far more important information concerning the spring offensive. This sounded like highly significant news, and again Mata Hari must have heard about it before leaving Paris. If she wanted to pass it on knowingly—that is, *as a spy*—then she would have done so at the earliest possible moment, in November. As it turned out, she confessed in Paris to having told the Germans about the spring offensive and other vague items on her return from London—she had dug it up out of six-weeks-old French newspapers and made up the rest from memory. In Madrid, after all, talk about the war was not restricted to spies. In 1916 *everybody* talked about the war, and the Allies could hardly have been expected *not* to plan a spring offensive.

The last bit of news contained in the amplified versions of the intercepted telegram is, as we know, even farther wrong. Mata Hari had not been in France for the first time in March 1916. She was there in December 1915, and by March 1916 she had been back in Holland for nearly two months. At the hearings that took place after her arrest, Mata Hari was to point to this discrepancy as proof that she had never met the German Chief of Espionage before her return from England, and that he had known nothing about her.

Weighing all these discrepancies in the telegrams from Madrid to Berlin, all these superfluous details, lengthy explanations, and one might even say irrevelant chitchat, there is only one way to explain it: Von Kalle may have been an efficient officer and even a competent embassy attaché, but his experience as an intelligence officer was in inverse ratio to his capabilities as a military man. Moreover the Germans were, of course, happily innocent of the fact that the French had broken their radio code, and as such von Kalle went gaily ahead with the sending of his exaggeratedly informative messages.

On her arrival in Madrid, Mata Hari moved into the Palace Hotel, where she did not meet but was the immediate neighbor of a professional sister of hers—a *real* spy. Marthe Richard (also called Richer) was a young Frenchwoman who, having lost her husband early in the war, had been recruited by Captain Ladoux himself for his activities. It was at his request that she had gone to Spain, where she had been able to infiltrate the German circles so effectively that before long she was the mistress of the German Naval Attaché—who was the head of one of the spy rings.

After the First World War Marthe Richard became famous and was decorated in 1933 by the French government with the Legion of Honor "for services rendered." A film was made about her life, and both she and Captain Ladoux wrote books about her adventures.

In her own book, *My Life as a Spy*, Marthe Richard describes how she was a close neighbor of Mata Hari. The maid one day came into Marthe's room and told her that the woman next door was "an artist." "French?" asked Marthe Richard. She was not, answered the maid. "She is an English dancer, and her name is Lady MacLeod."

After this the maid picked up a note from Marthe Richard's desk which was to remind her of a meeting for that afternoon, and told her "not to leave scraps of paper lying around—those were the Chief's orders." Consequently, according to Marthe Richard's own deduction, the maid at the Palace Hotel—also serving the room next door—was a German agent. Yet this maid knew nothing about Mata Hari, but *did* know about Marthe Richard.

While Marthe was the mistress of the Naval Attaché—Herr von Krohn—there was another gentleman on the German embassy staff whose initials were equally "von K."—the Military Attaché von Kalle. As fate would have it, he too headed an Intelligence section for the Germans in Spain, and was the gentleman Mata Hari had gone to see when she arrived in Madrid on the return trip from London.

The mix-up between the two chiefs of Intelligence, both German, both attachés at the embassy, and both with the initials *von K.*, was clearly asking for trouble. It resulted in an unlimited series of mistaken identities in all the books and articles on Mata Hari. Usually von Kalle is the loser, for nearly everywhere von Krohn is mentioned as Mata Hari's lover and spy-ring boss. (Von Kalle was a *Hauptmann*, or Captain, with assignments as Military Attaché at both the Madrid Embassy and the Lisbon Legation. He resigned after the First World War with the rank of Colonel. When I inquired about him in 1963 at the German War Archives, they not only sent me a list of his various appointments, but with typical German punctiliousness informed me that "Kalle in the officers' roster was not mentioned with the aristocratic 'von.'")

How very little was known about Mata Hari's presumed spying in Madrid is perfectly described by Marthe Richard herself, who, after all, should have known something about what was going on. As late as April 1917 the French spy-ace still had no notion

about Mata Hari's visits to von Kalle, and by then only read about
it in the Paris newspapers. The chapter she devotes to it in her
book mightily enhanced the later *Von K. versus Von K.* controversy among the Mata Hari writers.

Since the French authorities had held up the news about the
arrest for quite a while, Marthe Richard read about the case
many weeks after Mata Hari had been put in prison. At the same
time she discovered, due to wrong reporting in *Le Matin,* that
Mata Hari in Madrid had been the mistress of Marthe Richard's
own lover, Hans von Krohn. She therefore had every right to be
furious, and rushed into her friend's office to berate him in no
uncertain terms.

"Don't deny it!" she yelled at the head of the Naval Intelligence.
"It won't get you anywhere! I understand everything now. That
dancer stayed at the Palace Hotel at the same time I was there!"

Von Krohn showed a totally perplexed face and remarked that
"Mata Hari was perhaps a spy in the service of the Military
Attaché—von Kalle—or maybe even the Ambassador himself."

Marthe Richard called her lover's attitude "hypocritical," and
said: "One doesn't invent things like that, not even in the newspapers. And moreover Mata Hari has declared that she knows
you!"

"If you won't believe me," said von Krohn, "then I'll show you."
He opened the safe and took out a large book full of photographs.
On the back of each of these was a spy's name, his or her serial
number, other descriptive detail, plus a short résumé of the
information they had supplied to their chief. Marthe Richard
looked at the pictures upside down, but mentions that with her
specially strong glasses "it would have been easy for me to recognize her." Yet Mata Hari's photograph was not in the book.

Von Krohn, by now definitely set on convincing his mistress,
took out another file, containing "the agents employed by the
embassy." And Marthe Richard, in a book written and published
in 1935, quoted him as saying, "I can assure you, Marthe, that she
is not employed by any of our agents in Spain. But inasmuch as

she is Dutch, she may be a member of her own country's Intelligence service."

(While German denial as to Mata Hari's espionage can only be accepted at face value, it must be mentioned for the record that Major General Gempp, in a signed article in *"Heer und Wehr,"* the military section of the newspaper *Schwäbische Merkur* of June 14, 1929—eleven years after the war ended—wrote the following about the effectiveness of women spies in time of war: "Cases like the one of the unhappy dancer Mata Hari, who for that matter has accomplished nothing for the German espionage service, were tremendously exaggerated." The only note about Mata Hari still in today's (1965) archives of the German Foreign Office is in a file marked *"Agents,"* and was written in January 1920 by Freiherr von Scheliha. Its partly wrong information mentions that she had been born on Sumatra, was known there as a dancer, and had been the wife of a Dutch colonel from Arnhem. She danced at La Scala and in Paris, and was shot by the French. The report must have been supplied by the German consul in Amsterdam, who later on helped to thicken the Mata Hari plot.

The only German who, as far as I know, tried to take some credit for knowing about Mata Hari's "activities" was a certain Justin Herre, who had emigrated to the United States shortly after the First World War. Herr Herre claimed to have been a German spy in France, and to have met Mata Hari during the war in Paris in a certain Café Mariano in the Rue de Rivoli. In 1923 this gentleman, in a letter that smacked disgustingly of pre-Hitler Nazi feelings, wrote from New York to one of Mata Hari's relatives in Holland: *"With* Mata Hari Germany would have won the war! Count von Moltke knows about Mata Hari, and so does the Kaiser—I took care of that. The French Jews and niggerdogs have stolen all her money." While the German Kaiser in 1923 was still alive at the small castle in the village of Doorn in Holland, to which country he had fled in 1918, Mr. Herre's knowledge of German history must have been slight, for he apparently did not know that Count von Moltke, former favorite of the Kaiser and former Chief of Staff of the German army, had died in 1916.)

Whether or not von Krohn knew about Mata Hari is, at this point, of no importance. The point is that Marthe Richard, who by 1935 surely had no reason to defend Mata Hari, wrote about her scene with von Krohn the way she did. She was, after all, in danger of her life. She knew that she herself was spying for France, and she knew that her state of intimacy with the Naval Attaché—on which her spying activities depended—was at stake. Even though she may not have liked the man (she only "rendered services" in the interest of her country) her scene of jealousy was real enough. She was definitely convinced that von Krohn had another mistress—Mata Hari. Therefore we can certainly believe her description of von Krohn's reaction in the face of her accusation. And even if von Krohn were playing a game, and only feigned not to know, it still proves that Marthe Richard herself during all the time she was in Madrid was totally unfamiliar with Mata Hari's presumed activities.

Enter another gentleman. He is Colonel Denvignes, chief of the Intelligence Section of the French embassy in Madrid. Having met Mata Hari in the company of two attachés of the Netherlands Legation, first at the Palace Hotel and then at the Ritz, Mata Hari told him about her experiences at Falmouth, adding that she had informed Captain Ladoux, but was still waiting for his further instructions. Taking advantage of her presence in Madrid, and Mata Hari having told him that she had gone to see von Kalle, Colonel Denvignes asked her to sound out von Kalle on various subjects, including more details about the German use of submarines along the coast of Morocco, which von Kalle had mentioned to her. At the same time, Mata Hari explained later on in Paris, the aging Colonel made amorous advances to her, asking for a bunch of violets and her handkerchief as a souvenir.

In the meantime Mata Hari, limiting the Colonel's advances to the flowers and the handkerchief, started to get annoyed about the silence from Paris. She had, all things considered, not been on a pleasure trip to London. Her annoyance turned to indignation when she was told by a Spanish friend of hers, Senator Junoy, that he had been advised by a French secret agent to break off his friendship with her.*

Mata Hari, who had not hesitated to cut up mattresses and throw a wardrobe down the stairs when she was angry, again took immediate action. She went to Colonel Denvignes' office to ask him for an explanation. The Colonel had just left for Paris, and his replacement told her that he knew nothing about the whole business.

Mata Hari's impulsive nature took charge. She had been wronged and, having already planned to go to France anyhow, she rushed off to Paris that same night—January 2, 1917. This was a matter that had to be followed up to the bitter end. She *had* to know who was telling her friends behind her back to be careful about her and to stop seeking her company.

Had Mata Hari had the slightest suspicion, the decision to go to Paris could only have come to her in a state of complete insanity. Ladoux himself had told her that the British suspected her of being a German spy; she knew she had been followed on various occasions; the British had arrested her and had prevented her from continuing to Holland; now her Spanish friend had warned her. If there were any feeling of guilt or any knowledge of playing a double game, only a demented person would have put his head into the lion's mouth under those circumstances. And Mata Hari was far from crazy. Yet she went to Paris.

The only possible explanation is that Mata Hari was playing her association with the French straight. It was a game to her—a fascinating game—like being a Javanese princess born in Leeuwarden. Her attitude and action were a perfect continuation of

* In July 1925, Senator Junoy accused Raquel Meller, the Spanish-born music-hall artist who in the late twenties was the toast of Paris, of having betrayed Mata Hari to the French police because she suspected her husband (the journalist-writer E. Gomez Carrillo) of having been Mata Hari's lover. Gomez Carrillo's comment, as published in the *New York Evening Graphic* of February 6, 1926, was: "The whole story is pure fancy. Raquel Meller and I were not married until 1924. As such it is plain that my wife could not have betrayed Mata Hari in 1917."

her lifelong behavior. At school she had been the center of admiration with her carriage and goats, and she had impressed her girl friends with her clothes and manners. Now she had expected to impress the French with her ability of being of service to them—a demonstration of egocentricism that was entirely her own.

All this time she saw nothing, heard all, and said everything. What she heard on the left, she told on the right—with embellishments. She threw names around like sugared almonds at a wedding—names of people she had known, and names of people she imagined she had known. Instead of making up a biography of herself, she now made up stories for and about others—not understanding that this was no longer a game, that she was not talking to fairly gullible newspapermen, but that she had to do with hardboiled intelligence agents in wartime. At all costs she wanted to prove that she was important, that she could be of use. That is why she agreed to help Colonel Denvignes and went from him back to von Kalle, back to Denvignes and back to von Kalle once more, like a tennis ball. And now, being furious at the wrong that was being done to her, she rushed off to Paris to have it out at the head office!

But in Paris she got nowhere. The Colonel was already on his way back to Spain, and Mata Hari had hardly a chance to exchange two words with him on the platform of the Gare d'Austerlitz. This being so, she decided to tackle the lion in his den—Captain Ladoux owed her an explanation. But he too feigned innocence, and Mata Hari went off to seek solace with an old friend of hers, Jules Cambon, the secretary-general of the Foreign Office. She was lost for three days, and so, it is rumored, was M. Cambon.

For a whole month Mata Hari went on living in Paris as if there were not a cloud in the sky—except a very small one. Vadime de Massloff suddenly appeared on a quick trip to the capital, not only to enjoy the company of his mistress, but also to inform her about and ask for a possible explanation of some upsetting news he had received. Vadime had been called in by his superior officer, who had read a letter to him which he had received from the Russian Embassy in Paris. It warned him about the liaison between one of his officers (Vadime) and a dangerous *aventurière*. Mata Hari had no explanation, and could not understand who was behind the slanderous note.

After Vadime's departure she went on to enjoy the offerings of Paris, spending her days and sometimes the nights in the company of those males whom she had admired since childhood—the men in uniform. An infinite variety of them was available, for as happened after the liberation of Paris in 1944, all Allied troops felt that a leave visit to the French capital was the all-powerful medicine to refresh their morale.

The Paris season, notwithstanding the war (or perhaps on account of it) was gay. Between the Opera, the legitimate stage and variety shows, there were over thirty theaters to choose from. Mata Hari went to many of them, and with her Polish officer-friend, as Leo Faust indicated, she applauded *Mademoiselle du Far West* at the Folies-Bergère.

Captain Ladoux, inconceivably from his point of view, gave her one month's grace—during which time she might well have squandered (if she were a spy) all the secrets of France to the Germans. The delay was certainly not in the interest of the Chief of the French Intelligence Service, whose task it was to protect these secrets from being divulged. By the end of that month Captain Ladoux had no more evidence against her than at the beginning, and why he waited is another mystery. If Mata Hari were guilty in February, she was guilty four weeks earlier. Just the same Ladoux did nothing—yet.

There were some fallacious peace feelers in the air around that time, sent out by Germany, followed by the request on President Wilson's part to all belligerents to let him have their peace conditions. Mata Hari was at peace with everybody—except Ladoux.

On February 1, 1917, Germany shut the door against any possibility of an early peace by declaring the unrestricted U-boat warfare, which would bring the United States into the war two months later, on April 6. Twelve days after that first of February Captain Ladoux also shut the door—on Mata Hari.

In the morning of February 13, Police Chief Priolet entered her room at the Élysées Palace Hotel on the Champs Élysées. She did not, as the scene has been reported, disappear into the bathroom to come back in the nude in an effort at wholesale enticement of the intruders. There were five inspectors accompanying their chief. Mata Hari, bewildered, dressed and went along.

The accusation was read to her: "The woman Zelle, Marguerite, known as Mata Hari, living at the Palace Hotel, of Protestant religion, foreigner, born in Holland on August 7, 1876, five feet ten inches tall, being able to read and write, is accused of espionage, tentative complicity and intelligence with the enemy, in an effort to assist them in their operations."

She was taken to the prison of Saint Lazare.

Chapter 16

THE secret file which the French War Council compiled on Mata Hari was made available to the members of the Military Tribunal on July 24, 1917. It is a voluminous folder about six inches thick. Marked on the binding *"Affaire* Zelle-Mata Hari," it contains a lot of papers, a lot of words, a lot of documents, and no proof whatever.

The file was the product of one man, and one man only—Captain Bouchardon, the *rapporteur militaire* or Investigating Officer, who had built up his case during over four months of interrogation of Mata Hari and various witnesses. Whatever thin evidence it contains was construed out of hearsay and endless monologues by Mata Hari. One might in fact say that Mata Hari talked herself

into death. Captain Boucharodon, who had been selected for the
post of *rapporteur militaire* one week after war had been declared,
turned every story she told into a possible reason for accusation.
Every word she uttered was weighed by him to see whether it
might fit in somewhere to build up his case—and it was immate-
rial whether the word was true or not. In the end it was Mata
Hari's word against Boucharodon's—and Boucharodon who, according to various people, was an obsessed spy hunter, was sitting on
the stronger side of the fence.

Mata Hari's actual trial was of little importance, except insofar
as it dealt with the verdict and sentence. Yet nearly all writing on
the subject of her innocence or guilt is concerned with the trial
only, undoubtedly because it offered dramatic possibilities of the
"J'accuse" type, mostly based on rumor and hearsay, which would
impress the reader and the cinema public. But the real case was
Boucharodon's. He went about it with infinite patience, starting on
the same day the doors of the prison had closed behind his prospective victim, whom in his memoirs he called "a born spy, who
clearly showed that she was one."

Only three people participated in the hearings: Mata Hari,
Boucharodon, and *sergent-greffier* Manuel Baudouin, the recorder
who took down the questions and answers. Maître Clunet, the
lawyer, who, at Mata Hari's own request, had been appointed to
her defense by the Military Court, was only allowed to be present
during the first and last interrogation. This was the rule dictated
by military law, and Boucharodon kept himself to the letter of it.

The first cell Mata Hari was put in was padded. The director
of Saint Lazare was taking no chances with any possible suicidal
intentions of his prisoner. It was in this cell that the prison doctor,
Leon Bizard, met her for the first time. Dr. Bizard's mostly sober
account of his experience with Mata Hari is about the only factual
writing in all the literature on the dancer-spy's behavior that can
be accepted as credible. All other tales, such as her insisting
"upon having a daily bath in milk when it was almost impossible
to obtain that precious fluid for the young of Paris" (statement by

Major Coulson) or her dancing totally nude, or even fully dressed, in her cell, as reported by various other writers, must again be relegated to the rich field of fables.

During that first meeting between Mata Hari and Dr. Bizard, she complained bitterly about her surroundings. The only furniture in the sparsely gas-lit cell consisted of a mattress, and the light coming in from the outside was extremely dim. When the doctor asked whether there were anything she wanted, her answer was, "Yes, a telephone and a bath." The absence of bathing facilities or even sufficient water must have been maddening to a woman who like most Dutch had always considered cleanliness one of the great virtues—and being on friendly terms with a great many people of importance, she obviously would have liked to talk to them, not realizing that as soon as the prison doors had closed behind her, nearly all her friends—if indeed not *all*—deserted her, undoubtedly being of the opinion that any connection between them and a suspected spy in wartime might not only be harmful to their reputation, but even result in their arrest.

After a few days Mata Hari was transferred to a cell in another part of the prison—now destroyed, but then situated at the corner of the Rue du Faubourg St. Denis and the Boulevard Magenta—which was known as the Ménagerie, and which had been set aside for spies. Hygienic facilities were practically nonexistent, and Bouchardon himself was to write many years later that on the morning of the execution "we followed a long corridor, where the rats rushed between our feet." Exercise in the beginning was nil, but later on Mata Hari was allowed a daily walk in the courtyard.

Spending her days for the most part alone, Mata Hari was compelled to share her cell at night with one of the women inmates, who was allowed to perform cleaning and other light jobs in the prison. Food, during all this time of pre-trial imprisonment, was not too bad, although Mata Hari had to pay for it. Sister Auréa, in charge of the kitchen, usually served the meals herself: consommé and coffee for breakfast, a plate of meat and vegetables plus coffee for lunch, soup and a meat course for dinner. Wine was served with the midday and evening meals.

Mata Hari, according to Dr. Bizard, was a good prisoner who made few special demands. Her state of mind was variable and she was sometimes moody—which is hardly surprising in her condition. She missed human contact and above all conversation, and was grateful to anyone who came to talk to her. But the number of these people was obviously limited to a very few only: Dr. Bizard, his assistant-intern, Dr. Jean Bralez, and the Catholic and Protestant clergymen of the prison, Father Dommergue and Reverend Jules Arboux.

During the fourteen endless pre-trial hearings, Captain Bouchardon found that he had very little to go on. With the exception of the intercepted telegrams, which according to him dealt with Mata Hari, and which he himself did not know about till the seventh hearing on May 1, 1917 (at which time he decided that "it was an open-and-shut case"), he had nothing in his file but the reports from Ladoux's agents, the proof that Mata Hari did receive money from abroad at the Comptoir d'Escompte, the knowledge that she had tried to return to Holland, and a laboratory report on a few items which had been found in her room when she was arrested. Among them was a tube or vial that had greatly attracted the attention of the police, because it contained—according to a chemical analysis—a secret ink "which could only have been obtained in Spain." The other items in Mata Hari's room and purse had been the usual ones: powder, rouge, lipstick, cold cream, perfume.

The military authorities had made tests with the secret ink, and the result of these experiences is included in the file. It consists of a sheet of plain white paper on which some invisible lines had been written. It had then been torn in half from top to bottom, cutting each written line in two, after which the investigator had applied various methods to make the words on one half of the page visible. The test was successful, for this half shows the initially invisible words in a brownish tint. Since the test was made in 1917, it may well be that the color at the time was different.

The tube with this invisible ink that "could only be obtained in Spain" actually contained, according to the report from the laboratory in the secret file, oxycyanide of mercury. It is today, as it was in 1917, a well-known disinfectant that, with a doctor's prescription, can be bought at any pharmacy in the world. Modern medicine has advanced way beyond the oxycyanide-of-mercury stage for its disinfectants, but fifty years ago—sold in the form of tablets to be diluted in water—it was frequently used for feminine hygiene. And, like a great many chemicals, it can also be used as "invisible ink." But if a tin of milk had been found in Mata Hari's room, would the laboratory have come to the conclusion that this too was a secret ink, obtainable, for instance, only in Holland? As most boys know, one can write with milk on any kind of white paper, and by simply heating the sheet the writing will soon become visible.

Mata Hari herself was extremely direct and explicit when, during the hearings, the real use of the "secret ink" was brought up by Captain Bouchardon on April 12. "It is nothing but a product one puts into injections," she said, "to prevent the birth of children after each coition. It was given to me by a doctor in Madrid last December."

I asked a chemist how oxycyanide of mercury could be used as invisible ink. He made several suggestions, one of the most simple being the dilution of the chemical in water. Then, to bring up the color, the inscribed sheet must be covered with a blotter that previously has been soaked in any kind of sulphuric acid solution. Speeding up the drying process with a heated iron, the handwriting comes up beautifully.

While these preliminaries were going on, one might assume that Mata Hari would have tried to get in touch with the outer world. In London, as soon as she had been put in jail by Scotland Yard, she wrote to the Netherlands Legation. In Paris this did not happen, or if it did, the letter was never forwarded. This second supposition was probably the true cause of her silence, because as late as April, two months after her arrest, the Dutch Legation in Paris was still officially ignorant of the fate of their compatriot. And still on May 23 her own lawyer in The Hague, Mr. Hijmans, was totally in the dark as to her whereabouts.

Bouchardon, during the hearing that took place on May 1, stated in so many words that the police had kept her arrest secret, hoping that the Germans would continue to communicate about Mata Hari with their office in Madrid. For this same reason they obviously did not want word about the arrest to leak out via the Dutch Legation.

As late as June 22, 1917, in a letter to the Netherlands consul, Mata Hari (by then being allowed to write) mentioned that she had the impression that "in Holland apparently no one knows what has happened to me, although I have written to my maid"— Anna Lintjens. Consequently the prison authorities had not forwarded this letter. Another letter did get to its destination, but not any further than the prison office. Shortly after her arrest a letter was received, and kept in the court file, which said: "I am innocent, and have never committed any espionage against France. I therefore ask you to give instructions to let me go."

The Dutch Legation in Paris *did* know about Mata Hari's arrest by Scotland Yard in 1916. After the Foreign Office in The Hague in December of that year had been informed by their representative in London about what had happened, they had sent a nearly full copy of the London report to their Legation in Paris. In an accompanying letter they warned Paris that Mata Hari on her return to France might possibly contact the Legation. In that case, wrote The Hague, "the information on what happened to her in England would indicate reason to be prudent."

Now, during the second week of April, someone in Holland finally approached the Foreign Office and reported having been without news from Mata Hari for a long time. It was most likely Baron van der Capellen. As a result of this *démarche,* the following telegram was sent to Paris on April 11, under the signature of Foreign Minister Jonkheer Loudon: "Please inform by tele-gram present address of Margaretha Zelle alias Mata Hari. Last known address Plaza Hotel 25 Avenue Montaigne and please ask whether she has intention to repatriate soon." It is clear that nearly two months after she had been arrested, no one in Holland had the slightest idea that Mata Hari was in jail.

The Paris Legation apparently was still somewhat uncertain about Mata Hari's predicament. If they had heard rumors of her arrest, they were not informed of them by the French authorities, either at an earlier date, or immediately upon receipt of the inquiry from their Foreign Office. By sheer coincidence, a few days after the arrival of the telegram from The Hague, they finally received a first communication from Mata Hari herself, in which she asked to "please advise her maid" that she was "having difficulties in leaving France" but that "she should not worry." Dated April 16, the letter was delivered to the Dutch consulate six days later, on the twenty-second.

The fact that the Legation had not been officially informed about the arrest is evident from the wording of the cable they sent to Holland on April 23, the day following the receipt of Mata Hari's letter, but fully twelve days after arrival of the inquiry from The Hague. They explained that their information had been obtained *semi-officially* from the authorities at the Quai d'Orsay, the French Foreign Office: "Semi-officially we have been in-formed that she is imprisoned at Saint Lazare. She is suspected of espionage. The authorities investigate the case, which seems to be very serious." And by courier the Legation sent a letter to The Hague with the request to forward it to Anna Lintjens, re-assuring her about Mata Hari along the lines requested: "Anna should not worry."

One wonders what special reasons Anna Lintjens had to worry. Anna, of course, was *always* worried, as she had intimated when I saw her in 1932, and as her son confirmed to me in 1963. She worried about Mata Hari's restlessness and her constant travel in wartime on ships that might be torpedoed or hit a mine. Anna, who was now in her middle fifties, could not understand why Mata Hari would leave the quiet atmosphere of The Hague, where she could live in comparative luxury on the funds supplied by Baron van der Capellen, but preferred instead to roam around Spain and France.

Holland, during the First World War, prospered considerably as a neutral country doing business with both the Allies and the Germans—but food for the Dutch themselves was extremely scarce, and a rigid system of rationing had been instituted. In Holland, a country that was proverbially rich in dairy products, there was neither butter nor cheese, which had been substituted by bad margarine and some kind of worse cheese spread. White bread had become a luxury, meat was nonexistent, potatoes were soggy, eggs were of a preserved putrefied kind, stoves were heated with stone-hard newspaper-balls soaked in salty water, gas for cooking was available for only a few hours a day, resulting in neatly upholstered "hay cases" in every home to keep the food warm, and there were long lines in front of the municipal food kitchens every day. Even without the constantly bad news from the front, there were plenty of things in Holland to worry Anna Lintjens, who could only think that conditions in France were worse.

But there was undoubtedly more, as Mata Hari one day started to explain to the imperturbable Captain Bouchardon. And Anna, who obviously knew about the matter, must have shaken her head many a time when, and after, it originally happened. It could, she must have thought, bring nothing but trouble.

Mata Hari's tale concerned a visit she had received one evening from one of the German consuls in Amsterdam, who had asked her to spy for his country. After a few days of meditation, she had accepted his money in a mental exchange and payment for the confiscated Berlin furs, a matter that had irked her ever since it had happened. After which Mata Hari threw some bottles of secret ink which the consul had given her into the canal that goes from Amsterdam to the North Sea, and never giving it a second thought, had called the whole thing quits. As far as she was concerned, it was good riddance, and her Berlin account with the Germans was settled.

But by the time she poured out this amazing tale, she had been in jail for three and a half months, and had gone through seven long and exhausting interviews with Bouchardon, who even at this point was hardly any the wiser.

Bouchardon, forty-six years old, with thin moustache, high forehead, arched eyebrows, and rather thin face, was a patient interviewer. Very much the officer type, he had learned his profession during his years as prosecuting attorney in Rouen and Paris. In his legal profession he had consciously developed the maddening habit of suddenly getting up from his chair while talking to the accused. He would then walk up and down the room, stop at the window and tap with his fingers on the glass, causing a growing exasperation in the interrogated party. Besides this it seems that he was a perennial nail-biter. The system worked perfectly on Mata Hari, and Bouchardon wrote in his memoirs that on one occasion she exclaimed: "If you only knew, Captain, how you irritate me with that constant walking up and down!"

The first meeting between Mata Hari and her interlocutor took place on the day of her arrest, February 13. Bouchardon writes that he met her "one hour after Priolet had waked her up in her hotel on the Champs Élysées." He must have have been mistaken, for at the end of that first interview Mata Hari, as the court report shows, "protested against the conditions at Saint Lazare." Consequently she must have been taken to prison first, and only afterwards to Bouchardon's office. The latter therefore was equally or at least partly wrong when he said that Mata Hari, at the end of that first meeting, thinking that she was free to go, "smiled at me most graciously, after which she directed her steps to the door with a balancing of her body that was not devoid of a certain charm. But she was no longer free, and the staircase that led to the Dépôt (the prison belonging to the Palace of Justice) opened up in front of her. She turned towards me, a haggard look in her eyes, dumb with fear, bits of dyed hair sticking to her temples."

That hearing on February 13 was the first of a series of fourteen that lasted till June 21—over four months. All of them took place at Pierre Bouchardon's office at the Chancellerie, which communicates with and at the same time is separated from the Palace of Justice by various courtyards and corridors, with the main entrance on the Quai de l'Horloge along the Seine. The office was so small, writes Bouchardon, that "two chairs, a small desk and a bookcase with glass doors could hardly find enough room. One day we were sixteen in this office, which with difficulty could hold ten people. It felt like being in the *métro* during the rush hour."

Bouchardon started off easily: "Please tell us the story of your life." And from there on Mata Hari talked. She talked with that flair for self-dramatization which had been her trademark all along, and which did not even leave her in prison. Bouchardon himself admired her for it, and having one day personally taken down part of her testimony in shorthand, declared: "The language was excellent, and what subtlety of phrasing! What irony! What sharpness and presence of mind in her answers!"

Bypassing the earlier parts of her life, Mata Hari came immediately to the period that interested Bouchardon specifically—the months that led up to the beginning of the war.

"In April or May 1914," she started off, "I met my old lover again in Berlin, Lieutenant Kiepert, who invited me to supper. The next day a kind of blackmailing small newspaper commented on this meeting, saying that France had been victorious over the Austro-Hungarian empire, because Kiepert's wife was Austrian."

According to the newspaper, Kiepert's wife was not Austrian, but Hungarian, for Mata Hari had taken good care to paste the clipping in her scrapbooks. Marked "April 1914" and headlined in French *"On revient,"* the story said that "a former star of Berlin's glittering nights has apparently rediscovered an old love of hers. When Mata Hari, the beautiful dancer, said good-by to the rich estate owner K., who lives just outside Berlin, she took along a few hundred thousand as a farewell present. Whether the shine of the money has worn off or whether it is love that brought her back to her former friend, during the last few days they could be seen, apparently happy and closely intimate, in a private dining room of a fashionable restaurant in town. It would seem therefore that the lovely dancer with the Indian *nom de guerre* has gained a definite victory over Hungary."

As a result of this article, continued Mata Hari, the Lieutenant told her that he would not be able to see her any longer, but, he added, "I'll come and see you in Paris." Mata Hari answered that he would have to wait six months, because she had a contract at the Metropole Theater. Kiepert said: "You'll be in Paris before then, and so will I."

Mata Hari did not take his statement seriously at that moment, but on reflection thought it highly significant. "I wrote immediately to the French Minister of War (Messimy), who happened to be a friend of mine. In his answer the Minister said that his position in the government made it impossible for him to cross the frontier."

During May or June, Mata Hari went on, she became the mistress of a naval officer, a certain Kuntze, who was attached to "the hydroplane base at Prestig." (His name, according to information received from the German War Archives, was Paul Kuntze, born on November 12, 1883, and he was therefore seven years younger than Mata Hari. In taking down her statement, Sergeant Baudouin wrote "Prestig" as the name of the base. Mata Hari must have said "Putzig," which was one of the three prewar German hydroplane bases on the Baltic, not far from Danzig, the others being Kiel and Warnemünde). When Kuntze too mentioned an early meeting in France, Mata Hari felt that "this could be serious" and said to herself, "I really must let them know in Paris." She then wrote a letter to "one of my former lovers, the well-known pilot Henri Capeferet, the first one who flew over Paris." Again there was no reaction, and the days passed.

(*Sergent-greffier* Baudouin, who, according to Bouchardon, was a highly intelligent person and "one of his colleagues at the Paris Tribunal," was most likely not an expert on aviation. The "well-known pilot" and "former lover" was not Capeferet, but Henri Kapférer, the director-owner of the Astra Corporation, which started building dirigibles in 1904. Kapférer was known as one of the greatest zeppelin pilots in Europe.)

Bouchardon never interrupted his prospective spy but let her ramble along quietly, thinking that if he let her talk long enough, at some moment the truth—or what he *wanted* to be the truth— would finally come out.

"Towards the end of July," Mata Hari continued, "I was dining in a *cabinet particulier* with one of my lovers, the *chef* de police Griebel, when we heard the noise of a demonstration. Griebel, who had not been informed about it, took me along to the place where it was being held. An enormous crowd was holding a frantic meeting in front of the Kaiser's palace, yelling: '*Deutschland über Alles.*'

"Then came the declaration of war, and foreigners were rounded up all over Berlin. I could get out of my contract with the theater on account of *force majeure,* but the theatrical *costumier* started to sue me for eighty thousand francs for furs and all the jewelry I had with me."

She then went on to relate her adventure during the trip to Switzerland, where she lost all her luggage, her subsequent return trip to Berlin, and her final departure for Holland.

"Arriving in my native country I felt terribly ashamed. I had no money whatsoever. I did have an old lover in The Hague, Colonel Baron van der Capellen of the Second Regiment of Hussars, married and very rich, but knowing how much importance he attached to clothes, I could not go and see him without first replenishing my *garderobe*. That is why, on leaving a church in Amsterdam, I let myself be accosted by a stranger. He turned out to be a banker by the name of van der Schalk, who became my lover and who was very good to me and very generous. Making him believe that I was Russian, he showed me the whole country, not realizing that I knew it better than he did.

"By the time I was well fixed up again in clothes, I went back to Baron van der Capellen, who is still my lover today."

At that moment Mata Hari had a lapse of memory, because she told Bouchardon that she returned to Paris "in May 1915" in order to gather her belongings which she had left in storage.

"I traveled via England and Dieppe. I stayed at the Grand Hotel for three months (again a mistake) and became the mistress of the Marquis de Beaufort, who was staying at the same hotel—for really, I didn't like to be alone in Paris."

"With my ten packing cases I returned to Holland via Spain, because the British frontier was closed on account of troop movements—meaning that if this had not been the case, she would have returned to Holland the way she had come: via Dieppe, across the Channel, and from England via Harwich to the Hook of Holland.

Before ending her testimony on February 13, Mata Hari requested that "Maître Clunet be named my lawyer," after which she protested "against the conditions at Saint Lazare."

Bouchardon felt, especially because (as he wrongly remembered it) she showed fear on leaving his office when she discovered that the Dépôt instead of her hotel room was waiting for her, that he had won the day. (Mata Hari could never have seen "the staircase that led to the Dépôt" from the small office she had just been in, as Bouchardon describes it in his memoirs. The prison cells of the Dépôt, now destroyed with the exception of the historical part where Marie Antoinette spent her last days, were built on two floors a short distance from the offices of the Chancellerie and could only be reached via several courtyards.)

The next day, Bouchardon writes, "she had taken hold of herself again and put up a good fight."

Chapter 17

THAT next day was quite endless, and *greffier* Baudouin's hand must have been limp from writing it all down. Mata Hari talked about her stay in Holland, her second trip to Spain, a strange meeting aboard ship with a Dutchman whom she suspected to be the cause of some of her later troubles because she did not want to sleep with him, for which reason—she thought—he had denounced her to the British; then she told in detail about her first meeting with Captain Ladoux, her trip to Vittel, the interrupted voyage to Amsterdam on the *Hollandia*, and the return to Vigo. By then even Bouchardon must have been tired just from listening to her, although, as before, he did not interrupt.

The only thing Mata Hari probably liked about Bouchardon's small office was its warmth. The winter of 1916–1917 had been extremely cold, and the first night she spent in jail the thermometer had gone down several degrees below freezing. The cells had no central heating, and the temperature, if not the atmosphere, in Bouchardon's office must have seemed fairly cosy to her.

Mata Hari went on where she had left off on the previous day —back in The Hague. Again she was wrong about time and date, a circumstance that hardly ever happened during the later hearings, because she told Bouchardon that it was then, during the first part of 1916, that she tried to see her daughter "whom (she) had not seen since she was twelve years old." As we know, Mata Hari had met Non at the Arnhem railway station a good many years before her twelfth birthday and, corresponding with her husband in September 1914, she had tried once more—and for the last time.

Her sojourn in The Hague, she said, "*Se passa tristement*"— was very sad. Her lover, Baron van der Capellen, was off somewhere near the Dutch frontier on his neutral army duties, and it was difficult for Mata Hari to take another lover in a town like The Hague, where such matters could not be kept secret too long. In the meantime her Grand Hotel lover from Paris, the Marquis de Beaufort, begged her to please return to France. It was a sad state of affairs indeed for a woman of Mata Hari's temperament, and she finally decided to give in to the Marquis's pleading.*

"In June 1916 (it was actually on May 24) I embarked on the *Zeelandia* with the intention to return to Paris via Vigo and Madrid," Mata Hari continued. She then went on to describe in detail her adventure aboard on account of a Dutchman by the name of Hoedemaker, who was supposed to be a British agent "traveling up and down between Amsterdam and Vigo with the sole intention of denouncing Dutchmen, Danes, and Norwegians who were on their way to South America to pick up trade connections which the Germans had dropped. At Falmouth he would stand near the British officer who checked all passports and immediately certain passengers would be taken off the ship."

Anti-semitism during the earlier part of this century being a virulent disease which at times even contaminated the otherwise tolerant Dutch, another Dutchman, a certain Cleyndert, told Mata Hari "to be careful of that dirty Jew. He tells everybody that he has been in your cabin." Mata Hari told Bouchardon in elaborate detail how she had asked the ship's captain to make Hoedemaker explain on the boat deck in front of all passengers whether or not he had been in her cabin "and to offer his apologies." Hoedemaker said no, the other passengers said yes, and quite a fighting scene ensued, during which Mata Hari, "while the other passen-

---

* Although Mata Hari did not tell Captain Bouchardon, she had not been entirely without a love life during Baron van der Capellen's absence from The Hague. Marking a definite preference for young boys, there were at least two of these—aged seventeen and eighteen, but looking older—whom Mata Hari had casually experimented with during the spring of 1916, one of them staying at her house for two full weeks. Both men confessed their well-remembered happy indulgences to the author in 1964.

gers yelled 'Hurrah' and 'Bravo,'" slapped Hoedemaker in the face, "which made the blood come out of his mouth."

The result of it all was, said Mata Hari, that the Uruguayan consul, who sat next to her at the ship's dining table, warned her that "Hoedemaker will take revenge. You'll see what is going to happen to you at the Spanish border."

Getting off the ship at Vigo, Hoedemaker kept close to Mata Hari, who requested the assistance of two fellow passengers, an American and a Dutchman by the name of Rubens, please to keep an eye on him. But nothing happened, except that she saw Hoedemaker on the train, and once again at the Ritz Hotel in Madrid.

(Henri Hoedemaker committed suicide in 1921. Described by a member of his family as "an adventurous character," a vague story is known among Hoedemaker's relatives about "his having committed suicide because he thought Mata Hari was shot as a result of the information he gave the British.")

In telling the Hoedemaker incident to Bouchardon, and probably trying to make it sound as the initial reason for her later troubles, Mata Hari did not know that the British already had been suspicious about her for nearly a year. It did, however, result in the unpleasantness that befell Mata Hari when she tried to cross into France, as the consul of Uruguay had predicted. Wanting to board the train on the French side of the border at Hendaye, Mata Hari said that she "was bodily searched, after which I was brought to the office of the *police spéciale,* where three gentlemen subjected me to a detailed interrogation. They told me that I would not be allowed to enter France. I protested and asked for the reason. 'I don't have to give you any reason,' said one of the policemen, 'you can go to San Sebastian and ask your consul for an explanation.'

"The consul," said Mata Hari, "was a Spanish wine merchant, who did not understand anything about the whole business. I then prepared a letter for M. Cambon, the Secretary General at the French Ministry of Foreign Affairs, and the next morning, letter in hand, I went back to the Hendaye station. The men who had interrogated me the night before let me pass without any trouble."

In Paris Mata Hari went to the Grand Hotel, "but the Marquis de Beaufort wasn't there and could not get any leave. In the salon of Madame Dangeville at 30 Rue Tronchet I met a Russian officer by the name of Gasfield, who introduced me to his friend Captain Vadime de Massloff of the First Special Imperial Russian Regiment. He became my lover, and it was a great love on both sides. Massloff was stationed at Mailly (near Rheims) and came to see me whenever he had the chance."

Mata Hari then proceeded to inform Captain Bouchardon on her intention to go to Vittel, and from memory gave a detailed report of the conversation she had on her first meeting with Captain Ladoux.

"Around that time I wanted to go to Vittel, as I used to before the war. Hallaure, a lieutenant of the Dragoons,* whom I had known and who worked at the War Ministry, advised me to go to 282 Boulevard St. Germain. I was very well received by a gentleman in civilian clothes, Captain Ladoux."

Ladoux mentioned to Mata Hari that Vittel was situated in the Zone of the Armies, but Mata Hari explained that she had been there before, and even owed some money to a local doctor.

"It is very difficult for a foreigner to go there," said Ladoux.

"In that case," answered Mata Hari, "I'll go to Rome and Fiuggi, where the waters are equally effective."

"It is not that I want to refuse you a permit, but you'll have to answer certain questions, because you have been reported as being suspected. Aren't you trying to sell rice to the Germans?"

---

* In 1910, when Jean Hallaure did his military service, at the age of twenty-one, Mata Hari spent a few days with him in Dinan, in the Côtes du Nord province of Brittany. While there, she was photographed in Hallaure's uniform as an officer in the 13th *Hussard* regiment. The photograph was taken by the local pharmacist, Monsieur Clément, who, according to his grandson, was "a photo-fanatic."

"I told him the story about Hoedemaker. He laughed and continued his questioning."

"Who was the dark gentleman who traveled with you from Madrid to Hendaye?"

"He was the husband of the Russian dancer Lydia Lopokova [*] with whom I shared a compartment. The next morning he asked for permission to bring his wife her breakfast."

"What happened to you in Hendaye?"

Mata Hari told him, and Ladoux, as she explained to Bouchardon, said that it checked "with the details that had been reported to him." After which, said Mata Hari, Ladoux had asked her about the people she knew in Holland. As always, Mata Hari was quite frank—her love life had no secrets.

"I am the mistress of Colonel Baron van der Capellen."

"How does he feel about France?"

"He is a very elegant gentleman, who only likes what comes from France. He always writes me in French and in this letter which I received from him only this morning, he says: 'Marguerite, you who love France so much . . .'"

This was probably the opening Ladoux had been waiting for, and Mata Hari explained the rest of the conversation in great detail to the avidly listening Bouchardon.

"If you love France that much, you might be able to render us important services. Have you ever thought about it?"

"Yes and no, but one does not offer that kind of services without being asked."

"Would you be willing?"

"I have never given it any detailed thought."

"You must be very expensive?"

"That—definitely!"

"What do you think you are worth?"

"All or nothing. If one gives you the kind of important in-

[*] Later Lady Keynes, wife of John Maynard Keynes, famous English economist, who represented the British Treasury at the Versailles Peace Conference.

formation you expect, it is expensive. If one fails, it is worth nothing."

After that, Mata Hari explained, Ladoux told her to go and see M. Maunoury, who would give her the permit for Vittel. When she was leaving his office, he reminded her once again of what he had asked her: "As to the things I told you about, come and see me when you have made your decision."

Walking down the Boulevard St. Germain, Mata Hari mulled Captain Ladoux's proposal over in her mind, and decided to go and see her old friend Henri de Marguerie, who then told her that "speaking as a Frenchman" he was sure she could be of service to his country.

Fortified by de Marguerie's opinion, Mata Hari the next day went back to Ladoux and said she would accept his proposition.

"Let us see," said Ladoux, "can you go to Germany and Belgium? Have you any suggestion?"

Mata Hari was noncommittal. "I first want to go to Vittel. Let me finish my cure, and I'll come and see you on my return."

In Vittel, where Mata Hari said she arrived on the first of September, "I found that Captain de Massloff had been seriously wounded by poison gas, and moreover he had totally lost the vision in his left eye, and might go blind."

One night de Massloff asked what she would do if that actually happened.

"I'll never leave you, and I'll always remain the same woman for you."

Vadime's next words took Mata Hari by surprise and started her thinking. The Russian captain asked her to marry him.

"I said yes, and said to myself: 'I have it all worked out. I am going to ask Ladoux for enough money so as not to have to deceive Vadime with other men. I'll leave the Marquis de Beaufort, I'll leave Baron van der Capellen, I'll go to Belgium and do whatever the Captain asks me to, after which I am going to sell my furniture and art objects in Holland. Then I'll come back to Paris to the apartment I have rented, Captain Ladoux is going to pay me, I'll marry my lover, and I'll be the happiest woman in the world.' "

On her return to Paris around September 15, Mata Hari once more went to see Captain Ladoux, who complimented her on her excellent behavior in Vittel. He then came to the point: "How do you expect to operate?"

"In Germany or in Belgium?"

"Germany interests us less. You must go to Belgium. But how?"

Mata Hari remembered her lover from the early days after her return from Berlin, the banker van der Schalk, who had introduced her to Wurfbain, the man in whose office she had been insulted by Mr. Soet. Wurfbain lived in Brussels, said Mata Hari, did a lot of business with the Germans, and had promised her a wonderful time if she would accept his invitation.

As she explained to Bouchardon, Wurfbain had painted a beautiful picture of night-long frolics "in the *maisons fermées* of Brussels with Hungarian, German, and Belgian prostitutes." Wurfbain, continued Mata Hari, was the right arm of von Bissing (*Freiherr* Moritz Ferdinand von Bissing, the German Governor-General of Belgium), and Mata Hari explained her plan to Ladoux.

"I'll write Wurfbain, then go to Brussels with the best clothes I have. I'll frequent the German High Command, and that's all I can tell you. I have no intention of staying on for months and getting lost in small operations. I have one big plan in which I want to succeed—one only, and then I'm going to leave."

It was as if Mata Hari had said to Captain Ladoux, the Chief of French Intelligence: "I'll run this war for you—just trust me," but that was, of course, perfectly in line with all her actions; small things had *never* interested her.

The Captain seemed taken by her plan, said Mata Hari, and asked her "for what reason" she was going to serve France, this being a question which he put to every new applicant. Mata Hari had her answer ready.

"I have only one reason—to marry my lover and to be independent."

"The stake is worth it—and what about the money angle?"

"I want a million francs, but you will only have to pay me once you are convinced of the value of my services."

Captain Ladoux answered that it was a lot of money, but they had paid more at times and "if you render us the services which we ask of you, we'll know how to pay for them. We once paid someone two and a half million." He then said that there was something that bothered him. Had Mata Hari ever been in Belgium before? She answered that the last time she was there she went with Baron van der Capellen to the Exhibition of Miniatures.

"Have you never been in Antwerp?"

"No."

"And yet I know you have been there."

"No."

"And if I tell you you have been photographed in Antwerp?"

"Then I would laugh in your face, because neither before, nor during the war have I ever been there."

On leaving Ladoux's office, Mata Hari had some second thoughts about the interview, she told Bouchardon, because she felt sorry not to have asked for an advance for the clothes she was to take to Brussels, so that she might have been able to pay some money to the man who was installing her new apartment on the Avenue Henri Martin. That evening she sent off a letter to Captain Ladoux, pointing out the matter of an advance, and then waited for a phone call from him, for which purpose he would use the name of *Monsieur Dubois*. But no call came through, and Mata Hari, never lax to pursue a plan to the very end, returned to the Boulevard St. Germain. Ladoux was adamant, refused the advance, and explained that he wanted to see results first. Yet he was encouraging: "You'll get your million, don't worry."

He then asked her whether she could write him from Brussels

with secret ink, but Mata Hari felt that "these are tricks that do not go with my character, and moreover I do not intend to stay long in Belgium. But what exactly do you want from me?"

"I can't tell you yet, and shall have to talk to my superiors about it. In the meantime I would suggest that you return quietly to The Hague, and two weeks after your arrival you will receive a visit from someone who will bring your your instructions."

"How shall I recognize him?"

At that moment the Captain smilingly wrote something on a piece of paper which he folded twice. "He handed it to me and said: 'She'll tell you this.'"

"I unfolded the paper and read: 'A.F. 44.'"

Ladoux asked her whether she did not recognize the number, and Mata Hari said that she had never seen it before.

"But I thought it was yours."

Mata Hari was indignant. "Captain, I beg of you once and for all to stop the kind of insinuations that bother me endlessly, and that includes the information you receive from your silly agents and all the rest of that dirty business. If not, I can see that at a certain moment I won't feel like doing anything at all."

"If you could play a really important spy into our hands, whether German, Spanish, or Dutch, that alone would be worth 25,000 francs."

"I can't promise you that. I don't mind giving you information of military or diplomatic value, but I loathe to betray people."

Ladoux then told his new recruit to go and see M. Maunoury at the Préfecture de Police, who would arrange for her visa, and Mata Hari, her passport fixed up for a border crossing into Spain en route to Holland, left for Madrid, and went aboard the *S.S. Hollandia* at Vigo on November 9, 1916.

She now began to tell Bouchardon about the trouble she had encountered on her arrival at Falmouth.

"At Falmouth the ship was boarded by policemen, soldiers, and *suffragettes* who had to search the women. Two of them went so far as to unscrew the mirrors on the wall and to look under the bed. An officer interrogated me while looking me straight in the eye, after which he pulled an amateur photograph out of his pocket of a woman in Spanish dress with a white mantilla, holding a fan in her right hand, while her left hand was on her hip. She looked a little like me, but was shorter than I am, and somewhat stouter. I started to laugh, but my protests did not convince the officer. He said the photograph had been taken at Málaga, although I assured him that I had never been there. I was taken off the ship and was sent to London in the company of two of the *suffragettes*. At Scotland Yard a man entered the room in which I was waiting, and, calling me Clara Benedix,* told me to stand up. I protested as much as I could, but he insisted in calling me by that name. They took me to a little room where all my money and jewelry were taken away from me, after which, during four long days, three men in uniform asked me questions. A Belgian was brought in who talked to me in Dutch, and he had the nerve to tell the others that I spoke with a German accent.

"On the fourth day the three men said: 'We now know that you are not Clara Benedix. You are free to go, but you cannot continue on your trip to Holland. It is a general rule we have adopted in England for all Dutchmen. You have to go back to Spain.'

"On the first of December I went aboard the *Araguya* at Liverpool, and disembarked at Vigo on the sixth, where, at the Hotel Continental, I heard that Clara Benedix was a well-known German spy who spent a lot of time in Spain."

Mata Hari then went on to say that she had obtained this information from Martial Cazeaux, the French secretary of the Dutch consul in Vigo, and how she told him about a Belgian couple aboard the *Hollandia*, of whom the husband, M. Allard, was supposed to spy for Great Britain, while his wife worked for the Germans.

---

* The name is mentioned as "Benedict" in the French secret file. However, as my photostats of the Scotland Yard documents clearly indicate, the woman's name, according to the British Secret Service, was Clara Benedix.

The next day, still in Vigo, this same M. Cazeaux met her in town and asked whether she would like to go to Austria "for the Russians."

"I asked for one million one hundred thousand francs," Mata Hari told Captain Bouchardon, adding that she had mentioned that amount "more or less as a joke." Cazeaux found it expensive, but Mata Hari told him that if she "could save a hundred thousand men, it is worth ten francs a head, isn't it?" M. Cazeaux, whose position in this transaction was never fully explained by Mata Hari, said that "the Russians were also talking to the Americans, who were doing it for less," but she should go on to Madrid, where someone bringing one half of Cazeaux's visiting card—giving the other half to Mata Hari—would come to see her.

Chapter 18

I⊤ had been a tiring day, and both Mata Hari and Captain Bouchardon, as well as the hard-writing Sergeant Baudouin, needed a rest. Yet a certain line already started to take shape in Bouchardon's mind, as he explained in his memoirs later on.

The reports supplied by Ladoux's agents on Mata Hari's behavior in Vittel were totally sterile of any espionage activities. She had been there for two weeks only, and most of this time, according to all information available to Bouchardon, was spent with Vadime de Massloff. Yet Bouchardon came to the following conclusion as to what his victim had *really* done:

"In Vittel, where she had gone for the fake purpose of taking a cure, she continued to behave in the same way—with her head on the pillow." And "the same way," as Bouchardon had explained in a previous paragraph, was to sleep with countless men in uniform, from whom she then obviously extracted information which she supplied to the Germans.

But now, in prison, Mata Hari hardly was able to sleep at all. The strain of prison life was beginning to take hold of her, and on a Tuesday, in desperation, she wrote the following letter to Bouchardon:

Mon Capitaine,

My suffering is too terrible. My head cannot bear it any longer. Let me go back to my country. I know *nothing* about your war, and I have never known anything more than what was written in the newspapers. I have asked *no one* and *nowhere* for information. What more do you want me to say?

I repeat for the hundredth time that I have not done any espionage in France, and that I shall never do so. Do not break my health—I am so weak through life in this cell and on account of the lack of food. What purpose does it all serve?

My suffering must not last any longer. Let me go, I beg of you.

And Mata Hari signed her letter with her prison number: "Respectfully yours, M.G. Zelle 721 44625."

Two weeks went by before Mata Hari was taken out of the Saint Lazare prison to make a third trip to the center of Paris, where Bouchardon and his trusted *greffier* were waiting for her. It was now February 28, and as if not fourteen days but fourteen minutes had gone by, Mata Hari continued her endless tale of adventures—Bouchardon listening stoically as ever.

In Madrid she had been waiting in vain for any message from M. Cazeaux, but nobody turned up with the other half of the secretary's visiting card. Mata Hari had taken advantage of her stay in the Spanish capital to send a long letter to Captain Ladoux, in which she brought him up to date with the failure of her mission, and, not having been able to reach either Belgium or Holland, asked what she was to do next. She also wrote to

Anna Lintjens in The Hague, requesting her to tell Baron van der Capellen not to worry. After five days she sent a telegram to Vigo, asking Monsieur Cazeaux whether she should wait still longer, because she wanted to go to Paris. The answer came by mail, and she was told that "the Russian has gone to Switzerland" and would she please inform Monsieur Cazeaux about her Paris address.

Mata Hari, who was not accustomed to twiddle her thumbs for long, had already started to think about how to make use of her free time, and explained those thoughts to Captain Bouchardon: "Waiting for the answers from Paris and Vigo, I said to myself: 'What's keeping me from getting in touch with the Germans? I could build up some friendly relations with them that might lead to something.' If at that moment I would have found a way to sleep with the German ambassador himself, I would have done it. It is only in doing big things that you get somewhere—not by interrogating small-fry."

Mata Hari decided to act at once. She asked the hotel porter for the diplomatic yearbook, saying she was looking for the name of someone at the Dutch Legation, but instead turned to the page of the German embassy. There she noticed the name of the Military Attaché, a certain Captain von Kalle, and, she told Bouchardon, "It was only later that I found out that he had been promoted to Major." She "engraved" his name and address securely on her mind ("somewhere at 23 Rue Castellana or thereabouts") and was ready for battle.

"'We'll take the bull by the horns,' I said to myself. 'If it fails, nothing is lost, and if it succeeds, so much the better.'"

It sounded typical of Mata Hari, like the decision to start dancing and convince the world it was the real thing—but Captain Bouchardon must have begun to perk his ears, for the story now began to touch upon forbidden territory—the Germans.

That same day she wrote to von Kalle, informing him that she would like to see him, and asked when it would be convenient for him to receive her. Von Kalle's answer came the following day by messenger: "Madame, I do not have the honor to know you, but can see you tomorrow, Saturday, at three o'clock."

She was there at the indicated hour, and was introduced into the room where von Kalle was working.

"Madame," he said, "I do not know why you honor me with this visit. I am not in the habit of receiving women who might be sent to us by our enemies, but I noticed that was not true in your case."

"How did you discover that?" she asked with a smile.

"Because for at least ten months now I have been promoted to major, and our enemy's agents are fully aware of it. When you wrote me you must have used an old yearbook. I notice from your card that you are Dutch. Do you speak German?"

"Perfectly, as well as French."

"Why did you want to see me?"

"I have been under arrest for four days in England, having been taken for a German woman traveling with false Dutch papers. They insisted I was a certain Clara Benedix. What does it all mean?"

"You speak excellent German. How come?"

"I lived for three years in Berlin."

"You must know German officers?"

"A good many."

"Can you name some of them?"

Mata Hari mentioned several, and added that she had been the mistress of Alfred Kiepert. Von Kalle was informed about the liaison, and told Mata Hari that he had seen her at dinner at the Carlton Hotel, and knew about her accompanying Kiepert to the Silesia maneuvers. "So *you* are the woman he was so jealous of," he added.

He then explained that he knew nothing about her adventures at Falmouth, nor about Clara Benedix, because such matters were taken care of by Baron von Roland in Barcelona.

"The conversation having taken a rather pleasant turn, von Kalle offered me a cigarette and we talked about the Madrid high society. I was my most charming self. I played with my feet, and did everything a woman does when she wants to make a man fall for her—and I knew that von Kalle had fallen. At a certain moment he said, comfortably sitting back in his chair: 'I'm tired. I am busy with the preparation for a landing of German and Turkish soldiers from a submarine on the coast of Morocco, in the French Zone. It takes all my time.'"

Having left von Kalle shortly afterwards, Mata Hari confided her quite sensational news that evening to Captain Ladoux in a letter. She wrote him about the submarine along the Morocco coast, and about Baron von Roland being the head of the German espionage services in Barcelona. And she added: "I am waiting for your instructions; I can do whatever I want with my German."

The next evening, which was Sunday, Mata Hari had been invited to dinner by one of the attachés at the Dutch Legation, Mr. G. de With. Mata Hari met her host at the Palace Hotel, where he introduced her to an elderly gentleman "who had the ribbon of the Legion of Honor in his lapel, and who limped a bit." He was Colonel Denvignes, the French Military Attaché.

The evening after that, at the occasion of a gala dinner at the Ritz Hotel, Mata Hari was again invited by Mr. de With. Colonel Denvignes, who had been sitting at a different table, met her after dinner in the lobby and complimented Mata Hari for her ravishing dress. According to Mata Hari, continuing to unfold her involvement with the Madrid espionage circles to the eagerly listening Captain Bouchardon, Colonel Denvignes had said: "Madame, I have never seen anything as harmonious as your last night's entry at the Palace Hotel."

"He then sat down next to me on a bench and acted most amorously, so much so that it made me feel uncomfortable. From time to time I danced with the Dutch attachés, but on my return the Colonel would continue the conversation. At a certain moment he asked me where I came from, and I told him about the trouble I had had on my trip. He then asked what I was doing in Madrid. I said with a smile: '*Mon Colonel,* you do not have to worry, I am on your side.'"

"He shook me by the hand, and I went on: 'If I had known you one day earlier, I would not have taken the trouble to send my information to Paris, but would have handed the letter to you personally, and it would have arrived faster.'

" 'What information?'

"I told him all I knew, and also mentioned the name of von Kalle, and that I had found him a bit tired, but soft as a lamb. The Colonel said that the last time he had seen him, he too had the impression that he looked a bit pale."

The next day Mata Hari had lunch with a Spanish friend of hers, Mr. Diego de Leon, for whom at one time she had tried to sell some old masters in Paris, and who had promised her an eighteen-thousand-francs commission if the deal would come off. Mr. Diego de Leon having left her after lunch, Mata Hari went into the reading room of the Ritz Hotel, where the Colonel was waiting for her, "staging practically a scene of jealousy." He wanted to know with whom she had had lunch, and then said: "I've been thinking about our last night's conversation. Couldn't you find out where those officers and men have disembarked in Morocco?"

Mata Hari told him that "one could not rush things like that," but the colonel insisted.

"So I went back to von Kalle under the pretext of having forgotten to ask him something, and said: 'I intend to return to Holland via Switzerland and Germany. I know they are very strict at the German frontier, so I wonder whether you could help me to facilitate that part of the journey.'"

Von Kalle said he was sorry, but he could not do a thing, and then offered her a cigarette.

"I played the same game as on my previous visit, and before long I noticed that von Kalle became excited and rather daring. I said softly, blowing smoke into his face: 'And—still tired? Still weak? Still thinking about business?'"

" 'Don't even mention it,' he said, 'I won't feel at ease till the whole thing is finished.'

" 'But it must be quite a job to land people from a submarine on the coast of Morocco—where and how did you manage to do *that?*'

" 'Beautiful women should not ask too many questions,' " said von Kalle.

Mata Hari felt that she had been going too fast and turned the conversation to the great many photographs in his office—then left. Later that day Colonel Denvignes arrived to get the answer to his question. She told him that he had sent her "on a little boy's errand, and if I had not been intelligent, the whole matter would have been lost," and also advised him that "another time it will be better to let me do it my own way."

"The next day the Colonel came back after lunch and once again after dinner, and continued his amorous advances quite in public. The day after that he showed up once more, and said: 'I am very busy and have to accompany General Lyautey to Paris.' He asked me for my little bouquet of violets and my handkerchief as souvenirs, and wondered whether he could do anything for me in Paris."

"A lot," Mata Hari had answered. "You can go and see Captain Ladoux and his chief. Explain to them what kind of woman they are dealing with, and that they should be kinder to me and less secretive."

The Colonel promised to do so and said she could write him via the embassy, and if necessary could see his colleague the Marquis de Paladines. When Mata Hari told him that she had the intention of going to Paris soon herself, he asked her to phone him at the Hotel d'Orsay, and they would have dinner together.

Captain Bouchardon had been listening quietly, and now took an intercepted letter from his file, written by Mata Hari to a friend, telling him about the amorous advances of Colonel Denvignes: "The Colonel brought me a small bouquet of violets and asked me to wear them between my breasts for a whole day, saying that he would come and get them in the evening. He also wanted a ribbon of my corset, which he would pull out himself in the reading room of the hotel when we would be alone. He played a lover's game like a young man."

The letter, which was certainly not sent by Mata Hari in order to be intercepted, did convince Captain Bouchardon about the young man's fancy of the French Military Attaché in Madrid. Yet the whole meeting between Mata Hari and the French Colonel, because it fitted better into the final picture Bouchardon was to present about his spy, was completely reversed and became the opposite of what it actually had been.

"Mata Hari, audacious in all her actions," Bouchardon was to write in 1953,* "succeeded in approaching our Military Attaché, General Denvignes. She made him believe that she was in the service of France and brought him certain information which, she said, she had been clever enough to obtain from von Kalle during various visits to him. That information was, it is hardly necessary to say, outdated and without any value whatever, but the General, who had been totally subjugated by the *coquetteries* of the beautiful damsel, did not consider them as such. Having fallen in love like a second lieutenant, there was no end to his eulogizing of the new recruit."

Bouchardon's case was slowly taking shape.

"The day after the departure of General Lyautey and Colonel Denvignes," Mata Hari went on, "von Kalle sent me a letter at the hotel, asking whether I would like to come and have tea with him that same afternoon at three o'clock. I found him more distant—as if he had been informed about my meetings with the Colonel."

She soon found out *why* there had been a change of attitude on his part. Von Kalle told her that the French were sending

* Bouchardon actually wrote his memoirs in 1948. He died in 1950, and his daughter finally had the memoirs published in 1953.

radio messages all over, inquiring about the German landings in Morocco.

"They can easily have obtained that information from someone else," said Mata Hari, "and moreover, how do you know?"

"We know their code."

Mata Hari felt that she was losing her game and redoubled her coquettish enticements. But she understood that von Kalle had fairly well seen through her when he said: "One should forgive a lot to beautiful women like you, but if they knew in Berlin that the information came from me, there would be hell to pay."

"Seeing that he had become more submissive again," said Mata Hari to Bouchardon, "I decided to push things a bit. 'After all,' I said to myself, 'let's get it over with'—and I let him do what he wanted to do."

"Once his effusion was a thing of the past, he started off on a different subject." Mata Hari explained to the Captain that von Kalle had discussed the behavior of some of the men in the German army, which he said was cruel. Mata Hari had felt her way through the conversation, putting in a good word for the courage of the Germans. The French, von Kalle had said, were also courageous, especially some of their pilots. One of them had been landing spies behind the German lines lately, and he had picked them up again afterwards. But one of these days, von Kalle hinted, they would know all the details, because the Germans had excellently informed spies of their own in France.

Mata Hari asked him how they were able to get their information back to Germany, and when von Kalle said that there were many ways, she told him that she doubted this, because she herself had passed across many frontiers, and the investigation and checking of luggage and persons was such that it would be difficult to smuggle a pin across. "In England," she said, "they even checked the ribbons of my underwear."

Von Kalle put her straight; the Germans did not use women like *her,* but dirty people who could transport secret inks hidden under their nails or in their ears.

That evening Mata Hari wrote a twelve-page letter to Colonel Denvignes, telling him all about the French pilot, the secret inks and the fact that the Germans had discovered the code of the French radio signals. After which, having nothing more to do in Madrid, she decided to make preparations for her trip to Paris.

Two days later, on March 1, Mata Hari and Captain Bouchardon found themselves once more face to face. Continuing the story of her peregrination, she came to the episode where the letter from Spanish Senator Junoy had made her terribly angry, because someone had not only tried to bring their friendly relationship to an end, but had also attempted to blacken her behind her back. The Senator's reaction, said Mata Hari, had been that of a Spanish gentleman—as Junoy himself had indicated in his letter: "And that is," he had written, "why we warn you."

Her decision to leave for Paris now precipitated by the backhanded action of some French agent, Mata Hari left Madrid "on January 2, and arrived in Paris on the fourth." She had been quite surprised by Captain Ladoux's silence, she told Bouchardon, but since Colonel Denvignes was his superior in rank, she was sure that he had straightened things out.

Once in Paris and in her hotel room at the Plaza on the Avenue Montaigne, Mata Hari telephoned the Colonel at the Hotel d'Orsay. No one knew him there, nor at the Ministry of War, where she telephoned next.

"Tired of the run-around," said Mata Hari, "I dressed and went to 282 Boulevard Saint Germain, where an officer who was even taller than I am told me that the Colonel was leaving that same evening for Madrid."

Since Mata Hari was definitely set on seeing him, she went to the Gare d'Orsay at nine o'clock, only to be told that no one was allowed on the platform. She thereupon wrote a note for the Colonel, which she requested the employee at the office of the *Wagons Lits* to give to him. In it, she said that she absolutely *had* to see him, and would he please stand at the window of his compartment at the Gare d'Austerlitz, where the train would make a stop before leaving Paris. She then bought a platform ticket, but only found the Colonel after she had asked the sleeping car conductor to call him. The Colonel seemed like a different person from the one she had known in Madrid.

"Charming of you to leave like that, Colonel," said Mata Hari, "without even telling me. And our business? Did you see Captain Ladoux?"

"The Colonel," said Mata Hari to Bouchardon, "answered in a very tiny voice. 'I have seen him,' he said, 'but I saw more of his superior, Colonel Goubet. He told me that your information was most interesting and that you were an intelligent woman.'

" 'Is that all?'

" 'He also asked me whether I knew about your connections, and I said that I did not.'

" 'Why did you lie?'

"All the Colonel could answer to that was to say, in a plaintive little voice: 'Mon petit, mon petit.'

"That was all, for the train left and I remained on the platform in a kind of stupor.

"The following day I went to see Captain Ladoux, but the appointment slip on which I had put down my name came back with the word 'absent' written across it. The next day, after having waited for about an hour, I was given a pass for the following evening.

"I came back at the indicated time, which was six o'clock, and found the captain most bizarre. He was not smiling like the other times and seemed to be bothered about something. I asked him whether he had seen Denvignes and whether the Colonel had told him everything he had promised me to. He answered that he had hardly seen him, and that he had been told nothing—but he was surprised that I had gone to the French embassy in Madrid.

"I received a letter which smacks of blackmail—the letter from the Spanish senator," Mata Hari had said, "and when there is something I don't understand, I knock on any door."

She then explained to Captain Bouchardon how she had told the contents of the Senator's letter to Ladoux, who advised her not to forget that "she did not know him, and he did not know her." And Ladoux had added that it certainly was not *his* office which had sent the compromising letter to the senator, and if some subaltern agent had acted on his own, he would be sent to the front.

"That doesn't interest me in the least, but I believe that you have no reason whatever to have my work spoiled by the intervention of some little agent. If a French agent really sees something he does not like, let him go to the French embassy with his complaint, and not to a Spanish senator." Mata Hari was angry by now. "And besides that, I am very surprised by the kind of reception I get from you. Is this my thanks for the services I have rendered you?"

"What services? The information on Baron von Roland and the submarine?"

"You seem to forget about the radio code, the pilot, and the secret ink."

"This is the first time I hear about that."

"You mean the Colonel has not mentioned it to you?"

"I told you before that I have hardly seen him. You mean they know the code of our radio messages? The Military Attaché must have made fun of you."

"Even if there is only one chance in a hundred that my information is right, then it will be worthwhile to check on it."

"Of course! But I'm absolutely stupefied!"

"So am I. But I don't want to stay here any longer and want to go home. I have no more money to stay on in Paris."

"Stay another few days," said Captain Ladoux, "I'll ask Madrid to send me a report."

Going back to the hotel, Mata Hari picked up Senator Junoy's letter and dropped it at Ladoux's office. In the meantime she noticed that at the Plaza all her movements were closely followed by agents, who questioned the servants. When she telephoned, they listened behind the door. One time she received a letter which had been opened.

"By January 15, I sent a long letter to Captain Ladoux in which I asked him what he wanted of me. 'I'll do anything you want,' I said, 'I am not asking for any secret, I do not want to know your agents, I am an international woman—do not ask me how I want to work, but do not have my work upset either by your secret agents who cannot understand me. The fact that I want to be paid is only natural, but I want to leave.'

"With that letter I went to see Maître Clunet, who did not criticize the substance of it, but felt that the tone was a bit strong. Especially the word 'paid' shocked him. I said that as long as I was not ashamed to accept money, I did not have to be ashamed to say so—and I posted the letter myself on the Boulevard Haussmann.

"I got no answer, and went to M. Maunoury's office to ask him to get permission from Captain Ladoux to leave for Switzerland. It was my intention to go and see the German Military Attaché in Berne, to play the same game with him as I had played with von Kalle, and to bring all the information I could get to the French embassy. Monsieur Maunoury said that Captain Ladoux was on the Riviera and would not be back for three weeks, and without his permission he could not give me an exit visa.

"About that time I received a letter from Baron van der Capellen, informing me that he had sent me money once again, but that he could not continue to keep my house in The Hague going if I did not come back. And simultaneously I had a letter from my maid in which she advised me to come home, because the Colonel was longing for me very much. By now I had had enough of everything and went to the Foreign Visitors' Bureau, saying that I wanted to return to Holland via Switzerland. Ten days went by without any answer. On the twelfth of February I went back to the same office, where I was told that my papers had not yet arrived, and on the morning of the thirteenth I was arrested. That's all.

"Before I finish I want to protest once again. I have never spied against France, nor have I ever tried to. I have never written any letter which I should not have written. I have never asked any of my friends for information which did not concern me, and I have never gone to any place I was not supposed to go to. My original intention was to stay in France for only three months. At that time I only thought of my lovers. Any idea of espionage was alien to me. Only circumstances decided differently."

It had been a long speech, and Captain Bouchardon was to summarize those first four hearings in a single fairly cynical paragraph in his book: "During those four *interrogations* Mata Hari affirmed and reaffirmed the purity of her acts and of her intentions as to France. She in the service of the Germans! What a preposterous idea! It was really in *our* interest that she had gone to see von Kalle. Remembering that she had been one of the greatest courtesans of her time, she had captivated both the mind and the senses of that military attaché. After which it had been very simple to get information out of him, which she then brought to General Denvignes."

There was one statement in Mata Hari's testimony which escaped Captain Bouchardon's attention as much as it escaped Ladoux's, most likely because once again it did not fit into the structure of the case as he wanted it to develop: Mata Hari's actions were certainly not guided by the one prerequisite that should be among a spy's foremost qualities—the sense of secrecy. Having first told M. de Marguerie about becoming a spy, she now mentioned having gone for further advice to Maître Clunet, who, although an old and trusted friend, had nothing to do with the Foreign Service. And, since she did not mention any surprise on Maître Clunet's part when telling the story to Captain Bouchardon, it was likely that this was not the first time she had told the lawyer about her association with the French Secret Service.

Mata Hari having finished at long last, it was now Captain Bouchardon's turn. All he wanted to know for that day was where the five thousand francs had come from which she had received, via the Comptoir d'Escompte, at the Dutch consulate.

"The five thousand francs came from Baron van der Capellen," said Mata Hari. "The Dutch consul telephoned me on the fifteenth of January and said, 'The money has arrived; you can come and get it whenever you want.' I went to the consulate on the sixteenth and without further ado M. Bunge gave me five bills of one thousand francs each. That money certainly came from Baron van der Capellen, whom I had asked for it from both London and Madrid."

There was one last question: How and where had she met Dutch Consul Bunge? Mata Hari had her facts and dates straight: "I have met M. Bunge during my first trip back to Holland via Lisbon."

(The date checks with Mr. Bunge's movements, about which I was informed by the archives section of the Netherlands Ministry of Foreign Affairs. Mr. Otto David Eduard Bunge had been in the Dutch consular service since 1910, and had spent a year and a half in San Francisco, till December 4, 1915. Then, before taking up his post in Paris, he returned for a brief period to Holland. Having come home through the Panama Canal on a Dutch ship which made stops in Portugal and Spain, Mr. Bunge must have been aboard when, in January 1916, Mata Hari embarked in Lisbon with her ten packing cases full of household goods.)

On March 9, when the next hearing was supposed to take place, Mata Hari did not feel well and sent a letter to Captain Bouchardon asking him please to postpone the appointment: "Would you kindly put off the hearing till next Monday? I feel too sick to get up. Maybe I will feel better in a few days."

On the twelfth the postponed hearing did take place. Captain Bouchardon was still trying to feel his way around and, having heard Mata Hari's side of the developments, now came to the examination of various documents that had been found in her room at the time of her arrest. All visiting cards, of which Mata Hari had been such an avid collector, were bundled together on a piece of string. The names of a good many of the men whom Mata Hari had counted among her friends were by now known to the captain, but others had not been mentioned during the preceding four sessions.

Bouchardon picked up a first card, belonging to a certain Chief Sergeant of Cavalry George Jouis, stationed at the Aviation Training School at Cazeau in the Gironde province. According to Mata Hari she had met him on the platform of the Austerlitz station on the evening when she went to see Colonel Denvignes. Sergeant Jouis had asked her whether she would be kind enough to be his army godmother—sending him gifts to the front.

Another card belonged to Captain Henri des Maraudes, whom Mata Hari identified as a prewar friend who sometimes had accompanied her when she went riding in the Bois de Boulogne.

Card number three mentioned the name of a Russian Lieutenant Colonel, Patz-Pomarnatzky. She had met him in the dining car of the train between Bordeaux and Paris on her return from Spain.

Lieutenant Henri Mège, the next candidate, had stopped Mata Hari in the street one day, when she left Captain Ladoux's office. He had asked her for a date, but the meeting finished innocently with a cup of tea at the Plaza Hotel.

A certain Pierre Arrienceaux, living in Hendaye, was an officer whose duty it was to check the passengers in the train at that frontier post. He too wanted to meet her later, but again nothing came of it, Mata Hari said.

Captain Bouchardon then took a parcel of letters, most of which were written by Vadime de Massloff. Others came from a British captain by the name of Kingsell. They had met at the Savoy Hotel in London after she had been freed from Scotland Yard, explained Mata Hari, and the Britisher had been rather insistent.

Three letters signed E. W. de Jong were sent to her, she said, by a Dutch newspaperman who wanted an interview about her adventure at Falmouth. She had refused.

(Egbert Willem de Jong had been London correspondent for the Amsterdam newspaper *Algemeen Handelsblad* all during the war. It was probably Mata Hari's letter in which she declined to grant him an interview which Mr. de Jong had shown to the Netherlands Minister in London, and which the latter had mentioned to The Hague when he referred to his having been informed "from a private letter" which he "most confidentially" had been given to read, that she "wanted to avoid everything which might spread the knowledge of her adventure.")

The last letter was simply signed "Pierre." That was the same Pierre Arrienceaux who had wanted to date her in Hendaye, but she had never answered him because the tone of his letter was "too ordinary."

Chapter 19

CAPTAIN BOUCHARDON now thought it would be a good idea to give Mata Hari some time to reflect on what she had told him thus far. She had been in jail for exactly one month, and had related her side of the story. It had been a straight tale of travel, love, love-making and espionage-intrigue, out of which international mélange the Captain had already picked certain items which fitted into his scheme and job, which was the catching of spies. For the next four weeks Bouchardon did not ask for his suspect. She had nothing to do but stay in her cell, take her daily walk in the prison courtyard, talk to her lawyer, the doctors, the priest and the minister, and think.

Her thinking was greatly concerned with Vadime de Massloff, from whom she had had no news since she was arrested. The Russian officer, like Baron van der Capellen and so many other people, had no idea where she was. Her only contact with the outside was via Captain Bouchardon and Maître Clunet, and it was the former who finally was able to give her some news of her Russian lover: he had been severely wounded, and had written her a letter in which he reproached her for having forgotten him. The letter had been delivered to Captain Bouchardon, who had communicated its contents to Mata Hari. And thus her thinking during that month of rest from interrogations was suddenly focused on Vadime. In desperation she sent a letter to Bouchardon:

I thank you for the news you have given me of Captain de Massloff. I am terribly worried and am constantly crying. Please be good enough to try the Hospital at Epernay. I beg of you. I suffer so much thinking that he is perhaps dead and that I was not near him. And he even thought that I had forgotten him. You have no idea how I suffer. Please let me out of here, I cannot stand it any longer. . . .

But there was not a chance of setting Mata Hari free, and on April 12, she was once again brought to the Chancellerie, where Bouchardon now started the attack.

"Till now," he said, "we have let you talk without interrupting you, and you have had every possibility to develop your system of defense in the smallest details. We now would like you to answer some questions. The first one is this: When for the first time you went to our office of counterintelligence at 282 Boulevard Saint Germain, weren't you a German spy?"

Mata Hari was surprised. "But of course not, Captain—and moreover, when I went to the Boulevard Saint Germain, I went there to try and get a permit to go to Vittel."

Bouchardon now started to tie in Mata Hari's love life with what he was sure in his own mind were her spying activities: "Our question should not surprise you. Didn't you say yourself that you were an 'international woman' and didn't you admit that shortly before the war you had intimate relations with Lieutenant Alfred Kiepert of the eleventh Regiment of Hussars at Crefeld?"

"The fact that I have had relations with certain people in no way implies that I have done espionage work. I have never done any espionage for Germany, nor for any other country, with the exception of France. As a professional dancer I certainly could be in touch with people in Berlin without any of the suspicious motives which you seem to attach to it. And moreover, I gave you the names of those various people myself."

There was little else of importance that day, one of the shortest among the hearings. Before she was taken back to prison, the subject of the contents of her handbag and the various articles found in her room was brought up, and Mata Hari put Captain Bouchardon straight as to the use of oxycyanide of mercury; it was not to write with, but simply served to counter the after-effects of coition.

Again there was an interlude of several weeks, during which Bouchardon let Mata Hari's stories crystallize in his somewhat one-track mind. Every German she had been in contact with became a new link in the chain of mostly imagined evidence on which he was trying to convict her. He forgot, or feigned to forget, that his prisoner had really known many of these people through the years and that she could have talked to them on a great many subjects. Yet he was convinced, or became convinced, that every time she talked to a Frenchman it was only to obtain information—and every time she talked to a German, it was either to hand over this information, or to receive new orders.

Having been in prison for two months, Mata Hari now finally received permission to contact the outer world, but only via the local Netherlands Legation. Thus on April 16, 1917, she wrote the afore-mentioned letter to the consulate, which was received on the twenty-second:

I beg of you to be good enough to help me. For the last six weeks I have been imprisoned in Saint Lazare, accused of espionage, which I have not done.

Please do whatever you can for me, and I shall be most grateful. If you can advise my maid without mentioning my arrest, but only in telling her that I am having difficulties in leaving France and that above all she should not worry, then please do write this letter for me. Name and address are Anna Lintjens, Nieuwe Uitleg 16, The Hague. I assure you that I am half crazy with grief. Please also ask Count van Limburg Styrum, the secretary of our Legation, to do whatever he can for me. He knows me and knows about my close friends in The Hague.

The letter was signed Marguerite Zelle McLeod–Mata Hari, and contains one wrong statement, probably due to the monotony of prison life. On April 16, when she wrote the letter, she had not been in jail for six weeks, but nine.

While wondering how to proceed, Captain Bouchardon received some new information from the War Ministry, which, as far as he was concerned, decided the case once and for all. As he was to write in his book: * "I brought her back time and again to the one document which constituted her condemnation to death."

This is, in Bouchardon's own words, what happened and how he proceeded: "The investigation was stalled, when on April 21, the War Ministry added to the file the text of the intercepted telegrams which had been exchanged between von Kalle and Germany between December 13, 1916, and March 8, 1917." (Bouchardon does not indicate why the War Ministry, having this information available, waited for over six weeks to hand it to the one person who should have been informed about it from the very beginning: Captain Bouchardon. The delay was prob-

* Pierre Bouchardon, *Souvenirs*, published by Albin Michel, Paris, 1953.

ably due to the French War Ministry's reluctance to hand over vital intelligence information even to a military investigator, since in doing so the accused, if he were a real spy, might find an opportunity to inform his superiors in enemy country about the secrets obtained by the government of his captors. In our case, Mata Hari, if she were indeed the spy the French thought she was, might have tried to inform the Germans, via some accomplice, of the fact that the French had broken the German code.)

To Bouchardon the case suddenly became crystal clear. "Margareth-Gertrude Zelle had furnished von Kalle with a whole series of information. What information? I do not believe that I am authorized to reveal it, inasmuch as I am still bound by professional secrecy. All I can say is that it was considered by our services, and especially by Supreme Headquarters, to contain a part of important truth. It confirmed, in any case, that the spy had been in touch with a number of officers and that she had cleverly been able to ask them certain perfidious questions. At the same time her association with other circles had enabled her to get information on our political situation."

What indeed was the information which Bouchardon declared not to be allowed to reveal in 1953 (or in 1948 when he wrote it), this information which Supreme Headquarters had declared to contain "a part" of true facts? It dealt with the already mentioned spring offensive of 1917, which everybody knew would be coming anyhow, and it dealt with the talks between Briand and Princess Marie Bonaparte concerning the King of Greece.

And thirty-one years after Captain Bouchardon had finished with the Mata Hari case, he felt that he could make only one positive statement about the document that condemned her to death: "*in any case* she had been able to ask certain perfidious questions." He is therefore doubtful about all the rest. And while the information Mata Hari gave von Kalle was important enough to shoot her, the information the French got on the submarine off Morocco and the German breaking of the French radio code was "outdated" and of no importance.

"On May 1," Bouchardon continues in his book, "I decided to put my cards on the table. And since I had to play a careful game, I closed my door to everyone, spreading the news that I had gone to the prison in Fresnes for some hearing. Thus while the press was looking for me elsewhere, I shut myself with my *greffier* and Mata Hari inside a sort of cave where the convicting evidence of the Third War Council was heaped up. It was an emotional duel, but for once the spy defended herself badly. Great actors do have such moments of weakness. Did not she even go so far as to insinuate that von Kalle had been paying the staff of the Hotel Ritz and had ordered someone to open her mail in order to find out about the people she corresponded with?"

Captain Bouchardon's horrified amazement about such treacherous acts on the part of the Chief of German Espionage in Madrid seems rather childish. It can be accepted for sure that all warring embassies in Madrid were paying the staffs of the hotels in town to spy on anyone who checked in and out—and that included the French embassy as well as the German.

But Captain Bouchardon had a job to do, and he did it, "notwithstanding she used every trick in the book: cries, tears, smiles, indignation, invective." Her reaction to his treatment was violent, he was to write: "'How can you be so without pity,' she said while stamping her feet, 'to torture a poor woman like that and ask her such vile questions!'"

On May 1, Bouchardon faced his opponent in a different kind of mood. He now had all the trumps in his hands—according to his own theory. He started that day with the preliminary question: "You have mentioned in one of our former hearings that you were not able to tell von Kalle anything military or political of importance, because you had left France forty-three days before. We would like to tell you that even after forty-three days some information can still be precious."

"I repeat that I did not go and see von Kalle on my own account. I did not even know his name and rank, and I had no specific idea in mind. Captain Ladoux had asked me to prove my honesty and capability. Finding myself back in Madrid after my Falmouth adventure, and receiving no instructions whatever, I said to myself, 'If I go ahead on my own and take up contact with the Germans, the Captain will pay me when I get back to Paris.'

"I did not try to hide anything, for I kept Captain Ladoux informed by post. Although I may not have mentioned the Military Attaché by name, I did tell him that I had been in touch with a highly placed person at the German embassy. On top of that I told everything to Colonel Denvignes and I brought him three pieces of important news. But I now presume that while the Colonel did mention this information when he got to Paris, he did so without indicating from whom he got it. If the French were dissatisfied with my services, they only had to refuse my visa for re-entry into France when I wanted to come back. That would have been more correct."

Now Bouchardon played his big trump—the one he considered her death warrant: "For the last few days we have had the material proof in our file that you have played the most audacious comedy with our counterespionage services and with ourselves. You are agent number H-21 belonging to the Central Information Bureau in Cologne, sent to France for the second time in March 1916; you have feigned to accept the offer from Captain Ladoux and to accomplish a trip to Belgium on his behalf. During the month of November 1916 you received in Paris the amount of five thousand francs, coming from Germany. And finally, you have furnished von Kalle with complete information on a certain number of subjects of political, diplomatic, and military importance."

Mata Hari was far from beaten by these revelations: "You are making the same kind of mistake as Captain Ladoux when he insisted that I was agent AF-44 from Antwerp, or the British, who insisted that I was Clara Benedix. You take me for someone else. There must be confusion somewhere. Captain Ladoux and the British also thought that they had the proof in hand, but the evidence showed them differently. And I repeat once again that I did not go to Boulevard Saint Germain on my own account."

"Well, then—if we must convince you, I would like you to know that we have the complete text of a message which von Kalle sent to Berlin on December 13, and which arrived at its destination. What did von Kalle say? 'Agent H-21 belonging to the Central Information Bureau in Cologne, who was sent to France for the second time in March, has arrived here. She has feigned to accept the services of the French Espionage Bureau and to carry out a trial mission to Belgium on their account. She wanted to go from Spain to Holland aboard the *Hollandia* but was arrested in Falmouth on the eleventh of November because she was mistaken for someone else. Once the mistake was recognized, she was sent back to Spain because the British continued to consider her suspect.' That is you, isn't it? You have given us enough details on your mishap in England to be sure about the identification, and if that person is you, then you are also agent H-21. Don't try and tell us that you have been able to fool von Kalle about your earlier affiliation with the German espionage service and about your imaginary inscription number, for von Kalle did not fail to obtain his proper information at the right places. On the twenty-third of December 1916 he received the order to pay H-21 three thousand francs. You had asked ten thousand for your information. What information did you give von Kalle which was well enough appreciated in Berlin to pay you, if not ten thousand, just the same three thousand francs? For von Kalle paid you thirty-five hundred pesetas and advised Berlin accordingly on December 26, 1916."

"Spain is full of German agents," said Mata Hari, "and there can be mistakes in any telegram. Maybe von Kalle wanted to find out who I was and what kind of people I knew. He may have employed members of the staff at the Ritz Hotel to go through my mail and to get information on me. Moreover I would like to point out that a certain Mademoiselle Blume was also arrested on the *Hollandia,* a German woman who came from Holland. That arrest did not take place on the trip *I* made, but at some other time."

"There is no possibility of any confusion of personalities, for agent H-21 told von Kalle that her maid lives in Holland and that her name was Anna Lintjens."

"Von Kalle may say whatever he wants to. He may have obtained information from my telegram, the way I told you. When I send a telegram, I give it to the hotel porter, without going to the post office myself. In any case, I am not agent H-21. Von Kalle did not pay me a penny and the five thousand francs which I received in November 1916, as well as those which I got in January 1917, came from my lover, Baron van der Capellen."

"You might as well stop telling us your stories about Baron van der Capellen—we now *know* in which way and through whose intermediary you received your money from the German espionage service. For we have two more communications from von Kalle, dated December 26 and 28, 1916. The first one says: 'H-21 will request by telegram via the Dutch consul in Paris that a further amount be paid to her maid in Roermond and wants you to advise Consul Krämer in Amsterdam about same.' In the second telegram he says: 'H-21 will arrive in Paris tomorrow. She requests that an amount of 5000 francs be sent to her immediately at the Comptoir d'Escompte in Paris through the intermediary of Consul Krämer in Amsterdam and her maid Anna Lintjens in Roermond, to be paid in Paris to Dutch consul Bunge.'

"Thus you first received five thousand francs on November 4, 1916, and once again the same amount on January 16, 1917. To that we have to add the thirty-five hundred pesetas which von Kalle confirms having paid you. That makes, in two and a half months, nearly fourteen thousand francs which the Germans paid you. We are, of course, far from the one million which you had the audacity to ask *us.* But those amounts indicate through their importance the kind of services you rendered the Germans and the position you held among German spies. In any case they prove that your maid has been an intermediary in the whole setup and that all the letters which she sent you and in which she mentioned the various funds as coming from Baron van der Capellen is sheer comedy."

Mata Hari tried to explain: "I have written and even sent telegrams from the Ritz Hotel to my maid, asking for money. I am really the mistress of Baron van der Capellen, a colonel of the Second Regiment of Hussars, a married man, and who, in a small country like ours, where censorship is very strict, has always asked me never to send him letters or telegrams in which there would be mention of tenderness or money. My maid is a most honest woman who has been in my service for eight years; she knows about my love life and has always served as intermediary with the Colonel."

(In 1963, talking with Anna Lintjens' son, he told me that his mother once came home "with a large amount of money, all in bills." He did not know whom the money came from, but was sure that his mother had been in The Hague.)

"On my return from Vittel," Mata Hari went on, "my finances were very low. I had made a mistake in the amount of money I had taken along from Holland, and on top of that Captain Ladoux did not pay me anything and made me stay a month longer than I had intended." (She had returned from Vittel in September, and did not leave for Holland till early November.) "Why then should it be strange that I asked my lover for more funds?

"I do not recall having mentioned to von Kalle any of the things he put in his telegram of December 13, but I do remember that he himself made certain allusions as to the Greek Prince. He said there were efforts to dethrone Constantine and to replace him with Prince George. Apparently he had this information from the King. I remember I answered that I had read something about a scandal in which the Greek church in Paris was mixed up."

Captain Bouchardon now proceeded to read the further information contained in von Kalle's telegram of December 14, which dealt with the Belgian spy Allard, a matter of secret inks, and a landing at the mouth of the river Scheldt.

"I have certainly not spoken to von Kalle about the development of a secret ink by the French," said Mata Hari. "And as far as the Belgian Allard is concerned, I do not believe that I mentioned him to von Kalle, but I did mention him several times in Vigo, or perhaps in Madrid at the Ritz, where people were always listening. I never mentioned anything about a landing at the mouth of the Scheldt, simply because I knew nothing about it."

Bouchardon came back to the subject of the British agent: "We would like to point out to you that for a person who has offered to serve France, it is rather a peculiar way of helping them when you openly mention in front of hotel employees, of whom you yourself say that they have an indiscreet curiosity, that a certain Allard is a British spy."

(Bouchardon showed a strange streak in his thinking whenever it suited his purpose: he did *not* accept Mata Hari's statement that von Kalle might have paid the employees at the Ritz to check on herself and her mail, a statement which he had declared to be quite preposterous, yet he immediately *did* accept the possibility that these very same Ritz employees might have reported to von Kalle about Mata Hari's mentioning Allard as being a British spy. Not only did he accept this idea, but it would be used as one of the reasons to have her executed.)

Bouchardon then went on to say that "the information on the secret ink was of great importance," because it meant that the Germans had been told that the French had discovered the composition and use of some of their highly secret inks, a discovery the French had not made till October 9, 1916—and that, Bouchardon must have figured, was just one month before Mata Hari had left Paris for Spain.

Mata Hari went back to an earlier argument of the Captain: "You always say that I offered my services to the French counterespionage. That is not true—I did not offer Captain Ladoux anything. *He* asked *me* to work for him, and I only accepted nearly a month later, after some deep thinking. At the time I had some great plans, but did not know whether I would succeed. In any case, since I was not to be paid till afterwards, I did not steal anything from the Captain. And as to that ink, I swear that I know absolutely nothing about it."

"What secret ink did the Germans give you before you saw von Kalle?"

"I repeat that I have had no contact with the Germans before I saw von Kalle. That is as good a reason as any not to have had the ink you are talking about."

"Well, then—let me just put the documents in front of you. Not knowing that you had been arrested, Berlin sent the following message to von Kalle on March 6: 'Please let us know whether agent H-21 has been told that for all communications she should use the secret ink which was given to her, and whether she has been shown that this ink cannot be developed by the enemy.'

"Already on December 23, just to bring you up to date, the German espionage sent the following message to von Kalle: 'The secret ink which H-21 received cannot be developed by the French if the stationery before and after the use of the ink has been treated according to instructions.'"

"I do not understand anything about your story with those secret inks," Mata Hari countered his statement. "I have never used any secret ink, and as a matter of fact, where would I have put it in England, where they searched all my luggage and where all my toilet articles were chemically checked? And moreover, I am not agent H-21."

Bouchardon was not finished: "We ask you to consider carefully everything you obliged us to bring up today. You have mentioned certain information which you gave to either Colonel Denvignes or Captain Ladoux, and on the value of which, by the way, we must carefully reserve judgment. But could you act differently? It was difficult for you to continue living in Madrid the way you did and to go on seeing von Kalle knowing that you could be constantly followed by our agents, without thinking simultaneously about the explanation you eventually would have to give us. And therefore, in order to explain your visits to the Military Attaché and to circumvent our suspicion, you were simply *obliged* to act as if you were handing the French certain information. It is the very basic principle of any espionage game, and you are far too intelligent not to have thought of it."

"I can only repeat what I've said before—I never did make any offer to the French out of my own free will. And I am not an expert on the subject of espionage, because I never thought of it till Captain Ladoux brought up the subject. I have no idea what one must do and what one must not do. I clearly told him: 'Captain, when I give you any information, be sure to check before making use of it—I shall simply give it to you the way I hear it.' And when he offered me French secret inks, I refused. After all, it would have made a very nice present for the Germans, if I had been working for them.

"And when he suggested putting me in touch with his agents, I again refused. But if I had been in the service of the Germans, would I not have jumped at the chance to deliver their names to them?

"When I saw that Captain Ladoux was somewhat suspicious, I said to him: 'I don't want to know any of your secrets—just let me go my own way. I only ask one thing of you: leave me alone.' 'That's all right,' he said, and we shook hands on it."

"Just the same," said Captain Bouchardon, "it seems to me that you cannot deny the correctness of the information which von Kalle sent so scrupulously to Berlin. When for instance, on the twenty-third of December, 1916, he informed his chief that H-21 had requested that she immediately be sent five thousand francs to the Comptoir d'Escompte in Paris via the intermediary of her maid, he didn't invent anything—for the money arrived on the sixteenth of January 1917. You must therefore have given him precise instructions, which he faithfully transmitted to Berlin."

"I had wired Anna Lintjens from London and Madrid, telling her to ask the Baron for money."

"But that still does not explain how von Kalle, without having received exact information from you as to the amount, intermediary, and name of the bank, could have transmitted those details to Germany."

Mata Hari stuck to her argument: "Someone may have tipped him off on the contents of the telegram to my maid."

Chapter 20

At the end of the hearing on May 1, Bouchardon must have thought that he had the case solved, and he would say as much later on, basing his judgment exclusively on his own inference and conclusion: "Before her departure from Paris the double-agent received, through the intermediary of the Dutch consul, the amount of five thousand francs on November 4. That money, as anyone will have to agree, came from Germany." What he meant was, of course, that he *wanted* everyone to agree. And he furthermore decided that "the investigation was virtually closed." Yet while the intercepted telegrams did point to von Kalle as being somehow, perhaps, mixed up in the payments, Bouchardon had no proof whatever that in reality the money did *not* come from Baron van der Capellen. In fact, while Captain Bouchardon did everything possible to pin Mata Hari down on this point, and while these transfers *did* come under discussion at the trial itself, yet not one single word in any of the eight points on which she was to be condemned would mention the word payment, or funds, or money, or anything that could be construed as being even slightly connected with it. Captain Bouchardon, notwithstanding his personal conviction that he had solved the case, apparently could not convince the jury of this point of view—the only one on which he had some proof.

Giving Mata Hari nearly three weeks to think over the revelations contained in the telegrams, he called her again on May 21. This time he found a different Mata Hari in front of him. She had been thinking hard.

"Today I want to tell you the truth," she said right at the beginning. "If I did not tell you everything before, it is only because I felt somewhat ashamed."

"Around May 1916 I was home in The Hague, when the doorbell rang. It was rather late and when I opened the door I found myself face to face with M. Krämer, the German consul in Amsterdam, who had written that he would be coming to see me, but without saying why."

(Krämer's name has never been spelled right anywhere, not even at the trial. According to the German Foreign Office in Bonn, in a letter I received from them in January 1963, his name was Karl H. Cramer. On November 2, 1914, with the title of consul, he had been put in charge of the German Official Information Service in Amsterdam as a sort of press attaché attached to the consulate, where he remained till December 24, 1919. Before the war "his profession had been merchant," he was born in Bremen, and died in 1938.)

"The consul had heard that I had requested a visa for France. He started the conversation as follows: 'I know you are going to France and wonder whether you would render us some service. We would like you to gather information down there which you feel might interest us. If you agree, I am allowed to pay you twenty thousand francs.'

"I said that it wasn't much. 'That's right,' he said, 'but in order to get more, you would have to show us what you can do.' I did not give him any definite answer, but asked for time to think it over. After he had left, I thought of my expensive furs which the Germans had kept in Berlin and that it would be a fair exchange to get as much money out of them as possible. Consequently I wrote to Cramer: 'I have thought it over, you can bring the money.' The consul came back immediately and handed me twenty thousand francs in French bills. He also said that I would have to write him with secret ink. I objected that I didn't like this very much, especially because I would have to sign with my name. He answered that there were certain inks which no one could read, and that all I had to do was to sign my letters H-21. He then gave me three small bottles, marked 1, 2, and 3. The first and the third were filled with a transparent liquid, while the second bottle was blue-green, a bit like absinthe. He then moistened a sheet of paper with number one, wrote with number two, and cleaned it all off with number three. 'That is the way you proceed,' he said, 'and then with ordinary ink you can write me a plain letter on the same sheet of paper, and you can address all your letters to me at the Hotel de l'Europe in Amsterdam.' "

Bouchardon must have thought that by now he had caught his spy practically in the act, but he had not yet heard the end of the tale.

"Having the twenty thousand francs in my pocket," said Mata Hari, "I bowed M. Cramer politely out of the front door, but I can assure you that I never wrote him one single word from Paris. I should add, by the way, that once our ship was in the canal which goes from Amsterdam to the North Sea, I dropped the three bottles in the water, having first emptied them."

Mata Hari went on to explain that when she talked to Captain Ladoux later on, he had wondered why his counterpart in the German Intelligence had not recruited her for his service. "For the simple reason that he didn't know me," Mata Hari had answered. This had made Ladoux suggest: "If only you could arrange that some day—but that's for later." Mata Hari's own reaction to this future plan had been that Ladoux "would get anything he wanted from her." But Ladoux had insisted on her first proving to him to be worth her salt, "and when we are sure of you, you can be sure of us."

Mata Hari had considered this a great loss of time, and had said to herself that as long as Ladoux did not want to pay, there was no reason for her "to reveal her great secret to him and to tell him what she had in mind—all just for nothing."

"Then, when he asked me whether I wanted to go back to Holland via Switzerland or England, I chose the second route because I certainly did not look forward to the prospect of having to go via Germany, where they could ask me what I had done with the twenty thousand francs without giving them anything in exchange. If at that moment I had had anything on my mind which might have made me suspect to the French, I certainly would have accepted the offer to go back home via Germany.

"Once in Madrid, the circumstances obliged me to act along the lines which you know by now. Captain Ladoux had not paid me anything. He had abused my confidence, and I had only a few hundred pesetas left. Some women in my position would probably have stolen; I received not a word from Paris, and my hotel bill kept going up and up. It was then that I went to see von Kalle, who knew nothing about me. I wanted to try and see whether I could manage to safeguard my trip through Germany without being arrested."

Mata Hari explained how, in order to gain von Kalle's confidence, she told him she had had an offer to spy for the French. "I then made up some information for him which I got partly out of old newspapers and partly composed from memory—information which was of no importance whatever and which could not do any harm to France. Von Kalle then cabled his superiors to ask whether he could pay me any money. I had asked for ten thousand francs, but Berlin refused. I don't know whether a later message did authorize the Military Attaché to pay me.

"It is true that von Kalle paid me three thousand five hundred pesetas, but I would guess that it was his own money. He had committed some most intimate acts with me in his office, and had offered me a ring. Since I don't like that kind of thing, I had declined the offer, and I suppose that he gave me the three thousand five hundred pesetas instead.

"As to those two payments of five thousand francs, perhaps that money did come from Cramer, because before I had left Holland I had told my maid that in case I sent her a telegram asking for money, she could go to the Hôtel de l'Europe and ask for Cramer, but only in case it was impossible to get in touch with the Baron. I cabled my maid in October 1916 and had the telegram sent via the Dutch consulate. And I sent a similar telegram in January. But I doubt whether Anna had to go to Cramer, and I believe that the money simply came from the Baron, because that's what she wrote me."

(This statement by Mata Hari shows up her highly peculiar way of thinking. In confessing to Bouchardon that she had instructed her maid to contact Cramer in certain cases, she actually tried to convince him of her innocence. For, having told him that she had not done anything for the twenty thousand francs paid initially, it should—in her mind—be obvious to Bouchardon that she certainly had no intention of doing anything for some further payment either. Furthermore her amazing confession was proof of that other extraordinary trait in her character, which always convinced her—and *only* her—that wherever and for whatever purpose money could be obtained, it did not matter what she got it *for*, but it only mattered whether she did anything *for it*.)

Bouchardon had been listening quietly, and he must have thought that he had found the answer to his problem. "We take good note of your confession," he said, "but would like to give you a very simple exposé of what *we* are thinking: When you were talking to *our* people, you carefully kept your relations with Cramer hidden, as well as the number H-21 he had given to you, and the mission he had trusted you with. On the other hand, when you were talking to von Kalle, your first move was to tell him that you had acted as if you had accepted a mission from the French. Now whom did you serve under those circumstances? Whom did you betray? France or Germany? It seems to us that the answer is simple."

Mata Hari was not defeated. "If my attitude towards the Germans and the French was different, then it was because I wanted to hurt the first, a plan in which I succeeded, and help the second

—a plan which was equally successful. After all, I couldn't expect to get permission to travel through Germany for selling them a bottle of vinegar! I was obviously obliged to make them believe that I was on their side, while in reality the French were leading the game. Once I had obtained certain information from von Kalle, I tried to see Captain Ladoux three times on the Boulevard Saint Germain. If I had been able to see him, I would have said: 'Here is a free sample of what I am able to do. Now it's your turn.'"

Bouchardon: "Unfortunately one can find another explanation for your actions. It was impossible for you to visit von Kalle without risking being seen by one of our agents. You therefore simply *had* to make your preparations, so as to be able to say to us, 'I am going to see van Kalle, but am doing it for *you*.' Anyone who is familiar with espionage knows that whenever a German agent finds himself in a situation like yours, the enemy always supplies him with certain information in order to gain our confidence—but while that information is true, it has lost its value by the time he tells us about it."

"I assure you that your way of thinking is worth absolutely nothing. I had never done any espionage before. I have always lived for love and for pleasure. I have never purposely associated with people who could give me information, nor have I tried to find access to certain important circles. And let me point out to you that the information I got from von Kalle was neither old, nor unimportant. Colonel Denvignes told me that Colonel Goubet found it most interesting."

"You just said that you knew nothing about espionage. That ties in very badly with those great secret plans of yours for which you wanted a million."

"I had only mentioned people I knew in France—but I would have been able to build up connections in Belgium which, under Captain Ladoux's guidance, would have led to great things. And besides, the whole idea of becoming a spy and the plan to spy for both countries simultaneously was all Captain Ladoux's—not mine."

Captain Bouchardon had much more in his file: "You have been under surveillance in France since June 1916. From the reports we have on you, we have noticed that at the Grand Hotel you tried principally to meet officers of various nationalities who were on their way through. Thus on the twelfth of July you had dinner with an officer who must have been Lieutenant Hallaure.

"On the fifteenth, sixteenth, seventeenth, and eighteenth of July you shared a room with a certain Belgian Major Beaufort. On the thirtieth of July you were in the company of a Major Jovilčevič from Montenegro. On August 3, you were seen with Second Lieutenant Gasfield and Captain de Massloff. The fourth of August you had dinner at Armenonville with Captain Mariani, an Italian.

"August 16 you had dinner at the Gare de Lyon with a French staff officer, Captain Gerbaud, who was leaving for Chambéry. On August 21, you went to Armenonville with a British officer. The twenty-second you had lunch with two Irish officers, James Plunkett and Edwin Cecil O'Brien. On the twenty-fourth you lunched with General Baumgarten. On August 31, you had lunch at Armenonville with an English officer who had arrived that morning, James Stewart Fernie.

"Without wanting to accuse your informants of anything more serious than imprudence, your daily meetings with all those officers could have supplied you, in adding two and two together, with an overall knowledge that would have been interesting to the Germans."

Mata Hari: "I love officers. I have loved them all my life. I prefer to be mistress of a poor officer than of a rich banker. It is my greatest pleasure to sleep with them without having to think of money. And moreover I like to make comparisons between the various nationalities. I swear that the relations I have had with the officers you mention were inspired by nothing but the feeling and sentiments which I have just described to you. And moreover, those gentlemen came to see *me*. I've said yes to them with all my heart. They left thoroughly satisfied, without ever having mentioned the war, and neither did I ask them anything that was indiscreet. I've only kept on seeing de Massloff, because I adore him."

Mata Hari's story made no impression on Captain Bouchardon. He disbelieved that she never talked about war. He disbelieved that "the uniform" had had an attraction for her ever since she had lived in The Hague and had met John MacLeod, and he consequently felt it his duty equally to disbelieve her story that many of these men had been her lovers because she *preferred* them to civilians.

Bouchardon wanted clarification on some statements Mata Hari had made during earlier hearings. Why, for instance, had she not informed Baron van der Capellen that she wanted to go to Vittel for her health?

"Because I really *had* to go to Vittel, as I used to before the war. If before my departure I wrote the Baron that I felt fine, then I did this because he is the kind of man who never wants to hear about people who do not feel good. He needs a mistress who is gay, healthy, and permanently cheerful."

As to the Second Lieutenant whom she was seen with on January 5, 6, and 7, that was M. Mège. And the pilot she had dined with she had met in the street. He had invited her to supper, but she could not remember his name.

The American, Moore? He had been after her, but "I didn't like him because he had such bad table manners. He said he was a munitions salesman."

Mata Hari's prewar friend Hallaure had been interrogated by Captain Bouchardon, and had made several uncomplimentary remarks. She found it "not very chic of him" to slander her "now that he knows that I'm in trouble." It was true, she said, what he had told Bouchardon about her having been arrested in Germany as a Russian spy. But the woman who had alerted the police had never set eyes on her, and the Germans had let her go immediately.

Hallaure had commented on his conversation with her before her trip to Vittel. Mata Hari was indignant: "I have never said that Hallaure gave me the idea to go to Vittel, but I want to state once again that it was my health that made the trip necessary. As to my going to the office on the Boulevard Saint Germain, I did not know that foreigners needed a special pass for the Zone of the Armies, and I simply did what Hallaure had advised me to do."

Before ending this interview, Bouchardon once again returned to the subject of the twenty thousand francs Cramer had paid her.

"If you really did nothing for Germany after having received that money from Cramer, you would have easily been found out when you went to see von Kalle. Answering his first telegram about you, Berlin would immediately have said that you had fooled them and that you were no good as an agent. But we have the text of all messages exchanged between von Kalle and Berlin during a whole month, and Berlin has never made any allusion to a betrayal on your part."

Mata Hari had the last word for that day: "I have no idea what Berlin answered, but they certainly could not have said that I *have* done anything for them."

Chapter 21

The following day Bouchardon continued the attack, again starting off on Mata Hari's conversation with Cramer and her subsequent meetings with von Kalle. According to him, the whole association with the Germans was an open book. According to Mata Hari, he was reading a lot on the pages of that book that had never been printed there.

"You can hardly expect us to believe that Cramer gave you twenty thousand francs without your having proved to them that you were worth that much money. Germany gives nothing for nothing, and the funds which they usually supply their agents as travel expenses are far below the amount you got. You must consequently have worked for them previously, and our reasoning is confirmed by your own statements, as made to von Kalle. We know from his first telegram that you were sent twice to France to spy for the Germans. You have talked about the second trip. Now let's talk about the first."

"One doesn't simply send a woman like me off on a trip, a woman who has a home and a lover in Holland, without supplying her with funds. And as to my first trip to France, it had nothing whatever to do with Cramer, and I told von Kalle only that I had twice *been* in France—not that I was *sent* there."

"Why did you make use of the Dutch consulate to send Anna Lintjens your two telegrams in which you asked for money? There must have been something mysterious in those telegrams, or you would have used regular channels. Didn't you use the consulate at other times as well, specifically to send information to Cramer?"

"I assure you that I only used the consulate for those two telegrams. It was quicker that way."

Coming back to the argument of the previous day, Bouchardon pointed out that if Mata Hari had really done nothing for the twenty thousand francs she had received from Cramer, she would hardly have risked telling von Kalle that she was spy H-21. And according to Bouchardon's interpretation of the intercepted telegrams, H-21 was certainly not considered a traitor.

"Just the same I could not commit suicide! I had no more money. I thought that in giving von Kalle some information— information that had no value at all—I might somehow get back into their good graces and get my permit to go home via Germany."

Bouchardon had by now more or less completed his questioning, and brought in his first witness: Captain Ladoux. The Captain had previously made his own deposition during an interrogation by Bouchardon. He now had to try to make his arguments stick. But while Ladoux knew all, or nearly all, about Mata Hari, she knew nothing about Ladoux's dealings with Scotland Yard.

In his deposition Ladoux had stated among other things that Mata Hari had already been in the service of the Germans before her first trip to Paris in December 1915.

"When I came to France in 1915," said Mata Hari, "I was not in the service of the Germans. I only went to Paris to get my linen, but I admit that on my return Cramer, whom I had known since January 1915, asked me a number of questions on general and political subjects. I remember that I did not tell him anything concerning the military. It is difficult after such a long time to recall exactly what he asked and what my answers were. The Germans are always like that in Holland—the moment someone comes back from France, they're on top of him, they cling to him like flies and ask questions about Paris."

Mata Hari was asked whether she had any remarks to make on Captain Ladoux's statement. She did indeed: "Captain Ladoux promised me a million francs if I succeeded."

According to the Captain, the matter had been discussed with a slight nuance: "When Zelle-MacLeod told me that she could actually penetrate as far as German Headquarters, I asked her whether she really believed that she could get us information on the operational plans of the German army. When she answered in the affirmative, I said: 'For that kind of information we would pay a million.' I would like to add, and I cannot insist enough on that point, that MacLeod never mentioned a word about her being in the service of the Germans under the number H-21."

"In the first place I didn't dare," Mata Hari commented, "and secondly I did not consider myself as a German agent at all, because I had never done anything for them. Captain Ladoux was never against my coming back to France when I asked for my visa in Madrid—why not?"

For a man who had asked Mata Hari to spy for him, the

Captain made a strange reply: "It was neither my job to oppose MacLeod's re-entry into France, nor to authorize the trip, any more than I had to answer her letters. Since MacLeod spontaneously decided to return to France, I took advantage of the opportunity to expose her, and in doing so I simply accomplished my duty."

"I had no more money—I just *had* to go through France to try and get back to Holland. And I would like to add that from a certain point of view Captain Ladoux had indeed engaged me."

Ladoux disagreed. "MacLeod had not been engaged. An agent is only engaged when he has received a mission, a number, means of communication, and money. MacLeod had only received an *indication*, because she returned to Holland anyhow, to wait till an agent of the French Secret Service came to see her, and this agent might eventually have given her instructions."

"The Captain has been more affirmative than that. Do you think I would have accepted if he had said nothing more? He knew perfectly well that I would go to Belgium and get in touch with the German High Command."

Captain Ladoux refused to give an inch: "It is exactly because I did not know how true Zelle–MacLeod's statements were as to her ability to penetrate the German High Command, that it was impossible for me to charge her with a mission before our Intelligence Service in Holland, who would have to use her anyhow, had given me a report on her."

This statement by Ladoux was, of course, quite ambiguous. For either he was convinced that she was a German spy, and then he might conceivably have accepted her ability to penetrate the German High Command, where she *might* have been able to get information for the French as a double agent, or he was convinced that she was not a German spy, and then he could have trusted her. Mata Hari understood this perfectly, and logically answered: "I asked you for a million *after* I had succeeded. You were not losing anything."

Ladoux simply confirmed the ambiguity of his earlier statement: "One can only charge an agent with a mission when one is sure of him. I was very suspicious about MacLeod."

"Why then did not you ask me to put all my cards on the table? You have been meandering about my having to prove first what I was able to do, and as a result of that I kept mum."

"I have constantly asked you during our conversation to tell me all you knew about the German organization. I even asked you several times whether you knew the Fräulein * in Antwerp who heads the German espionage system in Belgium against France and England. You have always answered me that you did not know her."

"I did not tell you about my plans because you did not want to pay me, and as such there was no reason for me to divulge my great secret."

"But since you say that you were so devoted to France, it would have been better to tell me everything."

"Whatever you say, one thing is sure: I have never fulfilled Cramer's mission."

Here Bouchardon intervened in the verbal duel with one of the most amazing statements uttered during the hearings: "As far as that is concerned, we would like to point out to you that according to our laws maintaining such contacts with the enemy is equivalent to the actual transmitting of information."

Mata Hari exploded. "Then your law is frightful! If I had known that, I would never have come back. I have never had the intention of giving the Germans any information. Captain Ladoux refused three times to see me last January when I came to see him on the Boulevard Saint Germain to explain everything."

Ladoux to Bouchardon: "By then it was impossible for me to see MacLeod, because I already knew that she was in the service of Germany and all that was left to be done was for the military authorities to interrogate her. When MacLeod went to see Colonel Denvignes at the Gare d'Austerlitz, he already knew what we

* Miss Schragmüller, the famous "Fräulein Doktor."

had discovered from the intercepted telegrams. He could only answer the accused in an evasive manner when she asked him questions."

Bouchardon wanted to know why Ladoux had left the choice about the return to Holland via either Germany or Spain up to Mata Hari.

"Because I wanted to know whether MacLeod was hiding anything from me. She preferred Spain for reasons which I am not familiar with." Ladoux added however that the trip via Spain was *generally* preferred by people traveling from France to Holland, because it was more comfortable, and there was less transfer of luggage. For once Mata Hari agreed with her adversary, but pointed out that she had chosen Spain also because the trip via Germany did not appeal to her for the reasons already indicated. Before the end of the hearing that day, the two would have one more opportunity to share an opinion. Mata Hari stated that she would like to point out once again that Captain Ladoux had promised her a million if she were able to get hold of the plans of the German General Staff.

"That's right," said Ladoux.

"And the idea of working for both the French and the Germans was equally the Captain's."

Captain Ladoux, who thus so drastically had drawn a line under his association with Mata Hari, a few months later would have the opportunity to save the life of both his victim and a good number of his own countrymen—an opportunity that was thrown aside either by him personally or by the French government or by both.

The incident was related to me in April 1965 by Monsieur Léon Corblet, by then eighty-six years old, the the same person who back at the beginning of the First World War had arranged the desk job at the *Deuxième Bureau* for his friend Jean Hallaure.

On his return to Paris from one of his many trouble-shooting missions for the Army's Intelligence Division, M. Corblet had met his old friend and protégé, who told him about an amazing suggestion they had received from the French embassy in The Hague. The Embassy had been notified that six or ten French school teachers (M. Corblet was no longer sure about the exact number) had been taken prisoner by the Germans in occupied northern France, accused of having supplied vital information to the French forces. To try to save the lives of these unfortunate people, the Embassy in Holland had suggested to Captain Ladoux that Mata Hari might be exchanged for these French citizens.

Hallaure told Monsieur Corblet that he himself most strongly doubted Mata Hari's guilt and had done his utmost to have the exchange arranged, even though there was no certainty whatever that the Germans, yet to be contacted via the Embassy in Holland, would accept the French offer.

According to Hallaure, the attempt was nipped in the bud when the idea was flatly rejected by the then Prime Minister of France, Alexandre Ribot. As a result, the teachers were all shot by the Germans shortly after Mata Hari's execution by the French.

The twenty-third of May was the third day in a row that Bouchardon put the suspect through his grilling. There was no doubt left in his mind as to her guilt. "The case was perfectly clear," he was to write later. And this being so, Bouchardon changed the tone of his questioning. He did not ask Mata Hari any more what had happened, but instead he *told* her. His was the truth, and all Mata Hari had to do was to say yes.

"We would like you to recall the questions Cramer or other Germans asked you when you returned from your first trip to France, for we fear that he was not the only one. We are sure that you won't have to make a great mental effort, and you will tell us simultaneously what the answers were. Cramer's twenty thousand francs indicate the importance of those questions and answers."

"I repeat that Cramer gave me those twenty thousand francs as an advance on my trip of May 1916. They had nothing to do with my previous trip, which had no connection with Germany whatever, but which I only made to get my stored linen, clothes, silverware, riding equipment, and so on. Cramer certainly had to pay me money for having disturbed me late at night, leaving his filthy bottles with me and telling me to get information for him. Upsetting me for one single evening like that was worth twenty thousand francs.

"I agree that on my return from that first trip Cramer came to tea, and that he asked me questions about Paris, but it was a purely mundane conversation. I told him that British officers in Paris made a rather bad impression on their French colleagues, that they treated them without any *politesse* or elementary good manners, but that the Parisians treated *them* like kings, serving them before anyone else in restaurants and tearooms and charging them only moderate prices. I agreed with M. Cramer that the French at some later moment might regret having let the British in, because they might not want to leave any more. I told him about Raemaekers, the cartoonist who made anti-German drawings after first having drawn anti-French and anti-British cartoons."

The rest of Mata Hari's talk with Cramer had touched upon the impossibility of merchants in The Hague going to France on business, resulting in greater business with Great Britain.

Bouchardon then wanted to know why Mata Hari had sent a telegram to her maid through the intermediary of Consul Bunge, knowing that von Kalle had already asked Berlin for money.

"When after several days in Paris I still had not received anything, I became worried and on the eighth of January I gave Bunge a telegram. But I still believe that the money came from Colonel van der Capellen, for that is what Anna wrote me."

"Where is that letter?"

"At the Dutch Legation."

"The first telegram indicates that H-21 belongs to the Cologne Espionage Center, but a later telegram, dated December 25, indicates that H-21 was also in touch with Antwerp. In fact Antwerp cabled von Kalle about you, and was of the opinion that you could have done far better for the twenty thousand you got from Cramer, and the five thousand francs of November 1916. But they did *not* say that you had done nothing."

But neither had Antwerp indicated that Mata Hari *had* done anything, a circumstance which Bouchardon, making his accusations in a carefully affirmative vein, did not touch upon. According to him, Antwerp's authorization to von Kalle to pay her three thousand francs simply proved that *everything* he claimed to have happened before was true. Yet he did not seem entirely sure even of this, as was clear from what he said next: "But *anyhow*, Antwerp knows you, and knows that you were given the secret ink. They even asked whether you could go to Switzerland and write from there." It meant: even if the foregoing is not true, one thing is sure—they know you. What was probably more true was that Antwerp knew about Mata Hari through Cramer, which checked with her own statement: "I swear that I only dealt with Cramer. I have no idea which office he belongs to, for I never asked. And I have never been in Antwerp. I know no one in that city."

From the answer to his next question Bouchardon should have understood that Mata Hari had told the truth when she said that she had never met von Kalle before she went to see him in Madrid. For he wanted to know about her trip to France in March 1916, which was the month von Kalle had indicated in his first intercepted telegram to Berlin.

"The date in that telegram must be a mistake. Von Kalle must have mentioned March instead of May, for I did not get my passport till around May 12. The mistake was probably caused by my speaking German, for May and March are fairly similar in pronunciation in that language."

Next to Captain Ladoux, the most important witness Bouchardon had seen was Colonel Denvignes. The Colonel being in Madrid, Bouchardon read his sworn statement to Mata Hari.

"There are certain things in his statement that are true," she said, "and I would even say that on the whole everything did happen the way he describes it. But the Colonel very cleverly twists the nature of our relationship. He forgets to say that he has been running after me to the extent of making himself ridiculous. Twice a day he came chasing me at the Ritz, having tea or coffee with me in front of everyone, and calling me *"mon enfant, mon petit."* I agree with him that I have not been his mistress. But on the other hand he proposed that I come and live with him, because I would cheer up his home. A man of the rank of Colonel Denvignes should not throw the first stone at a woman in her misery, the more so because he asked me to be his mistress. I told him that I belonged to a Russian officer, whom I was going to marry. And he asked me to have dinner with him at the Hôtel d'Orsay in Paris.

"As to his belief that I belonged to the German Intelligence, I would simply like to say this: it is totally ridiculous. If he had actually thought so, he would never have shown off with me in Madrid the way he did. He even kept a bunch of violets and a ribbon of mine as a souvenir."

Following Colonel Denvignes, a manicurist from the Hotel Plaza had been interviewed by Bouchardon as another witness. She testified that Mata Hari had told her not to like the Belgians and the British, and had said something about Verdun.

Mata Hari agreed that she might have mentioned the two indicated nationalities while she was having her nails done, "but only talking about their behavior at the hotel. And I certainly didn't mention Verdun."

Captain Bouchardon spent the following week interviewing various other witnesses for the prosecution, and having sworn statements made by those who could not come to Paris—among whom figured Vadime de Massloff. Mata Hari, during the same week, on May 29, wrote a letter to Bouchardon in which she asked him:

Mon Capitaine,

Please promise me to *come back* to the report Colonel Denvignes has made. You were reading it rather quickly to me and I was too bewildered by the Colonel's lies, which he passes off as "the whole truth," to enable me to answer as I *should* have and as I *want* to. Please give me the opportunity to answer this report *point* by *point*.

Thus when she faced Bouchardon once more on May 30, the French Colonel's testimony took up most of the hearing. The Colonel, in his own opinion and statement, had seen through Mata Hari from the beginning. *She* had come to see *him*. At one time during their conversation she had mentioned the names of the Crown Prince and the Duke of Cumberland, who was the son-in-law of the Kaiser. This, the Colonel claimed, proved that she was a spy. He also disclaimed to have asked Mata Hari to return to von Kalle, and had testified that he himself had told her about the landing in Morocco. Moreover he gave a different version of their conversation at the Gare d'Austerlitz, after which he most uncomplimentarily finished his statement to Captain Bouchardon by saying that Mata Hari, after all, had only been after people's money, and that she did not amount to much.

Mata Hari, in discussing the Colonel's statement with Bouchardon, proceeded to answer the accusations one by one:

"I would first like to state that the Colonel asked to be introduced to *me*. If he claims that Mr. de With, the attaché at the Dutch Legation, had told him that my name was Mrs. MacLeod, then I would like to point out that everybody in Madrid, where I have danced, knows that Mrs. MacLeod and Mata Hari are the same person. I would like to add that the next day around two thirty M. Denvignes was sitting in the reading room of the Ritz, knowing that I usually went there around that time. He received me with these words: 'Guess whom I've come for?' 'Maybe for me,' I answered. After that he complimented me on my dress and asked whether I would dine at the Ritz. I said yes.

"That evening, during the after-dinner dance, I was in the company of M. de With and M. van Aersen, when the Colonel came in. He took advantage of the two Dutch attachés' dancing with other women to remain all night long in my company. He asked me what I was doing in Spain and why I had not gone directly to Holland. It was at that moment that I told him that I was on his side, and that if I had known him earlier, I would have given him the information which I had just sent to Paris. After that I told him about what had happened at Falmouth.

"I did mention the Crown Prince and his brother-in-law, the Duke of Cumberland, but only to say that the Prince has a stupid smile and that he was constantly at odds with the Duke, whom I know very well and whom I can see whenever I want. I met him while I was the mistress of von Kiepert, and he frequently came to dinner at my apartment.

"As to the conversation which the Colonel says took place later that evening, I would like to point out that it took place two days afterwards, *at least* two days afterwards, and that it was totally different from the way he describes it. I have explained that meeting with von Kalle during the hearing of February 28. And I must insist on stating that the second time I went to see von Kalle it was at the special request of the Colonel.

"I have neither mentioned any Francophile groups in Catalonia, nor did I talk about my own position in Germany. I did tell the Colonel about Captain Ladoux's constant niggling, how he negotiated and did not understand what he could get out of me. And it was not M. Denvignes who *asked* me to get him information on the landing in Morocco. He knew *nothing* about that. On the contrary, *I* gave him that information and he was perplexed by it. So much so, that the following morning he came back to ask whether I could get more details. It is absolutely untrue that he asked me to get him precise information on ways and means to stop such a landing. The man is positively dreaming! And it isn't true either that I told him that in France I lived only for my art, and in Germany exclusively for pleasure.

"He gave me to understand that he might be able to get me a contract at the Madrid Opera, to which I answered that after the war I would like to go back to Paris to live.

"I have never talked to Monsieur Denvignes about the morale of the various people at the German embassy, for the simple reason that the only person I had met there was von Kalle, and all I said was that I had found him tired and in not too good a physical condition.

"The Colonel totally belittles the information I gave him. He is wrong, for when I gave the same information to Captain Ladoux on January 5, he seemed utterly amazed and said textually: 'I am absolutely stupefied!'

"As to our last conversation, the one at the Gare d'Austerlitz, I have given you an exact account of what was said. If my text differs from the Colonel's, then I'm sorry—but the conversation took place exactly as I told you.

"As to the Colonel's appreciation of the value of the information I gave the French and the Germans, I can only stand on what I have said before. And regarding the last phrase of the Colonel's statement I have only one word to say: the witness speaks out of malice and lover's spite. As a matter of fact I am convinced that it was the Colonel, knowing that de Massloff was my lover, that it was *he* who was behind the letter which the Russian Military Attaché wrote to the Colonel of the First Russian Imperial Regiment, warning him that I was a dangerous *aventurière* with whom de Massloff should have nothing more to do."

Having finished with Denvignes' statement, Vadime de Massloff's testimony was read. In essence he declared that his affair with Mata Hari had not been of any importance, and that he wanted to make a clean break with his mistress in March, only to find that she was in jail. Captain Bouchardon asked whether she had any comment. Her answer was short:

"I have nothing to say."

Chapter 22

A FTER the hearing of May 30, Mata Hari's fate, as far as Bouchardon was concerned, was sealed. If it had depended on him, the trial could have started the next morning. No matter what Mata Hari had said in her own defense, no matter the contradictions in both Ladoux's and Denvignes' statements, no matter the irrelevancies of some of the witnesses, like the manicurist, who were apt to construe *anything* Mata Hari had said as proof of her spying, Bouchardon was convinced. (When I talked to Mata Hari's ex-maid at the Château de la Dorée in 1962, she too said several times: "I always knew she was a spy!" She knew no more about it than the manicurist.)

Bouchardon did not believe that any money Mata Hari had received could possibly have come from Baron van der Capellen —even the five thousand francs she had been paid in Paris before her departure on the ill-fated return trip to Holland. Thirty-one years later he still stuck to his original idea, still confirmed that Mata Hari had been *sent* on two *missions* to France for the Germans, instead of having come—the first time most certainly—to get her household goods. He repeated this in his book:

"Did not Margareth-Gertrude Zelle herself declare on December 13, 1916, when talking to von Kalle, that she already had accomplished two missions to France? Indeed her passports confirmed that she had made a first trip to Paris in December 1915.

"Mata Hari had accepted a mission from Cramer. She received from this consul, if she did not already have it, the number H-21, three bottles of secret ink, and twenty thousand francs. She then returned immediately to France, where she associated with a great number of officers. Later she collected the money of two checks, each of five thousand francs, and moreover received from hand to hand thirty-five hundred pesetas. Thus there was not the slightest doubt that: (1) the twenty thousand francs from Cramer were payment, or an important part anyhow, for previously performed services; (2) the first check of five thousand francs, paid more than one month before her conversation with von Kalle, was payment for previously supplied information, different from what she was to tell him personally later on; (3) the two sums she received after that (the thirty-five hundred pesetas and five thousand francs) were her salary for that later verbal information."

The remaining three hearings therefore had only little bearing on Bouchardon's conclusion. On June 1, he asked questions, with a variant, on matters he had already touched upon, trying to clarify certain points. Von Kalle, he said, had wired Berlin on December 13, saying he would send detailed information by code or letter. Bouchardon wondered what these further messages or letters had been about, and asked Mata Hari to tell him. There was little she could elaborate on, and instead she reconfirmed her nonaccomplishment of the Cramer mission: "From the moment I threw away the three bottles of ink, I felt somehow purified as to any German espionage, and by that same act I lost all contact with them, as well as the number H-21 which they had given me."

She was questioned about a certain gentleman of about twenty-five who had come to her hotel on the day of her arrest, and about the director of a bank in Berlin. "Unknown," said Mata Hari about the first. As to the second, his name was Constant Baret, he was a Frenchman, and had been one of her lovers. But not so Cramer, she said, who had never propositioned her towards that goal. She had been introduced to Cramer early in 1915 by Wurfbain, and she could never have received the consul at her home in The Hague before her return from Paris, because till then the house had lacked all comfort; she had no linen, no silver, could not even have served a cup of tea, and certainly no meal.

Once more Bouchardon said that 20,000 francs was a lot of money—the Germans never paid that much. As proof of that he could mention a certain French officer who had been willing to spy for the Germans, had asked 20,000 francs, and had been politely refused. Mata Hari was quick to point out that there was quite a difference between a Frenchman who *offered* his services, and a person like herself, whom the Germans "had run after, because they thought—wrongly—that I was able to give them important information."

Once on this subject, Mata Hari elaborated: "In the first place the confiscated furs in Berlin were still bothering me, and all I did therefore was reimburse myself. And as to telling von Kalle that I had feigned to accept a mission from the French, I *had* to tell him some story like that, or he would have wondered how I could have made two trips to France in the middle of the war. Moreover I had to give him some explanation for the company I kept in Madrid—including your Military Attaché."

Vittel was discussed once again: "I only took care of my health and of Captain de Massloff—I hardly exchanged any words with the other patients. And I did not tell you any lie when I said that I had been living in a château in Touraine. It was the Château de la Dorée in Esvres, during the years 1910 and 1911. Rousseau, my lover, had signed the lease, but I paid for it."

The one-before-last hearing on June 12 brought little news. Bouchardon discussed another letter Mata Hari had sent him since the preceding interrogation, and Mata Hari protested that the French had arrested her without giving her an opportunity first to have an interview with Ladoux at his headquarters. And she requested her old friend Henri de Marguerie to be called as a witness. She "had dined practically every night with him" when she was in Paris in 1915. After all, she "had told him about the offer from Captain Ladoux," and he had advised her to accept.

When Mata Hari went back to her cell that afternoon, she had nothing to look forward to but the last meeting with Bouchardon. It took place on the first day of summer, June 21, in the presence of Maître Clunet. Mata Hari made a last effort to convince Bouchardon that Captain Ladoux had either definitely engaged her, or that at least she had every reason to believe that their conversation had meant far more than what had been declared by Ladoux.

"If my meeting with Captain Ladoux had taken place in the private room of a restaurant, then his thesis might have had some value. But it took place in an office belonging to the War Department, and afterwards he sent me to another official office, the one of M. Maunoury, to have my exit visa arranged. And, moreover, I would like you to consider the position I was in: Captain de Massloff had asked me to marry him. I wanted to live with him—in France. Inasmuch as he was Russian, I could not, in fairness, ask for money from anyone but the Allies. I therefore promised my help in all loyalty to Captain Ladoux—I only asked him not to inquire as to how I wanted to proceed. Today, when I am interrogated for the last time, I shall tell you what I had planned—and you will finally understand how grand and beautiful the idea was which I had in mind, and to what an extent Captain Ladoux was denuded of any kind of foresight.

"I had been the mistress of the brother of the Duke of Cumberland, who, as you know, had married the daughter of the Kaiser. With the Duke himself I had some intimate relations as well. I knew that the Duke's brother-in-law, the Crown Prince, had made him solemnly swear that he would never reclaim the throne of the kingdom of Hanover. He did swear this, but only for himself—not for his descendants. He and the Crown Prince hate each other violently. It was this hate which I intended to exploit in the interests of France—and in my own interest. So you can see what services I could have rendered you!

"I would have resumed my relations with the Duke of Cumberland and would have done all I could to detach him from Germany and get him over on the Allied side. It would have been sufficient to promise him, in case of an Allied victory, the throne of Hanover.

"Before I came to France I never thought about espionage. It was only in Captain Ladoux's office, while thinking of my coming marriage, that I suddenly conceived this great idea. All my life I have acted spontaneously. Little things never interested me. When I conceive great things, I go right at them.

"I can state with pride: All my trips to France have been totally devoid of any suspect contact. I have never written any letters which even in the slightest degree could be interpreted as dealing with espionage. I have only dealt with honest people. I have asked no one any questions about war. Not one single person can have told you that I have asked him anything on that subject. My conscience is absolutely clear. I left your territory with the idea in mind to do in all sincerity what I had promised.

"If I had wanted to do anything for the Germans, I would have stayed here. The fact that I intended to return to Holland proves that it was my intention to follow through on what I had promised. And to accomplish this I was obliged to contact the Germans. It was only with that purpose in mind that I went to see von Kalle, and remembering what I had read in forty-three-days-old newspapers, I made up some kind of story. Anyone with even the slightest bit of intelligence could have done it.

"At the same time, in order to give Captain Ladoux a sample of what I was capable of, I obtained information from von Kalle which was of definite interest to France. That is, at least, how it was considered by Colonel Denvignes, who hurried to transmit it to Colonel Goubet, giving him to understand that he himself had been able to acquire it.

"To sum it up, I have supplied von Kalle with nothing but outdated news, and have given your country information that was topical and entirely new. At least it was that when I gave it to Colonel Denvignes. As the situation is now, he gets all the honor, and I am in prison."

It had been a good speech, and Mata Hari had finally been able to explain what she had been thinking about when her preparations were so suddenly brought to a halt. Her plan involving the Duke of Cumberland had been based on a bit of German history that dealt with the royal succession in the kingdoms of Hanover and Braunschweig. On November 1, 1913, the throne of Braunschweig went to Kaiser Wilhelm's son-in-law (married to the Kaiser's daughter Victoria Louise since May of that year), who was Ernst August, Duke of Cumberland. On his accession to the throne he also became Duke of Braunschweig and Lüneburg, and as a descendant of the British Royal Family he moreover had the title of Prince of Great Britain and Ireland. His grandfather, George V of Hanover, had lost his throne to Prussia in 1866, and the whole family lost their rights to their British title on November 8, 1917, when all foreign princes of English blood who were fighting against Great Britain were stricken from the English peerage.

As Mata Hari had correctly explained, her friend the Duke of Cumberland had renounced his ancestral rights to the throne of Hanover, and she had figured that he might be interested in regaining those rights.

The Duke, who was born in 1887, and with whom Mata Hari had divulged she had had "some intimate relations," was the father of the present Queen-Mother of Greece, Frederika. His brother, who, as Mata Hari had confessed, had been her lover, was George Wilhelm. Born in 1880, he died in 1912. By 1907 he was therefore twenty-seven, Mata Hari was thirty-one, and the Duke of Cumberland was nineteen. During the same period, in addition to the Duke and his brother, Mata Hari had also been the mistress of Herr Kiepert.

Chapter 23

AGAIN it was the cell at Saint Lazare that awaited Mata Hari. She was still full of hope, for despite the violent clashes with Bouchardon, she felt that none of his conclusions could have any real value. Besides von Kalle and Cramer, all the men she had known had been friends or lovers—nothing else. No one could believe that her conversations with these men had touched upon dangerous subjects, that she had meant any harm or that she had wanted to spy for Germany.

At that moment she was only vaguely familiar with the fact that none of the men Bouchardon had talked to had been able, or had wanted, to defend her. Some of them had explained that their conversation had never touched upon military matters. But none of them had said that they did not believe her to be a spy—neither Messimy, the twice-former Minister of War, who even Bouchardon thought had been one of her lovers, nor even Jules Cambon, the Secretary-General of the Foreign Office.

Mata Hari's optimism was caused by her not understanding that it had been her fatal mistake to try to work out an espionage system of her own. Other spies who were double agents were acting as such with the full knowledge and cooperation of their respective governments or principals. Mata Hari had followed the same course, at least in her own mind, but without informing the French, or without having had the chance to explain to Ladoux.

The hearings being closed, Bouchardon had started to write his report, keeping in mind his personal verdict of "guilty," and changing negative answers into positive statements. Captain Ladoux, for instance, had insisted that Mata Hari tell him about Fräulein Doktor. Her negative answer had been ill received. She just *had* to know the spying Fräulein in Antwerp, because Cap-

tain Ladoux had thought so, and Captain Ladoux was infallible—
until he too went to jail.

Bouchardon deftly mixed facts with probabilities, taking note
of certain qualifications of Mata Hari which, though not *making*
her a spy, were convenient to a spy. "Speaking five languages," he
was to write, "having lovers in all capitals of Europe, being known
to everyone and finding everywhere discreet accomplices, Mata
Hari could flatter herself to be a really *international* woman."

Elsewhere Bouchardon would recall how Mata Hari, having
been taken along by *chef* of police Griebel to the demonstration
in front of the Kaiser's palace, "on the first of August 1914 had
cruised along in her lover's car, and in that carriage, as if she were
sitting in a front box, had witnessed the display in favor of the
war right under the Kaiser's windows."

According to Captain Bouchardon it all added up to one thing
only: "To say it shortly, the case was nothing but a *flagrant délit*"
—meaning that she was caught red-handed.

During those long hot summer days Mata Hari, waiting for the
trial date to be fixed, had nothing to do but to think about past
and future. The past had very acutely caught up with her in the
form of some letters from Holland, but while the hearings were
still in progress, she had had little time to give them much
thought. Now she had, temporarily at least, all the time in the
world—and the letters meant nothing but more trouble.

Late in May the Netherlands Legation in Paris had forwarded
a first letter to her—via the director of the prison—which came
from the firm of C. H. Kuhne and Sons in The Hague. It dealt
with an unpaid bill for clothes and furs.

"She owes us the amount of three thousand two hundred and
eleven guilders and eighty cents since October 1915," wrote
Messrs. Kuhne & Sons, "and notwithstanding our multiple efforts,
we have been unable to get in touch with her." Anna Lintjens had
informed them, they wrote, that Mata Hari was living at the
Grand Hotel in Paris, either under her own name, or under that

of Mata Hari, and would the Legation please be good enough to try and make her see reason.

Two weeks later, on May 23, Mata Hari's lawyer in The Hague sent off a letter on the same subject, trying to protect his client's interests. He enclosed an invoice from Kuhne & Sons, and "as Madame Zelle's address is probably known to you," Mr. Hijmans requested the consul to forward the invoice to Mata Hari. The lawyer was clearly worried about what might happen to her property in case she did not pay promptly, for, he wrote, "inasmuch as it might be the intention of the Kuhne company to have her properties attached, I would appreciate if you would let me have her answer as quickly as possible."

On June 14, one week before she was to confront Bouchardon for the last time, the consul sent Hijmans' letter on to Saint Lazare. So now, as if she did not have enough trouble, Mata Hari had to think about unpaid bills in The Hague from a fashion house that might sell her furniture in order to get paid for clothes which she had bought two years previously.

Feeling quite sure that her imprisonment would only be temporary, Mata Hari made every effort to protect her interests and possessions in Holland. Baron van der Capellen would certainly be good enough to help her in this situation—which should have been the least of her worries. And surely the people in The Hague would not make her sleepless nights worse by the added thoughts of having no home to go back to when all this was over. And so Mata Hari, on June 22, the day after she had finished with Captain Bouchardon, wrote a fairly angry letter to the consulate in Paris, with the request to inform the parties concerned.

"Kindly write Mr. Hijmans at Nieuwe Uitleg 19 and explain to him what has happened to me," she started her letter. "I have the impression they do not know in Holland, in spite of the fact that I have written to my maid. They think that I am in Paris to amuse myself, and that I do not intend to come back. As I have property in The Hague and connections which I cannot lose, I would appreciate if you would inform my lawyer about the accident that has befallen me.

"I suppose nothing serious can happen to me, the more so because I have a charming house in The Hague and have no other debts than the one with the *couturier,* which happens to every woman. The *couturier* has to *wait.* I cannot accept a bill which is five hundred guilders too high, and on which seven hundred guilders have already been paid, without first checking the various bills which I have from them, and on which most likely some other items have also been paid already. The *couturier* does not have to worry. He will receive the money I owe him, with interest, if necessary, but I am in prison on account of a war accident. The interrogations have been continuing since February 13, 1917. It is impossible for me to handle my affairs at this moment.

"Please ask my lawyer, Mr. Hijmans, to call my elderly maid to his office. She must go and see my lover Baron van der Capellen, and ask him to pay one thousand guilders to Kuhne, without however accepting the full amount of their bill as being exact— and let Kuhne keep quiet and stop sending letters either to my home or here, because I cannot answer them.

"Kindly ask my lawyer whether everything that concerns my house in The Hague is in order, whether the rent and the taxes have been paid, so that at least I do not have to worry about *that.* What has happened to me is terrible, but I am innocent, so it will all be cleared up."

As an afterthought she wrote in the margin of her letter: "My bill at Kuhne's can never be more than a maximum of two thousand guilders."

By now the government in Holland began to take a slight interest in the case, and on June 30, Mr. Hannema, the secretary-general of the Ministry of Foreign Affairs, sent a telegram to Paris in which he said that he "would like to be kept closely informed," adding that "various Dutch newspapers have published articles about the arrest of the afore-mentioned lady"—who by then had not been just recently arrested, but had already spent nearly five months in jail.

The Paris Legation either had nothing to report (although if they had been in touch with Maître Clunet they could certainly have wired back that the hearings were finished), or they simply had not had any contact at all with the lawyer. For it was not until several weeks later that there was a first exchange of letters between them. On the morning of July 24, Maître Clunet, answering a note from the Legation, informed them that he had added the two communications from the Legation to his client's file. And he further informed them that "it is today at one o'clock that she will appear before the Third Military Tribunal at the Ministry of Justice." The proceedings, he expected, would last two days. Maître Clunet could hardly have informed the Dutch representative any later about the date and time of trial—and most likely the Legation had not even taken the trouble of inquiring.

The two communications Maître Clunet had received that morning were bitterly ironic. Mata Hari herself, with all the phantasmagoric thoughts that must have gone through her mind during these more than five months in jail, had not forgotten about the matter. On July 16, she had requested the Legation to forward to her lawyer a letter "written in Dutch on violet-colored stationery and signed Anna," which "I left at your office one day," and to which was attached "a stop-over ticket for the S.S. *Hollandia*."

Having been held up in transmission by censorship at the prison, Mata Hari's letter crossed with the documents the Legation had forwarded to Maître Clunet. Both of these dealt with Mata Hari's interrupted trip to Holland in November 1916. While throwing away money by the handful, Mata Hari had her father's businessman's mind as to money that was due to her. And having returned from England to Spain instead of continuing to Holland, the unused part of the steamship ticket was left and it was worth money.

Both answers to her inquiry had reached Maître Clunet on that morning of the trial. One was a letter dated July 22, from the Paris office of the Royal Dutch Lloyd, commenting on a letter they in turn had received from their head office in Amsterdam. Reading like a shockingly bad joke, the letter said: "At the request of M. Mata Hari the Royal Legation hereby remits to Maître Clunet a steamship ticket number 52272, with an attached stop-over ticket number 32242 of the Royal Dutch Lloyd, as well as a copy of a letter sent to the Netherlands Minister by the Lloyd's agent in Paris, authorizing M. Mata Hari to receive the amount of 328 francs"—(and the accompanying letter from the Royal Dutch Lloyd supplied the details)—"the company having decided to refund to M. MacLeod, passenger aboard the S.S. *Hollandia* of November 13, 1916, the amount of the value of the unused ticket for the section of the trip from Falmouth to Amsterdam."

Chapter 24

THE trial of Mata Hari started at a time when the war situation in France had reached a desperate level, and not since the thunderous German advance towards Paris in 1914, when the French government fled to Bordeaux, had morale probably been so low. Loss of human life on the battlefield all through 1916 had been frightful, and the outbreak of the Russian revolution in St. Petersburg in March 1917 had dealt the Allies a heavy blow. Although the Kerensky government kept Russia fighting on the side of France and England for a while, the situation on the eastern front quickly deteriorated.

In April and May 1917 the British had broken through the enemy lines at Arras, yet their gallant action brought no improvement in the situation, because the Germans brought their advance to a dead halt. Finally, after General Robert Nivelle's ill-fated

French offensive in the Aisne and Champagne had similarly been stopped by the Germans, inflicting slaughterous losses on the attackers, mutiny spread through the French lines in May and June 1917, ultimately reaching sixteen army corps. Their physical endurance weakened to the point of despair by the losses they had sustained during 1916 and by the disastrously cold winter that brought along 1917, and their morale increasingly undermined by defeatist and pacifist propaganda which emanated from clandestine subversive centers in the rear, the troops, taking their cue from the Russians in revolt and singing the "International," marched with red flags. Some of the men, often indiscriminately selected as the leaders of the mutiny, were courtmartialed, condemned to death—and immediately executed—by hastily organized front-line army courts. The result was that the total disintegration of the French army seemed only a matter of weeks.

Faced by this the government precipitously replaced General Nivelle as Commander-in-Chief by General Henri Pétain who, mercilessly repressing the mutiny, finally succeeded in bringing the chaotic situation back to a semblance of normality, re-establishing order among the rebellious troops. Only a miracle saved France from the fate that would befall her twenty years later, and without Pétain's relentless action Kaiser Wilhelm in 1917 might well have victoriously marched down the Champs Élysées at the head of the triumphant German troops, as Hitler would do in 1940.

The desperate seriousness of the crisis in France during that early summer of 1917 was afterwards clearly stated by the then Minister of War and later Premier Paul Painlevé, when he said: "There came a day when between Soissons and Paris there remained only two regiments on which we could count."

The overall situation was worsened by the losses at sea from sharply increased German submarine activities. To sustain French morale it was necessary to turn the public's attention away from conditions at the front. A scapegoat somehow had to be found, and a strongly enforced spy hunt was one of the means the government had at its disposal. At least *some* of the blame for the course of events could be written off as being due to their nefarious activities. Within a comparatively short span of time several spies were arrested, brought to trial, and shot.

The atmosphere of suspicion was such that Captain Ladoux himself ended up in jail by October 1917, accused of espionage by a certain unscrupulous Pierre Lenoir, who—with money supplied by the Germans through one of their agents in Switzerland—had bought the Paris morning paper *Le Journal,* which he then sold to a group of equally unscrupulous anti-government Frenchmen. It was perhaps some consolation to Ladoux that Lenoir later on was executed when it was discovered that he himself was a spy, but in October 1917 it was still only Ladoux who was arrested. He was provisionally freed, but remained at the disposal of the Army authorities. On January 2, 1919, Ladoux was again jailed, to be tried on May 8 by the same Third War Council who by then had quite finished dealing with Mata Hari. Although he was acquitted, it is significant of the psychosis of suspicion that dwelt in France, that the Chief of the Espionage and Counter-espionage Division of the Army could be seriously suspected of actually doing what he was supposed to prevent. It can be compared hypothetically to putting J. Edgar Hoover in jail on suspicion of subversive activities.

As a result of all this, the accusing fingers that were pointed at Mata Hari were accompanied by strong words when the trial opened. Major Émile Massard (the one who had called Mata Hari "of Jewish extraction"), Commander at Headquarters of the Armies of Paris, was present during the full duration of the trial as representative of the Paris Military Governor, General Dubail. Massard is the only person who, not being under oath, has written an eyewitness account of the proceedings, unfortunately only five years later, and apparently from memory. He quotes Lieutenant Mornet, the Trial Counsel, as having said of Mata Hari: "The evil which this woman has caused is incredible; she is perhaps the greatest spy of this century!"

Massard's estimate of Mata Hari's earnings as a spy was as high as his opinion of German remuneration for those who served them was low. He coldly estimates that she received "during the first two years of the war more than seventy-five thousand francs" from the Germans, "which is enormous, if one takes into consideration that ordinary agents never received more than a few thousand francs."

Captain Bouchardon had his own pre-delivered epitaph; he variously described his victim as a woman "whose facility of languages, innumerable connections, remarkable intelligence and innate or acquired immorality all contribute to make her suspect. Without scruples, accustomed to make use of men, she is the type of woman who is born to be a spy."

Characteristic of the general feeling is a statement made in the thirties by Marthe Richard, who declared that she "might easily have finished like Mata Hari, instead of being awarded the Legion of Honor." She too, during her spying activities in Madrid, had often been left without news and instructions from Captain Ladoux for long periods of time.

Marthe Richard made her statement to Paul Allard, a French writer who tried to unravel the Mata Hari mystery and who in 1933 published a book about his findings entitled *Les Enigmes de la Guerre*. Allard, after having talked to as many people who knew about the trial as he could find, came home with statements that were totally different from those made in 1917. Colonel Lacroix, who in 1932 was Chief of the *Conseil de Guerre*, which then kept a close watch on Mata Hari's file, conceded that he had read its contents. According to Allard, the Colonel found "no tangible, palpable, absolute, irrefutable evidence." And even Bouchardon, who by now had a cooler head than back in 1917, could verbally no longer give a positive answer as to Mata Hari's guilt.

Paul Allard summed up the general feeling quite adequately. "I have read everything that has been written about the famous dancer-spy—and I am just as far advanced as before. I still do not know what Mata Hari has done. In fact nobody knows what

Mata Hari has done! Ask the average Frenchman, or even the more intelligent Frenchman what Mata Hari's crime was, and you discover that he does not know. He is only convinced that she was guilty, but he does not know why."

Under the virulent temper that pervaded France in July 1917, the atmosphere at the Palace of Justice, when the Military Tribunal assembled there on the twenty-fourth to sit in judgment on Mata Hari, was a peculiar one. The echo of the recent front-line mutiny was still reverberating between the walls of the building on the Ile de la Cité. On the one side of the Court of Assizes room sat Mata Hari, still innocent till declared guilty—but already a spy. Across from her sat the jury, composed of a president and six judges, military men all. And in between lay Captain Bouchardon's report, on which the jury had to decide.

But as a result of the general feeling of suspicion, and notwithstanding the presentation of mostly circumstantial evidence only, the jury had neither the opportunity nor the courage to give a negative answer to the charges. Bouchardon's accusations, all prepared and ready, making every innocent move suspect and every suspicious move guilty, could only be answered by a conviction. And yet there was a difference of opinion among the judges which, under the circumstances, required courage. On three questions out of the total of eight one of the members of the jury voted *Non*. And one of these questions, number seven, was the most important of all—and was the one on which she was undoubtedly condemned to death. All other questions were fairly irrelevant. Yet there was so much doubt on that question number seven that a military man, in the atmosphere of Paris in 1917, had enough strength of character to differ with his fellow members of the jury.

A human life was at stake—of little value perhaps in a war where losses of hundreds of thousands of men had become commonplace. But this was a life that was to be discussed in front of people who had to weigh evidence. This required time for thought and discussion, and in Mata Hari's case there was very little of either.

The trial started on July 24, at one o'clock in the afternoon. At seven that evening a recess was called till the following morning at eight thirty. That same day everything was finished. And included in those one and a half days of work was the time necessary for such purely legal procedure as the seating of the jury, the opening speech, the reading of legal documents, summing up by the trial counsel, pleading by the attorney for the defense, and deliberation of the jury. Considering all this, and Maître Clunet's speech alone having taken up many hours, very little was left for proper presentation of the case, the listening to witnesses for both the prosecution and the defense, cross-examination, and proper investigation—which, of course, was really not necessary. Bouchardon had done all this for the jury before the case ever came to court; Mata Hari was condemned by the pre-trial file, and the jury only confirmed the conviction.

The following are the eight questions on which the jury had to pronounce judgment by the end of the second session on July 25:

1. The afore-mentioned ZELLE Marguerite Gertrude, divorced wife of MACLEOD, called MATA-HARI, is she guilty of having entered the entrenched camp of Paris in December 1915, or in any case within the period of the statute of limitations, to obtain documents or information in the interests of Germany, an enemy power?

2. The same, is she guilty, while in Holland during the first six months of 1916 or in any case within the period of the statute of limitations, of having delivered to Germany, enemy power, and notably to the person of Consul Kramer, documents or information susceptible to damage the operations of the army or to endanger the safety of places, posts, or other military establishments?

3. The same, is she guilty, in Holland in May 1916 or in any case within the period of the statute of limitations, of

having maintained intelligence with Germany, enemy power, in the person of the afore-mentioned Kramer, in order to facilitate the projected task of the enemy?

4. The same, is she guilty of having entered the entrenched camp of Paris in June 1916, or in any case within the period of the statute of limitations, to obtain documents or information in the interest of Germany, an enemy power?

5. The same, is she guilty, in Paris since May 1916 or in any case within the period of the statute of limitations, of having maintained intelligence with Germany, enemy power, in order to facilitate the projected task of said enemy?

6. The same, is she guilty, in MADRID (Spain) in December 1916 or in any case within the period of the statute of limitations, of having maintained intelligence with Germany, enemy power, in the person of the Military Attaché von KALLE, in order to facilitate the task of the enemy?

7. The same, is she guilty, under the same circumstances of time and place, of having delivered to Germany, enemy power, in the person of said von Kalle, documents susceptible of damaging the operations of the army or to endanger the safety of places, posts, or other military establishments, said documents or information dealing in particular with interior politics, the spring offensive, the discovery by the French of the secret of a German invisible ink, and the disclosure of the name of an agent in the service of England?

8. The same, is she guilty, in Paris in January 1917 or in any case within the period of the statute of limitations, of having maintained intelligence with Germany, enemy power, in order to facilitate the projected task of said enemy?

Mata Hari, who for the duration of the trial had been moved to the Dépôt at the Conciergerie, next to the Palace of Justice, did not know what was in store for her when she entered the Court of Assizes room on that afternoon of the twenty-fourth of July. She wore a low-cut blue dress for the occasion, with a three-cornered hat. Having walked through the various courtyards and climbed the spiral staircase to the second floor of the center building, she entered the courtroom through a low door on one side. The moment had come to face the jury.

The seven gentlemen she saw on the jury bench were all members of the Third Permanent Council of War of the Military Government of Paris, and as such they had all been appointed by the Military Governor.

Having sworn "to guard religiously the secrets of the deliberations," and presided over by fifty-four-year-old Lieutenant Colonel Albert Ernest Somprou of the Garde Républicaine, their names went from the simple to the aristocratic. The lowest in rank was Second Lieutenant of the Seventh Regiment of *Cuirassiers* (Cavalry) Joseph de Mercier de Malaval, who remained in the service till 1945. His participation in the Mata Hari trial either must have left no impression—which seems improbable—or he must have felt ashamed of it. According to his wife, whom I talked to in 1963, "he had never told (her) of his association with the trial at all."

None of the members of the jury are alive any longer. Fernand Joubert, who was Chief of a battalion of the 230th Regiment of Territorial Infantry, was born in 1864. Captain of the *Gendarmerie* Jean Chatin, already on the nonactive list by 1914, was born in 1861. Lionel de Cayla, who lived on the Champ de Mars and who was apparently the only Parisian among the jurors, was born in 1862 and served in 1917 in the army as a captain of the 19th Squadron of the *Train des Equipages*. Henri Deguesseau, born in 1860, served like Joubert as a lieutenant in the Territorial Infantry, but in the 237th regiment instead of the 230th. The seventh man on the jury was Adjutant of Artillery (12th regiment) Berthomme.

Besides these seven men, Mata Hari faced Lieutenant Mornet, who as trial counsel represented the *Commissaire du Gouvernement,* plus Adjutant Rivière, the *commis-greffier* (clerk of the court) who was to keep notes of the proceedings. On Mata Hari's side, sitting just below in front of her, was her lawyer, Maître Edouard Clunet, aged seventy-four.

At the start of the trial the hearing was open to the public, which therefore was present at the far end of the room when Mata Hari was brought in "free and without handcuffs," to be addressed by the President of the Court. As was usual, Lieutenant Colonel Somprou had the required law books in front of him: the Military Code of Justice, the Criminal Instruction Code, and the Ordinary Penal Code. Everything was going to be based on the Articles in the books.

Asked to give her name, Christian name, date and place of birth, civil status, profession and address, Mata Hari declared that she was called "Zelle, Marguerite Gertrude (as recorded by the French clerk in the minutes), forty years old, born in Leeuwarden (Holland), divorced, dancer, and living before her arrest in Paris at number 12 Boulevard des Capucines," which is the address of the Grand Hotel. (The main entrance at that time was on the Boulevard, and was only later on changed to the Rue Scribe. And while Mata Hari thus gave the Grand Hotel as her official Paris residence, it is sure that after her return from Spain she did not live there any more, but instead moved to the Plaza Hotel on the Avenue Montaigne, as was also indicated in the telegrams from the Dutch Foreign Office to the Paris Legation. Yet the French records indicate that on her arrest she was staying at the Palace Hotel on the Champs Élysées. If so, she must have moved there from the Plaza.)

The president of the court then asked the clerk to read the order of the trial and the convocation of the Military Tribunal. This was immediately followed by a request from Trial Counsel Mornet to have the hearing closed to the public "because the publicity might endanger the safety of the state." He also requested that "publication of the report of the hearings be prohibited." Maître Clunet was asked to give his opinion on these requests, after which the jury left the room through the doors in the corner to Mata Hari's right, to discuss the questions in private.

Returning to the courtroom and their seats on the bench, Lieutenant Colonel Somprou proceeded to read to the trial counsel, facing Mata Hari across the room, and to the public on her far left, the details of the jury's deliberations and the decision they had come to: "After having heard the attorney for the defense, the president of the jury asked the following questions: (1) Is there reason to order the hearing to take place behind closed doors? and (2) Is there reason to prohibit publication of the report of the hearings in the *Affaire* Zelle?"

"The votes having been taken separately and conforming to the law on each one of these questions, the jury, considering that the dissemination of the hearings would endanger the public order—believing, moreover, that it would be equally dangerous for the public order to allow publication of the report of the *Affaire* Zelle—declares unanimously that there is reason: (1) to have the hearing closed to the public, and (2) to prohibit publication of the report."

This being so, the audience was requested to clear the court. All precautions were then taken to make sure that not a word of what was going to be said would reach unauthorized ears, for which reason guards kept the public at a distance of thirty feet from all doors leading to the courtroom. The secrecy was complete, and the interrogation could begin.

Mata Hari, sitting on the long side of the room, faced the seven high windows giving on to the north. Right above her, against the wall, was the clock, next to which a bust of "Marianne," symbol of the Republic, looked down on accusers and accused. High up on the wall above the jury was a large empty frame which once had enclosed a picture of Christ—removed in 1905 when France decreed the separation of church and state. The press box on Mata Hari's left was empty too, and so by now was the space reserved for the public.

Trial Counsel Lieutenant Mornet, a very thin and large-bearded vegetarian who never drank alcohol and who after World War II would be prosecutor of Marshal Pétain, started off by telling Mata Hari that she had always been seen in the company of men in uniform—that she apparently had very little interest in civilians. This, of course, was bypassing a good number of Frenchmen outside the military whom she had known as well. But in Bouchardon's report little weight was thrown in their direction.

Mata Hari explained that the uniform had always held a great fascination for her, ever since and even before she had married her husband. This made very little impression on the jury. Veering away from a subject which was no argument for conviction anyhow, the questions turned to Mata Hari's trip to Vittel. She admitted frankly, as she had done during the pre-trial hearings, that she had had two objectives: to drink the water for reason of health, and to see her lover Vadime de Massloff.

Taking a cue from Bouchardon, Lieutenant Mornet wondered why she had told a lie: When Ladoux had asked her why she wanted to go to this spa, she had answered that she planned to take the cure. Yet at the same time she had written to her lover in Holland, Baron van der Capellen, that she felt fine.

Mata Hari's explanation was the same as before: it was the kind of white lie any woman in her position would use. To get permission from Ladoux to go to Vittel she used the real reason —her health. On the other hand, there was no reason to bring this to the attention of Baron van der Capellen.

Then money entered into the conversation, the twenty thousand francs from Consul Cramer and the payments via the Comptoir d'Escompte, of which the second check for five thousand francs was in the file right in front of Lieutenant Mornet. What was this money for, the Lieutenant wanted to know—and how did it happen there had been other payments?

Mata Hari told the story as she had told it to Bouchardon: she had been paid because she had been the mistress of these various men. Mornet felt that the payments were high for such service.

Mata Hari disagreed. To a woman who had had horses and villas at her disposal, who had earned ten thousand francs at the Paris Olympia at the very start of her career, a woman who had a home in The Hague and who before this had been living in a villa in Neuilly-sur-Seine, in a château near the Loire, and in first-class hotels all over Europe—to such a woman small amounts of money were of no interest. And, Mata Hari pointed out again, the money she had received at the Comptoir d'Escompte was sent to her by Baron van der Capellen. Only one payment came from von Kalle, the one of thirty-five hundred pesetas. And there was one more thing the Lieutenant should know about the payment from von Kalle—it had not been his own money; he had used government funds to pay his mistresses, government funds that had been put at his disposal to pay his spies with. Did Mata Hari perhaps mean that von Kalle had paid her for other things than spying? Exactly; he had paid her as a lover pays his mistress, and the money he used for this purpose was actually intended for intelligence purposes.

Mornet was not impressed. He stuck to the point which Bouchardon had brought forward: the Germans generally paid their spies very little. No men would pay her large amounts of money just because she fulfilled some physical needs. If von Kalle paid her thousands of pesetas or francs, that could only have been for services rendered—services which had endangered France, and none other.

Marthe Richard, if she had been called as a witness, would have been able to confirm Mata Hari's story. As she confessed a good many years later in her own book, the Naval Attaché in Madrid, von Krohn, had bought her a going-away present. She wrote that the day after she told him she would return to France for good, "he offered me a solitaire which he bought at a jeweler's shop in Barcelona." And when Marthe Richard, just before leaving Madrid, told the German ambassador that she had been von Krohn's mistress, she said to him, according to her own statement: "I bring you evidence that he kept me with the money he had at his disposal to pay his spies with."

Lieutenant Mornet changed his attack. If she did accept twenty thousand or thirty thousand francs from the Germans—for whatever purpose—why had she asked a million from the French? Again Mata Hari had her answer ready: because now she really planned to help—help the *French*. And with the connections she had, she could be of real service; she was now *willing to spy*, and that was worth a lot of money.

It made no impression on the jury, and Mornet came to his next subject: Why had she kept it a secret from Captain Ladoux that she had had an offer from Cramer in Holland? And why had she told von Kalle that she had been accepted as a spy by the French?

Mata Hari felt that Lieutenant Mornet made no sense at all— or that he certainly did not understand what goes on in a woman's mind, who is not only *allowed*, but who *has* to use various stratagems to attain her goals. There was no reason whatever to tell Ladoux about the Cramer proposition, she said, because she had taken the money and had not given the Germans anything in return. And as to von Kalle? Colonel Denvignes had *asked* her to get information from him—*for the French*. And by then also wanting to get back to Holland, after her return from London, she had hoped to get a permit from him that would enable her to reach The Hague via Germany. After all, she knew only too well by then that she could not go via England!

She was obstinate, because she now understood that the men she was facing were trying to send her to jail. Logic was on her side, she felt. And logic it seemed when she threw a question back to the jury: Would she ever have returned to Paris if she had felt even in the slightest way guilty of espionage for the Germans after having been arrested by Scotland Yard? This would have been utter folly!

What about her number H-21, which was mentioned in the telegrams from Madrid, and which she herself had mentioned as having been brought up during her conversation with Cramer in The Hague? That did not mean a thing—that had been Cramer's idea, and she had paid no further attention to it.

The subject seemed exhausted. Lieutenant Mornet had covered the ground which Captain Bouchardon had prepared for him. Yet there was no real evidence for any of the subjects the trial counsel had touched upon, except where it dealt with Mata Hari's having spoken to certain people. But neither these Germans, nor the money she had received was positive proof of spying or of endangering the security of France, for nothing really indicated what the money had been paid *for*.

Yet to Lieutenant Mornet and the jury the case was progressing satisfactorily. Germans and money were involved—and that, in the Paris of 1917, could go a long way.

The moment had come to call the witnesses. Lieutenant Mornet announced that two of them were unable to appear—Captain de Massloff and Lieutenant Hallaure. Some authors, including French historian André Castelot, claim that these two important witnesses did testify in person. Castelot in fact writes that *"Mata Hari had begged* (the court) *not to call Massloff as a witness."* He then went on to say that *"just the same she had to endure this ordeal."* M. Castelot obviously had the wrong information, for it is *not* true that de Massloff testified in person, as is clearly stated in the minutes of the trial: "The witnesses, Captain de MASSLOFF and Lieutenant HALLAURE, not having been able to be approached to be given their warrants, the War Tribunal, at the equal advice of both parties, has ordered that the hearings will proceed without them."

Jules Cambon was at the bar, standing halfway between Mata Hari and Lieutenant Mornet straight across the room from her, and facing the jury. He had no comment, except to say that she had never pried him with questions of either political or military importance. Asked why she had cited him as a witness, Mata Hari gave the obvious answer: M. Cambon had been ambassador in several important posts, and had occupied, and was still occupying, one of the highest positions in France. To the jury, however, his statement meant little; hearsay about absent Germans and reports from dubious agents put more weight in the scales of justice than a strictly personal opinion of one of the top civil servants of France.

Adolphe Messimy, who had been Minister of War at the outbreak of hostilities, and who had written to Mata Hari in Berlin to say that he could not come to see her, had also been cited as a witness for the defense. By now a general, M. Messimy did not show up in court. His wife instead had written a letter to Lieutenant Colonel Somprou, explaining that her husband unfortunately was suffering from rheumatism, which made it impossible for him to leave his room. And besides, she wrote, the whole thing must be a mistake, for her husband surely had never known the indicated person.

According to Bouchardon, the Messimy letter, when read before the jury, caused the only gay moment during the sessions. Mata Hari laughed, and her laughter was contagious. "That's a good one!" she exclaimed, "he hasn't known me! He's got some cheek!"

(As there had been two "v. K's" in Madrid, there were two M———y's in the French cabinet in 1914, the Minister of Interior, M. Malvy, and Messimy, the War Minister. In March 1926, accused by a newspaper of having been on intimate terms with Mata Hari, Messimy declared that "fourteen years ago this woman, through all the means of seduction of which she was capable, tried to establish herself as my mistress." There was nothing to it, said Messimy, as he had only written to Mata Hari to say no. The incriminating letters on official ministerial stationery having been signed "M———y," Messimy's colleague, Malvy, had previously been mistaken for Messimy. In 1917 Malvy was accused of high treason by Clemenceau, and was banished to Spain for five years. On his return he was rehabilitated, the *M———y–Messimy* truth by then having been established. In 1926 Malvy became once more Minister of the Interior, but on entering the

Chamber of Deputies he was again accused of having been Mata
Hari's lover, and fainted dead away.)

Several other witnesses were called—the manicurist, a fortune-
teller, Henri de Marguerie. None of them said anything that
could add substance to arguments either for or against the accused. By the end of the first afternoon in court the "Case of the
Army Against Mata Hari" still rested on one argument only:
Captain Bouchardon's file.

And so at seven o'clock in the evening of that twenty-fourth
day of July 1917, during which the Germans bombed Nancy
"without causing casualties" and the Allies retook the California
plateau in the Chemin des Dames area, "the repose of the members of the tribunal and the defendant being essential, the president, by virtue of Article 129, Paragraph 1 of the Code of
Military Justice, declared the hearing suspended and ordered the
continuation for the following morning, July 25, 1917, at half-past
eight, at which time he invited the members of the Council of
War to be present. He then ordered the guard to accompany the
accused, who was taken back to prison."

Mata Hari, for the second time that day, covered the ground
between the courtroom and the Conciergerie—down the circular
staircase extending along four floors to the basement, and through
the tunnel and courtyards to the Dépôt, where the cells with their
iron bedsteads were situated on two floors.

Going home that night, the members of the jury had nothing
but impressions to take with them—impressions of a woman who
had lived brilliantly in the Paris of the earlier part of the twentieth century, and who had had many lovers. The only other
impression they had was one of guilt based on an accumulation
of accusations.

Chapter 25

THE following morning saw a repetition of the proceedings of the previous day: the members of the jury took their places at eight thirty, the law books were once again deposited before Lieutenant Colonel Somprou, Mata Hari was brought into the courtroom in the company of Maître Clunet, and, as before, the public was requested to leave.

Things were proceeding at a very fast pace now. Lieutenant Colonel Somprou requested the clerk to read the statements from witnesses who had not been able to appear in person. Included was the deposition from Vadime de Massloff, explaining that the affair with Mata Hari had really meant little to him—he too was afraid; after which both Mata Hari and Maître Clunet were asked whether they had any comment.

The trial counsel, Lieutenant Mornet, took the floor. He painted Mata Hari's sinister behavior in eloquent words and demanded that "defendant Zelle be declared guilty of all acts brought against her." Again Mata Hari and her lawyer were asked whether they had anything to say. It was very little—they could only repeat previous statements. Mata Hari maintained that she was innocent, after which Maître Clunet pleaded "not guilty" in an emotional but not very convincing appeal that lasted the greater part of the afternoon. Yet all the words that were spoken on this second day of the trial hardly meant anything—they were nearly exclusively words required by law: testimony *had* to be given; summing up *had* to take place; the defense counsel *had* to make his speech, all according to certain paragraphs in the three law books that were permanently displayed on the bench.

During all this talk the temperature between the four high walls had become fairly oppressive. The thermometer that afternoon rose to a humid 82 degrees, and a thunderstorm which might have cooled off the atmosphere brought only very little rain, hardly enough to wet the Paris pavement.

President Somprou now declared the hearings closed and ordered the defendant to be removed from the court to the Prisoners Room on the same floor, while the jury retired to decide on its verdict. The seven men did not need much time. The trial minutes do not indicate the exact length of their deliberation, but Massard mentions that it took them forty-five minutes in all to vote on each one of the eight questions, plus the verdict. Elsewhere half an hour is mentioned, and even ten minutes only. Accepting the longest time indicated—Massard's—it makes an average of five minutes per point.

Voting was done from the lowest grade up, with Lieutenant Colonel Somprou each time voting last. The members of the jury were unanimous in their opinion as to Mata Hari's presence in certain places at certain times. Not even Mata Hari herself had denied that she had been in Amsterdam and The Hague, Paris and Madrid.

But taking each of the eight questions separately, one notices a strange repetition of the strongly negative opinion of the one member of the jury who had the courage to say three times: "*Non.*" He acquiesced in the accused's presence in those places at those certain times. He even agreed that she had spoken to Germans in each one of these locations and had "maintained intelligence with the enemy," or "had tried to obtain information and documents." But every time his opinion was asked on whether she had *disposed* of such information, he categorically said "No." To the other six members of the jury, speaking to Germans and giving them information was all the same. The seventh member drew a sharp line: there was no proof.

The first question somewhat insidiously asked whether Mata Hari had entered *the entrenched camp* of Paris in December 1915. She had, not crawling on all fours protected by the dark of night, but quite normally on a regular train and with a valid visa. The answer was a unanimous *yes.*

The second question asked whether during the first six months of 1916, in Holland, Mata Hari had given documents and information to Consul Cramer. The seventh man answered with a definite *no*.

The third question asked whether she had talked to Cramer in May 1916. All seven members of the jury were convinced of it; Mata Hari had said so herself. The answer was unanimously *yes*.

The fourth question asked whether she had returned to Paris in June 1916 with the *intention* of obtaining information. Again the answer to this statement was a unanimous *yes*.

The fifth question, contrary to number four, asked whether she actually *did* talk to Germans in Paris in the summer of 1916. The seventh man again said *no*.

The sixth question asked whether she had talked to Germans— von Kalle—in Madrid in December 1916. All seven members of the jury said *yes*.

The seventh question asked many things: did she tell von Kalle about the French discovery of the German secret ink; did she inform von Kalle on secrets of French internal politics; did she tell von Kalle about the spring offensive, and did she give von Kalle the name of a British agent? To six members of the jury all these things were definitely proved. The seventh man again differed of opinion. Six said *yes*, the seventh man said *no*.

The eighth question asked whether Mata Hari had talked to Germans in Paris in January 1917. By now the seventh man must have felt intimidated. This question was essentially the same as number five. Only the year was different: January 1917 instead of May 1916. This time, for no apparent reason, the seventh man also voted *yes*. It seems strange that while the jury confirmed— in questions five and eight—that Mata Hari had actually "maintained intelligence with the enemy *in Paris*," none of these German agents had been caught, brought in as witnesses, or been brought to trial. Nor was Mata Hari, of course, ever *seen* talking to them. The jury simply confirmed what Captain Bouchardon had suggested.

Now a peculiar thing happened to the seventh man on the jury. He had courageously expressed his opinion on all important accusations against Mata Hari. None of them, he felt, was proved. But finally he must have lost his courage. For when the president of the court, Lieutenant Colonel Somprou, asked for a vote on the sentence, this seventh man changed his mind. He had most categorically absolved her of all action that marked her as a spy. Yet he asked to have her shot, and "the Council unanimously condemns the afore-mentioned ZELLE Marguerite, Gertrude, to death."

It was not all—although the rest was of no real importance. "In the name of the people of France . . . the Council condemns defendant to reimburse the state for all costs" of the trial.

To bring the case to conclusion, Lieutenant Colonel Somprou ordered the trial counsel to have the sentence read to the accused in the presence of an armed guard. Mata Hari had hoped to be acquitted. She might have thought of being sentenced to jail. Death had never been on her mind.

The reading by Adjutant Rivière, the court clerk, took only a few minutes. Maître Clunet, according to Massard, wept. And Mata Hari, taken aback, repeated several times: "It's impossible! It's impossible!"

She then regained control of herself and signed a request for a re-examination of the legality of the trial before the Council of Revision. It was another step on the way to the end.

(Paul Guimard, one of the latest pseudo-truth writers on Mata Hari * repeats the fictional story that she was condemned unanimously on all eight points. But M. Guimard happens to be wrong on a great many other points as well, having apparently been inspired in his writing by the tales as related mostly by Heymans and Gomez Carrillo. He not only confirms the premarital sexual relationship between Margaretha and her fiancé, resulting—as it did not—in the birth of their son Norman six months after the

* "Un Drame d'Espionage en 1917," as published in Du Premier Jazz au Dernier Tsar, Editions Denoël, Paris, 1959.

wedding, but he also tells his readers the fable of the "Chief" of the German police, repeats the story of the Belgian spy shot by the Germans, and for good measure decides that after a sojourn of two months in Vittel—instead of two weeks—she was called to the office of Captain Ladoux, "who ordered her to leave the French territory immediately.")

In condemning Mata Hari to death, the jury had totally by-passed her real course of action, which was a very simple one. She did what every other double agent would have done, and what Ladoux himself had suggested for later. She did this so cleverly that even von Kalle fell for her game. She accepted the money from Cramer, believing in her own bizarre way that as long as she did not do anything for it, no one would bother about it, and no one would ever hold it against her.

Cramer reported her acceptance of his offer to Germany with some dubious and scant information, as dutifully reported in 1920 in the Agents' file of the German Foreign Office, where it was obviously copied from the previous wartime records ("born in Sumatra"), and Cramer equally informed his superiors in Antwerp about his negotiations with her, including the news of the handing over of the twenty thousand francs. Thus Antwerp was later able to inform Berlin that "she could easily have done better for the twenty thousand francs she had received"—for which in fact she had done nothing but give von Kalle some worthless information.

All this would have been fully sanctioned by the French Intelligence Service if Ladoux had known about it beforehand. In that case Mata Hari, like Marthe Richard, might equally have been decorated with the Legion of Honor, and would have been a French heroine for ever after. But Ladoux was out for revenge, and explained every move by Mata Hari as an act of treason, instead of as "services rendered."

He furthermore refused to let her continue on her trip to Holland, where he would have been rid of her. This he was not inclined to do, for she would then have been out of his reach and he would not have had the satisfaction of revenge. That is why he asked Sir Basil Thomson to send her back to Spain, where she was within easier reach.

Mata Hari walked blindly into the trap, and once in Paris, Ladoux was able to correct his loss of face vis-à-vis Sir Basil. Ladoux's honor thus was saved, and another spy, who could be pointed to as having been the cause of so many French setbacks, was shot. For Ladoux it was a satisfactory solution. That Mata Hari lost her life in the process was of only secondary, or even of *no,* importance.

Chapter 26

AFTER her one night at the Conciergerie, Mata Hari now went back to cell number 12 at Saint Lazare. Being sentenced, the rules were changed, and two extra beds were put into her room, which during the night were occupied by female prisoners on voluntary guard duty. She was allowed to read and smoke, but did little of either. Two nuns took care of her—Leonide and Marie, and especially with the former she became very friendly after a while. Every morning at five o'clock Sister Leonide used to bring her coffee, much appreciated by Mata Hari, whose early morning coffee habit went back to her childhood.

The new rules also brought an end to the daily walk in the prison courtyard, which Mata Hari had been allowed before the trial started. The impossibility of having even that little bit of fresh air made her suffocate. Cooped up in her cell, she asked Dr. Bizard please to intervene for her with the authorities.

"I cannot stand it any longer," she wrote one Monday morning to the doctor in a letter which, as was her habit, she left undated. "I need some air and exercise. This will not prevent them from killing me if they absolutely want to, but it is useless to make me suffer, closed in the way I am. It is too much to bear."

According to Dr. Bizard (he and his assistant, Dr. Bralez, were the only males to see her practically every day during all the time she was in prison), she never received flowers or sweets, as has been variously reported. Mail—the few letters sent to her via the Netherlands Legation—now had to go through the office of Lieutenant Mornet, because as Maître Clunet was to inform the Legation shortly after the trial, "No letters can be transmitted to defendant without the authorization of the trial counsel's office." Maître Clunet's information was prompted by a letter from Anna Lintjens, addressed to Mata Hari in care of the Legation, which had been forwarded to her lawyer for transmission to Saint Lazare.

By now the Netherlands government was following the case with close attention. Three days after sentence had been pronounced, on July 28, the Foreign Ministry requested their representatives in Paris to try and have the verdict reduced to a prison sentence in case the Council for Revision confirmed the legality of the trial.

The Council saw no reason to doubt its legality. Maître Clunet, who had gone to the Council's office on the Boulevard Raspail on Thursday, August 16, was told that the case would be heard on the following afternoon at two o'clock, ten days after Mata Hari's forty-first birthday. Although Maître Clunet was present at the hearing, there was nothing he could do. Since he was not inscribed to plead before this court, Maître Monnard, the president of the lawyers at the Court of Appeals, had named another lawyer, Maître Bailby, to defend Mata Hari's case before both the Council for Revision and the Court of Appeals.

"No violation of the Law having been committed during the proceedings and the decisions of the Third War Council, the request for revision has been rejected," was the message Maître Clunet sent to the Dutch Legation on August 17. Now only two possibilities were left to save Mata Hari from execution: the Court of Appeals and eventually a request for pardon to the President of the Republic.

The Hague kept watch from a distance, and on the last day of August another cable was sent to Paris: "If judgment Mata Hari is maintained, please take steps to have request for pardon presented before execution."

Mata Hari, for the first time since she had been arrested, began to see the futility of the efforts to save her. Understanding the situation better than anyone, the fight had gone out of her. All those on the outside saw nothing but guilt and acts of espionage that had been justly dealt with. Mata Hari, the only person who really knew what had been going on, looked at it from a completely different angle. She, after all, had been *present*, and while she felt that nothing she had done justified the decision taken, she understood only too well how it came about. All those who were supposed to be her friends had deserted her—out of fear, out of jealousy, out of revenge perhaps. People whom she knew innocently had become dangerous companions; conversations which were private and intimate had become acts committed to divulge secrets of state; things that were simple became complicated; actions that were plain became guilty, and Mata Hari knew that explanations were of no avail. The war had changed everything —small things had become big, and appearance had become reality.

Her downcast mood became tragically evident in the one long letter she wrote to the Netherlands Legation on September 2, 1917. She was not resigned, not even desperate—she simply felt alone and deserted.

"I beg your Excellency to please intervene for me with the French government. The Third War Council has condemned me to death and it is nothing but a grave error."

She then heavily underlined the next words, which stand out strongly from the rest of the letter:

"There are some outward appearances,

but no acts, and all my international connections are necessarily the result of my profession as a dancer, and nothing else.

"At this moment everything is wrongly explained and the most natural things are greatly exaggerated.

"I have asked for the revision of the case and have appealed against the judgment, but inasmuch as they would have to discover juridical errors, I do not think I shall get satisfaction.

"After that only the request for pardon from the President of the Republic remains. Since I truly have not done any espionage in France, it is really terrible that I cannot defend myself.

"Jealousy—vengeance—there are so many things that crop up in the life of a woman like me, once people know that she finds herself in a difficult position.

"I am well established in The Hague. My connections are known to Count van Limburg Styrum, who certainly will give Your Excellency some information on myself, if you desire it."

And again she signed: "Măta Hări—M. G. Zelle McLeod."

In addition to the depressed tone of the letter, it contains an extremely strange statement. Its contents indicate that as late as September 2, the date of the letter, Mata Hari had not yet been informed by her lawyer that the Council for Revision had rejected the appeal. For she clearly writes that she has "asked for revision of the case"—which revision had already been rejected two weeks previously.

Maître Clunet was not taking as active an interest in his client's case as articles and books written then and later try to make us believe—unless he did not tell her about the rejection in order to save her feelings, which seems doubtful. Clunet had been in love with Mata Hari, in fact is supposed to have been her lover; he had known her for many years, was in tears about his client's fate, pathetic in his pleading and inconsolable in her condemnation.

All, or nearly all, of this is true. But it would seem that although Maître Clunet was thoroughly interested, he was also fairly ignorant about pleading a case before a military tribunal.

This idea is strengthened by what took place before the Court of Appeals when the case came up on September 27, the total time spent on discussion being exactly fifteen minutes.

Speaking for the court, Counselor Geoffroy requested that the case be dismissed without further discussion. Then Mata Hari's lawyer, Maître Reynal (instead of Maitre Bailby, who was originally supposed to speak for her, as had been indicated by Maître Clunet) explained that he had read the file. Maître Reynal was apparently not very interested in doing anything else to help his unknown client; he nonchalantly pronounced a phrase which is occasionally used by lawyers in France who are not paid for the job they have been assigned to, and who therefore at times may take little interest in the case. Maître Reynal, representing a person who had been condemned to death, stood up and said: *"Je déclare m'en rapporter à la sagesse de la cour."* The phrase, in legal terms, signifies absolutely nothing. Its only meaning is: "I have seen the file, I have nothing to say, and leave the decision to the court."

Maître Reynal had one more phrase to add: he told the court that Maître Clunet "insisted" that he ask for a postponement of the hearing, and would the court please hear Maître Clunet himself. Maître Reynal, with these words, washed his hands of the whole thing.

Maître Clunet never got a chance to say a word. The president of the Court of Appeals explained that only lawyers who were inscribed at that court were allowed to speak. Maître Clunet was not, and could therefore not be heard. And as to the postponement of the hearing, "this could not be ordered, because the file had been distributed three weeks previously."

It meant that if Maître Clunet had wanted to request a postponement, he should have done so earlier.

There were only a few minutes left of the total of fifteen, and Solicitor-General Peyssonnié went through them perfunctorily. There was only one question to be discussed, he said, and that was the question of competence. "We have to decide whether in time of war crimes of espionage and intelligence with the enemy come under the competence of the Council of War. The *juris prudence* is unanimous in answering this question in the affirmative. Case dismissed."

The Netherlands Legation telephoned Maître Clunet on September 28, expressing concern about what might happen next. The lawyer explained that "there were another two or three weeks left [undoubtedly meaning: before the execution] and there will still be plenty of time to talk about the *affaire*." The communication, brought to the attention of the Dutch Minister in writing, seems to indicate a feeling on the part of the lawyer—contrary to the feeling of urgency on the part of the Legation —that there was certainly no reason to rush things.

Maître Clunet was not getting paid for his work. Even though Mata Hari had *requested* his services, he had been *assigned* to her defense by the Order of Lawyers, and after the telephone conversation on the twenty-eighth, he took good care to bring this angle of his involvement clearly to the attention of the Legation.

"In answer to your request," he wrote on the following day, "and on account of your interest in your compatriot, to whose defense I have been appointed without pay by the President of our Order, I am sending you herewith today's edition of the *Journal of Tribunals*"—which contained the decision of the Court of Appeals.

The Legation immediately informed The Hague, and the answer did not take long. It consisted of seven words. Signed by Foreign Minister Loudon, the Dutch government cabled on Saturday, September 29: "PLEASE ASK PARDON PERSON INDICATED YOUR TWONINETYTWO."

It was therefore neither Queen Wilhelmina nor the Prime Minister of Holland who intervened for Mata Hari, as has been previously reported. Nor was it, as Major Massard wrote, Maître Clunet. It was, as it had to be, the Dutch Foreign Office. Its request was transmitted in writing to the French Minister of Foreign Affairs at the Quai d'Orsay on Monday, October 1.

"*Monsieur le Ministre*," wrote Netherlands Minister *Ridder* de Stuers,

> I have been charged by my government for reasons of humanity to ask for the pardon of Madame Zelle Mac-Leod, known as Mata Hari, who on July 25 has been condemned to death by the third Council of War and whose appeal has been rejected on September 28 last by the Criminal Chamber of the Court of Appeals.
>
> I have the honor to request the obliging intermediary of Your Excellency in order to remit to the President of the Republic this request from the Government of Her Majesty and I would be grateful if Your Excellency would let me know the reaction with which it has been received.

The same day, following an early morning telephone conversation, a special delivery letter was sent to Maître Clunet, informing him of the action taken, and a cable was dispatched to The Hague, saying that the request made in their telegram number 223 had been "carried out immediately."

Nothing happened—except that back in Holland, on October 3, John MacLeod married his third wife, Grietje Meijer.

On October 13, the Foreign Office in The Hague cabled Paris, stating that six Dutch newspapers had announced Mata Hari's execution, and would Paris please answer immediately, so they could "prevent further comment." This was Saturday, and not a word had been forthcoming from President Poincaré, nor from the French Minister of Foreign Affairs. In fact, the French government had snubbed the representative of Her Majesty the Queen of the Netherlands. They had sent their answer to the lawyer.

On Monday morning, October 15, when the Dutch Legation opened its doors, a message was waiting from Maître Clunet—

"the request for pardon had been rejected." By that time Mata Hari was already dead.

Chapter 27

DURING the eighteen nights that passed between the rejection by the Court of Appeals and the day of execution, Mata Hari had been able to sleep in comparative tranquillity only three times—the three Saturdays. She knew that on Sundays there were no executions. Nearly every other night she asked Sister Leonide whether she thought she could sleep quietly—which usually she did not.

At six o'clock in the evening of Sunday the 14th, Major Massard at Paris Army Headquarters received his copy of the order of execution, signed by Captain Bouchardon. The final act was set for the next morning. Later that evening, when Dr. Bizard was informed of the order, he decided to pay a casual visit to Mata Hari's cell in the company of Sister Leonide. They talked about meaningless things, and the Sister asked Mata Hari "how she used to dance." Mata Hari did a few innocent steps, which through the years in various reports became an exalted dance in the nude.

Outwardly, she remained master of herself. There were no tears, and during all this time of waiting there was no despair—except, according to both Dr. Bizard and Dr. Bralez, once in a while a statement of nonunderstanding of the French people. Had she said *"Ces sales boches"* in Holland on her arrival from Berlin, it now became *"Ah . . . ces Français."* It was not an expression of dislike, as the phrase she had used for the Germans, but more one of incomprehension.

Yet even Dr. Bizard, who on the whole gave a moderate account of his patient, towards the end could not suppress some feeling of antipathy. To him her attitude was not what the French call *cran*—a sort of mixture of courage, disdain, and cold-bloodedness—but suddenly he felt that "till the end she had played her part of courage and indifference." It was therefore not real courage, but just an act—as if being brave in the face of death could be anything else.

On Monday morning Captain Bouchardon arrived at Saint Lazare shortly after four o'clock. A car had picked him up at his home on the Boulevard Péreire at four sharp. Dr. Bizard and his colleague Dr. Bralez arrived nearly at the same time, while Massard came a little later, at 4:45. It was a cold morning; the temperature was 35 degrees Fahrenheit. The news of the execution must have reached the press, because instead of the usual crowd of about thirty people, the number that would assemble for a "normal" execution, there were in the estimate of Dr. Bizard "at least a hundred, both civilians and military," plus a number of soldiers sleeping on the pavement. And Massard counted about a dozen journalists.

Assembled inside the prison were other officials: Captain Thibaud, chief recorder of the War Council, who had been picked up at his home on the Place Vaugirard at 4:30, Trial Counsel Mornet, Lieutenant Colonel Somprou (who ordered everyone to stay downstairs), and, of course, Maître Clunet, plus Major Julien, chief of the *parquet* of the Third War Council, Dr. Soquet, the medical officer, M. Estachy, director of the prison, and General Wattine, the solicitor general.

Maître Clunet said that he was too nervous to go upstairs and asked Somprou please to tell Mata Hari that he was there. The Lieutenant Colonel did not feel like playing messenger and told the lawyer curtly that "if he had anything to say, he should do so himself."

The gentlemen were taken to Cell Number 12 by Sister Leonide, who, opening the door, indicated the center bed as being Mata Hari's. She was not sleeping normally; Dr. Bizard, on the previous night, had given her a double dose of chloral, a colorless liquid soporific. The two other women, sleeping in beds alongside Mata Hari, opened their eyes when the door moved—and understood. They started to cry when Mata Hari was shaken to make her wake up as well. Shocked into consciousness, she supported herself on her arms and leaned forward. Her eyes were frightened—then she, too, understood and became perhaps the quietest person in the cell.

It was only now that she was informed about the rejection of the appeal for pardon. There was a short silence, and again Mata Hari repeated the words she had spoken when the sentence had been pronounced nearly three months before: "It's impossible! It's impossible!"

According to Dr. Bizard, Mata Hari had to console Sister Leonide: "Don't be afraid, Sister—I'll know how to die." The men left to give her a chance to dress. Only Dr. Bizard remained in the cell. Sitting on the bed to put on her stockings (and again the description is Dr. Bizard's), her legs showed high up, and Sister Leonide wanted to cover them. It was Mata Hari who had the presence of mind required under the circumstances: "It doesn't matter, Sister, this is really not the time to be prudish."

The doctor offered her smelling salts. "Thank you, Doctor," she said, "you can see I don't need them"—and she asked to speak to Reverend Arboux. The two remained alone in the cell for a short while; then the pastor left, apparently under a high emotional strain. The others re-entered. Dr. Bralez, the intern, claims she asked him what kind of weather it was, and that he answered, "beautiful." It seems doubtful, for it was not. It was a foggy morning, and visibility on the outskirts of town was hardly three hundred feet.

Mata Hari was ready. She put on a pearl-gray dress, a straw hat and veil, a coat loosely on her shoulders, and her best shoes —good shoes had always been her passion. She wore no jewelry. It had been taken away from her when she was arrested in February. Finishing her toilette, she put on her gloves and thanked the doctor for all he had done. Once more she consoled Sister Leonide, who was close to tears. A last question was put to her, a question that has given rise to fantastic tales ever since. The question is, according to French law, not compulsory—for as the wording indicates, the condition it deals with should be *stated* by the prisoner. Article 27 of the first chapter of the French Criminal Code (since June 1960 changed to Article 17) stipulates that "if a woman condemned to death declares and is found to be pregnant, she will only be executed after the child is born."

According to Dr. Bizard, Mata Hari had said nothing, but Medical Officer Dr. Soquet asked "whether she had reason to believe herself pregnant." Since she had been in jail for eight months, the question was fairly superflous, and Mata Hari's reaction was one of obvious surprise and denial. The emotional scenes, written by a good many imaginative authors, in which Maître Clunet was the man who invoked the article and who declared himself to be the father, are—again—sheer invention.

On leaving the cell, the chief guard wanted to take her arm, but Mata Hari shook him off, offended, declaring that she was neither a thief, nor a criminal. After which she took Sister Leonide's hand to walk towards the office on the first floor, called the *Pont d'Avignon*, where she was officially handed over to the military authorities.

It was here that she asked permission to write a few letters, supposedly three, of which one was addressed to her daughter. What happened to them has remained a mystery. She is supposed to have given them either to the director of the prison, to Maître Clunet, or—as Henri Lecouturier, who later on was charged with the sale of Mata Hari's jewelry, had heard—to the Protestant minister. It is definite that Mata Hari's daughter never received any message from her mother, as is clear from a letter which John MacLeod wrote to the Netherlands Legation in Paris on April 10, 1919, asking for a death certificate which his daughter Non needed "for eventual marriage plans. . . . Not a word of farewell from Madame Mata Hari to her child reached us, although—according to the newspapers—she wrote two letters immediately before she died. We have consequently given up hope of ever hearing anything." Nor are the two or three letters in the French secret file.

Dr. Bizard stood only ten feet behind Mata Hari while she was writing, ready to intervene. But she finished her letters quietly and quickly—it had taken ten minutes.

Accompanied by the military gendarmes, Sister Leonide and the Reverend Arboux, Mata Hari entered the automobile that had been waiting for her. It was a long trip from the center of Paris to the suburb of Vincennes, but the streets were empty at this early hour and the cars moved quickly. The walls of the Château of Vincennes, part of which was used as military barracks, loomed up in the semidarkness, still filled with a slight fog. The temperature, instead of rising since the middle of the night, had dropped another degree to thirty-four Fahrenheit.

The cars slowed down to pass through the narrow gate of the château, stopped for a moment at the fourteenth-century dungeon on the right, then gathered speed to cover the rest of the one-third-of-a-mile-long courtyard, passing by the sixteenth-century chapel a little farther on the left.

One of the soldiers who purportedly took part in the execution wrote a sensational story in 1963 for an Italian magazine in which he mentioned that from the guards' room they "could see the automobile penetrate into the courtyard," after which he described how Mata Hari was shot in that very same courtyard. The tale is fiction.

Mata Hari was not shot in the courtyard of the Château of Vincennes, or in the dungeon, or against the walls or in the dry moat surrounding the castle. She was executed at the polygon of Vincennes, a vast cavalry maneuvers ground that started at the other end of the inner court, beyond the château itself.

The automobile passed through the arcaded walls at the far side of the château and slowly penetrated the rain-soaked wooded and hilly area of the polygon, to come to a stop near the assembled troops. A trumpet was blown, and Mata Hari helped Sister Leonide, who prayed aloud, out of the car. Side by side the two women walked towards the pole that indicated the place of execution—then separated.

Twelve soldiers of the Fourth Regiment of Zouaves, lined up in two rows of six, faced her. Off to the right stood a group of four officers. Close to them were Sister Leonide, Reverend Arboux, and the doctor. Farther back, behind the execution squad, stood the troops, composed of cavalry and artillery units, and soldiers belonging to a front-line regiment. Captain Thibaud, in his function of Chief Recorder of the War Council, standing close to Mata Hari, read the sentence: "In the name of the people of France . . ."

Mata Hari refused to be bound to the pole, and the rope was loosely strung around her middle. She also refused to be blindfolded. The officer in charge raised his sword, and the sound of twelve rifles exploded in the deathly stillness of the morning.

Maréchal de logis Petey, of the Twenty-Third regiment of Dragoons, walked over to give the inert body the *coup de grâce*. Captain Robillard, a doctor at the Béguin Military Hospital in Paris, checked to make sure.

It was six fifteen. The sun had come up four minutes earlier, at six eleven. Mata Hari, the Eye of the Day, was dead.

Later that morning Maître Clunet telephoned the Netherlands Legation, which informed The Hague—and with that the floodgates of fantasy, rumor, and make-believe opened up. Only one month after the execution the Dutch government became concerned by an article that appeared in a German publication. It charged that Mata Hari had been a lady in waiting to Queen Wilhelmina. Jonkheer Loudon, the Netherlands Foreign Minister, in a personal telegram to the Paris Legation informed them that "I have ordered contradiction of this absurd rumor." He also requested the Paris representative "to try everything possible, in case the French press also spreads this rumor, to have the newspapers point out that the indicated person was not a lady in waiting and had nothing to do with the royal court."

The owners of Mata Hari's house in The Hague, two sisters, wrote to Paris in December 1917, wondering whether anyone known to the Legation—"her daughter perhaps"—could continue to pay the rent, inasmuch as "due to the shortage of apartments in town, this is an excellent time to sell or rent the house." They soon got their chance: Mata Hari's furniture and possessions were sold by auction on January 9 and 10, 1918. Baron Eduard Willem van der Capellen had kept himself far from the house of his former mistress; he had not even collected a photograph of his, which figured prominently among the items for sale.

John MacLeod, in various letters to the Foreign Office in The Hague and to the Paris Legation, tried to get information on what had happened to his ex-wife's earthly goods, because "on account of her high living" he had concluded that "she possessed a not unimportant fortune." And as his daughter's guardian he wanted to have it brought to the French authorities' attention that legally a part of this fortune was due to his child.

All her possessions, he was informed by the Paris Legation (which got this information from the French Foreign Office) including "everything that had been in her room at the hotel, as well as her jewelry from the prison at Saint Lazare, had been sold at auction on January 30, 1918," and "the net amount of the sale was 14,251 francs and 65 centimes." Equivalent to about $2500 today, the money had been used "to pay the French government, which had privileged rights to it, to defray the cost of the trial."

John MacLeod was equally informed that after due and thorough research it had become clear "that the deceased had not disposed of her goods, and had not left a will." John's reaction was bitter: "My daughter would have been the sole heir of the properties of her mother, if everything which that woman left behind, thanks to the good care of the French Republic, had not totally disappeared, without leaving a trace. They certainly have divided the spoils beautifully."

Even if Non had inherited her mother's money, she would not have had much use for it. John MacLeod, in his last letter to Paris on April 10, 1919, the one in which he requested his ex-wife's death certificate "for eventual marriage plans" of his daughter, had also indicated that she intended "to leave soon as a school teacher for the Dutch East Indies." By then Non had already passed her medical examination for the tropics. Exactly four months later, on August 10, 1919, she was dead. The day before, accompanied by her stepmother, she had gone to buy some silk muslin for an evening dress to wear aboard ship. She had been in perfect health, only a bit undecided in making her choice —which was strange for her. Non went to bed at eleven o'clock that evening. The next morning Grietje MacLeod–Meijer found her dead in bed. During the night she had suffered a sudden cerebral hemorrhage.

Her father survived her for more than eight years. Nearly seventy-two, he was buried next to his daughter at the cemetery of Worth-Rheden near Arnhem. The grave carries a simple headstone without the family name: "Our Non—born May 2, 1898, died August 10, 1919—and her Father, born March 1, 1856, died January 9, 1928."

All the others are dead too: the pathetic Maître Clunet; Captain Ladoux, who had started it all at the request of the British; Captain Bouchardon, who, giving the finishing touch to Ladoux's work, had felt a strange professional compulsion to pursue the case to the only end he saw fit, and who had signed the death warrant; Lieutenant Mornet, who cut short all explanations and protests; Lieutenant Colonel Somprou and his members of the jury, as well as most, if not all, the men who shot her. Every one of them rests quietly in his grave, wherever that may be— except Mata Hari.

Enveloped in the clouds of suspicion that hung over France in 1917, not one of her former friends had the courage to claim the body and give it a decent funeral. The remains were taken to the dissecting room of one of the Paris municipal hospitals, where her so much wanted, disputed, and admired body underwent post-mortem operations in the interest of medical science.

And thus all that is left of Mata Hari is some unglamorous ashes somewhere in France—the dust of a woman who had started life in a quiet provincial Dutch town, and who had liked music, poetry, and red dresses, plus, later on, money and men— and who could not live without either.

Index